SISTERHOOD

D1564849

Sisterhood

JESSA CALDERON

LUMINARE PRESS
WWW.LUMINAREPRESS.COM

Printed in the United States of America

Luminare Press
442 Charnelton St.
Eugene, OR 97401
www.luminarepress.com

LCCN: 2022902347
ISBN: 978-1-64388-935-1

In loving memory of Julia Bogany and Barbara Drake who worked endlessly with love for their people to keep our culture thriving and make us proud to represent our culture in our everyday lives.

Contents

Foreword

This book is a mix of Fiction and Non-fiction. Although U.S. History will have you believe that nothing was worth noting on this continent prior to European: Spanish/French/American (English) invasion, there was a rich culture amongst Native Nations. People of high intelligence, they were doctors, healers, botanists, astronomers, astrologers, good cooks, artisans, hunters, gatherers, story keepers and tellers, artists, singers, dancers, grandmothers, grandfathers, parents, children, leaders and so much more. Science continues to come out with facts that back up what our families have been saying about our truths for generations, proving the history books wrong. The sad fact is that almost no one listens to Native people until science and archaeology state it as facts. By then, the damage is always already done. Although this is a mostly fictional book, I am sharing truths of some Native histories and even truths of the tragic modern events that take place with some of these characters.

There is much more rich history in our cultures that I did not fit into this book. As a young woman growing up in the Los Angeles Unified School District, I have seen firsthand how our stories were being sugar-coated and fictionalized, from stories such as the California Missions, all Natives supposedly crossing the Bering Strait, to our mysterious disappearance in the 1800s. It is time for us to hold institutions and school districts such as LAUSD accountable for working with Indigenous voices of each Nation that they are discussing and or should be discussing. Our children shouldn't have to feel ashamed, embarrassed, or invisible in their homelands. That is unacceptable.

My hope in writing this book is that those who read it will have a better understanding that we still exist and we are everyday people too, that our youth will be proud to be themselves and not hide their identities any longer, that education and political entities have Natives at the table with a voice that is finally heard, that people Ancestrally connected to Central and South America can be proud to be Indigenous as well, that those who claim Chicano can be proud of their Native heritage without forcing erasure stories on other Natives with their fabricated story of Aztlan (there is an older belief/story of Aztlan that does not create erasure to other Nations.), that we can each take away healing points and move forward knowing that we are all worthy of health, peace at mind and heart, love, and success no matter how hard of a life we've had, if possible, get some land back for those of us non-federally recognized Nations as well as federally recognized Nations, and most importantly that we can work together and heal the earth for the sake of the next seven generations. Can I get a Lelelelelele?

Narrator Intro

What up, though? My name is Robert. My homies used to call me Pleito because I was always getting into fights and shit. As much trouble as I liked to get into, I also enjoyed learning and school. I secretly enjoyed writing essays and short stories in English class.

I was a well-known gang member in the apartments where I grew up. Honestly, the apartment complex that I was raised in, pshhh man, it ain't no muthafuckin' joke. Making it out of the hood alive isn't in the cards for some of us. A grip of the homies will make it out in handcuffs. A few of the homies and residents will find decent jobs to get them by.

As for myself, I didn't make it out the hood alive. I was gunned down by two of my bitch ass enemigas July 16, 1993. July is when the streets start to get really hot in more ways than one, know what I mean? I was active as fuck too, so it was just a matter of tiempo before that shit caught up with me. I left my mom and baby sister Suzy behind. I felt gatcho in my last seconds of life because I thought, "I should have been the one to step up and take care of my jefita and hermanita. Instead, I was chillin' in the calles and running amuck. But from where I stand now, I can see that everything is happening as it should. I can't do too much for them from here, but I do keep an eye on my familia.

When I died in '93, I was three months away from turning seventeen. I would have graduated high school in 1994 had I not been gunned down. And I mean it, I would have graduated, unlike most of my homies who were too cool for school and dropped out.

Enough about me though, I'm gonna share a few stories with you about some events and experiences that went down with a few of the homies from the apartments where I grew up. The stories that I share today mostly take place after my death and revolve around a clika of homegirls who lived in the complex. Why do I wanna tell you about this group of females, you ask? Because these girls are what are known as: "A product of the barrio." Despite the odds against them, these ladies made it out of the hood with much success.

One of these girls is my baby sister Suzy, and I'm proud as fuck of her ey. When I speak to you about my baby sister and jefita, I'm gonna try to talk about them as a narrator instead of a relative, so there's no confusion. Right now, as I sit here and tell you their stories, these girls are between the ages of sixteen and eighteen. I'm gonna share pieces of these girls' life stories from youth to the very end because, well, I know what happened. I have seen it in the hall of records. Do yourself a favor and grab a seat, cause shit's about to get real.

DRIFTING

The sun was beginning to rise. Lori sat up from the slab of concrete where she was sleeping. She walked to a hidden area in the apartments, pulled out a water bottle, toothpaste and toothbrush from her duffle bag and began to wash her face and brush her teeth. Lori wet her hair then put the container, toothpaste, and toothbrush back in her bag. She pulled out a comb. Lori combed her hair as she walked over to Gabby's apartment to wait for her to come out and kick it.

Lori had recently found herself in an unstable situation in her life. A week prior, Lori's brother Andre had broken the lock on her room door and stole her old cell phone, a camera, and a boom box radio. When confronted by Lori, he denied that he did it. Andre had mass addictions to alcohol, weed, and cocaine. Lori told her parents about her missing things. Lori's dad Ray argued with his son and kicked him out of their home. However, that appeared useless as Andre found himself sleeping in his car, sneaking into the apartment to shower and steal things while his parents were away at work.

Only three days had passed that Ray kicked Andre out, when Lori's mom Toni walked up to his car and told him to come back inside. Lori was upset and began to argue with her mother about how she was enabling his bad habits. Toni told Lori, "If I want my babies to live at home with me, then

I'll have my babies live at home with me, if you don't like it, you can leave." Lori felt so rejected with that statement that she went to her room, packed a duffle bag of clothes and necessities then left.

Lori hung out with the youngsters until two or three in the morning. After the last youngster called it a night, she slept outside around the apartment with her head on her duffle bag for a couple of nights. One night, she was hanging out with the guys from the hood, when one of the O.G.'s spotted a man who had been walking around the apartments acting like a tough guy towards the kids.

The O.G, who went by the name of Stroller, walked up to the tough guy and banged on him. The guy said he didn't want any problems. Stroller said with an aggressive voice, "Know where the fuck you're at ese. You're in my hood. Let me catch you walking in my hood again; it's on sight." The guy nodded and sped off.

About fifteen minutes passed, and the tough guy went walking down another path behind Lori. In disbelief, Stroller said, "Mother fucker. Come on, little homies." Stroller and two of the youngsters ran up on the guy. Stroller socked the guy in the face. Before the guy could hit the floor, Stroller grabbed him by the collar. Stroller grabbed his gun out from his waistband and pistol-whipped the guy three times.

Although Lori heard everything, she never once turned around to witness. She sat there gripping onto her bag, with her eyes closed and her teeth clenched. Stroller walked back to Lori and said, "Come on, little mama, let's bounce." With nowhere else to be, Lori threw her duffle bag over her shoulder and left with the guys.

They jumped into Stroller's car and headed to one of the big homies cantóns. This big homie was known as Big

Creeps. The guys and Lori all got out of the car and went to the back house to kick it. Creeps had been on one. Cocaine was his drug of choice.

When they walked in, Creeps' son was tired and acting up. Creeps had told his son to lie down, but the kid was antsy because people were there. Creeps started shouting and went to hit his son. He slapped his son in the face. Lori was scared for the kid because Creeps was a big vato.

Lori remembered a trick Gabby taught her about instantly calming someone by squeezing the back of their neck and sending them love. Lori attempted it on Creeps hoping it would work. Creeps melted in Lori's hands, instantly relaxing. He then apologized and talked calmly to his son, who was quietly sobbing. Soon, his son lay down to sleep.

After a while of chilling and drinking at Big Creeps pad, Lori had to go pee. The bathroom didn't have a door, so Stroller told all of the homies to put their backs to the bathroom. He said, "If anyone peeks at her, you're getting a putaso." All the guys turned their backs while Lori, feeling very uncomfortable, tried to go pee. She shouted out, "Man, you guys are making me nervous. Can someone start whistling or something?" The guys started whistling a little tune. As Lori began to pee, she said, "Ahh, that's better."

After an hour more of chilling at Big Creeps' pad, Stroller received a phone call. He told Big Creeps they were going to shake the spot. The guy on the other end of the phone call told Stroller to come through to check out some straps. By the time they reached the guy's house, not too far from the apartments, Lori had grown tired. Also, the thought of being around drunken guys with guns didn't sit right with her. She told the guys that she was going to walk home. The guys told her to be careful. Lori walked a little bit further up the street and lay on the sidewalk. Gripping her duffle bag, Lori fell asleep.

About thirty minutes after lying down to fall asleep, Lori was awakened by a foot to the side of her rib cage. She glanced up to see a man's image standing over her. It was Stroller, angrily he asked, "The fuck you doing laid out like this?" Lori said nothing. Stroller sighed and picked Lori off the ground, saying, "Come on, I ain't leaving you out here."

Lori got in the backseat of Stroller's car. Stroller turned to the youngster sitting in the backseat named Lil' Blue asking him, "You know where I found her?" Lil' Blue had his eyes squinted at Lori as he asked, "Where?" Stroller explained that he went to take a leak up the street and spotted her sleeping on the floor.

To Lori, Lil' Blue asked, "What the fuck's wrong with you, man? Why didn't you go home like you said you were?" Lori looked down at her feet as she replied, "I've been sleeping out on the calles for a few days now." Stroller said, "Naw, that's bullshit mija, you can sleep in my car. I'll leave it open for you for now on."

Lori's eyes watered up as she said, "Thanks, Big Homie, but I don't wanna bother nobody, that's why I didn't say shit." Lil' Blue snapped his lips and told Lori, "C'mon man, you know you can stay with me anytime, sis." Lori nodded her head, still looking at her feet. Stroller said, "Go ahead and sleep in here, for now, Lil' mama. You're safe here." Lori said nothing more; she leaned against the door and fell asleep.

Around 2:30 in the morning, Lil' Blue woke Lori up saying, "C'mon, let's go home." Lori silently got out of the car and followed Lil' Blue into his pad. When they got to his room, he said, "Go on and sleep on the bed man, I'll sleep on the floor." As she went to lie down, Lori quietly said, "Thank you, brother."

The next morning Lil' Blue woke Lori up with an egg sandwich on a paper plate. She sat up and took the plate. Lori sat with her feet up on the bed, and her knees bent, holding the plate with one hand and taking bites of her sandwich with the other. Lil' Blue asked, "So you gonna break it down for me or what?" Lori rolled her eyes and told Lil' Blue precisely what lead to her sleeping outside like that.

Lori said, "I'm thinking of staying with my tía so I can finish out the last semester of school here. But at the same time, I don't wanna start no shit between her and my mom." Lil' Blue said, "Naw man, just tell her that you can't stand living with Andre. She'll take you in."

Lori nodded, she said, "Yeah, that could work, I'll hit her up later today. Hey, thanks for letting me crash here, carnal," Lori lifted the sandwich, as she continued, "And for the sandwich." Lil' Blue replied, "Símon. You can take a shower. When you're ready, we'll go smoke a bleezy." Lori agreed. A real shower sounded terrific to her right about now. Lil' Blue handed her a towel and waited for her in the living room.

Lori met Lil' Blue in the living room when she was ready. He smirked and said, "You can leave your duffle bag in the room, man, ain't no one gonna jack you here." Lori looked down at her bag and let out a single soft laugh. She walked to his room and placed the bag by his door.

Lori and Lil' Blue stepped out to the staircase to blow some smoke. They were on winter break, so they had nothing but time to kill. Lori said, "Now that I'm washed up and looking decent, I think I want to go apply for jobs." Lil' Blue asked, "You wanna go walk around the shopping center and apply?" Lori said, "Yeee, I'm down with that." Lil' Blue went inside to grab some pens. Together they walked around filling out and turning in applications.

On the way back to the apartments, Lil' Blue asked, "Don't you think it'd be dope to work at six flags?" Lori thought about it for a second then replied, "Mmmaaaybe, like if you're working the rides. But showing people their pics or anything else, prolly be weak as fuck." Lil' Blue agreed and said, "That's what I was thinking. I'd be macking it to the morenitas every day as I check their butts, I mean belts, belt buckles."

Lori lightly shoved Lil' Blue as she laughed out, "Yooze a fool." Just as they were walking to the staircase of Lil' Blue's pad, Lori received a phone call. After she hung up the phone, she explained, "It was the guy from the jewelry section at Stan's clothing, he asked me to go in at 4:00 p.m. today." Lil' Blue excitedly said, "Fuck yeah. I knew you would land something."

Come 3:45 p.m., Lori started walking over to the jewelry shop. When she got there, the jewelry owner briefly ran over sales and prices. Lori sold four items in the first twenty minutes. Then a man walked in speaking Spanish to Lori. Lori responded, "I'm sorry, yo no hablo español." The guy turned and walked away. The jewelry owner asked, "You don't speak Spanish?"

When Lori said no, the man said, "I only hired you because I thought you spoke Spanish." Lori replied, "Well, you didn't ask me." The man said, "I thought all you Mexicans spoke Spanish." Lori responded, "Well, jokes on you, I'm the Native American that was forced to speak English. Maybe next time, don't assume." He reached into his pocket and pulled out a twenty-dollar bill. Handing the money to

Lori, he said, "You can go home now. I don't need you here." Lori's eyes opened wide. She felt shocked and offended. She said nothing else and walked out of the store.

Lori entered the apartments and walked around. When she spotted Lil' Blue, his jaw dropped. He asked, "What are you doing back so soon?" Lori told the guys what happened. They all laughed, then Lil' Blue angrily responded, "That's some racist ass bullshit. If only these fools knew whose stolen lands that they're on. And that both Spanish and English are languages forced on us. All of these settlers should be speaking Native American languages. The ignorance is too real." Lori agreed, then shrugged her shoulders and said, "Well, hey, at least we can buy a dub sack." Lori and Lil' Blue smirked at each other.

Stroller walked up to the guys and said, what's up. He was coming home from work. He looked over to Lori and said, "Well, if it isn't La Drifter!" Lori shook her head as she rolled her eyes, and then said, "Home is where the heart is homie." Stroller gave a sly smile and nodded. He truly understood that saying. He excused himself to go home, clean up, and grub.

Around 7:30 in the evening as Lori and some of the youngsters just finished smoking a blunt, someone whistled. It was the whistle that signified cops were in the apartment. All the guys scattered like roaches when the lights turn on, to avoid the police. Lori ran toward the alley behind the apartments.

Once she hit the ally, she began to walk. A man dressed in black told Lori to stop. Lori turned to look at the man and continued walking. The man ran up to Lori and grabbed her right arm. Lori wiggled her arm away and shouted, "Get away from me!" The man grabbed her arm again this time, with a harder grip and grabbed her left arm as well. The man cuffed her and asked, "Why would you walk away from a police officer when he asks you to stop?" Lori responded, "How do I know you're a cop and not some weirdo rapist? You're not even wearing a uniform. Plus, you didn't show me your badge."

The man asked, "Why should that matter?" Lori asked him, "If your daughter was walking alone, and a strange man tells her to stop and grabs at her, what would you expect her to do?" The man grew irritated, exclaiming, "We're talking about you." He began patting her down and reached into her pockets. Lori shook her body and kicked her leg. She asked the officer, "Shouldn't you call a female officer over to reach into my pockets like that perv?" The man replied, "Hey, watch your mouth."

Just then, two male officers walked up. One cop had Lil' Blue, and the other officer had Grimz. The police lined the guys up to the right of Lori. The guy who had his hands on Lori's cuffs asked Lori, "Do you know these guys?" Lori looked over to her right, sounding disgusted, she said, "Eew hell naw I don't know them."

She glanced at the cop holding Lil' Blues wrists, asking him, "Do you know this guy behind me?" The officer said nothing. Lori continued, "Because he came at me all crazy. Claiming to be a cop but didn't flash a badge or nothing. And he patted me down like a female cop, digging into my pockets and such." The cop that Lori was talking to wouldn't even look at her. Lori then asked the policeman behind her, "Are you done harassing me or what?" The cop asked, "Do you live here?" Lori said, "Yes."

Then the undercover asked Lori where she was previous to their encounter. Now sounding annoyed, Lori sighed then answered, "Man, I'm coming from my girlfriend's house. Look, you dug in my pockets and found nothing, you haven't given me a reason as to why I'm in handcuffs, am I under arrest?" The cop replied, "No, you're not under arrest. I'm going to let you go. But next time, when we tell you to stop, you need to stop."

Lori replied, "The next time you tell a young woman in a dark alley to stop while undercover, flash your badge. Otherwise, you're just a creep for all they know." The cop took the cuffs off and let Lori go. Lori turned and slowly walked away. The other officers patted down the guys and found a small sack of weed on Lil' Blue. They questioned the guys for a little bit. Grimz and Lil' Blue talked respectfully knowing that they would go to jail or get a beat down or both by talking the way Lori had. The cops took the sack of weed and let the guys go.

Lori met Lil' Blue at his pad. They went to his room and talked. After about an hour of talking with Lil' Blue, Lori said, "I guess I should get to my tías house before it gets too late." Lil' Blue asked, "Did you ever call her?" Lori admitted that she didn't call her aunt because she didn't have the number. As Lori grabbed for her duffle bag, Lil' Blue said, "Well, if for whatever reason she isn't home or you can't stay there, bring your ass back here." Lori agreed. She gave Lil' Blue a hug and a kiss on the cheek as she wished him a good night.

Lori walked for about thirty minutes until she got to her aunt's house in Arleta. Arleta was one city over just South West of Pacoima. When Lori arrived, her aunt Jenni was sitting with her two sons watching a movie. Jenni opened the door and welcomed Lori in. Lori and Jenni sat at the kitchen table and talked. Lori explained that she needed space from her brother. Jenni told her niece that it was okay for her to stay as long as necessary. So long as she helped out around the house and with the boys. Lori agreed.

Lori spent the next few mornings looking for a job. She would spend her afternoons at the apartments. She tried to be at her aunt's house by the early evening. Within a few days, Lori began working at an Asian cuisine restaurant in Arleta. Her shift would be Monday-Thursday from 9:00 a.m. to 3:00 p.m. just until school started back up. Then they would consider adjusting her hours. Her job paid her under the table.

Although Lori loved walking to work, she bought a used beach cruiser bicycle off of her aunt's neighbor for sixty dollars. When Lori rode her bike to the apartments for the first time, she spotted her friends Suzy, Slick, and Isela. Her homie Slick was the first to say, "What-chu got on my 40 foo?! Haha, what's up fuckin' D-Bo?" Lori laughed and said, "Better knock it off, before you get your chain ganked, and knocked the fuck out like Red foo."

Suzy laughed, then, she told Lori, "Ey, but low key ma, your bike got that little D-Bo squeak goin' on for real." Lori laughed and said, "Ugh, I know, huh? I need some WD-40 or something. I'll be fixing this bike up little by little. More importantly, though, I wanna save up for a car." Suzy asked, "What are you thinking of getting?"

Lori responded, "Shoot, I don't even care. I'm down to get a little used Honda like Gabby. But I don't know how soon that would even happen unless my job was for sure willing to keep me when school starts up. Then again, it's better for my body and the environment if I fix up and ride this bike around." Isela agreed, "Yeah, that's true. Maybe at least ride around until you start college." Lori said, "Or something. Well, I'll be back. I'm gonna go see what's up with Lil' Blue."

Slick hissed as he tightened his jaw and pulled his lips back, exposing his teeth. Lori squinted at him as she asked seriously, "What Slick?" Slick said, "The cops took him in this morning. They said that he matched the description of a shooter, and they found a strap on him." Lori tossed her head back and looked up to the sky. She looked back at Slick, who had a stern look on his face, ensuring that he wasn't joking. She let out a big exhale as she said, "Fffuuuck."

Isela trying to ease Lori's mind, said, "We don't know if he was the shooter or if his gun matches the one used in the shooting. Until they determine that, they only have him for a strap." With her lips pressed together, Lori nodded her head. Lori excused herself and rode her bike to Lil' Blue's pad; she sat at the stairs outside his door. She prayed hard for Lil' Blue. Twenty minutes passed, Lori stood up and rode back to her aunt's house.

On the days she worked, Lori would come home to make dinner. She spent most of her days off from work at the apartments unless her aunt needed a babysitter. Lori kept tabs on Lil' Blue's court results. She found out that his gun and bullets did match the gun and ammo in question. The judge charged Lil' Blue with assault with a deadly weapon. Lori would keep in touch with Lil' Blue through letters. Aside from missing him, she began to find satisfaction in her daily life.

LORI

L ori lived in Arleta from eight years of age until she was twelve years old. Work had begun to slow down for her father, who worked in construction. As soon as summer vacation began, her parents moved Lori and her brother to the apartments just a few weeks before her thirteenth birthday.

Walking around the apartments, Lori saw Gabby and Suzy passing by on their scooters. Lori walked in the direction that she had seen the ladies riding in. Soon she came across Suzy, Gabby, and Isela. Lori decided to introduce herself and talk to them. Isela was the first to say hi. She shook Lori's hand as she said, "Hi Lori, I'm Isela. These are my friends Gabby and Suzy." Gabby and Suzy followed suit by shaking hands and saying hi.

Isela then said, "You kind of look familiar, don't you dance Jingle?" Lori admitted that she did. Isela told Lori that she went to pow wows and danced too. Lori laughed and said, "I know who you are. You look different outside of your fancy shawl regalia." Isela giggled. Isela mentioned that Gabby was Indigenous to the area as well. The girls felt an instant connection from that moment. The girls spent the next two hours talking to each other until Lori excused herself to go home. Lori spent her summer vacation meeting and hanging out with the kids in the apartment.

Lori danced Jingle dress at the pow wows since she was six years old. She learned to dance and make her regalia from an Ojibwe woman. Lori didn't compete; she just danced for the people and took her dancing really serious. People would often ask her to pray for them when she danced. She did so every time with love in her heart and loving thoughts for the people.

Lori's bloodline stemmed from the Yoeme also known as Yaqui tribes. Her seven times Great Grandpa on her mother's side came to California as a colonized soldier from Sonora, Mexico. His job was to help the Spaniards colonize the Native tribes of Southern California down to the far north of what is now Sonoma, California. He settled in Duarte, California. That is where he met his wife who coincidently, was Yoeme from Sonora as well. She had been kidnapped and enslaved. She eventually became a runaway who slipped through the corrupt European enforced system's cracks and was getting by.

The two fell in love and never forgot their roots. Like most other Natives on the West Coast, they raised their kids to claim that they were Mexican in public. It was dangerous at times to be a dark skinned Mexican, but it was dangerous all the time to be "Indian."

Indian was a name that was forced on to the Indigenous people of North, Central, and South America by the first European invaders. Although the people weren't from India, neither were they treated God like (referring to the story some tell of the meaning of the Spanish word Indios) by the Europeans.

During the twenty six years of colonial invasion from the Mexican rancho period of their children's adult years, there was a standard system in place where the Natives worked the fields for business owners; on payday, the business owners handed out alcohol. Whether or not the Natives took the alcohol or got drunk, the owners would still call the sheriffs and claim the Natives to be drunk. The Natives would get picked up by sheriffs and incarcerated for intoxication.

They would stay in confinement until it was time to go back to work. The business owners would then pay their bail and make them work off their debts. In this way, the Natives remained slaves and could not leave the ranches. In the mid-1800s as Americans took hold of the ranches, Mexicans (including the California Natives who were trying to fall through the cracks) worked hard labor for little to no money. They would often be deported to Mexico when the work was done. Some California Natives were sent to Mexico.

The Americans were deathly violent to the California Natives. Although America ceased much of the land under Mexico's ruling, (as I mentioned earlier California was not initially taken from the Natives of Mexico, their ancestral colonization is another story in another place and time) there were still California Native Families living from the land, especially in Northern California.

If European American invaders found a Native family living freely on the land, they took it upon themselves to either torcher and kill them or forced them into slavery. Much like the Catholic Spaniards, the Christian Americans stole and claimed the land in the name of Jesus and the doctrine of discovery.

Lori's dad, Ray's family, was from the Pascua Yaqui Tribe of Arizona. Ray's relatives' lives were disrupted by the same missionary system that came for Central America and most of California. Their history, like all Turtle Island people, was a difficult one, in dealing with colonization.

With the brainwashed fear of going to hell, many Native families incorporate their Native teachings with the Catholic/Christian teachings. Though many disagree with the mixed teachings, many others are content with the way they honor both teachings. And in some cases, Native truth has been hidden in some of the religious teachings by Native peoples long ago.

Lori's grandfather from her father's side came to San Fernando as a young boy. Lori's grandmother was born and raised in San Fernando. Lori's Father Ray met her mother Toni through mutual friends at a Native social gathering. Five years after Ray and Toni met; the two were wed and continually moved around the San Fernando Valley. They weren't ecstatic to live in the apartments, but it was affordable on Toni's salary. Her father Ray got paid in cash, so it was Toni's checks that the apartments went by. Lori and her brother changed three elementary schools because of the moves that Lori's family frequently made. But they were able to stay in the same middle and high schools.

Although Lori had many friends come and go, the girls that she met in her first week at the apartments would become her lifelong friends. Isela's parents and Lori's parents knew each other from the pow wows. To both sets of parents, it was comforting to be so close to other proud Native people. They would grow closer over the years.

In Sylmar, Lori cheered for a pop warner team named The Golden Bears from the time that she was six until she was thirteen. Her brother played football for the same divisions that she cheered for every year. Since Lori was twelve years old, she had been taller than most girls on her teams. Lori always found herself either being the base or the spotter for the stunts. She used to dream of being a flyer, but that day never came.

At ages fourteen and fifteen, she was on an all-star team founded by the valley's pop warner board. During the last year of all-stars, she frequently complained of pain in her left leg during practice. Still, she hit hard during competitions. After each competition, she cried from the pain in her leg. Still, they always took first place.

When all-stars came to an end, she wanted to try out for the J.V. cheer squad at her high school, but the pain that she had been living with in her lower left leg since she was eleven was becoming more painful each day. Eventually, at the age of fifteen, she was walking home from school; the pain became so unbearable that Lori couldn't put any pressure on her leg without the urge to scream in pain. She asked Isela to push her to get home. Isela walked behind Lori, forcing her to go forward.

Finally, they made it home. Lori fell to the floor in her room, crying hysterically. She decided to grab a crutch to see if it would help her walk. It was excruciating still, but the pressure on her leg minimized enough to walk. Her mother realized something was seriously wrong. Up until then, the doctor put it off as inflammation and nothing more. That doctor had prescribed Lori to take Ibuprofen four times a day for the swelling three years prior. Lori did as prescribed for two weeks before deciding her doctor was clueless.

Toni finally took Lori to a leg specialist where they would discover a giant cell tumor was the cause of the pain. The doctor scheduled surgery for extraction. Lori went to the children's hospital first thing in the morning. There, they tested the tumor to find that it was benign. After finding that the tumor was benign, they surgically removed the lump. It had eaten out part of her calf muscles and the tibia.

Once removed, the doctor used a bone cement to replace the missing bone and bone marrow.

The bone cement put in place of the bone, expanded and gave the last of the original standing bone a fracture. It took time for Lori to heal. She would choose to smoke weed and eat edibles but refused to take doctor prescribed pain killers. Lori was grateful that her best friends came to see her at the hospital.

Although she drank on occasion, ate edibles, and smoked weed, Lori seemed to do well in school, even living amongst so many druggies and gangbangers. Her brother Andre used to drink and smoke with her now and again. But after moving into the apartments, he eventually began drinking more and doing coke with some of the other kids he hung around. Andre and Lori began to grow a little distant from each other.

Lori was sad to see her brother doing so terribly with his addictions. Especially because Native American people already had a bad rap of being lazy, alcoholics, and drug addicts. But most of these Native kids struggled with life in the western world. Teachers and Joes off the street would tell Native kids; Natives didn't exist, they were going to end up dead or in jail, pregnant by 13, or never amount to anything but a low life druggie.

That stereotypical kind of discouragement and expectation was common. It was a struggle for many Native children to ignore. All Lori could do was to speak up against it. Furthermore, pray for her brother as well as all of the other kids facing this kind of discrimination. At the same time, she continued to lead by example while finding and working on her own self.

Lori also held a lot of empathy for the Earth that she called Mother. Her parents taught her that Mother Earth has a spirit. And everything that comes from her has a spirit as well. From rocks, plants, water, insect, animal to the human, all are related in the sense that everything contains energy. Lori watched her parents stand for the protection of Mother Earth. They also stood for civil rights. Her parents stood against the desecration of sacred sites, burial sites, oil extractions, natural gas extractions, water damming, pollution, and deforestation, to name a few. It was always a scary stance as corporations repeatedly proved through violence that they had no concern for citizens or the Earth.

Once when Lori was eight years old, a man flicked his cigarette butt out of the window. It landed near Lori's feet. The butt was still lit. Lori picked it up, looked both ways then ran across the street to the car that was now sitting at a stop sign. Lori tossed the lit butt in the man's lap as she shouted, "Sir, you dropped something!" The man threw his gear into park and opened the door. Lori ran across the street to her mother. Her mother stood very serious, although she was laughing hysterically in her mind.

The man grabbed the cigarette butt and began shouting at Lori's mother, "What the fuck is wrong with your kid?" Toni asked, "You have the nerve to ask what's wrong with my daughter after you littered? Are you aware that you can get a ticket for littering? Or cause a fire by throwing a lit cigarette out of the window? Or that it will wash into the ocean? So don't you dare come cussing at me when you were the one in the wrong."

Lori took a step forward and said, "I just want you to take care of our Mother Earth, sir." The man glared at Lori. He realized he was in fact in the wrong. But he was angry at the way Lori called him out on it. His anger began to lift as he said, "You're right. I promise to throw away my cigarette butts the right way from now on, kid." Lori smiled and said, "I realize asking you to quit altogether for the sake of your own health would be pushing it, so I'll just say, 'Thank you.'" The man laughed and told Toni, "You're raising her the right way." Toni smiled and nodded her head in gratitude to the man. He walked back to his car and drove off.

Despite the typical family dysfunctions, Lori loved her immediate family very much. She found herself living with them on and off as she continued to grow physically, mentally, emotionally and spiritually.

BACK YARD BOOGIE

Suzy had her headphones on listening to her favorite Carlos Santana album "Abraxas." She sat on the steps outside of her apartment. Suzy smoked a bowl to unwind from another day of house work. She loved smoking bud while she allowed her mind to get lost in the music, which was easier to do when her apartment was clean, and dinner made.

Isela and Lori were joking and laughing on their walk back from the candy store. The 'candy store' was someone in the apartment complex who decided to sell candy out of their apartment. Suzy spotted the two ladies, so she whistled to get their attention. The two ladies walked over to the staircase to join Suzy, they hugged her and then took a seat on the steps below her.

Suzy asked Isela, "What did you buy me, loca?" Isela pulled out a tube of Lucas Pelucas. Isela tossed the container in Suzy's lap. Suzy glanced down at the container in her lap and said, "Oh hell yeah, good looking out baby girl." Holding the pipe out to Isela, Suzy offered, "Here I'll trade you for a couple of hits." Isela grabbed the piece from Suzy's hand and hit it. Isela held the pipe up to Lori silently offering Lori a hit, Lori shook her head no.

Suzy's mom Lisa pulled into their parking slot about 320 feet from where the girls were sitting. Isela put the pipe in her pocket out of respect for Lisa. Lisa got out of her car and approached the girls. The girls and Lisa greeted each other with a smile and a "Hello." Changing her smile to a smirk, Lisa passed the girls on the stairs and implied, "Smells good."

Suzy asked, "You want some?" Lisa shook her head, retorting, "Nope, but that's the kinda shit I would rather you guys do inside the pad though, cause ain't nothing but little snitches around here." Lisa was referring to the downstairs neighbors and the neighbors across from them, who regularly called management and cops to complain about every little thing. The girls shrugged, and they slightly giggled. Suzy said, "You're right, mom, sorry. Dinner's on the stove." Lisa nodded her head and walked into the apartment.

Isela changed the subject anxiously, stating, "Oh yeah, it went down this morning. The juras raided, and snatched up Dooms and Weso." Lori gasped and responded, "Whaaaat? Awe man that sucks." Feeling bad for the guys, Suzy replied, "Awe fuck that's gatcho," as she shook her head side to side. Lori asked, "Why did they gaffle them up, though?"

Isela answered, "Honestly, I don't know, but I think they were mainly looking for Crimes because they went to his pad first and tore it up. Crimes wasn't home, but his moms let them in. I think Dooms and Weso were just in the wrong place at the wrong time. I hope they get released tonight." Suzy agreed, "I know. Dooms can handle himself, but poor Weso's so skinny he might get handled, for real."

Silence fell over the ladies for a couple of seconds, Suzy said, "I kinda wanna shake the spot. You guys wanna take this session to the jungles?" The ladies agreed. Suzy stood and walked to her screen door, shouting, "Hey ma, I'll be back a little later." Lisa shouted back, "Please be careful." The ladies walked down the steps and over to the center of their apartment complex. On the way, they ran into Miranda, who had just finished making weed drop-offs. Miranda greeted them with hugs and kisses. The ladies invited Miranda to join them in the jungles. Miranda walked with the ladies, who each found a seat on the bench where they sat talking.

Soon, Gabby approached the ladies. She handed Suzy a flyer to a party that would be going down that coming Friday. As she did so, Gabby exclaimed, "Tehoovet taamet my loves! Check this out. It sounds like a good time que no? Let me know if you fine ass females are down to roll up." Suzy read the flyer. She scrunched her shoulders, saying, "Hmmm, yeah, I don't see why not?"

Suzy passed the flyer to her right-hand side, Lori grabbed it, and after scanning it, she agreed to go too. Lori offered the flyer to her right-hand side. Isela looked to see who was hosting it, replying with excitement, "Oh hell yeah, hosted by my prima Stella's party crew. I'm definitely there." Miranda was the only one who opted out.

Suzy remarked, "Awe Miranda come on. It's always more fun when you roll." Miranda uttered, "Seriously, I would love to go, but I haven't got to see much of Miguel lately. I just wanna chill with him at home. Maybe I'll catch you guys the next time around." Gabby added, "Well, boo to you not going. But family does come first." She then looked over to Suzy, asking, "We can take my car if not, but do you think we can roll up in the van since the low-low is out of the question?"

Suzy answered, "I mean as long as it's running right, yeah, that should be fine." Gabby snapped her fingers. "Alright dope, it's going down. You know we need us a ladies night before school starts up again," Gabby spoke with excitement in her voice. Suzy rolled her eyes, saying, "Ugh, school, don't remind me."

The girls heard a gunshot, which sounded like it was in one of the parking lots on Pakooynga St. They watched some of the neighbors run towards the noise to see what happened. Miranda said, "These people are ballsy as fuck, to hear gunshots and run toward it so quickly. Like at least take precaution, but naw, all just to have the chisme first and shit." Gabby laughed, she said, "For reals, people don't think things through. I get making sure people are okay, but we all know that ain't what these chismosas are about."

Just then, Denise came running up. She sat down and panted as she insisted, "I was here the whole time." Suzy responded, "Of course you were." Gabby asked, "Where's your roll dawg?" Denise answered, "He's home chilling. He's been there the whole time too." Isela laughed and said, "Sounds good. But seriously, are you okay?"

Denise, still slightly panting, replied, "No, yeah, I'm good. It's just, shit was crazy man, I was in mama Sita's car looking for my iPod under the seat, and Clever was throwing some trash from the car away, right? Something told me to look up. I saw a dude with a bandana over his face walking towards Clever. I grabbed the strap and got on my belly, sure enough, he pulled out a cuete, so I shot him in the arm that he was holding the cuete. I threw the strap under the seat, locked the door, and we ran. I told all the nosey fucks running toward me as I ran, 'Run. He has a gun,' to take eyes off of us. I signaled for Clever to go home, I figured it would be best if we split up for a while."

Gabby asked, "Why didn't you shoot him in the head?" Denise responded, "Because it's broad daylight, so I just thought I'd give him a warning shot in case someone was watching." Gabby nodded her head as she said, "Fair enough."

Denise asked, "What was the topic before I rudely interrupted? Gabby handed Denise the flyer asking, "You wanna roll with us?" Denise read it. She knew her best friend Clever couldn't go because he was a cholito who stood out like a sore thumb, and they might end up fighting. Denise handed the flyer back, saying, "Naw, I think I got some family shit that day."

About twenty-five minutes later, two police officers walked up to the group of girls, one of the cops inquired, "Good evening, have you ladies been out here long?" Miranda replied, "Yes, sir, for about an hour now." The cop then asked, "Have you heard any gunshots since you've been out here?" Miranda insisted, "Yeah, I heard one shot and seen people running toward it, so we just sat here keeping an eye in that direction to be sure the shooter didn't come in, which he didn't. Why what happened?"

The cop replied, "We got called out about a shot fired but haven't found a victim or a suspect. Did you see anyone come in who appeared to be shot?" Suzy answered, "Sorry, officer, no one has passed by us other than these kids on bikes." The cops thanked the ladies for their cooperation and wished them a good night. The ladies said good night to the officers. Suzy reignited a conversation with the ladies.

A few minutes later, Denise thought out loud, saying, "I wonder if that fool hopped in a car with someone, or what? Cause if so, that means they probably saw who Clever and I are. Dang, I wonder if he's gonna go to the hospital or let it heal like nothing." Suzy agreed, she said, "I know, huh? He had to have come in a car if the cops haven't found a victim. Man, I bet his homies are gonna be clowning his ass about this." The ladies giggled and agreed. Denise jumped up, saying, "Well, I think I'm in the clear, so I'm gonna go to Clever's pad. I'll see you guys later. The ladies all said bye to Denise.

They hung out in the jungles for another ten minutes before a group of youngsters from the neighborhood walked up to join them. The guys greeted the ladies with handshakes then found themselves seated on a bench close to where the ladies were sitting.

One of the guys who went by the name of Young Creeps called Miranda over to where the guys were sitting. Knowing what he wanted, she reached in her bra and pulled out a sack of weed. Miranda stood up and walked over to the youngster who had called her. She lifted her chin, asking, "What's up, Young Creeps?" The youngster asked Miranda for a twenty sack of weed.

Miranda exchanged the weed for the money in a simple handshake. Young Creeps said, "Good looking out, homegirl." Miranda nodded her head, replying, "Símon," she walked back to the ladies. Miranda said, "Since I'm up, I think I'm gonna just go home." Suzy said, "Awwwwe, okay, ma, we'll see you tomorrow." Miranda replied, "For sure," as she hugged Suzy. She went down the line to embrace each of the ladies. Miranda turned to the guys and said, "Good night, mocosos." The guys all said good night to Miranda.

When Miranda got home, she told Miguel about the flyer party. He said, "Flyer party, huh? You should go and have fun, Lil' mama." Miranda replied, "Well, I mean, it sounds fun and all, but I was kinda hoping to kick it with you. I haven't seen you in aaages." Miguel said, "I know, it feels like that, huh baby girl? I'm sorry I haven't been around much the last few weeks, but jales keep coming up. I have a chance to make an easy fifty G's this weekend. When opportunities like this come along, I gotta jump on it."

Miranda scrunched her lips together and shifted them to the left, then smirked as she raised her shoulders and asked, "Well, you gotta do what you gotta do, right?" Miguel responded, "I mean I don't have to, have to, but I did arrange the deal already plus it's a quick vay-cay and payday. I wanna make as much as I can while I can, to have a stash for you guys. Do you wanna go with me and check out the scene while I handle 'biz'?" Miranda asked, "Where are you going, and for how long?" "Oregon. I hear there's beautiful scenery out there, snow and shit. I'll be leaving mañana. And I'll be back home by Sunday en la noche," Miguel answered.

Miranda gave Miguel a blank stare for a second before responding with an attitude, "What the hell kind of vacation? You're pretty much driving there and right back. Naw, I'm straight. I guess I'll kick back here." Miguel laughed. He said, "Well, it's more like a change of scenery then que no? Okay, mamash suit yourself, if you don't go with me, I think you should go to the party with your homegirls and have fun. And when I get back, I'll take you to dinner or bowling or anything that you wanna do." Miranda nodded in agreement, she scrunched her shoulders then said, "Yeah, fuck it, I guess I will."

The next day Miranda met up with Suzy and Gabby by the automatic gate near the corner of Glenoaks Blvd. and Pakooynga St. She told them that she would be able to make it to the party after all. Suzy said in excitement, "Yay! Oou, does that mean we can roll up in the Pimpala instead of the ghetto ass soccer mom van? I mean unless we're rolling mad deep." Miranda replied, "Well, count heads and keep me posted. Either way, I'll drive. That way, you can party." Suzy excitedly said, "Oh hell yeah, that's fiiirme loca. I'll get a headcount A.S.A.P."

Friday night came, Gabby and Lori knocked on Suzy's screen door. Suzy shouted, "It's for me, ma. I'm gonna bounce. And don't wait up for me." Lisa said, "Okay, mija quida te por favor." Suzy kissed her mom on the cheek as she passed her by in the living room. "I will, Mommy. I love you," Suzy told her mom. Lisa replied, "Love you too, mijita."

Wearing a light pink, skin-tight, long sleeve dress, Suzy opened the door to greet the ladies. She said, "Q-vo mis babydolls. Let's roll." The girls walked down the stairs. They began walking over to Miranda's house. They didn't get too far before Bouncer, one of the local neighborhood cholos, noticed the ladies.

Bouncer was with a young woman who came with her girlfriends to hang out with the guys from the neighborhood. Bouncer completely interrupted his conversation to ask Suzy, "Where the fuck you think you're going dressed like that?" Suzy walked up to give him a big hug. As she did so, she replied, "We're meeting at Miranda's, then off to a flyer party."

He sounded defensive as he asked, "You're gonna be walking in the streets dressed like that?" Suzy smiled as she shifted her eyes side to side with a look of feeling awkward written on her face, she lifted her arms in a shrug replying, "Uh, yeeeah. I don't wanna drive over there, get drunk and drive back. Why?" Bouncer asked, "Are you strapped?" Suzy responded with a giggle, "Nah, uh." Bouncer said, "Na man, I can't have you walking the streets dressed like that, it's not safe. I'm gonna have to get you a lil' cuete that you can carry in your purse sis."

Suzy knew Bouncer wasn't crazy for being concerned. Rapes and murders happened just about every day in Pacoima. Still, Suzy held in her laugh as she replied, "It's just right up the street carnal. It'll be fine." Bouncer replied, "Look, just please be safe. As a matter of fact," Bouncer pulled out a small handgun. He handed it to Suzy as he insisted, "Take this. And call me when you get to Miranda's. Then call me when your ass gets home. I don't care what time it is, just call me." Suzy took the gun, made sure the safety was on, and then fit it in her handbag. She gave Bouncer another hug, followed by a kiss on the cheek. She said, "Eh, I'll text you. I love you. And you be safe too carnal."

As the ladies walked away, Bouncer very seriously said, "Man, I'm gonna cop you a cuete for reals, though." Without looking back at Bouncer, Suzy threw her left hand in the air signaling thumbs up. Bouncer looked at the girl who he was previously talking to and shrugged as he said, "Sisters."

(Bouncer was a firme camarada of mine. We smashed together for days. When I passed away, he stood at my casket and promised that he would always keep a close eye on mi familia and treat them as his own. He stayed true to his promise. He has maintained a good relationship with both my jefita and hermanita.)

The ladies continued to Miranda's house. Suzy called when they were at the corner to ask Miranda to open the door. Miranda told them to go through the side gate, which led to the backyard. Isela was already in the yard, rolling a blunt.

The ladies walked to the backyard. They took turns greeting Isela with hugs and kisses. They all sat down around the table under the balcony. As Isela lit the blunt, Suzy anxiously said, "Shit, I forgot to bring my Visine, you know them stoner red eyes ain't attractive at all." Isela passed the blunt to her left. She then pulled a little bottle out of her purse. She threw it over to Suzy. Suzy said, "Oh, hell yeah, good looking out mujer." Giving a little wink, Isela said, "Don't even trip." The blunt and the Visine both made their way around the table.

Over at the party house, Stella's party crew was all set up and ready to throw their back yard flyer party. Tanya had just finished posting all of the info on the party lines. The ladies of the party crew huddled up. They decided who would be working which shifts for the night. They would be taking shifts in groups of two.

No matter what, two ladies would be at the door collecting the money and patting down the ladies, two guys would be with them to pat down the guys, two ladies would be working the go-go boxes, two ladies at the Nos tank and two ladies would be at the bar at all times.

When they weren't working at a station, they got to party it up with their guests. After the meeting, one of the ladies from the party crew shouted out their crew name, "Stylish Stunnas!" They all cheered out, "Stylish Stunnas!" The ladies laughed around for a bit before heading to their work stations.

Isela and the girls were all pretty much ready. They chilled at Miranda's house for a little bit. Before they left, they touched up their hair and makeup. By 9:45 p.m., the ladies were jumping in the car. Gabby, Lori, Suzy, Isela, and Miranda rolled up to the party looking beautiful. They walked to the front of the line, where they were greeted at the gate with mad love from Stella and Tanya. They were welcomed in and told to have fun.

Stella knew all of the ladies who came with her cousin Isela. Whenever Isela's family would have gatherings, Isela's friends always came over to hang out and eat. Stella often brought some of her friends to family functions too, including Tanya.

A young female, waiting in line to get in, shouted out, "Oh, cause there's not a line or what? Why didn't you search those bitches, but we all gotta wait to get searched?" Suzy looked to see who shouted that. The girl was mad dogging Suzy. Suzy gave a crooked smile to the girl then kept walking. Tanya spoke up, saying, "Hey, we're all here to have a good night, but you don't have to be here, you can leave." The girl rolled her eyes and stayed in line.

The ladies were impressed when they got to the back yard. The dance floor was big, extending past the porch. There were two go-go boxes set up on the dance floor outside of the porch. The DJ had a dope lighting and DJ system. Some of the ladies in the crew were serving liquor and beer at a bar. Beside the bar, there were two ladies with the Nos tank. Miranda walked straight to the dance floor and started dancing to the music. The other ladies walked over to the bar. After getting their drinks, they met Miranda on the dance floor.

The girl who had made the remark out by the gate walked in with her friends. She scanned the yard immediately, looking for Suzy. When she spotted Suzy, she snarled her lip and gave Suzy a dirty look. Suzy was too busy having fun to notice.

Some guys walked into the yard shouting out their party crew name. Following their call, Stella's crew shouted their party crew name out loud. The guys and ladies went back and forth, shouting their party crew names a couple of times. It was all in good fun. Gabby's brother Dennis walked in with his friends. Lori spotted him and tapped Gabby then pointed to Dennis with her lips. Gabby looked over to her brother. When they caught eyes, they both lifted their heads to each other as to say, "What's up."

The party was active; people were scattered around the yard, enjoying the music. Some folks had cups at hand filled with beer or liquor. Some had balloons filled with Nos, some had blunts filled with weed, while some gente had all of the above. There were females taking turns dancing seductively with each other on the go-go boxes. The DJ played dope music all night. Now and again, the different party crews took turns seeing who can shout their crew's name out the loudest.

Suzy and her friends were having a good time. They mostly danced with each other in a group. Now and again, the ladies would dance with a guy who would ask. Suzy walked back to the bar for a refresher. The guy standing next to Suzy recognized her from middle school. They crushed on each other then. He tapped on Suzy's shoulder. She looked up to see who it was. It didn't take long for her to recognize him; she smiled. In excitement, she shouted, "Oh my goodness, David. How are you?" They gave each other a big hug. He said, "I been good, girl. How have you been?"

They engaged in small chit chat before David offered to pay for her drink. They grabbed their drinks and walked toward the back of the yard, where the music wasn't as loud. Miranda glanced over now and again to make sure Suzy was fine. Judging by the huge smile on Suzy's face, she felt there was no reason to worry. Suzy and David showed complete interest in wanting to catch up on each other's lives up until that point. They both agreed that they thought of and missed each other.

The song "Lookout weekend" by Debbie Deb began to play. Suzy put her arms in the air, snapped her fingers and started swaying her body as she said, "Ooou, that's my song. Let's dance?" David nodded, yes. They walked over to the dance floor. Suzy walked up to her friends and started dancing with David.

The girl who had been giving Suzy the bad looks decided that she would keep pushing Suzy with her butt and hips as she danced wildly. Eventually, she stepped on Suzy's foot with her left high heel. Suzy grabbed the girls' leg before she could move her foot away. Suzy shoved her by the leg. The girl caught her balance then grabbed Suzy by the hair, and socked her in the face. She had a grip on Suzy's hair. Suzy's face was toward the ground. She lifted her arms to take some swings at the girl. With her fists, Suzy could feel the girls face at every swing.

One of the girls' friends was about to take a swing at the back of Suzy's head. Miranda pushed her shouting, "One on one bitch!" Miranda angrily looked the girl up and down. The girl didn't say a word, nor did she make a move. Suzy and her opponent made their way to the floor. Tanya caught wind of the fight going on. Tanya ran up to the rumble and broke it up. David reached for Suzy and picked her up. He and all the girls asked Suzy if she was okay, Suzy quickly nodded yes.

Tanya precisely knew what happened when she saw who the other girl was. Tanya told the girl and her friends that they had to leave. Some of the ladies from the party crew escorted them out. The girl was complaining the whole way out and wondering why Suzy didn't have to leave too. Tanya asked Suzy, "You good, mama?" Suzy felt around at her face. She replied, "Yeah. I'm good, mujer." Tanya nodded her head and walked away.

All of the girls showed concern for Suzy. She told them, "I'm cool. Keep having fun. I' m gonna step away for a breather." David walked Suzy off of the dance floor. As he did, David asked, "Damn, could that girl make it any more obvious that she straight up hated on you?" Suzy smirked.

She replied, "From the gate, literally!" Suzy combed out her hair with her fingers. She asked David how she looked. David said, "Gorgeous as ever."

Suzy said, "I'm so embarrassed that just went down in front of you, my bad, for reals." David shook his head side to side as he replied, "Na, don't be embarrassed. It wasn't even your fault. Now, if she mopped you up, I could see you being embarrassed. But damn, you put in work on that girl's face." Suzy smiled, asking, "For reals, I did?" David said, "Hell yeah, all she did was mess up your hair a little. But she walked away bleeding." Suzy said in a sad tone, "Aww, she did?"

Suzy quickly switched it up with a smile, saying, "Well, I guess that's what she gets. Anyways, enough about an unimportant subject matter. I wanna hear more about you. Why didn't you go to the high with us?" David and Suzy stood there and talked. About an hour had passed, Miranda walked up, saying it was about that time to leave. Suzy nodded at her and put her finger up, gesturing, "Just a sec."

David said, "I enjoyed catching up with you, Suzy. Is it okay to have your number to keep in touch?" Suzy gave David her phone number. They gave each other a tight hug as they wished each other a good night. Both of them walked away, smiling.

The ladies drove about four blocks away before Gabby's phone began to ring. It was one of her brother's friends. He said, "Dude, Dennis blacked out again. The cops rolled up, and the homies shook the spot with the quickness. Can you come to get us?" Gabby had her hand over her eyes. Shaking her head, she said, "I'll be right there."

Gabby told Miranda what happened. They turned the car around and went back to the party. The cops pulled off as

Miranda got there. "Do you need help, ma?" Suzy asked. "Na, I think I got this," Gabby replied. Suzy declared, "I'll go anyways."

The ladies hopped off the car and walked to the backyard. Suzy spotted Stella then shouted, "Great party, baby girl!" Stella laughed out, "Yeah, so I heard, you okay?" Stella asked Suzy. Suzy nodded, "Yeah I am, that was so random. But Gabby's brother is passed out in the bathroom, though. We came back to pick him up."

Stella's eyes widened. She looked over to Gabby, asking, "Oh, he's your brother? Homeboy scared the crap out of me. He hit the ground so hard that I think he might have a concussion." Stella gestured her hand for the ladies to follow her. Stella led the ladies to the bathroom.

Gabby's brother had begun to come to, but he was completely zoned out. He had a look of confusion on his face when Gabby called to him. Dennis' friend Joey was in the bathroom with him. Joey confessed, "He passed out, right as the cops got here. Everyone we came with booked it, but they didn't know Dennis passed out. The girls told me to bring him in here and lock the door."

Gabby rolled her eyes as she reciprocated, "This fool's such an idiot. I'm glad you stayed with him, though. Now, help me take him to the car, yeah?" Joey and Gabby lifted Dennis off of the floor. Both Gabby and Joey threw an arm of Dennis' around each of their shoulders.

Gabby thanked Stella for looking out for Dennis. They walked out to the car. On the way out, Gabby was scolding Dennis, "Dude, you need to kick back with all that powder, next time you might not be so lucky." Lori sat on Isela's lap in the backseat. Gabby put Dennis in the middle. Joey sat next to Dennis. Gabby sat up front on the passenger floor in between Suzy's legs. By the time they pulled up to the apartments, Dennis seemed fine. Gabby thanked Miranda for being the designated driver.

"We'll see you tomorrow, yeah?" Gabby asked Miranda. Miranda replied, "Yeah, ma, most likely." Suzy said, "Andale, drive safe. Have a good night, baby girl." They all wished Miranda a good night. Everybody got off of the car, as they walked on to the sidewalk they all wished each other a good night and split up.

The next day, Gabby brought Dennis breakfast to his room. He sat up to eat. Gabby sat on the edge of his bed, "How does your head feel?" She asked. "It's okay. It's kinda throbbing, though," Dennis replied. Concerned, Gabby insisted, "You know you scare me every time you do that stuff. I swear I think to myself, 'Oh my gosh, is this it? Is this the last time he's going to O.D? Do I gotta be the one to break the news to mom? Or do I get to have a brother for another day?'"

Dennis pressed his lips together as he listened. Gabby continued, "Next time it might not be a hit to your head, it might be a hit to my heart. I love you carnal, take it easy, uh?" Dennis nodded. "Thanks for breakfast sis," was all Dennis could manage to say. With her notebook in hand, Gabby kissed Dennis on the forehead and walked out.

Gabby walked toward the benches to smoke a morning bowl. Isela was on the steps outside of her apartment. She spotted Gabby walking, Isela whistled. Gabby walked over to Isela, who was blazing with her neighbor Johnny also known as Grimz. Gabby walked up, greeting them both with a "Good morning." In sync, they greeted her back, "Good morning." Gabby said, "I was just headed to the jungles to blaze a bowl." Isela said, "Well, here, hit this." They finished the weed that was in Isela's mini bubbler.

Isela asked Gabby how her brother was feeling. Gabby answered, "He says he's okay. I just left him at the pad." Isela said, "Good. Man, I swear that fool has more lives than a freakin' kitty cat." Gabby smirked, saying, "You ain't lying." Gabby reached over for the bubbler. She packed another bowl. Those couple of bowls had them all feeling faded.

Gabby asked Isela and Grimz what they were going to get into later in the day. Grimz said he was going to hang out with the guys from his tagging crew up the street. One of his friends was throwing a kickback. In a feisty tone, Isela asked Grimz, "Oh yeah, cause we don't want to go to a kickback, huh?" Grimz snapped his lips then said, "You already know, you guys are welcome to roll up." Isela said, "I was only teasin' you. I'm going to a family function in a few. You guys are welcome to join me too."

Gabby asked Isela, "Oh yeah? Where's this going to be at?" Isela pointed her lips towards the south, replying, "A'ya, in East L.A." Gabby shook her head, "I'm straight. I think I'm going to stick around here." Isela said, "It's all good. I'm anxious to go and see a couple of my cousins. It's been a cool ass minute since I've seen some of them." Gabby asked, "What is the get together for?" Isela replied, "They're having a coming of age ceremony for two of my little cousins. After the ceremony, we'll throw them a little fiesta."

Gabby said, "Oh, no way? That's what's up, mamash. I love that you guys keep the traditions going in your family." Isela responded, "We try, some more than others. I mean you see it; there are a lot of traditional activities still going on these days. But you got religious Natives, who refuse to participate, then you got the teenagers like us that should be continuing to learn and practice the ways and traditions, but we rather mess around and kick it with the homies. Most of us keep going in and out. It's just so much easier to be messing up in this western world than to be on a straight spiritual path. I know I'm not ready for all of that right now."

Gabby agreed, "I feel you. At least you acknowledge it. Now, as a teenager, I don't usually get involved with our ceremonial gatherings like before. I feel like I'd be disrespecting my Nation if I'm not walking the red road, yet still going to ceremonies after sipping on a beer or something. But I know one day soon I will walk the red road again. I guess we'll get there when we're ready, yeah?"

Isela smirked and nodded yes as she said, "I'm not gonna lie, I love our culture and traditions, but the everyday corrupt city life that's forced on us to live out here is what easily separates me from the ways that I should embrace. This western way of life completely disconnects us from the natural world. But yes, when we're ready, it will come easier. You know, when I stop kicking it with all of you horrible influences."

Gabby laughed. She said, "Yeah, right, because you weren't the one who smoked me out for my first time or nothing back in middle school, huh." Isela replied, "Fuuuuuck, I did, huh? Man, those were the good ole' days too."

Isela asked Gabby, "Colonialism aside if weed, alcohol, and money weren't an issue, would you do more things with your Nation?" Gabby said, "Absolutely, I would. Culture has had a positive influence on my views and my music. I know one day I'll give back, but I'm more interested in finishing school to do massage and music right now."

Just then, Isela's family walked out of their apartment. Isela's dad Andy wore creased blue Levi's, a creased black button up long sleeve dress shirt with white and turquoise ribbons, and some black leather boots. He had his black hair long and pulled back into a braid. He wore a black bandana around his forehead, tied behind his head just below the ponytail of his braid.

Isela's mom Grace wore a long white skirt, a beautiful turquoise blouse, and some white leather sandals. The ties of the sandals wrapped up and crisscrossed above the ankles. Grace wore turquoise earrings with a matching necklace. She wore her dark brown hair down, which sat just above her butt, wavy and thick. Isela's older brother Gil dressed like a rocker. He had long hair too, but he wore a higher ponytail on the mid-back of his head, he shaved the sides and back of his head.

Isela's baby brother Mikey dressed just like his dad. The only difference was Mikey refused now to have long hair due to all the teasing and fights at school. He had a fade. Isela said, "Whelp, I guess that's my cue. I'll see you guys later." Isela shook Grimz's hand. She stood up and hugged Gabby. Isela walked over to her mom's car.

Grimz told Gabby, "I'm gonna shake the spot too. I'll catch you al rato." Gabby replied, "Orale." Then she shook Grimz hand. Grimz jetted down the stairs. He headed over to his girlfriend's apartment.

Gabby took a stroll through the apartments. She loved the feeling of walking around in the morning. She walked over to the jungles. Gabby sat down on a bench. She closed her eyes, took a deep breath, and smiled as she exhaled. She opened her eyes and then turned to a blank page in her notebook. Without hesitation, Gabby began to write a song.

GABBY

B oth of Gabby's parents were from the Tataviam and Tongva Nations. Before the depressing mission era, the Tongva had been residing throughout what is now forcibly known as Los Angeles County, parts of the IE, parts of the Orange and Riverside County areas and four of the Channel Islands. (Before the European invasions, the people of these areas were better known by their family clans and the Villages where they were born.)

Whereas the Tataviam Nation lived mostly in Santa Clarita Valley up to the Antelope Valley's edge and often married into the families of the northernmost parts of the San Fernando Valley. All of the local Villages of these areas were known to marry about seven villages out, which included marriage with the Chumash and other nearby Nations as well. If I drew a map to show you where many of these California Native Nations' territories were when the colonizers invaded them, their borders might look more like a checkerboard rather than a straight line.

Both of her Nations have their monthly board meetings. They have been trying to become federally recognized for over a couple of decades. Their treaties with the United States were signed and disregarded. The BIA had since been making the act of federal recognition and land rights a difficult task to complete. It's felt as though the United States' goals and hopes have been to take every piece of land while eliminating the existence of the Native Americans through murder as well as the conversion of religion, lifestyle, relocation, blood quantum, and paperwork.

The United States' teachings of blood quantum also make it difficult for the offspring of those who were from federally recognized Nations to continue to be recognized when birthing kids of mixed Nations. Gabby's Nations were among many Nations in the United States whose treaties were signed but not ratified. According to what they called the 18 lost treaties, many families across California were to reside together on large isolated plots of land. After some families were gun forced to sign, they were escorted by wagon with American soldiers or forced to walk to the reserve. The fifty thousand acres set aside for Gabby's Nations is now known as Tejon Ranch.

The U.S. soldiers murdered some families before they could arrive at that reserve. After the forced relocation, the treaties would go missing, therefore becoming nonexistent. Indian Affairs superintendent Edward Beale who proved to be enemy of the Natives, claimed the treaty land of Fort Tejon for his own, ridding the Natives from the property. The treaties resurfaced fifty years later, never to be reinstated. Still, Native Nations haven't stopped declaring themselves as Sovereign Nations.

Nations also hold stories of land grants being removed by or wrongfully sold to the new coming people of great fortune and status such as Charles Maclay. These true stories result in death and homelessness for Native people.

Gabby's parents divorced when Gabby was three, but they kept a mutual understanding for the sake of their kids. Dennis was Gabby's older brother and only sibling. Both kids chose to live with their mother. Gabby's mother, Tiffany, was Tataviam and Tongva. Both Nations were known as Fernadeño after they became enslaved into the San Fernando Mission, along with some Serrano and Chumash people as well. Her Father was Gabrieleño.

Both Gabrieleño and Fernadeño are names that the First Nations people of the area had been forced into after the Spanish invasion and enslavement into the Missions. The Gabrieleño were mostly Tongva, although there were other surrounding Nations such as the Serrano, and Chumash nations who were also enslaved into the San Gabriel Mission.

Both of her bloodlines link her to the villages of Houtnga (El Monte), Pasheeknga (San Fernando), Pakooynga (Pacoima), and Chaguayanga (Castaic junction).

Gabby had raw talent. She was capable of writing songs within a matter of minutes. Once she started writing, it usually flowed smoothly. The quickest she had ever written a song was in five minutes. She also had plenty of notebooks that contained one or two-sentence rhymes.

When she got stuck on a song, she would go back to those sentences to see if she might fit any of them into her current writings. If she found a place to insert the sentences, she would cross a line through them to remind herself that she used it.

Songwriting was one of Gabby's greatest passions. She felt comfortable in the recording booth. She had already written and performed a couple of hooks for some of her rapper friends. Gabby always had fun writing hooks for other people. She made it look effortless. They would play the beat with their verse or idea for her. She would close her eyes and listen to the words while moving her head to the beat.

Gabby would open her eyes, place the pen on the paper, and scribble a few lines down. Gabby would start singing what she wrote to the beat until it sounded like a match. After singing it a couple of times, she'd say, "Okay. I think I got it." She'd sing it again with confidence. Everyone would agree that was it. Then she'd hit the booth and record it for them.

Being in the studio was like a high for Gabby. She loved the feeling of singing into the microphone. She loved listening to the finished product. It gave her a sense of pride. She had so far only recorded hooks for other people. Her cousin Mark had a studio set up in his room.

Mark made a deal with Gabby to trade recording sessions for hooks. She was itching to finish the process of recording her first solo album. Although she had a ton of songs, she wasn't quite ready to complete her album. Gabby was saving her money for beats and copyrights.

Like most kids of the hood, Gabby had a problematic and, at times, traumatic childhood. Gabby adapted to life around violence, drugs, and gangs. One of the O.G.'s in her neighborhood heard through some youngsters, including her best friend Tripps, that Gabby was down for them and that she should get put on the hood. The O.G. took a walk with Gabby to pick her brain and see where she stood.

Gabby explained to him that she had every intention to be a singer and a massage therapist. Gabby further expressed her fear of gang life getting in the way of her music career as far as travel went. The O.G. respected the words that came from Gabby's mouth. He told her he had never heard a youngster speak with so much assurance. He then said, "You got a good head on your shoulders. If anyone bothers you about getting put on the hood, let me know, they'll get handled."

It took a long time for Gabby to realize that the colonial enforcers influenced the behavior of her community from the trauma as well as lack of education and resources made available to them. After many conversations with Isela, she realized that much of the trauma came as a result of colonialism, which introduced harsh living conditions and behaviors such as rape, theft, enslavement, imprisonment, and murder.

Also, for generations, the colonizers have kept the laws one-sided. The first generation of colonizers went as far as making up laws to arrest Natives. As time progressed, they wrote laws that would only allow people of color to live in certain areas and not in others. They made sure alcohol was easily accessible to keep the Natives and Blacks from prospering or growing.

With all of the brainwashing and hatred showered on the community of color, the communities kept this vicious mental cycle of believing that they are supposed to live poorly and undeserving. With little income, the struggle to provide a home, food, or water, the majority of these families also never had or accumulated the resources to heal from these genetic and personal traumas. Few people throughout the generations do mentally and physically break free from these stigmas.

When she was seven, an elder starred into Gabby's eyes and said, "It's believed among spiritual beings that the human beings who endure some of the hardest and tragic experiences, will make for the greatest guides to healing, if, they can come to terms with their experiences." By the time she was eight years old, Gabby was aware of both of her abilities. She spent her days alone in ceremony, connecting to herself and learning more about her gifts.

Gabby's other gift and passion was bodywork, which she learned at the age of 8 while in ceremony with self. She had to wait until she graduated high school or become eighteen to take a massage course and become certified. In the meantime, people would ask her to help them when they were in pain. She didn't have a table or equipment. So she would lay a blanket on the floor and have them lay down. She would work on people of all ages and body types.

People were amazed at how fast their bodies would heal after she worked on them. In most cases, it was immediate relief. She didn't only help people through bodywork; she did energy work and guided mental healing as well. Often, Gabby sang or hummed to her clients while working on them.

People found it easy to talk with Gabby. It didn't matter who she was with; they felt a sense of comfort with her. They would instantly open up to her and find themselves speaking about their most personal and intimate life situations. Gabby would listen, only giving advice when asked. She loved the feeling of knowing that she carried the capability of helping people to heal.

Gabby often thought about ways to bring healing to Native country. Gabby, Lori, and Isela had endless conversations about what healing practices were needed and how to bring it to the community. Their community was filled with many very spiritual and ceremonial people as well as angry, hurt, and lost people. The mental healing and reversal of the colonial mindset are what they agreed was needed the strongest.

They often practiced techniques on each other. They would debrief amongst each other to figure out what worked best for each of them. Gabby practiced many of these techniques on her clients with a high success rate. Although some of her clients called her a healer, she would gently explain that she was not a healer but a guide, and that each of us has the ability within to heal ourselves.

REASON FOR EVERYTHING

Gabby recently had met an older guy from a nearby neighborhood. She secretly grew a crush on him. He went by the name of Deuce. Deuce thought Gabby was cute but only liked her as far as friends go. Deuce hung out frequently with his cousin George. George was infatuated with Gabby. George would ask Gabby out on dates or ask if she'd like to hang out alone sometime, Gabby always nicely said no. There was something about George that rubbed Gabby the wrong way.

As Gabby sat on the bench in the Jungles that morning, Deuce sent Gabby a text message. He asked if she wanted to chill with him and his cousins later that evening. Gabby wanted to see Deuce, so she texted him back, asking, "Sure. Where's this going to be?" Deuce said, "Up the street at my cousin's pad. George offered to pick you up. Is that cool?" Gabby thought for a second. She didn't want to be alone with George. Still, Gabby texted him back, "Yeah, I guess that's fine." Later that evening, George picked her up. They showed up to one of his cousin's houses.

Gabby was the only female there. She was laughing and joking with all of the guys. George poured her a couple of drinks throughout the night. Gabby eventually began to feel a little funny. She thought maybe it was because she didn't eat enough.

A little later that night, Deuce stood up. He said, "Alright, I got to bounce. I got some shit to handle." The guys said bye.

As Deuce began to walk away, Gabby thought to herself, "I should ask him to drop me off." She failed to ask him. A few minutes after Deuce left, Gabby tried to get up. She found it difficult as she was feeling weak. She looked over at George. "I need to go to the bathroom, but I can barely feel my legs," Gabby said with concern in her voice.

George helped her up. He wrapped his arms around her waist and guided her to the bathroom. George asked, "Do you want me to go in there with you?" Gabby replied, "No! No, I'm good, thanks." She closed the door and locked it. Moving slowly, Gabby pushed herself along the wall to the toilet. She felt like she was losing all control of her body. She managed to go pee. With the very little strength she had, she held on to the wall with both hands.

Gabby opened the door and looked at George with a worried look on her face. Gabby said, "I still can't feel my legs. Can you please just take me home?" George agreed. In the car, Gabby slurred, "Fuck, I don't have my keys." George replied, "I'll just get you a motel room." Gabby was feeling weaker by the second. It felt like extra effort to speak. She hadn't the strength in her neck to hold her head up. Slurring and whispering, Gabby managed to say, "No, that's okay. Just drop me off at my friend's pad." Again George insisted, "I don't mind. I don't want anyone to see you like this."

Gabby slurred, "Na, just take me to Pakooynga and Glenoaks." Within seconds of her request, Gabby blacked out. When she came to, she felt queasy. She reached for the door handle but was too weak to move her arm. She desperately felt the need to throw up. She purged a little bit of liquid in between the small gap of the door and the seat. George came back to the car from the motel lobby. Gabby sloppily told him, "I don't feel good, I threw up." Gabby still couldn't hold her head up. George said, "I got you a room for the night. I'll help you to get in there, and then I'll go home."

He started the car and drove into a parking space. He then put the gear in park. He turned to look at Gabby. Her head was down with her eyes closed. George smirked. He then got out of the car and walked around to the passenger side. He reached in to grab Gabby. Gabby had no control of her head, legs, or her arms.

George wrapped his arms around Gabby's waist, walking her into the motel room. Once inside, he laid her on the bed. There, George took off her sandals. He unbuckled her pants and slid them down her legs along with her underwear, which had a menstrual pad on them because Gabby was on her moon cycle.

Gabby barely able to move, tried to reach towards her pants. She looked into George's eyes as she quietly mumbled, "Please George. Don't. Just go home." He removed her blouse and bra. He began kissing Gabby on her neck. Gabby tried her hardest to fight and push him off. Unfortunately for Gabby, she was so weak it didn't matter how hard she tried to push, she was in no condition to fight the big guy on top of her.

He proceeded to take advantage of her. When he penetrated inside of her, Gabby began to cry. There was nothing else she could do. George looked in her eyes as he raped her. He wiped the tears off of her left cheek. George whispered, "Don't cry baby, I'm right here. I'll take care of you." Gabby continued to cry. She felt helpless and disgusted. Gabby went in and out of consciousness as George raped her.

Although George had drugged Gabby, he pretended that Gabby was his girlfriend. In his mind, he pretended that Gabby was consensual to the sex. He told himself that she would enjoy it just as much as he did.

It was about 1:20 a.m. when he finished. George got himself dressed, and then he left Gabby alone in the room. He got into his car, put the key in the ignition, and started the car. George sat there with a blank stare. About a minute later, he began talking aloud, "That shit didn't work. She wasn't supposed to know." George hit the steering wheel with his right hand as he continued, "FUUUCK, fuck, fuck. What if she remembers? What if she calls the cops?

"She was supposed to be my lady. She'll never want my fat ass now. FUCK. FUCK. Alright, okay. If she calls the cops or tells anyone, I'm gonna deny, deny, deny. It never happened. That crazy little bitch is making it all up." George stroked his right hand over his face, from his eyes, over his cheeks, and down his chin. He sniffed a deep breath of air through his nose. He then said, "Alright, fuck it then," as he drove off.

Gabby just laid there, still unable to move. She must have thought to herself and begged herself over a hundred times to get up. She would say things like, "Come on, Gabby, get up. Move. Just get up Gabby." A few hours went by. After attempting over and again to move, finally Gabby could feel her hands tingling. She took that as a good sign. At least now, she felt something. She continued at her attempts to get up. Eventually, she felt her body regaining some strength.

Finally, around 4:10 in the morning, Gabby had enough strength to move. She still, however, felt frail. She slowly crawled to the edge of the bed. She encouraged herself in thought, "You can get up. It's okay. You're okay, Gabby. Get up now." Gabby placed her feet on the ground, attempting to stand. She landed face down on the ground. "Aright, that's okay. I just gotta get to the bathroom now," Gabby thought.

Still lacking strength in her legs, Gabby crawled over to the bathroom, pulling herself with her arms. She reached towards the sink and tried to pull herself up. It took a few attempts, but finally, she stood on her two feet. Turning the water on, she splashed her face. She looked up to see her reflection. Gabby broke into tears. She stared back at herself, questioning, "What the fuck just happened? How could you let him do that to you? You didn't even defend yourself. You just fucking lay there. What the fuck's wrong with you?"

She shook her head. She then said, "Stop it, Gabby. It wasn't your fault. You were helpless in there. You didn't deserve what went down. He must have slipped something in your drink. Man, you've chugged liquor and been gone but never like that. You know what? At least you're still alive." Still slouched over holding the sink, Gabby continued sobbing. She slowly walked over to the shower trying to maintain balance. She turned the hot and cold knobs.

Feeling too nauseous to continue standing, she kneeled in the shower. Gabby cried uncontrollably as the water hit her. She reached over for the soap. She un-wrapped the bar of soap and began scrubbing herself as hard as she could. As dirty as she felt, no amount of soap could cleanse the feeling of internal disgust from her at that moment.

After 15 minutes in the shower, Gabby turned the water off and grabbed a towel. She dried up and got her clothes back on. She desperately wanted to get out of that room. She walked down the driveway of the motel and realized she was two cities away from home. Gabby didn't want to see anyone at the apartments. Holding her sandals in her left hand, she walked four miles to Miranda and Miguel's house. She felt it was too early to knock, so she lay on the doorstep.

Miranda got up and jumped in the shower. After she was dressed and ready for her day, she went to the kitchen to make breakfast. Gabby heard the noise of the pans. She got to her feet and tapped on the kitchen window. Miranda peeped out of the window to see who it was. She knew something wasn't right when she looked into Gabby's face.

Miranda opened the door to let Gabby in. Miranda asked Gabby if she was okay. Gabby, still in shock, told Miranda what happened. Miranda hugged Gabby tight, trying to console her. Gabby said as she cried, "I feel so gross. I feel like a fucking susia. Please, Miranda, keep this between us. I don't want anyone to see me differently." Miranda agreed.

Fighting back her tears, Miranda said, "Of course ma, that's your business to speak on. But for the record, you're not a susia. You are a woman now. I know that's not how you wanted to become a woman. And that's not how any child or woman deserves to be treated. Despite this unfortunate situation, you're a firme person. You still have your beauty and your good heart. Don't let him take that too mamas." Gabby said, "Thank you, Mujer." Miranda nodded, she said, "Come in the kitchen let me make you some breakfast."

Miranda pulled Gabby's arms and sat Gabby down at the kitchen table. The pans had been set out on the stove already. Miranda made some pancake mix with chocolate chips and walnuts. She then scrambled up some eggs. When the pans were warm, Miranda began cooking pancakes, bacon, and eggs.

Miguel came out to compliment the smell. Miguel could tell that Gabby had been crying. He didn't want to ask any questions. Instead, he politely said, "Good morning Mija." Gabby avoided eye contact with Miguel. She smiled in his direction, saying, "Good morning Miggy."

When breakfast was ready, Miranda served Gabby and Miguel first. She then served herself a plate and joined them at the table. Gabby said, "Damn, Miranda, I don't know what you did differently, but these are the best pancakes I have ever tasted." Miranda thanked Gabby, responding, "I used a little bit of cinnamon and a lot of love Mujer." Miguel added, "Can you believe that every morning my little sis gets up to cook? Bomb shit too, pozole, chorizo con huevos, huevos rancheros, tortillas hecho a mano. Man, whatever it might be, she hooks it up."

Gabby laughed. She insisted, "Shoot, in that case, I'll be over here every morning." Miranda welcomed Gabby's invite, "Anytime mamas. I learned from kicking it with Lita. I try to hook up dinner every night too." Miguel rubbed his stomach, saying, "Oooh, man, don't even get me started. This chick can throw down in the kitchen." Gabby said, "That's what's up. Not to brag, but I can microwave a mean cup of noodles." Everyone laughed.

After he finished eating, Miguel thanked his sister for breakfast. He walked over to her and kissed her on the forehead. Miggy then walked over to the sink to wash his plate. As he did so, he told Miranda what he had planned for his day. He wished the ladies a lovely day and headed out to start his shift.

Miranda asked Gabby, "Do you have any plans for today, ma?" Gabby replied, "Ugh, to dig a hole, crawl in it, and die." Miranda shook her head as she said, "That's what I'm afraid of, you're spending the day with me today. Like it or not. Listen, babe, what happened, it fucking sucks. That dude is a loser, a piece of shit who has massive issues. I know you don't want to hear this, but everything happens for a reason. You needed to experience this along with the confusion, emotions, and pain for some reason or another. Don't be a victim, Gabby. That's when he wins. Make a report if you need to, but forgive the situation for you, and go forward in a good way as you heal. You've gotten through this kind of stuff before. You're a strong warrior."

With tears in her eyes, Gabby shook her head, rolled her eyes upward, and replied, "You're so right. I don't want to hear that shit. But I know you're right about everything. I don't understand it now. I know, I don't wish this feeling on anybody. Not even my worst enemy." Miranda nodded in agreement. Miranda asked Gabby, "Do you believe in karma?" In an angry tone of voice, Gabby replied, "Fuck yeah, I do." Miranda said, "Me too. I believe that fool will get his. It might not be what I feel or what you feel he deserves. It's not on either of us to say what he deserves. But there has to be a balance between good and bad. When you're doing bad things, I believe you bring bad to yourself. I do believe that he will suffer for this."

Gabby shifted her jaw back and forth as she glared above Miranda's head for a moment. She then looked into Miranda's eyes. Very sternly, Gabby said, "I don't know, but fuck him." "Yup, but you still have to forgive the situation, yourself, and, if possible, him when you're ready. The sooner, the better for you," responded Miranda.

Gabby removed the dishes from the table. She walked over to the sink to wash them. Miranda went to the stove to grab the pans which she had used to cook breakfast. She took them over to the sink. Together they washed and dried the dishes.

Miranda said, "Okay, I had planned on sitting around weighing out weed sacks for a while. Scratch that thought. How about we do something random?" "Like what?" Gabby asked. Miranda Responded, "Well, we can go to Six Flags. Are you down?" Gabby inhaled deeply. For a moment, she thought to herself, "Ugh, I don't want to be in any big crowds. Don't be a bitch. It'll be better to get your mind off of it than to sit around thinking non-stop about it."

Gabby said out loud, "Okay. Yeah, I'm down." Miranda smiled, saying, "Okay, cool." Miranda gestured wait with her index finger. Miranda said, "Hold on, lemme just fix you up a little." Gabby gave Miranda a 'What the fuck?' kind of look. "Just a little bit," begged Miranda. She walked to her room to grab a brush, some bobby pins, and a makeup bag. She sat Gabby down at the kitchen table. Gabby said, "I don't know, ma." Miranda replied, "Just trust me."

Miranda combed Gabby's hair, slightly pumped, and pinned it on both sides of her head. She then combed it into a loose bun and pinned the bun in place. She looked at Gabby and agreed with herself by nodding her head and saying, "Mhm." Next, Miranda grabbed the eye shadow. She hooked Gabby up with eyeshadow, eyeliner, blush, and lip gloss. Next, Miranda curled Gabby's lashes. She took a step back and said, "Perfecto. Got you looking like a hot mama." Gabby blushed.

Miranda grabbed her keys and said, "Alright, we're good to go." They walked to the garage. The ladies hopped into Miranda's impala. As Miranda warmed the car, she asked Gabby hip hop or oldies? Gabby replied, "Oldies." Miranda put a c.d in the deck that had a mix of some bomb ass rolas. They cruised to the freeway and headed up to the amusement park.

When they pulled up to the parking entrance, Miranda gave the worker her season pass. The worker scanned her pass and handed it back. After they grabbed a parking spot, they walked to one of the ticket booths. Although Miranda had a season pass, she paid for Gabby's ticket with a hundred dollar bill. After purchasing the ticket, they went through the main entrance.

They glanced around as they walked passed all the shops. They walked up to a big water fountain. As a tradition, they took a couple of pictures together with their flip phones. Passing the kids' rides and a few others, they made their way to the first big ride. No sooner than they got in line, a group of young guys showed interest in the two young ladies.

One of the guys in the group asked Gabby, "Are you ladies from around here?" Gabby responded, "Yeah, sort of." The guy lifted his right eyebrow as if questioning Gabby's response. Gabby explained, "We live about 15 minutes away off of the 210 freeway. But this area we're standing on right now, is part of one of my ancestral villages." The guy nodded his head, saying, "Oh, okay. We drove in from Anaheim. I'm California Native too." Miranda said, "Shouldn't you be at Disneyland then?" The guys laughed. Another guy said, "We wanted to get on real rollercoasters." "Ah, I see. If I lived in Anaheim, you know where you could find me all the time," Miranda replied excitedly.

Gabby asked the first guy, "What Nation are you from?" He responded, "I'm Cahuilla and Tongva." Gabby excitedly replied, "No way? It's awesome to run into a Tongva brother. I'm Tongva and Tataviam." The guy smiled and said, "I knew it! You're too beautiful not to be Tongva." Gabby smiled shyly.

The first guy looked to Miranda, asking, "So are you here all the time?" Miranda replied, "Well, not aaaall the time. I try to come at least every two months." The guys said in sync, "Daaaaang, lucky." One of the guys asked, "Does that mean you have a season pass?" Miranda nodded her head, answering, "Mmhmm." The first guy put his hand out to Gabby and said, "Hi, I'm Robert, by the way." Gabby introduced herself as she shook his hand. She said, "This is my friend Miranda." Robert shook Miranda's hand, saying, "Nice to meet you." He pointed to his two friends saying, this is Ernie and Marcos. The ladies and the guys waved to each other, saying, "Nice to meet you."

Robert asked Gabby, "So what city do you live in exactly?" Gabby responded, "I live in Pacoima." "Oh, right on. I got a cousin who bangs Pacas." Miranda and Gabby laughed. Gabby asked, "Do you bang too?" Robert gave a sly smile and said, "Let's just say right here, right now, I don't." Gabby said, "It'd be better that you never do." Then she winked at him. He smiled.

Finally, they reached the front of the ride. With excitement, Robert said, "Alright, let's do this." The ladies got onto the back of the roller coaster. The guys sat in the cart in front of them. With their arms in the air, everyone was pretty much screaming, giggling, or doing both. After the ride, the ladies and the guys wished each other a good day. The guys went one way, and the ladies went the other.

Miranda and Gabby rode almost every roller coaster in the theme park. They didn't eat all day since breakfast. Around five o'clock in the evening, Miranda said, "I'm freakin' starving. You wanna go to eat." Gabby made a face as she thought about it. Before she could answer, Miranda said, "It's on me. Let's go to 'Outback.'" Gabby nodded as she replied, "Okay, yeah. I haven't been there in a cool ass minute."

The ladies walked out of the park and drove over to the restaurant. There was a waiting line when they got there. Miranda went in and made a reservation. When she came out, she said, "It's gonna take 30 minutes. You want to smoke a blunt before we eat?" Gabby pulled her head back, "Miranda, you don't smoke!" Gabby said in confusion.

Miranda smirked as she said, "Yeah, but you do, and I have a sack if you want to blaze." Gabby felt bad. Although she did want to smoke, Gabby said, "Naw, ma. I'm good. Thank you, though. You're the fucking best."

The ladies sat down on a bench outside the restaurant. They took that time to talk about goals and dreams. Gabby knew she would fall into being a massage therapist and an entertainer. Mostly she wanted to write songs and sing. Miranda had her mind on becoming a doctor. She hadn't yet decided what kind of doctor she wanted to be. She mostly wanted to choose between an obstetrician and a cardiologist.

The hostess called for Miranda. The ladies walked in to be seated. As they looked at the menu, Miranda said, "Ugh, I'm so hungry that everything looks bomb on this menu." Gabby agreed. When the waiter came to get their drink orders, Miranda first asked for Coconut shrimp. The waiter asked, "And to drink?" Both ladies ordered water with lemon. Gabby asked, "Can we go ahead and put our order in now?" "Yes, of course," The waiter answered. He then asked, "What will you have?" Gabby ordered chicken and ribs with broccoli. Miranda ordered a chicken salad and a bowl of soup.

When the shrimp arrived, the ladies excitedly ate them all up. The waiter walked up to Gabby with a mixed drink in his hand. He said, "Miss, there's a gentleman who requested that I bring you this drink. I do have to ask for I.D." Gabby replied, "Tell him I said thank you. But I don't drink." The waiter nodded and walked away. Miranda laughed, asking, "You don't drink, huh?" Gabby laughed too, and said, "C'mon, that's embarrassing saying that I'm underage." Miranda laughed, replying, "So what, you are underage. That's a bragging right."

Within minutes, the man who ordered Gabby the drink walked up. He put his hand out as he said, "Hello, my name is Adam." As Gabby shook his hand, she introduced herself and Miranda, "Hello Adam, I'm Gabby, and this is my friend Miranda." Adam shook Miranda's hand, saying, "Pleasure." He turned to Gabby and asked, "Do you mind if I join you for a minute?"

Gabby answered, "With all due respect Adam, I came to have dinner with my friend here. It's her birthday, and I would like to give her my undivided attention." Adam apologized, "I'm sorry to have interrupted." He glanced over to Miranda and wished her a happy birthday. He looked back to Gabby then said, "I have to say, you are a beautiful woman. Have a good night." Gabby smiled, thanking him. She wished him a good night as well.

Miranda kept a straight face. She leaned in, teasing, "Man, you're on a roll today." Gabby said, "What do you mean?" Miranda gave Gabby a face as to say, "Really?" Then Miranda revisited the day, stating, "Okay, homeboy at six flags had pinche babas coming out of his boca. All of his friends were all eyes on you. I guess you didn't notice all the other mafucka's that were staring and jocking on your ass over there today. And then this guy here looked hypnotized." Gabby rolled her eyes, saying, "Ugh. And I don't want anything to do with any guys right now." Miranda made a face of sympathy. She said, "I don't blame you, sis. I know in due time you'll heal and give some lucky guy a chance to show you how wonderful love can be."

The waiter brought their plates out. Announcing each dish, he placed them in front of the girls then said, "You ladies enjoy." They both smiled and thanked him. Throughout dinner, the ladies got back to talking about careers and schooling. Miranda had already applied to a couple of colleges of her choice. Gabby was planning on going to a trade school to become a massage therapist. Gabby figured that massage would be a more stable route versus music. The music would be recorded and performed in her free time.

After dinner, Gabby sighed, holding her tummy and said, "Thank you so much for dinner, ma. That food was bomb." Miranda winked at Gabby. "You're very welcome, Gabs. Thank you for spending the day with me, my love," Miranda responded. Gabby answered, "No, Thank you. This little break from reality was most definitely what I needed." Miranda smiled. The waiter brought boxes for the girls to take their leftovers home. He placed the check in the center of the table. After Miranda paid, the ladies got up and headed for home.

When Gabby got home, Dennis asked where she had been. Gabby said, "I spent the night with Miranda. Today we went to Six Flags." Dennis squinted his eyes in envy. Dennis said, "Awe must be nice, lucky ass." Gabby smiled and said, "It was. Good night." Gabby tossed her left overs in her brothers lap and went to her room. She locked the door behind her. She put her back to the door and took a deep breath. Gabby exhaled and walked over to the stereo. She turned the music on, low enough that it wouldn't bother anyone but loud enough that no one could hear her cry.

Gabby slowly walked over to her bed, plopping face down. Gabby quietly sobbed with her face hidden in her pillow. As Gabby cried, she flashed back to when she was four years old; she was playing hide and seek with some of the other kids at the apartments. One of the girls' older brothers grabbed Gabby by the arm, saying, "You're on my team." Gabby's friend Melly knew that her 13-year-old brother Greg was up to no good.

Melly was afraid of her brother. Still, she had Gabby by the other arm, crying out, "No, leave her alone, please. Just let her play with us." Greg replied, "Calm down. We are going to play." Greg shoved his sister, and sternly insisted, "Go hide." Greg excitedly pulled Gabby behind a building. He pulled up her shirt, revealing her tummy. Greg put his finger on Gabby's stomach. Gabby stood utterly stiff.

Greg said, "We're going to make a map to figure out the best way to go and hide. So let's see, we're here." Greg moved his finger down and then to the right of Gabby's stomach, saying, "Home base is over here." Greg slowly moved his finger down into Gabby's pants. As he touched her on what she knew as her 'Pee-pee,' he said, "And we want to be here." Greg began playing with Gabby's vagina. Gabby didn't know how to react. She looked like a deer caught in the headlights.

When Greg finished playing his "Game," he told Gabby nicely, "You can't tell anybody about this, okay? It will be our little secret. If you tell anybody about our secret, they're going to think you're a liar and then they're going to hate you. You can't even tell your mom because she'll hate you the most. She won't ever love you or want to talk to you again." Gabby nodded her head. She was scared and confused. She didn't know at the time precisely what just happened to her. She felt like what just happened was not okay. Gabby was afraid her mom would find out and truly would hate her.

Later that night, Melly angrily told her brother, "I'm telling mom what you did, Greg." He pinned her against the wall by her neck. Greg said, "Mom won't believe you. But still, if you tell her, I'm going to cut your little tongue out of your mouth. Do you want that?" Melly's eyes grew wide. She quickly shook her head. Greg let go of Melly's throat, and he said, "Good girl. Plus, your friend liked it, the same way you like it, Mel." Melly fell to the floor. She sat against the wall and cried as she held her head between her knees.

In the back of his mind, Greg was worried that Melly would tell their mom what he did to Gabby. Greg went to his mom and asked, "Mom, what would happen to a boy who touched a little girl in her private place?" Greg's mom showed concern in her face. She asked, "Why? Did you touch somebody?" Greg quickly shook his head, saying, "No, of course not. I was just wondering." Greg's mom said, "Don't lie to me. That question doesn't just come at random. What happened?"

Greg got scared and regretted asking the question. He realized his mother would keep grilling him. Greg said, "It's this girl, one of Mel's friends. I think her brother does it to her." Greg's mother asked, "What do you mean, you think?" Greg said, "Well, I think I saw him touching her." Greg's mom placed her hand over her mouth. She asked Greg which friend he was referring to. Greg couldn't think fast enough. He said it was Gabby. Greg's mother then told Greg, "You did the right thing by telling me. Go get ready for bed."

Greg's mom called the police station and told them that she suspected a neighbor was fondling his sister. Within an hour, the police were at Gabby's door. They pulled Gabby's mom Tiffany out and explained why they were there. Tiffany was concerned about both of her children. She opened the door and shouted for her son Dennis to come outside. The police questioned Dennis. When they finished, they thanked him for his honesty.

Tiffany said, "Sit on the couch and wait for me." Dennis went back inside the house. Tiffany asked the police, "Okay, you questioned him now what?" The policeman said, "We understand that there may not have been foul play. We still have to be sure. We want you to take her to the Doctors and get her checked for any signs of penetration or abrasions." We'll be able to close this report out depending on what the Doctor finds."

Tiffany asked, "Well, do I take her right now to the emergency or tomorrow to her doctor?" The policeman answered, "I don't want her to be freaked out. Take her tomorrow to her Doctor. Let the Doctor know why, and she should know what to look for. Give the Doctor our card and have him contact us." The officer pulled out a card and handed it to Tiffany. Tiffany's hand shook as she reached out to grab the card. She thanked the men then turned to go inside.

Tiffany went into the house and talked to Dennis. She believed her son wouldn't do such a thing. Tiffany also knew that kids were sometimes afraid to be honest with their parents. She didn't want to push the issue. Tiffany hugged her son and said, "I know you're a good boy papa. It's your responsibility as a big brother to take care of your sister." Dennis replied, "I know, mama. I would never hurt her." Tiffany said, "I know. Go ahead and go to bed. I'll see you in the morning." They kissed each other on the cheek and said good night.

First thing in the morning, Tiffany called Gabby's doctor's office to set the appointment. Tiffany got Gabby ready and took her to the doctor's office. The doctor checked her thoroughly. When she finished, she asked Gabby a series of questions. The questions were involving rape and molestation. Gabby suddenly knew why she was there, but she couldn't figure out how it got to this point. Gabby was afraid to let her mom find out, so she told the doctor that no one had ever touched her in such a way.

The doctor left Gabby alone in the room. She went out to speak to Tiffany. "There are no signs of penetration. Her hymen is still normal." Tiffany was relieved. She handed the policeman's card to the doctor. She said, "The officers asked me to give this to you. They need to hear this from you so they can close out the report." The doctor nodded her head as she took the card. The doctor replied, "You got it. I'm glad she's okay, Gabby is in the room waiting for you. We'll see each other soon."

Tiffany thanked the doctor as she shook her hand. Tiffany wanted to forget about this whole ordeal. She went into the room to get her daughter; neither of them mentioned the situation. Without saying a word, Melly and her family moved out of the apartments in a matter of weeks.

All through Gabby's childhood and teens, the images of Greg molesting her would play in her mind. Due to fear of rejection, Gabby didn't talk about the molestation. She was traumatized. Gabby often came across cycles of anger and depression within. More often than not, she felt abandoned or alone.

When Gabby was eleven, she finally revealed to Miranda what she had gone through. Miranda told Gabby that she was a resilient person for dealing with it so well. It helped Gabby a little bit to finally tell someone. Miranda kept Gabby's secret.

This time around, after crying and reflecting on the past, Gabby sat in her bed, staring blankly at the wall for a few minutes. She didn't think or speak. She just stared at the wall. Suddenly she reached over to her nightstand to grab a notebook. Gabby began to write. She wrote down everything that happened to her the night before, as she recalled it.

When she finished writing it all down, she began writing a song about it. Gabby wrote the song as a third party. First, the song contained a lot of anger. In the last verse, Gabby has the rapist killed by the young girl whom he raped. She knew this wasn't how the song would end. It did, however, make her feel a little better after writing it. When Gabby finished the first version of her song, she left the pen in the notebook. She then closed it and placed her book down on her nightstand. Gabby laid down, hugging her pillow. She cried a little more until she fell asleep.

Come morning, Miranda knocked on Gabby's front door. Dennis opened the door to greet her. Dennis pointed with his thumb over his shoulder as he told Miranda that Gabby was still sleeping. Miranda walked to Gabby's room and knocked. "Good morning, it's Miranda." Gabby unlocked the door and opened it slightly then went back to lie in bed. Miranda came in, closing the door behind her. Without saying a word, Miranda laid next to Gabby and hugged her from the back.

Ten minutes went by. Miranda broke the silence, asking, "Are you planning on hiding in here all day?" Gabby said, "I reeeally don't want to see anyone else besides you. I feel emotional as fuck, and I'm afraid I'm going to break down." Miranda said, "You just went through a lot. I don't blame you. But sis, you have to face 'em eventually. You know we all love you. And if you don't go out there, eventually we'll all be in here with you." Gabby said, "I know, I know. Oh man, good looking out on yesterday. It was nice being out of my element and getting out of my head for the day. I mean, there were a couple of times I caught myself thinking about it. But then I would check myself and try to be cool."

Miranda responded, "I had so much fun with you. Any time you wanna get out of your element like that, just hit me up. You know I got you." Gabby nodded her head. "So

I wrote something last night," Gabby mentioned. Miranda asked, "Really? Can I hear it?" As she pointed to her nightstand, Gabby said, "Pása me el cuaderno." Miranda reached for the notebook. She handed it to Gabby, who read the song to Miranda.

When Gabby finished reading it, Miranda said, "Wow, ma. That was vivid and deep aaand gory!" Gabby said, "I know, honestly, I don't like the ending. I feel like the song needs to bring healing to anyone else who may have suffered this type of pain. I just wrote that part in to help me feel a little better. But I'm going to rewrite it eventually." Miranda responded, "I get where you're coming from in this version. But I do agree that you can probably help others by letting them see they aren't alone in this fucked up world. This type of stuff happens way too often."

Gabby nodded in agreement, and then asked, "Well, I know you got shit to do today, is it cool if I get ready and just hang out with you?" Miranda answered, "Of course you can. That's exactly why I came over. My shift doesn't start until I say so anyway." Gabby replied, "Alright, cool. Here," Gabby handed Miranda the remote control for the television. Gabby said, "I'll be quick." She grabbed her towel and went to shower. After her shower, she came to the room to get dressed. As Gabby got dressed, she asked Miranda, "Are you down to go out to lunch? I'll pay." Miranda said, "Yeah, ma. That sounds firme."

When Gabby was ready, the two girls walked down to Miranda's car. "Where do you want to eat?" Gabby asked Miranda. Miranda thought for a second. Miranda said, "You know where I haven't been for a minute? Is Carrillo's in S.F." Gabby's eyes opened up wide. Gabby said, "Mmmm. That sounds good about now."

The girls took a drive to San Fernando. As soon as the girls sat down after placing their order, Miranda's phone rang. It was one of her clients asking for some weed. Miranda said she'd be right there. Gabby asked, "Should we take it to go?" Miranda responded, "No. Why?" Gabby replied, "Well, I just figured since you got that call." Miranda put her phone in her pocket. She then said, "Neh. They ain't going anywhere. First, I am going to enjoy my lunch and my time with you." Miranda winked and smiled at Gabby. Gabby shrugged her shoulders and smiled back.

After lunch, the ladies made their way over to Miranda's client to make a drop. On the drive over, Gabby's phone rang. It was Deuce. Gabby answered it nervously. He just called to make small talk. Gabby talked to him for a minute. Then she decided to tell Deuce what his cousin did. As she finished telling him, his cousin walked into Deuce's house. He asked his cousin if it was true.

George immediately became defensive. He said, "Hell nah, that bitch threw herself on me. She was all loose. You could tell she's a slut." Gabby said, "A woman can say yes to sex to a thousand different men. But if she says no to one and he still has sex with her, it's rape. He and I both know the truth."

Deuce and Gabby hung up on good terms. Gabby turned to tell Miranda what was said. Miranda had a look of anger in her face. She shook her head, saying, "Damn, that fool has some serious fucking problems. He has it coming though, so don't even trip off him." Gabby looked out the window and said, "I know who I am and what I have done in my life. That's all that matters to me."

Gabby never came across George again. She heard that he went to prison. Gabby wondered, but never learned for sure what he went to the pinta for. Eventually, Gabby got wind that George died in there. Gabby did see Deuce once in a while at the local shops. Deuce always seemed uncomfortable to see her. They would say a very brief hello and continue about their own business. In the back of her mind, she wondered if George went to prison for another rape, or if George possibly admitted the truth to Deuce. Because the few times she had seen him, Deuce had a look on his face as if he knew the truth and felt sympathetic toward Gabby. Gabby never brought it up with Deuce again.

It took some time before Gabby was ready to do the work to heal from George and Greg. When she was ready, she started by forgiving them for their actions. She forgave herself for finding herself in these situations of being molested and raped. She forgave her parents and brother for not being there to protect her. One by one, she thought about all of the issues that came up from these experiences: substantial trust issues, lack of self-love and worthiness to be loved, self-worth, abandonment, depression, and anger. One by one, she acknowledged these issues were part of the stories that she created out of her pain and fear.

Gabby finally came to the understanding that all of her experiences were predestined prior to her coming into this life. She was finally able to put the uneasiness to rest. Some days the memories of mental anguish did resurface, causing Gabby to drift back into a funk. Gabby would always set aside time to focus on the issues and heal. She would remind herself that she was beautiful inside and out. She would tell herself that she loved herself and was worthy of being loved by others. These experiences did help her to heal herself as well as be able to walk others through their healing journeys.

TAMALE SEASON

The girls had been on winter break for a week. December is about the time every year that most people in the valley seem to bust out either making or buying tamales until the New Year. Suzy and her mom would make up to twenty dozen tamales of chicken, beef, pork, corn, and sometimes pineapple or strawberry. They would also bake little apple, cherry, and blueberry pies then gift the food to their loved ones for Christmas gifts. For Suzy's mom, it was a tradition that began when Suzy's father passed away.

At that time, Suzy's mom Lisa had little money to her name. But she didn't want to show up to the family Christmas gathering with nothing. She went to the store to buy masa, meat, corn husks, as well as the produce that she would need to make the sauce for the tamales. Lisa put all of her love into making tamales and passed them out to her friends and family. Lisa felt so much shame because she couldn't give them anything more than tamales.

Lisa's loved ones raved over her tamales and requested that she make them every year. That brought so much comfort to Lisa's heart. From then on, she made annual tamales. As Suzy got older, she would help her mom to make tamales. When she was thirteen, Suzy asked if they could make pies from scratch to gift as well.

For Christmas and New Year's celebrations all over California, tamales always had a place at the dinner table.

Isela's grandmother hosted what they called a tamale line. In a particular order on both sides of the table, they would set out a bowl filled with corn husks soaking in water, a bowl of masa, a bowl of chicken in green sauce, a bowl of beef in red sauce, a bowl of pork in red sauce and a bowl of fruit filling.

One person would grab the corn husk and spread masa on one side of the husk. Then they would hand it off to the next person who then fills the masa with meat filling or fruit and pass it down, the next person down the line would close up the tamale and pass it to the next person who would stand the tamale up right into the pot. Everyone took shifts in this family preparation. They always had so much fun making tamales. But they all would agree that the best part was eating the result.

Christmas day arrived once again. The holiday was usually a reminder to everyone around the apartments that they were poor. Most parents tried to buy their kids at least one good gift. A lot of the kids would get shoes and clothes that they needed. The typical joke around the neighborhood was about at least having tamales to unwrap.

Although they didn't celebrate Religious holidays such as Christmas, Isela's family held Winter Solstice Ceremony around the 21st of December with their immediate family. It was kind of like their New Year. They also hosted an annual Winter Solstice gathering with their friends and family on Christmas day. For them, these holidays were focused more on bringing the community together while sharing love, laughter, and ceremony. After spending time with their families, the girls and other people from nearby stopped to hang out with Isela's family. Isela's brother Jared's (Rest in Peace) friends came by to show love. Isela's mom hugged them each extra tight. Gabby's mom and Lori's parents stopped in every year as well.

Isela's mom Grace had deer stew, pozole, fry bread, corn tortillas, assorted tamales, squash and corn with cheese, corn cakes, garlic lemon asparagus, fresh salsa, berry stew, pumpkin pie, pan dulce and a hot cacao drink all ready to serve up. Grace always loved cooking these big spreads because she knew how much food brought people together and made them happy.

The girls looked forward to Isela's mom's fluffy fry bread; it was a treat for them. Before eating, they placed food on a plate to offer to the spirits. While making this offering, everyone prayed in their way and thought about their loved ones who have transitioned to the spirit world. Isela's family focused on their ancestors, her great grandfather, who passed away when she was just nine years old and her brother who passed away last year.

After enjoying a delicious meal, everyone joined in playing family games and dancing to the music. They played a California walnut dice game while singing Tongva and Chumash songs that they learned from Isela's parents. They also played games such as trivia. Being surrounded by so much love and laughter, it was easy to forget that they were deemed poor by the westernized terms of thinking.

After a long, love-filled, and beautiful day, the girls always helped Isela's mom clean up, take out the trash, and put things away. After cleaning up, the girls and Clever hung out for a night session, talking, teasing, and laughing in Suzy's van for a bit before calling it a night.

SURVIVING ANOTHER YEAR

For the last three years, the ladies and Clever spent New Year's Eve at Denise's house. They agreed to do it again this year. Around 6 in the evening, Gabby, Suzy, Lori, and Clever packed up in Gabby's car with their backpacks, pillows, and blankets. Miranda rolled up separately with Isela and their sleepover gear, some arroz con leche, a bag filled with food for the morning, and a bottle of sparkling apple cider. Everyone dropped their personal belongings off in Denise's room. Miranda put the food that she brought in the fridge.

Denise made chicken enchiladas in green sauce, rice, beans, and salad. She also reheated tamales that her mom ordered from a family friend. She set out some salsa by the serving dishes. As the crew began to pile food onto their plates, Isela went to the fire pit to start the bonfire. Once she got it going, she set the chairs around the fire pit and went back inside to let everyone know that they can go chill by the fire.

As everyone stepped out to grab a seat around the fire, Isela served herself a plate of food. Denise started bumping the boom box that she had set up outside. She played an mp3 disc with a mix of hip-hop, R&B, classic rock, funk, old school, dance and oldies. She walked back to take her seat by the fire.

Isela asked Denise where her parents were. Denise answered, "They went up North to Bakersfield to stay with family and celebrate the New Year." Suzy responded, "Butt fuck Bakersfiiield? Why? There ain't squat out there to do." Denise laughed as she replied, "Yeah, there really isn't. More so cause we don't know the area. But I think that was their point. They just wanted to spend quality time with family. Oh, and get fucked up." Suzy responded, "Oooh, okay, I can see that. Are they only staying until tomorrow?" Denise answered, "Yeah, that was the plan. They'll probably be back late tomorrow night."

Just then, some old school started playing on the boom box. Suzy jumped up and shouted, "Oooh, turn that shit up! That's my jam!" Suzy walked over to the boom box to turn it up and started dancing on the porch. Gabby got up and joined her. Within a minute, everyone was on the porch, dancing and laughing.

After dancing to a couple of the songs that played on the boom box, Isela coned her hands around her mouth and shouted, "Weeeeed breeeak!" She grabbed her seat by the fire and pulled out her glass pipe, weed, and lighter. Everyone followed suit except Miranda, who went inside to grab the arroz con leche, cups, and spoons. She figured it wouldn't be long after they got high, that the munchies would kick in.

Miranda brought everything outside with her and grabbed a seat. The glass piece made its way back to Isela. She packed it one more time. When the pipe came back around, she asked, "Is everyone good?" Everyone agreed that they were stoned and thanked Isela, who then put her piece away.

Twenty minutes had passed before Clever asked Miranda, "What's up with that arroz con leche, though? Ha, an ese's got the munchies." Miranda handed the cups down with the spoons. When everyone had their cups in hand, Miranda walked around the circle and served the arroz con leche. After everyone had their serving, Miranda placed the container down and went to grab some wood. She placed three logs in the fire then went to sit down.

As the clock drew closer to midnight, Denise handed everyone a shot glass. She said, "Well, we ain't all fancy up in here, so I ain't got no kind of champagne for your asses. But we definitely hood up in here, so I do got tequila and shot glasses, what?!" After she handed out the shot glasses, she filled everyone's cup. Miranda grabbed her bottle of apple cider and filled her cup.

Miranda announced, "Before the clock strikes twelve, I would like to give a toast, we live in a neighborhood where people die young and often, from abuse, violence, and suicide. Every year that WE get to celebrate, it feels more like we are celebrating our survival of the previous Gregorian calendar year. That said, here is to surviving another year." Everyone held up their glass to salute and said, "To surviving another year." They all took a sip from their glass.

Gabby could hear the neighbors counting down from 10, excitedly she said, "Okay, here we go! The countdown's happening." As soon as the fireworks let off, they toasted and yelled out, "Happy New Year!" Everyone touched shot glasses and chugged their tequila, while Miranda chugged her apple cider. Then one by one, everyone gave each other hugs. With each hug, they said, "Surviving another year."

They hung out near the fire just a few more minutes until it died down. By that time, Denise suggested that they make their beds in the living room and put a movie on. They all grabbed their blankets and pillows, and then made their way to the living room. Denise put on a comedy to keep the mood up.

The next morning Miranda was the first one up. She went to the bathroom to clean up and get ready. Afterward, she went to the kitchen to start breakfast. Miranda made chicken pozole. While it cooked, she chopped up cilantro, onion, cabbage, and lemons for everyone to self-serve. Miranda began to warm the tortillas and place them in a tortilla holder to keep them warm. Miranda set tortillas on the porch table along with a bowl of salsa and chopped up fixings.

The smell of Pozole overwhelmed the house. It was a pleasant smell to wake up to. One by one, everyone took turns using the bathroom to wash up and get ready. Miranda grabbed enough bowls and plates to serve the Pozole. She placed the bowls on the plates and set them up for everyone to grab and help themselves.

One by one, the friends filled their bowls then went outside to put the fixings of their choice on top. They each grabbed a seat at the table under the porch. Everyone at the table was talking and laughing until they began to eat, then suddenly it got quiet. Suzy laughed and said, "That's when you know the food is good, when it gets quiet." Everyone agreed. "This pozole is bomb as fuck Miranda, gracias," Claimed Clever. Miranda smiled and sweetly said, "Thank you, and you're welcome."

After breakfast, Suzy volunteered to clean dishes. Denise offered to help her. The ladies stacked up bowls and plates then went inside to wash them. Clever asked, "Who's down for a game of pool?" Miranda agreed to play him. They walked over to the pool table to start the game. Isela said, "I'm gonna stay right here and pack a fat morning bowl."

Isela, Lori, and Gabby sat at the patio table and blazed. When they finished, Isela packed another bowl for Clever, Denise, and Suzy. The feeling amongst these friends was good. To them, this was how to start the year off right, full of love and laughter.

THE LAST SCHOOL DAZE

The early morning fog was drifting throughout the halls of their high school. The smell of coffee cake filled the air. Youngsters began to meet up around the cafeteria for their first day back to school. Some kids were excited to be back to school from winter break, others, not so much.

Cindy was sitting on a tabletop with her feet perched on the bench. Miranda, Gabby, and Suzy walked into the cafeteria together. They spotted Cindy sitting alone at "The Spot." Together they walked over to greet her. With loving energy, the three ladies gave Cindy a big group hug.

Miranda asked Cindy, "How was your winter vacation?" Cindy smirked as she replied, "The same as every break before it! I just chilled at the pad most of the time. I didn't do anything too exciting. What about you, ladies?" Miranda shrugged then said, "Just worked and hung out at the apartment most of the time. But we hit up the malls, parties, and six flags."

Gabby added, "Yeah, we went to six flags like a week ago. It was pretty chill." Cindy responded, "Luckyyy. Awe, well, I'm glad you guys made the best of your vacation." Miranda replied, "But of course, had to make the best of our last high school vacation. Next year we might not have time for all of that together."

With excitement in her voice, Cindy asked, "Oh man, I know, can you believe this is our last semester here?!" Suzy answered, "Yup. And I'm thrilled about it. I cannot wait to get to college and have some fun." Cindy smiled as she asked Suzy, "So do you already know what school you're going to attend?" Jason walked up just in time to hear the question. Before even saying hello, he interrupted, saying, "School of hard knocks Esa, thought you knew."

"Uuuy, Travieso. Good Morning pa. Good to see your crazy ass actually in school," said Miranda. Jason Replied, "What up, though? Oh, I won't be staying too long. I just came to meet up with the homies. Then we'll be going to our 'Back to school' kickback."

Suzy laughed out loud. She said, "I can't believe how serious you look when you say that. Really? A back to school kickback?" Jason lifted one eyebrow. He questioned, "What's wrong with that?" Suzy answered, "Well, that sounds like something you should throw the day before school starts. Otherwise, it's just a ditching party." Jason laughed at Suzy as he responded, "Damn Suzy, what the fuck do you do? Live your excitement through your mom's glory days? Ditching parties are from the '80s and shit."

Suzy rolled her eyes at Jason's statement. Suzy said, "Whatever fool. All I know is that I find more excitement at school with my homies versus where there's a bunch of drunk and doped up kids acting a fool while wasting their precious youth away." Suzy asked Jason, "Okay, so what I wanna know is; why do you meet up at school instead of the kickback?" Jason answered, "To protect the location duh. If I let people know ahead of time where the kickback is, it's most likely gonna get raided. So fuck that."

Miranda laughed and said, "Duh Suzy! Over here living under a rock! Acting like our kickbacks didn't go down in middle school. You must have been too drunk to remember, though." Suzy made a face as if she got busted. She laughed and teasingly shoved Miranda.

Jason said, "But hey Miranda, since you're here, can I get an eighth?" Miranda reached into her bra and pulled out an eighth of Kush. She shook Jason's hand, exchanging the weed with Jason for some cash. Jason said, "Good looking out, G." Miranda smiled and said, "Orale." Jason said, "Well, I'll catch you all soon." The ladies wished him a safe day.

One by one, friends began to surround and place their backpacks down on the lunch tables. They all greeted each other with hugs, air kisses or handshakes. The cafeteria echoed with the murmur of conversing and laughing.

The school bell rang. The kids grabbed their backpacks and started toward their first period. Some walked together as they continued conversing. Some of the kids hugged and agreed to see each other later.

Miranda had made a few sales on her way to her first period. By the time Miranda made it to her first class, she had already made a hundred and thirty-five dollars. She stepped into her first period history class with a bright smile. With a glow in her face, Miranda shouted, "Good Morning Mrs. Jimenez!" Her teacher, Mrs. Jimenez, said, "Good morning. Wow. I must say, it's rare to see anyone that excited to be back to school."

Miranda replied, "I just love school, Mrs. Jimenez. I find that it really and truly does pay to be here." In her head, Miranda laughed hysterically, but on the outside, she wore a big grin. Mrs. Jimenez said, "Well, I am very thrilled to hear that. Welcome back." Miranda smiled, and took a seat. Mrs. Jimenez was a chill teacher. Miranda knew that first period would be a breeze.

Suzy, on the other hand, had math for first period. Everyone knew her teacher, Mrs. Rank, to be a grouch. She didn't seem to give Suzy any problems yet. Mrs. Rank did not tolerate tardiness. All the kids who walked in after the tardy bell were sent to the auditorium room to hang out until first period was over. Isela had Mrs. Rank the year before and was drop failed because she was always just seconds or minutes late to class. Isela's mom wasn't even trippin' though because it was her fault that Isela was always late.

Mrs. Rank got straight to business. No questions on how their vacation was. She just expected the kids to know how to solve these math problems. If a student asked for any help, they were told, "It's a problem, solve it." Before class was over, the kids were assigned way more homework than they cared to receive. Suzy reviewed it and thought, "What a bitch." Suzy knew she could complete the assignments. She just wasn't happy about how much work it was. Suzy wondered if the other teachers would assign as much work as her first period teacher on their first day back. Or was it merely Mrs. Rank living up to her legacy?

First, second and third period came and went. None of Suzy's other teachers gave any homework. Both Suzy and Miranda were able to leave school at lunchtime. Because they took summer school the first three years for fun, they both had enough credits built up and only needed to take three classes each semester of senior year. The ladies met up at the same table from the morning. They hung out with their friends until the bell rang.

Suzy asked Miranda, "Q-vole mujer? You down to roll up the street, and I'll buy you a burger?" Miranda answered Suzy's question with a question, "Does that burger come with cheese fries and a strawberry shake?" Suzy replied,

"Baby girl, you can have whatever you like." Miranda responded, "Say no more. I'm there." The ladies signed themselves out at the front gate. They walked around the corner and hopped into Miranda's impala. The burger spot was only a few blocks up from the high school.

As the ladies waited for their meals in the drive-thru, Miranda suggested that they take the food to the cemetery to visit one of their close friends. When their order was ready, Miranda asked for an extra French fry holder.

They had quite a few friends and family members buried at the cemetery. There was one friend in particular from the apartments to whom they were both extremely close. His name was Luis. Luis passed away at the age of 14. He was walking home from the gas station when a green Honda rolled up on him. A guy jumped out and hit Luis up, saying, "Where you from Ese?" Deep in his gut, Luis knew what was about to happen. He put his head up high, stuck his chest out, and represented his hood with pride.

The guy dissed Luis' neighborhood. He then claimed his hood to Luis. As the guy reached for a gun at his hip, Luis threw a punch to the guys' face. The guy stumbled. Luis continued to throw punches. The guy pulled the gun from his pants, raised his arm, and shot Luis in the shoulder. He fired again at Luis' chest. When Luis hit the floor, the guy kicked Luis in the face. The guy ran back to the car and jumped in. The car dashed out of there.

Luis' homeboy Carlos was eating inside of the taco spot when he heard the first shot. By the time the guy was jumping into the car, Carlos had walked up to the window. Carlos was squinting to see who it was that got shot. He glanced around the guy and noticed that nobody had gone to check on him. Carlos pulled out his cell phone. He called for an ambulance as he ran out to check on the guy.

When he arrived at the body, he saw that it was Luis. Carlos' eyes grew wide, and he froze for a second. The situation suddenly became much more real. Carlos told the operator where to find Luis. As he ended the phone call, Carlos knelt beside Luis. Luis had no more life to him. Carlos glanced around again. People were staring from a distance, but nobody bothered helping at all with the situation.

Carlos began to angrily shout at the people who were just standing around and looking, "What the fuck is wrong with you? He's a kid, and you stand around and do nothing? He could be your fucking son or nephew. And you do nothing? Fuck you. Fuck you little fucking bitches!" Carlos placed his hand on Luis' collar bone. He whispered to Luis, saying, "I'm so sorry this happened to you, my boy. Fuck, my boy, I just saw you this morning. Shit hurts to see you like this. I pray you get to a place much better than this fucked up hell G." Carlos silently stayed knelt beside Luis until the ambulance came to get him. The EMT checked his pulse. They knew that Luis was dead; they stood by as the officers began their investigation, before taking Luis to the hospital.

Two police officers asked Carlos if they could question him. Carlos immediately and clearly said, "Look, I was eating in the taco spot when I heard the shots. I didn't know who shot or who got shot. I got up to look. I saw a body on the floor and no one else doing anything about it. I felt that calling for an ambulance was the right thing to do.

"When I got out here to check on the guy, I saw that it was my friend. His name is Luis Cardenas. He lives in the same apartment building as me just right there (Carlos pointed toward the complex). That's everything that I know." One of the officers nodded his head, saying, "You're a courageous kid." Seeing the agony and fear in Carlos' face, the policemen shook Carlos' hand then let him go.

Carlos slowly walked back to the apartments. He walked through a gate door off of Glenoaks Blvd leading into the parking lot. As he walked home, there was a group of friends hanging out. They all shouted hello's and what's up's in Carlos' direction. He silently walked right past them with his head down.

Isela felt something was wrong, being that Carlos didn't budge and kept his face looking downward. She called out to him, asking, "Hey Carlos, que paso?" Carlos stopped in his tracks. He lifted his head, looking straight ahead of him. Carlos then fell to his knees, placing his face in his hands. He began to sob uncontrollably.

Everyone in the circle rushed to and surrounded Carlos trying to console him. As he continued sobbing, he said, "Luis got shot on Glenoaks. He's gone. My homeboy, he's gone." Everyone was shocked and saddened by the news. Some of the other hood kids were angry and wanted revenge. But Carlos didn't have answers to any of their questions. The anger quickly turned to tears as they all mourned the loss of their childhood friend.

The girls pulled up to the cemetery. They drove up to the area where Luis' body rests in eternal sleep. Suzy carried the food. Miranda grabbed a blanket from the trunk. Together they walked up to Luis' memorial plaque. Miranda placed the blanket down on the grass for the ladies to sit on. Suzy placed the extra French fry holder close to the tombstone. Both ladies ripped a piece of their burger and put it in the French fry holder along with some French fries. The ladies sat there eating their food as they reminisced on the good and bad times that they shared with Luis.

Miranda mentioned, "Remember that time you were jump roping and Luis was throwing rocks at a wasps nest with Gabby, the wasps started chasing them, and they ran towards you yelling for you to run? It took a while for you to get why, but after you were attacked, you started running!" Suzy laughed as she responded, "How could I forget?! I was so mad at them for like a week."

Suzy's eyes began to welt with tears as she gazed off into the distance. She went on to say, "Man, I remember when my brother died, Luis kept asking when he was coming back. We both were too young to understand death. I just knew moms said he wasn't going to come back. I got tired of saying I don't know to Luis.

"One day the frustration built up, and I just started hitting Luis over and over screaming 'He's not, he's never coming back okay? So stop asking me, leave me alone!' Instead of being angry with me, he pushed through my swinging arms, threw his arms around me and hugged me tightly. He apologized over and over as we hugged each other so tight, and we cried together. I realized that he missed my brother just as much as I did."

Miranda rubbed Suzy's back and said, "It trips me out. How we watch our neighbors and relatives become gang bangers and lose the ability to think for their selves, get locked up, have early deaths, and the next generations who watch this, repeat the cycle instead of breaking it. I wish they would learn from the homie's mistakes. I'm tired of the painful losses. I want to see our people grow, prosper, and walk in unconditional love with each other.

"I know it's hard when the past of oppression pours into the present, causing so many of us to hate our circumstances and even ourselves. But still, I ask creator for the day that we take the system into our own hands and change it for the sake of our resiliency. I wish for our people to remember that these early Indigenous 'Gangs' were never intended to fight each other but to protect one another against the police and the U.S. Soldier and sailor brutality that they were facing in the 18 and 1900's.

"It's come a long way from that, and it hurts my heart. These guys are killing and claiming territory that doesn't even belong to them because the government took it away from us. Now we just rent to live on stolen land. All of this warring over territory, drugs, and money just doesn't make sense."

When they finished eating, they continued to reminisce with tears and laughter. An hour had come and gone. The ladies kissed the fingertips of their index and middle fingers, then touching their fingers to Luis' tombstone. With the same fingers, they felt their hearts. They stood up and headed back to the car to go home.

Miranda pulled up to the gate on Glenoaks and Pakooynga. The ladies gave each other a big hug. Suzy said, "Thanks for the ride, mujer." Miranda smiled, replying, "De nada, thanks for the grub." As she began to exit the car, Suzy looked back, saying, "See you later. Drive safe." Miranda responded, "Andale." Miranda reversed out of the driveway and headed over to her Brother Miguel's house.

Miranda settled at her desk to do some homework. Just as she finished up with her homework, her cell phone rang. It was a customer. She grabbed a couple of sacks of weed and drove down to the apartments. From there, she parked and walked down towards the liquor store. She met her customer near the store to make the exchange.

As she posted on a bench outside the burger spot, Miranda saw Isela's little Cousin Maribel with a couple of her friends passing along the sidewalk. Miranda whistled. The ladies spotted Miranda and began walking in her direction. Maribel told Miranda that they were headed to the apartments to drop off some birthday invitations to Isela and some friends. Miranda said, "Do me a favor pues, tell Isela to go get Suzy and meet up with me right here." Maribel agreed. Miranda hugged Maribel as she said, "Thanks, mija. See you later. Y quida te." Maribel nodded and smiled. She headed on to the apartments with her friends.

Suzy was sitting at the kitchen table, doing her homework when she decided to take a break to smoke some herb. Isela walked up to the front door of Suzy's apartment, proceeding to knock. When she heard the door, Suzy placed a curious look on her face. She placed the pipe down on the table then walked over to open the door.

Suzy was relieved to see it was Isela. Suzy opened the screen door and clasped Isela's hand, pulling her in for a hug. She invited Isela in with a gesture of her arm while saying, "You down for a sesh or what?" Isela smiled as she quickly replied, "Always down, foolia! I'll match you. How about that?" They walked into the kitchen together to blaze.

Isela saw the open textbooks on the table. She looked at Suzy and put her hand out to shake Suzy's hand hood style. Isela excitedly said, "That-shright loca! I know that it's only the first day of the last semester, but it's good to see you ain't ever fell off and blamed it on the yerba! Keep it up, love. You're close to walking that stage and getting your diploma mamash!"

Suzy blushed, turning her head off to the side. She then snapped her tongue against her pallet, coming back with, "Come on now! You know me. Making the honor roll, yet still causing des maaaadre. You're doing pretty well yourself que no mujer? How were the home studies today?" Isela answered, "Actually, really well." She paused to take a hit. She inhaled a few more times after taking the hit. With her lungs full of smoke, Isela exclaimed, "I just talked to my teacher," She exhaled the Kush smoke and continued, "I'm graduating in a month homie!"

Isela passed the pipe to Suzy and continued talking, "I'm on my last eight packets right now. As soon as I hand them into my teacher, I'll finally be done. Yay me! Ey, but I haven't even looked into college. I'm fucking up because I can't decide what I wanna do. I don't wanna waste my time and money, that's for sure."

After Suzy blew a cloud of smoke out of the window, she implied, "I feel you ma, if anything, do community college and work while you think about it. I applied to UCLA and CSUN, and I got accepted to both." Isela smiled, saying, "Hellz yeah Suzy! I'm so happy for you! Are you leaning toward one or the other?" Suzy replied, "Yeah, I'm leaning toward CSUN because it's close and convenient."

Isela asked, "What are you planning to major in?" "I still want to get into business. I think that'll be pretty down to be my own boss," Answered Suzy. Isela excitedly responded, "I know, right?! That's kind of where I am. And with all the skills we got homie, psssh. We got a variety of choices for our future businesses!"

Isela opened her eyes wide and said, "Hey, sorry to change the subject, but I just remembered, Miranda is waiting for us at the burger spot!" Suzy busted out laughing hysterically, exclaiming, "WOW, you would dawg!" Isela giggled as she suggested, "Fuck it; let's make this bowl to go." Suzy closed up her books. She neatly put them into her backpack and left her bag on the seat of her chair. Together, the girls exited through the front door.

Suzy and Isela exited through the back gate. To their left sat an elderly woman. The woman asked Isela in Spanish "¿Que hora son?" Isela politely explained to the women that she didn't speak Spanish. The elderly woman said, "Tienes un nopal en la fronte," which is an expression claiming Isela as one of her people. The woman continued, "Why aren't you proud to speak your language?" Isela said, "Soy Indígena de aquí, no soy de España. Are you from Spain? Cause Spanish is not the original tongue in Mexico. So if you're so proud maybe you should be speaking your Native language. Tehoovet Taamet, good day." Isela and Suzy continued walking.

As they walked up to the burger spot, they heard someone shout out, "Chaaaoow!" from the liquor store. Of course, it was Miranda. She had a brown bag in one hand. The other hand was in the air throwing up the P. It was kind of funny to see Miranda playing around throwing up gang signs. She always wore nice dress slacks or skirts, a beautiful blouse, and heels or cute flats. Her hair was usually done up cute. She often wore the 1920's through the '40's up-dos. Her favorite hairstyles involved pin-up curls, faux bangs, and wearing bandanas or scarfs in her hair.

The young ladies all smiled at each other and huddled up. Both Suzy and Isela hugged Miranda. Isela asked, "Orale, Miranda, you still down here, making your ends meet?" Miranda responded, "Best believe it homegiiirl! That's a given. Mafucka's know where it's at." No sooner than

Miranda said that, an older man walked up, asking for some yerba. They conversed minimally with each other. Miranda handed him a gram in exchange for a twenty-dollar bill. The man said, "Gracias, eh?" As he turned to walk away, Miranda replied, "De nada hombre."

All three ladies turned around to walk toward the apartments. Halfway to the complex, Isela said in a disappointed voice, "Aww snaps, we forgot to buy blunt wraps!" With a giggle in her voice, Miranda responded, "Ey, Isela, you doubt me too damn much." Miranda lifted two blunt wrap packages. She passed it over to Isela. Isela smiled at and grabbed the blunt wraps from Miranda's hand, then said, "And that my dear Miranda, is why we love you so much." Miranda smirked, replying, "Shuuuut uuuup! But I love you too doll."

The girls entered the apartments and sat on a slab of concrete fit for a bench. Suzy broke up some weed. When Isela saw that the bud was almost ready to be rolled, she began to prepare the blunt wrap. Miranda took a swig from her bottle wrapped inside a paper bag and continued to keep trucha for her homegirls.

Freddy, one of the residencies, began to approach the ladies. Before he got in front of them, Miranda acknowledged him by lifting her head as to say, "What's up?" Freddy returned the gesture to her. Freddy walked up, shaking all three of the girls' hands. He then asked Miranda, "Whatchyu sippin' on?" Miranda smiled big and said, "Some ice-cold H2O. Want some?" Freddy replied, "Ha-ha. No thanks. I was thinking maybe you were sippin' on some cervi." Miranda giggled, saying, "Come on, Freddy, how long have you known me? 11 years? And you seriously think I'd be sippin' all of a sudden? You crazy G, I'd rob a bank before I'd touch any kind of alcohol."

Isela's eyes opened up wide. She glanced over to Miranda, exclaiming, "Let me know when you're ready for that bank homie. I'm right there witchyu! We can donate a percentage of the money to some of the residents in need. Maybe even fix up the city, like these damn streets. Fix it right there on Glenoaks, where Suzy broke her foot in that pothole! Ha-ha!"

Miranda laughed and shouted, "Remember that?! She still crossed the street to buy her blunt wraps! She sat there in that very spot, rolled a blunt, smoked it, walked home later, fell asleep, then woke up in excruciating pain and drove to the hospital at three in the morning!" Miranda looked over to Suzy and said, "Psssh que Suzy, your just too G wit it mujer! Ha-ha."

Suzy smiled as she continued to lick and roll the blunt. Isela asked Miranda, "So what? We gonna hit a lick and be the 21st century female Robin Hoods O que?! Cause if so, I'm down." Miranda replied, "Daaaang Traviesa! I was just playiiing. Look at you about to start on the blueprints and shit! If super desperate times call, then we'll talk. Until then, I'm straight friend. I love my so-called freedom!"

Freddy shook his head side to side. He said, "You're too much, Isela. The crazy shit is, I know you're down to do some shit like that." Isela smiled at Freddy, shrugging her shoulders. She replied, "Hey, what can I say? I'm a product of my environment, homie. Plus, them banks been robbing our loved ones since day one." Everyone laughed and nodded at her comment.

Freddy found himself a seat in between Suzy and Isela. He turned his body toward Isela, then nudged her with his elbow saying, "Sup with Mikey, how's he doing these days?" Isela replied, "He's good. He is still good ol' Lazy, big pimpin' as always. Right now, he's probably with his girl of the day. You know Lazy, never planning on working a day in his life. Yet he's somehow finding ways to be on baller status though. Like, seriously?"

Freddy grinned, replying, "Yeah, your bro always had a way with the ladies. He never did care too much about whether they were sisters or cousins, huh? He's just out to get his, which he always seems to get, huh?" As Suzy lit the blunt, she said, "You know he had one girlfriend that we liked. You wanna know what happened to her? She left him! She was a smart one, I tell you." Freddy smiled and shook his head side to side. Suzy then took a big hit from the blunt and passed it to Freddy. Freddy hit the blunt and offered it to Isela. This order was how the rotation worked until the blunt was gone.

Right as the blunt finished, they heard Gabby singing her way around the corner. Gabby walked up with her beautiful smile. She took her headphones out of her ears and joyfully exclaimed, "What's up, ladies and gents! How is everyone doing?" Every one replied at once, "Good!"

Isela questioned Gabby, "Haven't seen you outside in a couple of days, ma, why is that?" Gabby gave a big smile in Isela's direction before replying, "Miranda knows! I've been spending the last few days with my cousin at his studio, recording hooks. Hopefully, soon he's gonna help me record some of my songs."

Suzy nodded her head as she listened to what Gabby was saying. Suzy was the first to say, "That's dope, Gabby. You are so talented and have such a beautiful voice. I'm glad you're going to do something with it. You know other than just entertain us by taking our song requests." Isela said, "Yeah, and don't go forgetting about us little people when you get big either." Gabby laughed and said, "Thanks, ladies. Y'all are my childhood sisters. You know I could never forget any of you. Anyway, this project is simply to get my feet wet. I even started rapping on some of the tracks."

Miranda said, "Eeee, you're trying to show Isela how it's done, huh? Ha-ha naw, it'll start as getting your feet wet, but I know it'll develop into something bigger for sure. Cause you got mad skill homegirl." Gabby flashed a smile and said, "Thank you, Miranda." Isela added, "You rapping too now, huh? We're not just childhood sisters we hood sisters! Na, but seriously, we gotta drop a track together, just for fun." Gabby replied, "For sure, I think it's only right we do some songs together, sis."

Suzy asked, "What is it like being in the studio?" Gabby blushed as she replied, "Okay, so, it's not exactly a professional studio. My cousin grabbed an old stand up fiberglass shower that my uncle was throwing out; he flipped it upside down and ran the microphone cord through what was once the drain. The microphone hangs down in the shower. But yo, the sound is banging. And he uses an old dusty computer, but it gets the job done. We have fun creating. No doubt about that."

Isela said, "If you love it, that's all that matters. I mean honestly, we all gotta start somewhere. At least you're making moves." Just then, Denise walked up with her best friend, Clever. Clever was holding the handlebars of a beach cruiser next to him. He nudged the kickstand of the bike down with his foot. Denise and Clever shook hands with everyone in the circle then they blended within it. Isela smiled at Denise and Clever, asking, "Firme bicicleta homies. Where are y'all cabrones coming from?" Denise and Clever glanced at each other and together, began to tell the story:

Denise started, "So Clever said that he wanted to smoke me out, right? His thing was we had to blaze in the jungles though. I'm like alright fuck it then, let's do this. We start walking down the ave..." Clever cut in, saying, "This dirtbag mother fucker on a BIKE, grabbed on Denise's titties! I'm like 'aw hell naw, that fool ain't getting away,' we chased him for what? Seven seconds before that putio went down! We bombed on that fool recklessly and came up on this bike, among other things." Miranda, excitedly raising her voice, said, "That's exactly what he deserved. Most females would be stuck on stupid like, 'what the fuck just happened?' Good for you, Maldita."

Suzy asked Denise, "Dang, did you have your burner on you?" Denise patted her side. She kept her gun in a holster under her arm. Denise said with an attitude, "That fool ain't worth no valas, you feel me? He got what he deserved, though." Suzy nodded, responding, "That's what's up. Crazy though, that fool had no idea that fucking with you could have got him killed. So what Miss Maldita? On to the jungles it is then?" Denise replied, "Yeah, I guess so. After all, that was the plan."

Denise glanced at everyone, asking, "Are you guys migrating with us?" Suzy said, "Yeah, let's do this. I got ends on a bleezy or whatever." Freddy stood up, saying, "Na, I'm outs. I'll see you guys later." He shook everyone's hand then went into his apartment to grub and play video games.

The others made their way to the jungles, which was just about nine hundred feet away. There is a half-circle of benches covered by shade and surrounded with grass. It's usually a pretty chill place to kick it so long as the neighbors or enemies aren't out hating or out to put in work.

Every one grabbed themselves a seat. Suzy and Denise were on blunt patrol, so they sat next to each other on one bench. As they rolled the bud, the surrounding homies conversed amongst each other. Isela and Miranda got to talking about car shows.

Miranda told Isela, "You know, there's a car show coming up right around the corner. Please tell me we're putting money aside so we could get it crackin' playgirl?" Isela replied, "I'm on it. I put some time into new designs. Now it's just printing the Tees. So we'll most definitely set up shop."

Miranda said with excitement in her voice, "I can't wait to see your new creations. I think we could put our minds together to create some new classic oldie shirts. The last ones we created sold the quickest at that last show. Let me know how much feri you need me to drop." Isela replied, "But of course, I'll text you a quote."

Isela looked over to Gabby, asking, "What's up, though? Are you gonna roll with us this year?" Gabby began to nod her head, but before she could give an answer, Clever interrupted the conversation by asking, "What the fuck? Why don't you guys ever invite us, youngsters, to go with you?"

Isela responded, "Because lil' homie where and when we go, we go to have fun. Where ever you travieso looking ass fools go, there seems to be some drama. Now don't get me wrong, I know you wouldn't start anything. And I would love to take you to the kind of places we go. But YOU decided to bang lil' homie, not me. That means there's a lot of places you won't be able to go. I mean,"

Isela shrugged her shoulders and said, "You can go, you're just more likely to throw putasos or get shot at if you do. That means we throw putasos right there with you or risk getting shot at if we choose to bring you. You know we wouldn't leave you hanging, but that shit right there, ain't the business."

Clever shaking his head side to side, said, "That's crazy. The only time we get to have fun is at a muthafuckin' hood party." Isela smiled at Clever. She shrugged her shoulders again and said, "Hey, we all make our own life decisions. You're not restricted from having any fun. It just depends on what you call fun. You can always go hiking, kayaking, to the snow or camping at a beautiful site away from civilization." Clever nodded his head in agreement.

He then replied, "I would like to try all that white boy stuff, but I don't have that kind of money. It's all way too far too." Isela replied, "First of all, menso, you're Indigenous fool. Our people didn't always have malls & city noise. Camping, hiking, and canoeing were more of a lifestyle; it was sort of how our people lived on a day to day basis. Secondly, this is California fool. You don't even need to travel too far to get to places like that. And camping is pretty cheap. After paying for a site, you don't need a lot of money. Of course, you wanna have food, a tent and a sleeping bag."

Clever snapped his tongue against his palette and responded, "Awe, you see, I don't have any of that stuff." Isela said, "You accumulate it little by little. Look, I have a tent that fits like ten heads. All you need is a pillow and two or three blankets plus warm clothes. It gets pretty cold at night. Save like six bucks every day, until Friday. And I'll take you camping in two weeks. I just have to make the reservations."

With excitement in his voice, he replied, "For reals? I'm down. Are you gonna teach me how to fish, Isela?" She shrugged her shoulders as she lifted her arms off to the sides. With a laugh in her voice, Isela said, "Yeah, don't trip lil' homie I'll teach you." Without actually coming forth and saying it, Suzy and Denise gave each other a look as if to say, "I wanna go too." Suzy said, "What's up my love, you said this tent of yours fits ten people right?" Isela replied, "Yes. But I only have room in my bucket for five." Denise said, "Well, that's fine by me baby girl, count me in on that five." Suzy shouted out, "Yayeah, count me in as well por favor!" Gabby added, "Me four."

Isela turned over to look at Miranda. Miranda said, "Look, I would love to go, but I know y'all. You're going to make me do all the cooking and cleaning. If I go, I would just wanna chill." Miranda shifted her eyes side to side and continued, "But none of you hoodie's seem to know how to do it like me, so I can't let y'all starve! Come on now. I'll roll-up." Everyone laughed and cheered for Miranda's commitment to go.

Suzy then said, "By the way, Isela, we can take the van. That thing just sits there most of the time anyway." Isela replied, "Aight, that's firme. So how about we meet up here in the jungles on that Friday around 3:30 after school? Everyone, please be sure to get your stuff together the night before, that way you're less likely to forget anything. And like I told Clever, save some money every day. When everybody is here, we'll pack it up and hit the grocery store to buy some breakfast, lunch, and dinner for the trip. I figure Friday we can eat out before we get up there." Everyone excitedly agreed on that plan.

The blunt began to make it's rotation as they continued talking about camping. Suzy said, "Okay, so you can count on me for the foil, pots, and pans plus cooking utensils. I'll also bring dish soap and a sponge." Denise said, "Well, I have some knives, forks, paper plates, and cups leftover from the last party we threw. Oh, plus two flashlights I can contribute." Isela said, "Okay, cool, that helps out a lot. I have three fishing poles. I also have the ice chests. If you guys can think of anything that could come in handy, like a chair to sit around the fire, bring it."

Suzy asked Isela, "I don't have a chair, should I buy one?" Isela responded, "I have three extra chairs if that helps." Denise said, "I have three chairs too." Suzy nodded her head, "Okay, cool then," She replied. The blunt was gone, and with it, the sun. Gabby stood up, saying, "Well, I would love to stick around, but I gotta make dinner for the bro and me." Gabby walked around and gave everyone a hug and kiss on the cheek. Gabby said, "Good night, fam," as she walked away. Denise looked over to Clever and gestured her head to the left, saying, "You ready to bounce too?" Clever nodded his head, yes. Denise and Clever made their rounds saying good night.

Clever walked Denise (with her new bike) to her house. They hung out in the back yard and shot some pool. Clever loved spending time with Denise at her pad. He felt safe there like he didn't have to watch his back.

A half-hour passed by, Miranda smiled at the two young women and said, "I gotta go. I'll see you ladies tomorrow for sure. Suzy, pick you up at 7:15?" Suzy replied, "Yes, please." Miranda gave them both a hug followed by a kiss on the cheek. They wished each other goodnight as well.

Isela and Suzy stayed to talk for a while longer. After all, they don't get to hang out at school anymore. Evenings and weekends are the only time they see each other during school days since Isela dropped out after fighting with her English teacher the year before.

That situation was messy: Apparently, this teacher just did not like Isela. Their energies clashed every single day. That teacher had a very negative vibe about her, Suzy would agree. One day this teacher decided she had enough of seeing Isela's face in class. Isela asked to correct some spelling on the board.

The teacher tilted her head and got this strange twitch in her eye. She ran toward and attacked Isela. Isela saw it coming and immediately stood up, getting into a boxing position. Isela let the teacher take the first swing, and then she and the teacher fist fought.

Although Isela was beating her teacher's ass, she became so caught up in the moment that she wouldn't stop. Isela hovered over her teacher, who was now on the floor, taking swing after swing. Suzy talked her into calming down, as Isela began to calm, Suzy grabbed Isela and sat her down. Suzy checked Isela's face and bloody knuckles asking if she was okay.

Isela sent the teacher to the hospital with a broken nose and a concussion. Since Isela had no significant injuries, aside from swollen and bloody knuckles, the school and police decided they would take affirmative action. The police arrested Isela and wanted to build a case to lock her up despite her claims of innocence. The school decided they would expel her. Since Suzy was in that class too, and she witnessed the entire thing, she pulled as many of the kids from that class together that she could, they went down to the police station to fill out statements. Isela's mother was furious when she went to pick Isela up from the station.

The police asked Isela if she wanted to press charges. She said no. Her mom wanted to press charges and whoop that woman's ass for attacking her child. Isela told her mom, "Look, mom, if you press charges, we're going to have to live at court for who knows how long. Don't we do that enough with Mikey getting into trouble? Plus, we have enough to deal with, like Jared's death. I fucked her up bad mommy."

With pain in her voice, Isela pleaded, "Let's just go home, please." Isela's mom's eyes began to tear up. She hugged her daughter tight and took her home. Isela thanked Suzy a thousand times a day for a few days. She knew if Suzy didn't speak up, no one else would have, and she'd be sitting in Juvenile hall. Suzy would always say, "That's what true friends are for. I know in my heart that you would have done it for me." Isela always agreed.

After the massive ordeal with her teacher, the school sent Isela an apology letter explaining that the teacher was fired and invited her back to school. Isela decided instead to take up home studies. Her mom pretty much let her do whatever she wanted after that. Grace treated her daughter as a grown woman who can make grown woman decisions. Isela excelled in the home studies program. She loved that she could wake up, open her book, and be in class.

When she first started, she turned in an entire semester's worth of work in less than two months. She decided with the way she was getting by in school, that she would look for a job. She had a family friend named Tim, who had started up a side business. He had a silk-screening shop in his garage where he printed T-shirts, bandanas, and banners.

Tim also had a day job working for a major corporation in Van Nuys. Isela approached him, explaining her situation. She offered to help him with silk-screening while he worked during the day so he can have more orders than just the ones he did over the nights and weekends. Tim said he wasn't interested in hiring Isela to help with his business.

Within a month of Isela promoting his business, Tim had received so many business inquiries that he didn't want to turn away, but he was overwhelmed. He decided to call Isela and offer her the job. Isela learned the ins and outs about silk-screening quickly. She was cranking out orders for shirts and bandanas mostly. She made banners about once or twice a week. On her downtime, Isela studied and did her homework. If she didn't have homework to do, Isela would work on new designs.

Within four months of Isela working with Tim, they talked about opening a shop where they'd make and sell their designs. After a couple of weeks of shopping around, they decided to open up a shop on Van Nuys Blvd. Isela became the day manager of the shop. Together she and Tim hired two people. One person was to work under Isela's supervision, and the other was to work under Tim's guidance. Isela was delighted with the way her life had transitioned. Everything seemed to have fallen into place. Isela's relationship with her mother was also growing stronger.

SUZY

Suzy lived in the same apartment her whole life. My mom and dad were both Purépecha from Michoacán, Mexico. My mom, Lisa, was born in San Diego, California. Her parents moved to California four months before Lisa was born. They relocated to Pacoima when Lisa was 12. My dad, Hector, was born in Colima, Mexico. He moved from Colima to Arizona when he was six. He moved to North Hollywood, California for work when he was sixteen.

My dad met my mom at her job; she was waiting tables at a Mexican restaurant. When he met my mom, the diner she worked at suddenly became my dad's favorite restaurant. Hector worked in construction for a man named James until he (my dad) died. Our dad overdosed on heroin when Suzy was just four months old. I was eleven years old. I found my dad lifeless on the kitchen floor. I was angry with him about it. I hated him for being selfish and leaving us.

I thought Suzy was lucky because she wouldn't have any memories of our dad. I was wrong; she hurt because she knew that every child was supposed to have a father. I was very protective of Suzy. Aside from missing a father she never knew, she was a happy child. She was always laughing. Moms and I loved her and spoiled the shit out of her as much as we could afford to.

Suzy was six years old when I died. I stuck around for a little while after I passed away. But I have responsibilities

I have to tend to here. I watched Suzy grow distant from a lot of her friends, and worst of all, my mom. Suzy didn't know how to handle my death. She had her good and bad days. Sometimes she was so bad that she lashed out on my mom or her friends. Both my mom and Suzy spent a lot of nights crying themselves to sleep. My mom often felt like she lost her husband, son, and daughter.

When she was 9, my abuelita from my mom's side, went to live with my mom and Suzy. Suzy loved my abuelita's stories and her cooking. Abuelita taught Suzy how to cook and make tortillas. Four years after moving in, Abuelita passed away naturally in her sleep at the age of 87. Abuelita's passing devastated Suzy.

When she was 13, I dropped a book in front of Suzy at the Pacoima library. Suzy stopped in her tracks, a little weirded out that the book fell at her feet when no one was around to push it. She picked up the book and read the back cover. It was a self-help book that also talked about dealing with death. Suzy decided to check the book out and read it. She read the book cover to cover three times before returning it. That book opened Suzy's eyes and changed her life; Suzy had a better understanding of life, including its tragedies. She began to grab control of her life from there on out.

Suzy began to love more openly, starting with herself. Reading the self-help book led to her learning more about her inner spirituality which eventually led her to the laws of the universe. She became intrigued by the way that the universe worked. She studied the twelve laws of the universe thoroughly. Suzy would sit outside and talk for hours with Isela and sometimes Lori and or Gabby, who all had open minds about things like spirituality and the laws of the universe. Isela and Gabby helped Suzy work through childhood and ancestral genetic traumas.

Suzy started putting the universe to work for her. She wrote motivating mantras that read things like, "You are divine energy with the ability to vibrate on a loving frequency. Share your frequency with all those you cross," and "Today is a fresh blank canvas, paint the picture you would like to see." She posted mantras all over the walls in her bedroom and bathroom.

When she was 14, Suzy kept a notebook with notes in it, which she tried to read every morning before starting her day. The notes read;

"I respect The Law of Devine Oneness. I am a product of my thoughts, words, and actions. I understand that my thoughts, words, and actions can directly affect me, those I love, and the universe as a whole because we are all interconnected through the Devine web of life.

"I respect The Law of Vibration. I understand that energy is an infinite source. Frequencies surround us on a constant. Vibrating on a high loving frequency is a choice. Vibrating on a low energy frequency is also a choice. I understand that vibrating on a high frequency will lead me toward a more productive and fulfilled life. I will attempt to walk in love today as I tune in to the higher vibrating frequency.

"I respect the Law of Correspondence. I understand that the habits and ideas that I fall into now will carry into tomorrow. If I realize habits or thoughts that I want to change, I will take action to change them now, as I understand that these habits have a direct effect on me, those I love, and the universe.

"I respect the Law of Attraction. I understand that like attracts like. If I think, act and feel positive, I will attract positive experiences, ideas, and feelings towards myself. If I choose to think, act, and feel negative, I will attract negative experiences, ideas, and feelings towards myself. Today I will think positive and loving thoughts. Therefore, I will attract positive and loving experiences. I further understand that life is a balance of good and bad. In this case, it is about how I choose to perceive experiences that determine them to be negative or positive. In hardship, I will seek the lesson in the experience.

"I respect the Law of Inspired Action. I understand that it is my responsibility to take action in meeting my goals big or little. When setting big goals, I will set small goals to reach the heights of the bigger goal. Today I choose to work out, eat healthily, and read a book. I understand that these small steps will help me reach my ultimate goal of health and intelligence. Every day I will set goals and take action to achieve them.

"I respect the Law of Perpetual Transmutation of Energy. I will talk lovingly to myself and everyone around me. I will encourage myself and those around me to be our best selves. I understand that the way I perceive myself and the universe around me will affect how others perceive me. I know that my body contains water and energy, both of which are capable of transmuting. I am what I believe I am. I am beautiful inside and out. I am healthy inside and out. I am loved inside and out.

"I respect the Law of Cause and Effect. I understand that every cause has an effect. I understand that every effect will become the cause of something else. I understand that the universe is always in motion. What I do today will have an impact on my future and the future of others. I choose to think about my actions before making a move. I choose to be a positive impact on myself and others.

"I respect the Law of Compensation. I understand that I am compensated in direct proportion to what I put into the universe. If I put blessings out into the universe, I will receive blessings. If I put pain and hate into the universe, I will receive pain and hate. I choose to put love and blessings into the universe. Today I will do good deeds. Today I will receive blessings. I am grateful for my blessings.

"I respect the Law of Relativity. All things are relative. It is in the act of comparing and creating meaning that I can determine anything good, bad, hot, cold, etc. Today I will practice non-judgment. I will not compare myself to others, be it body image or material possessions. I will try to let everything and everyone just be.

"I respect the law of Polarity. I understand that everything has an opposite. Because I know what it is to suffer through the loss of loved ones, I know what it is to appreciate the life I have. Because I know what it is to have hard days, I can appreciate it that much more when I have good days. Which end of the spectrum I dwell in, is my choice. As I overcome all obstacles and situations, I acknowledge that I will be learning and growing every step of the way.

"I respect the law of Rhythm. I understand that everything vibrates to certain rhythms. These rhythms include the seasons in nature, stages of life patterns, and even love as everything moves in cycles. Like a pendulum, the energy of the universe is continually moving. When something moves far to the right, it will eventually swing back to the far left. Sometimes I will experience amazing things. Other times I will experience devastating things. Regardless of my experiences, I will attempt to be open-minded to the fact that nothing is constant in life.

"I respect the law of gender. I understand that there are two significant types of energy, one example being masculine and the other being feminine. I understand that I contain a certain amount of both energies. I must learn to balance these energies within me.

"These laws all correlate. These laws each affect me whether I recognize it or not. I am grateful for everything I have and everything I am. I am grateful for my blessings of yesterday, today, and tomorrow. The life that I exist in is beautiful."

Sometimes on the days that Suzy skipped reading these notes, she would notice herself being a little sluggish. The days that she read them, she rolled out of bed and onto the floor. Suzy did a minimum of 50 pushups, 50 triceps dips, 100 backward crunches, and a minute of planking on the floor.

By the age of 15, Suzy had a routine of working out every morning. When she first began to work out, she started with calisthenics exercises because that was all she knew. Soon, Suzy learned about weight lifting, adding it to her regimen. Every Saturday, she jogged to the park.

There, Suzy jogged four miles then jogged back home and stretched. Sometimes one or a few of the girls would join her. Suzy's relationship with moms finally came into existence, and it was healthy.

For her sixteenth birthday, moms got Suzy a gym membership and threw her a party at my Uncle Saul's house. They hired a D.J. for music. They served rice, beans, potato salad, green salad loaded with vegetables, and marinated grilled chicken for dinner. My family and all of my sister's friends were there to help her celebrate.

Moms bought Suzy a carrot cake. They sang Happy Birthday, and Suzy blew out the candles. My mom explained herself by saying, "My daughter likes to eat healthily, so we decided a carrot cake was healthier because it had a vegetable." Everyone laughed. As she laughed, Suzy rolled her eyes and shook her head side to side.

Suzy began to hit the gym up every day either at five in the morning or in the evening. She felt great as she took good care of herself, from her golden-toned brown skin and long wavy brown hair to the healthy food and the way she dressed. Suzy took pride in her appearance, and it showed, she turned heads everywhere she went. People stared at her often.

Although sometimes it was awkward the way some people stared, she would usually smile and say hello. People, including kids, would ask Suzy if she was famous or a model. Because she heard it so much from strangers, friends, and family, Suzy would eventually entertain the idea of modeling.

When she was 16, Suzy's first taste of modeling was for the clothing store that Isela ran. Suzy posed in some of their tee-shirts. The images were converted into posters and hung in the window and on the store's walls.

When Isela would sell her shirts and bandanas at Lowrider shows, she brought Suzy's posters. Somedays, Isela would bring Suzy to model the clothing. Suzy would pose for pictures with the cars as well as people. Often people asked Suzy to sign their posters. Suzy became published in 4 magazine issues from these shows.

The older Suzy got, the better life seemed to get for her as well. Of course, she had some bad days in life, including her share of breakups and funerals. Still, she was able to evaluate and get through everything that she faced with a deeper understanding.

CLEVER AND DENISE

Clever lived with his mom and two brothers. His mother, Rosita, was born and raised in Highland Park, California. Her family was Rarámuri or Tarahumara from Chihuahua, Mexico. Clever's dad Daniel was also born and raised in Highland Park. His family had Mayan roots from Yucatán, Mexico. Clever's parents knew each other since elementary school.

They began dating in their senior year of high school. They were a happy couple until Daniel lost his job. He grew insecure and isolated himself from his family. Daniel left when Clever was nine years old to go and be with another woman. Soon after, he had another family with the woman and never reached out to Clever or his family.

Denise was an only child. Denise's mom Adelena was Mexica and Iipay or Kumeyaay. She was born in San Diego, CA. Although her immediate family lived and worked in San Diego, the Iipay family from her mother's side lived on Santa Ysabel reservation. Adelena's father was from Tenochtitlan. Denise's father, Jorge, was born in San Diego. He was of Mexica descent. Jorge's parents both derived from Mexico City, Mexico, as well.

Denise's parents grew up together in San Diego. They knew each other since elementary school. They began dating in the sixth grade and have been pretty inseparable since. When they were weeks from high school graduation,

Jorge proposed to Adelena, who agreed to marry him soon after they graduated. Jorge's work brought them down to the San Fernando Valley. Because they knew young love well, Denise's parents were very receptive and open to Denise's relationship with Clever.

Denise and Clever were best friends since the seventh grade. Clever was good friends with Miranda, who was good friends with Denise. Miranda was a grade older than both Clever and Denise. One day Clever walked with Miranda to the cafeteria. They went to the student store to buy a bag of hot fries and flavored water. When they dipped the corner to chill and eat, they ran into Isela, Suzy, and Denise. Clever knew Suzy and Isela pretty well because they had all grown up together in the apartments. Denise was a face he had seen around, but he never dared to speak to her.

He shook the girls' hands and then introduced himself to Denise. Clever was still known as Danny back then. (He didn't receive his name Clever, until the eighth grade.) Denise smiled shyly. She introduced herself and shook his hand. Clever spent the rest of lunch talking to Denise while trying to get to know her. When the bell rang, he offered to walk her to her next class.

Both of them carried big smiles as they walked to Denise's fourth period. When they got there, Clever asked if he could hug her. Denise gave him the okay. Clever leaned in for a hug. Denise hugged him back and kissed him on the cheek. She thanked Clever for walking her to class. Both kids walked away, still smiling big. Denise and Clever both had grown secret crushes on each other that day. For a while, neither of them let the other know. But it was pretty obvious.

For the rest of the year, Denise and Clever spent their mornings, lunches, and sometimes, after school time together. The following year, Isela, Miranda, Suzy, and Gabby went on to High school. By then, Clever and Denise were in eighth grade together. They would walk together to the apartments and hang out every day after school. When Denise would go home, Clever would hang out with the guys from the local neighborhood gang.

Eventually, hanging out with the neighborhood gang meant becoming active for Clever. It began with him going with them to smoke weed and tag. As the activities progressed, Clever liked the rush that he received from the gang bang activity. He knew what they were doing was wrong. He knew if they ever got caught by the police, they would all be in trouble. He also knew of the possibilities of facing death due to the lifestyle he was choosing. He figured when he died; it would be by the gun. Still, Clever was living in the moment.

One of the O.G's noticed that Clever was rolling with the youngsters to bust missions. The O.G pulled a youngster named Spooky aside and told him, "You guys can't be letting him roll with you like that if he ain't from the hood Ese." Spooky replied, "He's down though Big Cholo." Big Cholo replied, "I don't give a fuck how down he is homes. If he's going to be smashing with you guys like that, he has to be banging the hood. You either put him on or tell him to take his little ass the fuck home."

Spooky nodded. He replied, "Dispensa big homie. I'll do it right now." Big Cholo said, "Bring him to me. I wanna talk to him first." Spooky walked over to Clever and said, "Hey Danny, the big homie wants to talk to you." Clever nodded his head. He knew what it was regarding.

Clever walked over to Big Cholo. Big Cholo began to talk. He let Clever know that he noticed Clever was kicking it too hard with the neighborhood. He told Clever kicking it with the guys like that was a no-no if he wasn't from the hood. Big Cholo asked Clever, "Are you trying to be from my hood, youngster?" Clever replied, "I don't know."

Big Cholo snapped at Clever as if he was offended, saying, "The fuck you mean you don't know? You can ride with my lil' homies, but you don't know if you want to be from my hood Ese? You're with the business, or you're not. So what the fuck you gonna do? You wanna turn the fuck around and leave my hood like a little bitch, stop kicking it with my little homies, maybe even get a warm-up every time you run into them?" Clever shook his head no. Clever stuck his chest out, then responded, "I wanna be from the hood."

Big Cholo relaxed his tone of voice, "That's more like it lil' homie. I'm gonna let Trigger know. He'll make sure you get put on tomorrow. What time do you get out of school?" Clever replied, "I get out at three." Big Cholo said, "Alright check this out, when you get out of school, come straight here to this spot. The homies will meet you and handle business. Tomorrow when I see you, you're going to be from my hood, right?" Clever nodded as he responded, "Yes, sir." Big Cholo laughed and said, "I like the respect, but I ain't yo' daddy and I ain't the juras, you ain't gotta go calling me sir. Go on and get the fuck out of here, lil' homie."

Miranda noticed Clever talking to Big Cholo. She waited nearby for Clever. Miranda walked beside him and quietly asked, "What was that about?" Clever told her. Miranda sounded defensive as she begged Clever not to get jumped in. She placed all of the consequences before Clever. Clever listened to Miranda. He sat quietly without arguing until she finished.

The following day at lunch, Clever told Denise that he would get jumped into the neighborhood that day after school. Denise asked Clever, "Why?" Clever said, "I like the thrill of doing the things that we do. They take me to bust missions, we tag, they get me high, and let me carry their burners. And the guys I roll with make me feel like family."

Denise shook her head. She said, "Do what you feel you gotta do, Danny. Just know that I don't think it's a good idea." Clever looked down at his feet. He said, "Miranda already tried to talk me out of it last night. The truth is, all the shit I already did, I got myself in too deep. I can't just kick it and bust missions and not bang. They're making me feel the pressure.

"The big homie says I have to get put on the hood or don't go around the apartments anymore, or I'll get jumped every time I do. How can I not go around when I live there? I don't wanna commit to the hood. But at the same time, I guess I do wanna do it." Denise gave Clever a big hug. Clever said, "I'm sorry, Denise. I know you're disappointed in me. Today after school, I want you to go straight home. Or go anywhere else but with me. I don't want you to see this." Denise said, "Okay." She then walked towards the door to enter her class.

After school, Clever walked alone to the apartments, he stepped into the gate and dipped the corner to the right. Denise was sitting on a staircase with her head in her hands. Clever grabbed her arm, helping her to stand on her feet. Clever asked, "What's wrong?" Looking down, Denise responded, "I been thinking about this since you told me, Danny. You're my best friend. We do everything together. If you're gonna get put on the hood," Denise looked straight into Clever's eyes as she continued, "So am I."

Clever shook his head no. He said, "Denise, I can't let you do that. You don't know what it's really like inside this world. It's too dangerous for you." Denise snapped her tongue against her palate. She said in a raised voice, "How are you gonna tell me it's too dangerous for me? Yet, you're out there every day. And now you're gonna get put on Danny? Fuck that. If you get put on, I get put on."

Clever threw his arms around Denise and hugged her tight. He started to cry as he said, "I fucked up already. I'm in too deep. You, you have your whole life ahead of you. I'm not gonna fight with you about this, Denise, but I don't want anything to happen to you. If anything happens to you, it's on me. I can't have that on my conscience."

Clever pulled away enough to look into Denise's eyes as he continued, "You're my best friend, and that won't ever change. But you don't have to do this. Pleeease, please don't do this." Denise hugged Clever tight too. She said, "You're my right hand, Danny, you made your decision, and I made mine. Whatever happens, we're gonna be in this together." Clever didn't say another word. He pulled away from Denise and wiped his eyes.

Clever began walking to the center of the apartments, where the guys agreed to meet up. Denise walked with Clever. They met up with and shook the hands of all the guys that were there. There was one older cat named Trigger. Trigger was there to oversee everything. He let Clever know what he was going to face. He was the one that gave the guys the okay on jumping in Clever.

The three guys that were going to jump Clever in were a little older than Clever, two of them were fourteen, and the other was fifteen. Trigger said, "Okay, lil' homie, this is how it's gonna go down. These three homeboys are gonna jump you in. You can swing back, or you can cover your face. It's on you. I'm gonna count to thirteen. Once the thirteen seconds are up, you're gonna shake hands with these guys. Clever nodded in agreement.

Trigger looked at the boys and said, "If he goes down, I'm gonna stop counting. Let him get back up. And go at it again. Mi entiendes?" The three boys nodded, and then surrounded Clever. Trigger gave the word to start swinging. Trigger started counting to thirteen. Clever mostly socked up the fifteen-year-old because he was in front of Clever.

The other two were taking side shots on Clever's face. Once in a while, Clever got a swing on one of the other two. Clever went down at 10 seconds. He jumped up quickly. Denise had her hand in a fist pressed against her mouth while she watched. She was biting down on her index finger. Finally, Trigger counted to thirteen. Clever shook the boys' hands. Trigger walked up to Clever and shook his hand. He then wrapped his arm around Clever's shoulder and said, "Welcome to the family lil' homie." Clever nodded his head.

Denise stepped forward. She looked into Trigger's eyes, and then said, "Alright, I'm next." Pointing at Denise with his thumb, Trigger looked over to Clever and asked, "Is this hyna serious?" Clever glanced down to his right side. He nodded his head yes. Trigger asked Denise, "Why do you want to be from my hood, mija?" Denise looked in Clever's direction as she answered, "Because we do everything together. If he's gonna be banging and putting in work, so am I."

Trigger asked Denise, "Are you willing to shoot someone?" Denise said with an attitude, "If they're from a gang, yes. They ain't innocent, right? They chose to live the life. So yeah, I guess I'd have to say fuck 'em." Trigger smiled. He said, "Are you trying to get trained in or jumped in?" Denise gave Trigger a look of disgust. She answered with a question, "What the fuck? Do I look like a hoodie?" She then said, "You got me fucked up, I'm getting jumped in." Denise pointed her finger at the three boys who jumped Clever. She said, "These fools can put me on." Trigger laughed. He said, "These guys ain't gonna put you on, mija."

Trigger jumped on his phone. He called up a young female who was from the hood. Her name was Shady. Trigger told her to roll up with another girl from the hood named Dreamy. Those were the only two young girls from the hood. The guys didn't like females to be from the hood. Sometimes girls came in handy.

Shady and Dreamy were down for whatever. They both rolled up within four minutes. Dreamy wore khakis with a tight black wife beater. She had a black and white bandana over her shoulder to match her shoes. Her hair was black and straight, and she wore black liquid eyeliner on her eyelids. Dreamy was a gorgeous young woman. Shady wore jeans with a loose black T-shirt. Her T-shirt was tucked in and folded out over her jeans. She wore black and yellow shoes. Shady wore her hair in a ponytail. She also wore silver hoop earrings. She too, was beautiful and didn't wear any makeup.

Shady asked Trigger, "What's up?" Trigger said, "Ey, check it out, this hynita wants to get put on the hood. I wouldn't mind having her banging my hood, la neta. She has that don't take shit from anybody kind of attitude. Low key, I like it." Shady looked Denise up and down a few times. She introduced herself to Denise and shook Denise's hand. Denise said, "Nice to meet you, Shady, I'm Denise." Shady said, "Okay, cool. This here is my partner in crime Dreamy." Dreamy shook Denise's hand. In a soft voice, Dreamy said, "Check this out, Denise, we're gonna take a little walk, c'mon, let's do this."

Shady and Dreamy walked around the corner with Denise following behind them. They sat down on a bench. Shady patted her hand on the bench, in-between her and Dreamy. She said, "Have a seat, Denise." Denise sat down between the two ladies. Dreamy told Denise, "So tell us why you wanna get put on the hood."

Denise said, "To be perfectly honest with you, this thought never crossed my mind until earlier today. My best friend told me today that he was getting put on. Nothing I said was gonna stop him. I told myself fuck it then, if he's gonna get put on so am I. I mean, we're together all the time, you know? If something goes down with him, chances are I'm gonna be right there anyway. If I know I'm gonna end up putting in work with him; I figure I might as well bang too." Dreamy shrugged her shoulders, asking, "That's why you wanna get put on?" Denise nodded her head, yes.

Dreamy nodded her head, as well. She then said, "It's not that bad to be a female from the hood. We bust a mission here and there with the guys, but it isn't often. They usually ask us to be getaway drivers and stash things for them like drogas and fuscas. Any other work we put in is on us." Shady added, "But once you're on, it's por vida. You can't just wake up one day and say I don't want to be from the hood anymore; it just doesn't work like that."

Denise said, "I understand. That's why I was mad at Danny for his decision. But it is what it is. He just got put on. Now it's my turn." Shady said, "You seem like a cool lil' hyna. If you want this, we'll jump you in today. But, you're gonna have to smash with us for a while, so we can see what you're about. If I don't feel like you're hood material, I'm gonna jump you right back out." Denise said, "Fuck it. Let's do this then." Shady said, "Alright, firme. We're gonna walk back to where the guys are, and we'll jump you in right there 'kay?" Denise nodded her head.

The girls walked back to the spot where the guys were. Trigger asked Shady, "So what's the word, mija?" Shady nodded her head, saying, "It's a go." Trigger responded, "Okay pues, thirteen seconds, handle it." The girls took flight on Denise. Denise blocked as many hits as she could. She swung back as often as she could too. She clipped both girls in the face a few times. She got hit pretty badly, also. When the thirteen seconds were up, both Shady and Dreamy shook hands with Denise and welcomed her into the hood. Trigger shook her hand and welcomed her in as well.

Trigger told Denise, "For the next few weeks, you're gonna be rolling with these two ladies. When the time is right, they're gonna be the ones to decide on what to name you. Okay?" Denise nodded her head. With the little breath she had left, she said, "Okay."

The following day after school, Denise was walking out of the front gate with Clever. Shady and Dreamy were waiting for her across the street. Dreamy whistled. Denise glanced over. She spotted the girls then told Clever, "I guess I gotta go post up with those two." Clever said, "I'm sorry, Denise. I didn't want this for you." Denise replied, "Don't be sorry. I made my decision. Just take my bag to your pad, and I'll see you later." Denise gave Clever her backpack then hugged him. Together they crossed the street then split up.

Denise shook both of the girls' hands. Shady asked Denise, "Sup mujer, how was school?" Denise vaguely smiled as she replied, "It was alright. You know, school." Dreamy asked Denise, "So you ready to spend the day with us?" Denise glanced to her left; she could see Clever's back.

He was walking toward a back entrance to the apartments. She let out a breath and replied, "Yeah, let's do this."

The ladies walked down Pakooynga St. They passed a park and walked into some apartments across the street. These apartments were a government housing building. The girls walked around for a couple of minutes. Eventually, they ran into five girls standing around talking. These girls wore tight jeans. They had rubber bands around the ankles of their jeans, also known as "pretty girl" style.

Some of the girls wore flats, and some wore tennis shoes. Two of the girls wore tight shirts. The other three wore T-shirts big enough to tuck into their pants and hangover. They all had their eyebrows skinny and drawn in. Some of them wore dark brown lip liner. One girl pointed with her chin, saying, "Check these bitches out." The group of girls turned to see Dreamy, Shady, and Denise.

 In sync, the group of girls walked up to the other, one of them asked, "Where you bitches from?" Denise claimed her newfound hood. The girl that asked where they were from then said, "Fuck your bitch ass hood," She claimed her neighborhood. Denise socked her in the jaw. As Denise pounded on the girl's face, Dreamy and Shady took flight on the other girls.

Denise knocked that girl out cold. She turned around and grabbed the closest girl to her. The girl that Denise grabbed was swinging at Dreamy. She was about four inches taller than Denise. Denise's arm swung upward, dazing the girl out in one shot. That female sat on the floor, looking confused.

Dreamy sat on one of the girls' chest taking face shot after face shot. Shady had knocked a girl to the floor; her head hit the pavement so hard she tapped out. Shady was now working on the last chick. Shady knocked that girl out. Her body looked like wet spaghetti as she fell to the floor. Shady looked down at the girl who had looked confused and told her, "When your bitch ass homegirl wakes up, you can tell her that's what happens when you diss on my hood." The girl nodded her head quickly. She now had a look of fear on her face. Dreamy, Shady, and Denise turned away and walked back to the apartments.

When they reached the apartments, they walked back to the bench where they sat and talked to Denise the day before. They sat the same way too, with Denise in the middle. Dreamy said, "Now that you're from the hood, you're going to be creating enemies. Those girls we just laid out, they're our rivals. Now, when you walk around, you have to walk with eyes on the back and sides of your head. These bitches might send their little homegirls to jump you in school. Always be on your toes and ready for anything."

Shady said, "You did real good over there. You saw how there were five of them hoodies and only three of us?" Denise nodded, yes. Shady continued, "That's because most hoods jump in anybody they can so that they'll be deep. That's not how we roll; there's only a few of us. But we are street smart. We all know how to throw blows and shoot a gun. Now and again, we lose a soldier. But that's just part of this life. In this hood, we hardly ever jump in females. Do you know why?" Denise responded, "Because bitches are drama?"

Shady nodded as she said, "Ding, ding, ding. Bitches are drama that set people up. They turn on their hoods for camoté. Some bitches are just not made for this life. But all too often, these hoodies wanna try to be a part of this lifestyle. Now and then, you'll meet a lil' hoodrat claiming our hood. I guarantee it's because they got trained by the homies. Those girls have no self-respect. They don't get my respect, or anyone else's from the hood. The homeboys let em kick it so they can cack 'em down.

"We let 'em think that they're from the hood. But you'll never see them groupies at a junta. There are a few older ladies that used to bang the hood. But they're grown, doing the whole mommy and or career woman thing. That stuff gets a pass because they already earned their stripes. They did their dirt and put in work when they were young, so no one trips on them now. Once in a while, they'll stop by to check on shit. You're gonna have to meet them so that you don't ever trip on the wrong person, cause you will get checked for that. We'll take you this week to meet them." Denise nodded as she took it all in.

Shady asked Denise, "Do you know what a rat is?" Denise nodded her head, yes. Shady said, "Do you know what happens to people who rat?" Denise shook her head no. Shady then said, "If it's a cholo who rat's out on anyone, they will end up dead. If they do it to get less time, they try to go to p.c, which is protective custody. They know what they did was wrong. There'll be paperwork on them, and they won't live long in general pop.

"If it's a woman that doesn't live the life who pulled rat, she usually gets her ass beat pretty badly depending who and what she ratted on. If it's a man who doesn't live the life, he's most likely to die too. If you ever pull rat on anyone and the hood finds out, you will die. And Dreamy or I might have to be the ones to handle you. Do yourself a favor and don't rat ever, not on your homies, not on your enemies. If you need something done, you do it yourself. These cops will only shit on your name." Denise nodded her head in agreement.

Dreamy asked Denise, "Do you smoke weed, drink, or do any other drugs?" Denise shook her head no. Dreamy said, "That's good. Keep it that way. No one will ever get on your case for drinking or smoking weed. But you will get a warm-up if we find out you touched anything from heroin to crystal. I wouldn't suggest you ever touch alcohol either. That shit is the reason why good people get caught up or caught slipping. Your mind isn't right when you're on that stuff."

Denise asked, "What do you mean, why not?" Dreamy said, "When you smoke yesca, you'll be a little slow. You'll be lazy. But you'll still be able to handle yourself in a sticky situation. If you have to run or something, you'll be able to. You might kill your high, but you can do what you gotta do. With alcohol, your reaction time is way too slow. You'll most likely drink more than you should, you'll think you're doing something right, but you're not, you'll have horrible balance. When you're drunk and try to run, you'll probably fall or not get far, possibly passing out.

"There also have been occasions where girls have drunk way too much, they pass out and get taken advantage of by guys. It's just better not to do it. You wanna be on your toes at all times. You wanna be completely aware of your surroundings and what's going on around you at all times." Denise nodded her head and said, "Okay. I understand everything you're telling me."

Denise spent two weeks every day with these girls learning about hood life from the female perspective. They got into plenty of fights. They'd go to low key places to teach Denise how to shoot. The girls robbed a couple of cars. They would take the vehicles on some quick missions. Then they brought them to a guy who the girls knew. He would pay cash for the cars they brought in. He would disassemble the vehicle and sell the parts to cheap mechanics.

Denise would go home around dinner time to eat dinner with her family, and then she'd lock herself in her room. She would sneak out of the window to kick it with Dreamy and Shady. Denise never complained or hesitated to do any of these things. In her mind, she would say, "Forgive me for the sin I am about to commit. I do not want to hurt the innocent."

The fighting she didn't mind. She was getting down with girls from other gangs. When Denise spotted a girl looking G'd up, she would take the initiative to hit her up. After the girl would say her hood, Denise would claim hers if the girl wasn't an enemy, Denise would shake hands and be on her way. If the girl were an enemy, Denise would put in work on the girl's face. Denise didn't feel good about any of the stealing. She felt someone worked hard for what they had, and stealing it was crossing the line.

After two weeks of hanging out with Denise, the girls decided on a name for her. They picked her up from school. The girls walked into the apartments. Once they stepped foot in the gate, Shady began to tell Denise, "Well, you hung in there with us for two weeks mujer, you didn't bitch or cry once. You were down for whatever. And times we witnessed you do some crazy shit by yourself. That's what's up. You smashed on a grip of faces; we give props to you on that one. Dreamy and I have decided to name you, Maldita."

Denise nodded as she listened. Dreamy said, "You did good kid. I know you miss your bestie. We won't keep you away anymore. But if something needs handling, it's mando you are gonna have to get your hands dirty 'kay?" Denise looked Dreamy in the eyes as she said, "Símon. Just get at me, and I'm there." The girls shook hands. Shady said, "We'll catch you alratos, Maldita." Denise replied, "Orale. Stay up."

Denise walked over to Clever's apartment and knocked on the door. Clever answered the door. He gestured for her to come in. He closed the door and locked it. They sat on the couch and picked up remotes to play a video game. After a while, Clever asked Denise, "Are you hungry?" Denise laughed. She said, "You are, huh?" Clever nodded his head, yes.

Denise asked, "You want me to make you a grilled cheese?" Clever smiled and nodded his head again. Denise went into the kitchen and made two grilled cheese sandwiches, one for each of them. She also put some carrot slices and grapes on the side of the plate. She knew a sandwich alone wouldn't fill Clever up. Clever thanked Denise. He took a bite of his sandwich then let out a big sigh of relief. As he savored his bite, Clever slowly said, "I missed this." Denise laughed. She agreed, "I know, right?"

Everyone knew Denise and Clever were best friends. Behind closed doors, they would flirt. At the beginning of their sophomore year of high school, they finally hooked up. It all started one day when Denise was teasing Clever about his laugh.

Denise told Clever, "You look so tough, but you have this goofy laugh that just softens your appearance. It's so funny to watch this hardcore looking vato with such a dorky laugh." Clever tried so hard not to laugh when Denise said that. He wore a big smile instead. Clever grabbed Denise by the waist, pulling her in close. Clever leaned down toward Denise and finally kissed her. Denise kissed him back. She placed one hand around Clever's shoulder. She gently placed her other hand on the back of his head. They kissed each other passionately for a few minutes.

Finally, Clever slowly pulled his head away to look Denise in her eyes. His jaw trembled as he quietly said, "I've wanted to do that since the seventh grade." Denise smiled. She then asked, "So why did you wait so long?" Clever replied, "I was afraid. Mostly because I think we were just kids who weren't ready for a relationship. I was worried if I hooked up with you, that we would break up, and I would lose your friendship. I wasn't ready for that either. Right now, it just felt so right.

"Denise, I want to be with you forever. I want you to be my lady." Denise smiled. She combed the hair on her right side behind her ear. She gave the nod as she looked into Clever's eyes. Denise said, "Clever, I have always been your girl. I want to be your lady too." Clever held Denise just a little tighter. He said, "So did we just make it official then? You're my lady Denise?" Denise smiled and nodded as she replied, "Yes. I'm your lady." She wrapped her arms above his shoulders and hugged him tightly.

Denise pulled away, placing her hands on Clever's shoulders. She gave him a stern look. Raising her right eyebrow, she said, "But Clever with all due respect, I don't want anyone to know we're together. Not because I'm ashamed. Because I'm not, you're my best friend. I don't want people knowing because they get too interested and involved. I want to be with you forever too. I think the best way to do that is to keep us on the low." Clever agreed.

Clever said, "I know where you're coming from. I can respect that." They hugged again. Both of them were extremely happy that this day had finally come. They kept their relationship a secret for over a year. Clever walked to Denise's house every morning to walk with her to the bus stop. Together they'd take two buses to get to school.

After school, they always met by the back gate. Then they'd take two buses to get home and walk to the apartments to hang out together.

Whenever Denise was at Clever's pad and the time came for Denise to go home, Clever always walked her. Denise lived in a house around the corner from the apartments. Clever lived in the apartment complex. Every time, she would tell him not to walk her home. Every time, he would say something like, "You're crazy if you think I'm gonna let you walk alone. I wanna see to it that you get home safe." Denise always agreed.

Once they got to her house, she would usually say something like, "Okay, you got me home safe. Now I gotta walk you home to see to it that you get home safe." Clever would laugh and hug her tight. Denise loved to breathe deep when Clever hugged her. She thought he always smelled so good. She often told him, "There's something so comforting about being in your arms and smelling your scent. It feels like home." It made Clever feel good at heart when Denise said things like that. He wouldn't say anything. He'd just hold her tighter.

Clever wasn't good at expressing himself with words. He always showed her how he felt with kind and loving gestures. He would dedicate Denise love songs that expressed what he felt. He would buy her romantic cards and text her links to YouTube videos. Denise would click the links which would re-direct her to the song or video. After Denise would hear the song, she'd text him back with hearts and say things like, "<3 <3 I love you too hermoso."

Clever sent Denise texts every morning saying good morning. Even though they both knew he was going to walk over there to see her. He also sent her texts every night, wishing her a good night. Denise loved getting those texts. She looked forward to them.

Because they knew him since his middle school days, Denise's parents accepted Clever like a son. It was no shock to them when they found out their daughter was seeing him. Because it reminded them of their young love, Clever was always welcome in their home with open arms. The only rule they held was if Clever and Denise were going to hang out in her room, the door had to be wide open. Denise and Clever spent most of their time in the back yard, living room, and kitchen. They usually just went into Denise's room when she was going to change clothes and or shoes.

Rosita, Clever's mom, absolutely adored Denise. Denise called Rosita "Mama Sita." Rosita often told Denise, "You're like the daughter I always wanted." Denise would smile and say, "Awe, I love you like a mom. I'm glad we're as close as we are." Rosita would agree.

Denise enjoyed spending time at Clever's place. She would help his mom cook dinner for him and his two brothers. Rosita worked as a secretary in an Attorney's office in West Hollywood. She made pretty good money. They lived a little poorly because Rosita would pay her rent, bills, fill up on gas and food once a week, buy her kids the clothes and shoes that they needed, and the rest went to her savings for a house. She refused to flash her money.

Rosita told herself before she could even look at houses that she had to save sixty thousand dollars. Rosita was getting close to her goal on her savings. She would often tell Denise, "Mija, when I'm ready, I want you to do the house shopping with me. I want you to live with us. I'll even give you two the master bedroom." Denise would say, "I'll help you, mama Sita, but that master bedroom should be yours.

After all, you're working hard for it." Rosita would smile and say, "Uy, I don't care about how big my room is. I just want my babies to be happy."

Clever and Denise talked about moving in together one time. It was after Rosita brought it up for the first time. Clever thought it was a great idea. Denise said, "I will live with you if you want me to. I mean, I do want to live with you, but honestly, I'm afraid you're gonna get tired of me always being there. Maybe you'll get bored of me and tell me to leave."

Clever replied, "You're the least boring person I know. I have fun with you. And we're together all the time anyway. I think it would be a dream come true to wake up with you in the morning. I can give you a morning kiss instead of sending my morning texts. As far as telling you to leave, that'll never happen. I don't want you to go anywhere. When the time comes, I will talk to your parents and ask their permission and leave the final decision up to them." Denise smiled and said with excitement, "You're the sweetest man I know. I love you, un chingo." Denise leaned in and kissed him.

Clever and Denise spent the majority of their alone time together. They had many chances to have sex. Denise had told Clever one time that she would want to wait until they were married to have sex. Clever told her, "And when that day comes, it won't be sex, we'll be making love." Denise smiled and kissed Clever tenderly. She looked him in his eyes then said, "I love you so much, Danny." Clever replied, "I love you too beautiful."

Clever never made Denise feel pressured to having sex. He knew one day he would be the lucky man to take Denise's virginity. Clever also thought that if he ever pushed the issue, he would also be pushing Denise away. He respected Denise's wishes. Denise loved that Clever gave her so much respect. Clever was happy to spend so much time with such an amazing girl. He also felt that she deserved better. Clever spent every day of his life, making Denise happy.

Denise was happy. In her mind, Clever has always been the perfect fit for her personality. They rarely argued about anything. They laughed just as much as they talked. Denise couldn't see herself with any other guy.

MIRANDA AND MIGUEL

Miranda went outside to warm up her '63 impala. She was going to pick up Suzy and then head to school. Every time she saw her car, she couldn't help but smile. It reminded her of her best friend, Miguel, whom she called brother. Since Miranda was born, Miguel was her next-door neighbor in the apartments.

Miguel lived with his mother and his grandmother. Miguel's grandmother was born in Guanajuato, Mexico, to her parents, who were of the Guamare people. The Guamare is said to be a branch of the Chichimecas. When she was four months old, Lita migrated with her parents to El Monte, California. Lita met her husband in high school. He was a proud young Rarámuri man. His family came from Chihuahua, Mexico, long before he was born. After high school, they both settled into the typical factory worker positions. Soon after, they would have four children, including Miguel's mother, Ana.

Ana fell in love with Miguel's father, Juan. Juan was raised in the barrio life. His family didn't know much about their background. Just that they were once slaves of the San Gabriel mission and were identified by the Spanish as "Gabrieleños." Juan's sixth-time great grandmother was taken from her family at four years old by the Padre and soldiers. And his sixth-time great grandfather was taken from his family at five years old.

They only remembered what they learned in the mission, which mostly consisted of the Catholic religion. Both grandparents were taken from nearby villages, and they identified as Gabrieleño because that was how the Spanish called them. They both were, in fact, Tongva. They taught their children to never speak of being Indian. So their children were raised identifying as Mexicans.

Juan took on the Chicano lifestyle with his homies. He learned a lot of the Pachuco lingo from his Grandfather. Juan and his friends were big on cruising and partying. As Juan's relationship with Ana grew, he realized it would be best to move away from his homies, if he was going to settle down. They moved out to Sylmar to start a new life together. There, they would give birth to and begin to raise Miguel.

When Miguel was three years old, his father took him and Ana to a fair. It was a fun day. As they began to exit the parking lot, three men jumped out of a truck in front of them. One man had a baseball bat. He hit the windshield with the bat and yelled for Juan to get out.

With cars behind him and no other way to exit, Juan jumped out of the car, locking the door behind him. The three men began to jump Juan. Ana felt helpless. She desperately wanted to jump out and help Juan, but she was afraid to leave Miguel alone. She cracked her window and began to scream for help. The three men jumped back in the truck and sped off. By then, Juan was left for dead.

After his funeral, Ana knew she wouldn't be able to get by out there alone. Yet, she didn't want to burden her family. Ana went to the welfare office to apply for welfare and assisted living. That is how she wound up at the apartments.

When Miguel was five, Ana's father passed away. Ana convinced Lita to sell her home and live with Ana and Miguel.

Lita agreed to move in and help to care for Miguel while Ana worked. Miguel loved his walks to and from School with Lita.

Miranda's Dad Antonio was twenty-two, and her mom Laura was twenty when they conceived Miranda. Antonio was Tohono O'odham from Sonora, Mexico. He was Indigenous to the North American continent but was considered illegal in the United States. He moved to the U.S. when he was eighteen hoping to create a better life. Antonio began his paperwork but didn't realize it would take him years of processing.

Laura was Apache from New Mexico but knew very little about it. Like many others Laura claimed to be "Mexican." She was born and raised in Pacoima with her parents, who passed away in a car accident when she was fourteen. Laura's neighbor took her in to allow her to finish school with her friends.

When he was twenty, Antonio met Laura in the apartments and fell in love. Laura thought Antonio was cute, but she had her focus on school. When she graduated high school, Antonio asked if he could take Laura out to celebrate, Laura agreed. Antonio took Laura to a Mexican restaurant in Reseda. After dinner, he asked if she would like to dance. They danced until Laura had to go home.

Laura and Antonio fell in love. After a year of dating, Laura had gotten pregnant. She applied for an apartment of her own. Mid-pregnancy, she was approved for an apartment. Antonio moved all of their belongings. He placed everything exactly where she told him to.

When Miranda was only eight months old, Antonio got caught driving without a license or car insurance. The police took him in. Within a matter of weeks, Immigration and Customs Enforcement deported Antonio to Mexico. After a failed attempt at getting back into the states, he decided to make a life out there in Mexico. Laura refused to move.

Antonio often called to check on Laura and talk to the baby. Eventually, the calls from Antonio became less and less until Miranda and Laura stopped hearing from Antonio altogether.

Miguel's grandmother, Vero, would babysit Miranda while Laura went to school and work. Miranda would hear Miguel call his grandmother, "Abuelita." In due time, Miranda began to call Vero "Lita." Everyone thought it was so cute that eventually, Vero's name became Lita. Miguel was seven years older than Miranda.

By the time Miranda was six, Miguel had already started hanging out with the local gang members. Miguel never busted missions with the guys, nor did he drink or blaze with them. He also never got jumped in. Still, he was like family to the guys who he had grown up with around his age.

One day Miguel approached an older gang member who was standing alone. He said to the man, "Hey, Listo? I have high respect for you because I always see you making your money. I never once have seen you drink or get high. Above all, you always take care of your family. I was wondering, how can I be up on game like you if I don't wanna be from the hood?"

Listo nodding his head and smirking said, "I appreciate that lil' homie. You communicate well. You also give respect. That's important in this life. And it's rare for a youngster your age. Usually, these lil' punks need to get socked upside the head a few times a day. I like you, Miguel. I have respect for your familia. If you are serious about making money this way, I'll teach you what you need to know. But you HAVE to stay in school.

"To do what I do, you need to be educated in math and biology. If you can bring me your next two report cards and they carry good grades, I'll give you a decent amount to put you on deck. What you earn, you keep. But come back to me with all the money you make, to get a bigger sack. You do this a couple of times and watch your income grow. It's called flipping. Your goal is to flip fifty dollars into a hundred and so on. Understand?"

Miguel studied Listo and his words. He replied, "Yes, sir, thank you, Listo. You have no idea how much I wanna be like you." Shaking his head, Listo quickly responded, "Don't be like me lil' homie, be better than me. You're already on the right track by staying out of this gang and the crazy that it brings. Let slanging be temporary though. Use it as a tool to get you ahead. Be successful and show these youngsters it is possible to come up from nothing." Miguel smiled and said, "That's exactly what I wanna do. I'll make you proud, Listo. Thank you." To which Listo replied, "De nada lil' homie."

Miguel had always paid extra attention in class. He asked plenty of questions. He turned his work in on time. And above all, his grades were A's. So it was easy to prove to Listo that he was serious. Miguel brought his second report card with straight A's to Listo. Listo scanned the report card and said, "This is good stuff, lil' homie. Keep it up. I want you to keep bringing me your report cards with grades like these. Before I hand this to you, we have to cover some ground rules:

"Rule number one to slanging; never get high on your own supply. Smoking your own jale will leave you for broke and maybe even owing money, in this game, that can be dangerous. The second rule to live by, stranger danger, if you don't know them, don't do business with them. Why?

Cause he may be a rat, a cop, or a thief. It ain't worth finding out. Rule number three is really important. As much as you want to help a friend out, you don't wanna get burned for feria. So no fronts unless you don't mind losing out on feds or friends. Do you understand?" Miguel nodded his head, yes.

Listo gave Miguel his first scale and sack to slang. He turned the scale on and put a dollar bill on top. Listo said, "This is how I check the scales accuracy. If it reads 1.0, the scale is working correctly." He explained to Miguel how he would weigh the weed out on the scale. And he described the price ranges that went along with the weight. After that, there was never a day Miguel said he didn't have money. He flipped that fifty dollar sack given by Listo into a thousand dollars in no time.

By the time Miguel was seventeen, he had enough money to put a significant down payment on a new house. He thought of buying himself a car first. He used to see this older man cruising up Pakooynga St. every Saturday morning in a '63 impala bumping oldies. It was a blue and white two-tone. It had white interior seats. The car also had whitewall tires with wire spokes. Miguel would always tell himself he wanted that car.

One day he took a walk up the street looking for that car. He spotted it in a driveway. Miguel walked up to the front door of the house and knocked. When the door opened up, there was the man Miguel seen every Saturday. Miguel shook the man's hand as he introduced himself. The man's name was Pete. Miguel explained his reason for knocking. Pete would shift his eyes back and forth from the car to the kid in front of him, as he listened to Miguel speak.

Pete said, "I'll tell you what son, my wife, and I have been talking about selling, and we have been shopping around for a motorcycle. Now, it needs a little work, but the paint and interior are immaculate. I'll sell you that car for, hmmm, say fifteen." A little confused, Miguel asked, "You can't mean a thousand five hundred, right?" Pete laughed, he replied, "No son, fifteen thousand bucks."

Miguel replied, "Oh ha-ha yeah, that sounds more like what I was expecting to pay." Miguel opened up a backpack full of cash. He flashed it in Pete's direction. Miguel then asked, "May I come in?" Pete looked in the bag. His eyes grew wide. The corners of his mouth arched downward. Nodding his head, he agreed, "Sure, son, come on in, pleeease."

They sat at the kitchen table. Miguel asked, "While I count the money, can I have you fill your name out on these agreement forms for both of our records? Also, may I have the pink slip after we sign?" Pete was stunned that this kid sitting in front of him was as on point and outgoing as he was. It seemed to be rare with the young men of Miguel's generation. Pete agreed to get the paperwork started. He read the forms and nodded as he signed.

Miguel counted out hundred dollar bills and placed it in fifteen organized stacks of a thousand dollars on the kitchen table. They each signed the agreement forms, including an exchange in ownership paper that Pete signed over for the car. Miguel grabbed the keys along with the pink slip from Pete's hand. He then shook Pete's hand and said, "Thank you so very much. You have no idea how happy you just made me, sir."

Pete smiled and said, "You're very welcome. There's a strong drive inside of you son. I hope this car will drive you farther in life. Don't lose sight of where you're going. You'll get there." They shook hands once more. Pete walked Miguel outside and watched him start up the car. They waved to each other as Miguel took off in his new impala.

Miguel drove straight to the gas station. He then drove home to show his family his car. Miguel parked the low-rider as close to his apartment as possible; that way, it was visible from his front door. He opened the front door and called for his mom. Miranda was sitting at the kitchen table with Lita playing cards. In a very Mexican American accent, Lita said, "Uy, mijo don't yell for your mother like that. Go to her room and talk to her." Miguel replied, "Sorry, Lita. I'm just so excited to show you guys something." Lita asked, "What is it mijo?"

As Miguel walked past the kitchen to his mom's room, he said, "You'll see Lita." Miguel found his mom lying down on her bed reading. He said, "Ama, get up, please. I have something important outside that I would like to show you." His mom looked over to Miguel and thought about it for a second.

She then got up, put her shoes on, and followed her son. As they reached the kitchen area, Miguel excitedly told Lita and Miranda, "Come on, fam I'll show you!" Every one followed Miguel outside. "Look what I just bought off of a man up the street," Miguel said. His mom gasped, "Mijo, it's beautiful." Lita and Miranda were smiling and admiring it while they walked around it. Miguel told them, "I call her Blue Betsy. Get in the car you guys. Let's take a drive." They drove down Van Nuys Blvd. He decided to take his family out to eat. They wound up on Plummer St. at a little Mexican restaurant near the corner. He knew how much his mom loved that place.

After they ordered their food, they sat at a table by the window. Miguel told his mom, "Ama, if you don't have to work this following weekend, let's go to the beach. I'll drive." Miguel's mom smiled. She then replied, "Mijo I haven't been to the beach since you were 12. I would love to go."

Miranda asked, "Hey Miguel, what about me and Lita?" Miguel replied, "Are you kidding? You're the reason I want to go to the beach, mamita." Miranda responded excitedly, "Really, Miguel, really?" Miguel said, "Yes, mija, but we can't go to the beach without a bucket and a little shovel to make sandcastles. We have to go to the store and buy toys and food, okay?" Miranda excitedly replied, "Okay, Miguel."

They savored their food while enjoying each other's company. Then they drove back home. They pulled in to the parking lot. As Miguel put the gear into park, Miguel's mom told him, "I'm a proud mama mijo, thank you for dinner." Miguel replied, "Thank you, ama. That means the world to me. And you're very welcome."

That weekend Miguel came through with his word. He packed up an ice chest and took his family to Carpinteria beach for the day. They all had so much fun playing in the water and building funky looking sandcastles. Before they left for home, Miguel took Miranda to walk alongside the shore in search of sea urchins. That was a fun-loving day.

When Miranda turned 14, Miguel offered to buy his mom a house. His mom didn't want to move. She was content in her apartment. He tried to stay close to his family so they could always visit. So he bought a four-bedroom house under Lita's name just a few streets away from the apartments. Miguel listed Miranda as the beneficiary. It was a beautiful home, initially ranch property. The backyard was spacious. The previous owners added a 6 ft. deep pool and had a jacuzzi installed.

Miranda spent much of her time at Miguel's house. She would go to Miguel's home after school to do her homework. Miguel had given Miranda a key to get in. She also had a room there. He bought her a complete bedroom set, including a desk to study. When she would finish her work, she would help Miguel weigh out his supply and package it up. She learned a lot about business from him. When Miranda turned 15, she was confident that she could do what he did and make a career out of it until she graduated from college.

Miranda gained the courage to ask Miguel to let her work for him. At first, he said no. Miguel really did not want to see her follow in his footsteps, mainly because he understood the consequence if he had ever gotten caught up. He didn't wish for Miranda to take the kind of risks that he took every day. He hoped she would live a fairy tale life. But the more he thought about it, Miguel knew he was a hypocrite by saying no. After all, he was younger than her when he got started.

Miguel sat her down one day and explained his reasons for saying no. He then told her that he would rather her not slang at all. But if she were going to do it, he'd rather her slang under his guidance. He then shared with her the rules that Listo once told him.

Miguel said, "I want you to save as much money as you can from what you earn. Know that this money will pay for college. When you get to college, I ask that you get a part-time job. Once you get into a good steady job, I'd rather you stop pushing weight altogether, can you attempt that for me?" Miranda nodded her head, she replied, "Okay Miguel. I'll do that. Can I give you my money to keep in the safe?" Miguel responded, "Of course you can, Mamita." He got Miranda started in the so-called game. She did exceedingly well too. She made sure to only deal with people she knew.

Miranda also felt a sense of pride in knowing she always had money. She understood that American money was the way that man did trade to survive these days in America. Miranda personally preferred the idea of the barter system. She shared her wealth with people she loved and even with strangers all the time.

She also put a lot of money into her savings, as Miguel requested. Miranda started paying the utility bill for her mom when it came in the mail. She also began to buy the groceries for the house. Miranda's mom knew what her daughter was doing to earn money. She even knew if she demanded Miranda to stop, that she would only push her daughter away. Instead, she thanked her for her contributions and continued to pray for her daughter.

One night Miranda joined her mom in the living room to watch a show on their television. Laura tried to take part in a conversation. But it seemed all Laura could think about was her daughter's new hobby. She asked her daughter, "Mija, why do you feel you have to sell drugs?" Miranda replied, "Mom, it's not that I feel I have to. I actually want to do this. I like how I make more money an hour selling, than I could if I were working at the mom and pop clothing stores or bag girl at the grocery stores. I mean let's face it, right now those are the only jobs I can get, being that I'm just a high school student. Plus I only sell weed mom. I'm not hurting anyone."

Laura said, "Mija, I just don't want to see you go to jail and set your life back at all. Whether it's for a few months or a few years, I don't want to see it happen." Miranda responded, "Mom, I'm safe. I'm out of harm's way. I'm going to use the money to pay for college. I have been thinking of becoming an obstetrician or a cardiologist. Right now I'm unsure of which one. I'm leaning toward cardiologist, though. I am sure, however, that I'm just going to do it to help pay my way through school."

Laura pulled her head back, then replied, "Listen to my baby talk. You speak so knowledgeably, yet you're doing something not so smart or safe. It's not just the cops you have to watch. You have to watch out for snitches, and other dealers. Especially these lil' cholo's running around acting fools. They might try to rob you or kill you for shit."

Miranda laughed and said, "Mom, you watch too many movies. I'm selling petty weed sacks. Maybe if I was selling rock I have to worry about getting robbed. Plus, these lil' cholos all know me and respect what I do. Where do you think some of them get their weed from?" Laura shook her head side to side. Then she said, "Uy, cabrona, tu estas bien loca. And don't get at me like I learned this shit from the movies. Don't forget who was born and raised in the barrio foolia." And together they both laughed and left it at that. Miranda laid her head on her mother's lap. Miranda felt a little more at ease about slanging despite her mother's disapproval after that day.

Miguel taught Miranda how to drive Blue Betsy over at the Glen Haven memorial park. When Miranda was ready, Miguel took her and her mother to the DMV to have Miranda take her written exam. She passed the test and received a driver's permit. Miranda was so excited to have her permit that she did a little victory dance. Miranda took Miguel out to dinner to thank him and celebrate her accomplishment. Miguel, however, would not let Miranda pay the bill.

When Miranda was days away from turning 16, she walked to Miguel's house after school, as she did practically every day. This particular day when she walked in, Miguel was waiting for her. He wore a gigantic smile on his face. She squinted at him and asked what he was so happy about. Miguel replied, "Do you really want to know?"

Miranda anxiously said, "Of course I do, díga me por favor." Miguel responded, "Okay, well it's really something

I have to show you. I need you to wait in the bathroom. It's more of a surprise." Miranda laughed then replied, "YOU, want ME, to wait in the bathroom?" Miguel, still smiling big, said, "Yes, I want you to wait in there so that you can't peek." Miranda agreed.

She walked to the bathroom and waited for her brother to give the okay to come out. Miguel walked out to the garage. He opened it and took one last look at his '63 impala. He whispered to the car, "Thank you for all the work you put in for me. May you treat my sister well, and I'll make sure that she treats you right." The impala had a big sparkly white bow on the hood. There were two long thick pieces of ribbon running down the left and right sides.

Miguel walked into the house and shouted, "Okay, you can come out now." Miranda came out. She looked confused, seeing that Miguel was holding a bandana. There was nothing out of the ordinary around him. Miguel said, "It's not in here, I have it outside. I need to cover your eyes now." Miguel held up the blue bandana. Miranda rolled her eyes. Miguel put the bandana over her eyes. He then guided her out through the front door.

Miguel stood Miranda in front of the car. As he took off the bandana, Miguel said, "Okay, mamita, you can look now." Miranda's face lit up. "No freakin' way Hermano! You're not giving Blue Betsy to me!! Are you?" Miranda asked. Miguel replied, "Yes I am, happy birthday lil' mama." Miranda jumped up and down with excitement. She then jumped into Miguel's arms and hugged him tightly.

With enthusiasm, Miranda said, "Thank you, thank you brother, this is the best birthday gift ever! You're the best Miguel. You have no idea." Miguel smiled and said, "You're my world sis. I'll do what I can to make you happy and keep you safe. I have a few conditions for this gift though." Miranda stepped back then asked, "What is it?"

Miguel replied, "You need to take good care of this car. I'm going to show you how to check the oil, transmission fluid, and the radiator fluid. You're going to check it every couple of months. If the car needs anything I'll help you. I also ask that you graduate high school with nothing lower than B's in every class. I know you're getting A's now, and I hope you do keep it up. Lastly, I ask that you go directly into college or junior college after high school. That's all I ask of you."

Miranda asked Miguel, "Miguel, do you have faith that I can get through college?" Miguel answered, "Mija, you are so incredibly smart that you can go to an Ivy League school and come out on top. It's a matter of how much you apply yourself and how much faith you have in yourself." Miranda smiled then said, "Okay, brother, I am for sure going to do what you ask of me. Thank you, for everything you have ever done for me. Including this whip, you're handing down to me. Ugh, I love you un chingo carnal." Miranda threw her arms around Miguel again.

Miguel replied, "I love you too, hermanita, since the day your mom brought you home from the hospital, I knew you were a little angel who came to bless our lives." They hugged each other tighter. Miguel lifted his head away from Miranda and said, "You wanna go for a cruise in your new car?" Miranda responded excitedly, "Most definitely! Can I go swoop up some homegirls?" "Of course," Answered Miguel. Miguel took the ribbon off of Blue Betsy gently while Miranda warmed her up.

Miguel jumped in the passenger side. They both put their seat belts on. Miranda turned on the stereo. She inserted a Ralfi Pagan c.d. She slowly pulled out of the garage and the driveway. They pulled up to the apartments off of Pakooynga St. Miguel held up the gate opener and opened the gate. Miranda pulled in real slow. She drove around to the back of the apartments.

There, Miranda called Suzy and told her to come outside. Suzy came out and got into the car. She gave both Miguel and Miranda a kiss on the cheek. Miranda drove back toward the gate and pulled into a parking space just before the gate. Suzy called Isela and told her to come out. Isela got into the car and gave all three of them a kiss on the cheek to greet them.

Then Miranda asked, "You ladies like my new ride or what?" Both Suzy and Isela looked at each other; at the same time, they shrieked, "No way?" Suzy asked Miguel, "For real Miguel, you gave it to her already?" Miguel replied, "Yep. She received an early birthday present." Both Suzy and Isela excitedly responded, "That's what's up!" Miranda drove up to the gate. Miguel pressed the button on the remote to open it again.

Miranda drove to Van Nuys Blvd, and headed west. She made a right onto Woodman Ave. She took a left onto Devonshire Blvd. Then Miranda proceeded down Devonshire until they got to a restaurant called Nacho's. Everyone got out saying they were in the mood for a beef bean and cheese burrito and horchata to drink. Miranda asked Miguel if she could pay. He refused, as always. He said, "Mija, it's your birthday, so don't trip. I got it." Miranda kissed Miguel on the cheek. She then said, "You are the angel sent to bless MY life." Miguel smiled. He proceeded to pull out his wallet and pay.

Miranda filled some small paper cups of salsa and took them to the table outside where the girls were sitting. Miguel came out with his horchata at hand. He then gave the girls their cups to fill with the beverage of their choice. It was practically tradition that everyone would get a red beef bean and cheese burrito and drink some horchata when they went to Nacho's.

As they waited for their food, Isela asked Miranda what she planned on doing to celebrate her birthday. Miranda said, "I haven't put much thought into it." Suzy made a suggestion, "Why not go to the park to barbeque? I have that barbeque at home with the charcoal. We can all pitch in for the carne y pollo, and the drinks. Well not you Miranda it's your birthday." Miranda replied, "Pssshhh I'm not tripping I'll put in. I'm down for a barbeque." Isela then said, "Okay, I'll get the invites out, and we'll make it for Saturday." Everyone agreed.

Miguel stood up to get the food. While he was away, the girls told Miranda how lucky she was to have such an awesome big brother. Suzy said, "Not only is he smart and handsome, but he knows how to handle his biz, and he seems to always put his family first. Miguel is an amazing guy." Miranda agreed, saying, "I know, he really is the best. I love that man like no other."

Once the food was at the table, it was practically silent, that's how good the food was. They all thanked Miguel for their meal. They went back to Miguel's house because he had to get back to work. Miguel told them to kick back there as long as they wanted to. They decided to watch a movie on the cable box. First, Isela and Suzy rolled a blunt to smoke outside.

Miranda served everyone some strawberry ice cream while she waited for them to finish smoking. She hooked it up with nuts, sprinkles, fudge, and diced cherries. Although Miranda didn't drink or smoke, she didn't judge anyone for what they did. She just distanced herself from people who drank heavily or did drugs harsher than weed. She didn't mind being around people who smoked weed because they laughed a lot together. The girls came in ready for their ice cream and the movie. Miguel came back home halfway through the movie. He sat down and watched the rest of it with the girls.

When the movie was over, Miranda said, "Hey ladies, I don't mean to be a buzzkill, but with all the excitement I faced today, I haven't found time to do my homework. Is it okay if I take y'all home so I can get to it?" They agreed. Miguel told Miranda he had to make one more drop, and he could take the girls home. He asked Miranda to call her mom first to see if she was working the late shift.

When Miranda's mom worked a late shift, she would come home around the hours of 1:30-4 a.m. When that happened, Miranda would stay at Miguel's house. That happened to be most nights. Miranda called to ask if she would be home early. As usual, her mom was not planning to be home any time soon. So Miranda wished her mom good night and let her know that she would be at Miguel's house. Miranda kissed the girls good night and went to her room to study. That night after she finished her homework, Miranda fell asleep with the biggest smile on her face.

Miguel, Suzy, Isela, and Gabby put Miranda's birthday barbeque together for that weekend. Miguel bought her a cake to match her new impala. He also invited Miranda's mom, as well as his mom and Lita. Suzy brought the barbeque, charcoal and the meat. Isela brought an ice chest full of water, soda and beer. She also brought the rice, beans and tortillas. Gabby brought the potato salad, green salad and fruit. The ladies were responsible for inviting Miranda's friends. All of Miranda's friends from the apartments and school showed up. Miranda truly felt special. The day contained laughter, music, and fun.

In the evening they sang happy birthday to Miranda. After she blew out her candles, she decided to give a little speech, simply thanking everyone for taking the time out of their day to spend it celebrating with her. She gave Miguel and her girls a special shout out for everything they had done to make her birthday special. Her 16th birthday was a day she would never forget. Her entire year of being 16 was a good year.

Now at the age of 17, Miranda has been focused on graduating with a 4.0-grade point average. Miranda and her friends are all nervous yet excited, knowing that they are weeks away from completing their last year of high school.

ISELA

sela knew she was Indigenous to Southern California. Her parents Andy and Grace lived as close to their roots as western civilization would allow. Granted, they had to drive cars, work and buy groceries. Both of Isela's parents were of California Native Nations.

Her Father was Chumash, and her Mother was Tongva. Her seventh-times great grandparents were enslaved and baptized as young children. Grace's grandparents were forced into the San Gabriel Mission, whereas Andy's grandparents were forced into the Mission San Buenaventura. The Chumash, too, were forced to be labeled under Spanish imposed names such as Ventureño and Barbareño. Isela grew up around ceremonies, and what Natives call the pow wow circuit. The pow wows are Native social gatherings.

Andy's father played a significant role in keeping Southern California's social gatherings alive. They began calling them fiestas after their Native language had been beaten out of them. Before that, there were different names for different gatherings and celebrations. With the relocation act of 1956, Natives from around the U.S came to Los Angeles to learn modern trades and work.

These Native Nations from other states brought their dance styles and histories with them. They would gather together at open spaces to do their dancing and singing. That was when the Tongva and Chumash were exposed to the pow wows. The relocated Natives didn't know anything about or acknowledge the local Nations of the California areas for quite some years.

Isela's Grandfather made friends with some pow wow organizers, they would often have him be arena director at their pow wows. He always made sure there was a fire in the center of the arena, it was the Chumash way. He would bring in Chumash dancers to share their dances and stories during dinner break. It was through relationships made at these pow wows, that the understanding and acceptance of California Nations by other Native Nations would slowly begin to change.

At the pow wows, there are Northern and Southern-style drummers and singers who take turns singing their songs for the people to dance their many different styles. Isela learned to dance from a Seneca woman at a cultural workshop. They danced a fast-paced contemporary style called fancy shawl. Her mother wanted Isela out there dancing in their Traditional style. Grace worried because she saw how some of these Natives looked down upon the L.A. Natives as they never heard of these California Nations or recognized their styles.

When it came to competition dancing Isela's mom would sometimes avoid uncomfortable conversations by saying they were Shoshone as it had been told by archaeologists that they were Shoshonian who had similarity in language with Shoshone as well as other Nations around them, often called Uto-Aztecan language. Her parents were glad to have their kids be involved with the Native community.

Isela enjoyed hanging out with her pow wow friends. Isela also enjoyed being with family and friends at other Native gatherings and ceremonies. Her father and brothers sang beautiful songs. Other Nations of California sang creation, gathering, migration and island or ocean songs of their own, including her mother's Nation.

Both Tongva and Chumash women mostly used clapper sticks made of wood as well as rattles made of kelp or seashells. The men used those instruments as well as coyote gourds and the dipper gourds that were introduced by the South that they made into rattles. Some had rattles made out of turtle shells as well. While others had shuushar, which is the Tongva word for rattles made with deer hooves. Those rattles were originally brought out for certain occasions.

At social gatherings, the singers often stood in a straight row and sang. Some of the men would step forward and dance. The women danced and sang to the music as well. Isela loved dancing to her dad's songs; they always made her want to dance hard.

As she got older, some non-rez California pow wow's begun to set aside more time for some of the California Nations to come out and sing their social songs. This was previously more frequently done by the California Reservation tribes, who took turns hosting pow wows. Isela would sometimes join the women in their long ribbon skirts as they danced in rows across from the men.

Isela's parents grew close to many pow wow people. They got invited to go to a Sun Dance Ceremony in North Dakota on a Mandan, Hidatsa, and Arikara Reservation. There, Isela would participate uniquely for part of the ceremony. She and two other young girls took on the role of what was known as Tree Girl. The man who led the ceremony took to Isela. He adopted Isela as his Grand Daughter. She had a beautiful experience and would return quite a few times in her lifetime.

Although Isela was very involved in her culture, she lived in the city where culture was rare and, for the most part, lost. Many other children that Isela would play with at school or hung out with in the apartments didn't know much about their backgrounds. But Isela always made them question what their bloodlines were. They wanted to be as proud as she was about culture.

As Isela got into middle school, she began smoking weed and hanging around with the local neighborhood gang. The guys she hung out with thought it was cool that Isela knew her heritage, they didn't know or value their Native ways. Most of them claimed to be Chicanos or Aztec warriors without really knowing where their families were from.

As they got older, Isela and her brothers found themselves not wanting to go with their parents to the social or Ceremonial gatherings as much. Isela's mother, Grace, would tell her husband, "We have shown them the way, we cannot force them to partake in the traditional ways, they must want to. When you force it, is when they will rebel and never come back. When you let them decide, they will always return." Isela had lost a brother in a car accident on his way home from partying. Her father feared losing another child. He struggled with the thought of his kids being in the streets rather than with him, but he knew that his wife was right.

Isela's dad began teaching her how to box when she was four. He wanted her to have confidence and be able to defend herself. He also wanted her to be well rounded. Therefore he talked to her about business, healing, love, gangs, std's, drugs, alcoholism and disturbing violence that took place around them as well as to their ancestors after coming into contact with the colonizers. Andy told her crimes had at times existed pre-contact, but when they occurred, the criminals were immediately prosecuted. Depending on the crime, the community might kick them out of the village, forcing the criminals to fend for themselves. But he knew that the tragic events occurring in the community in today's day and age were repetitive traumatic cycles brought on by the invaders.

Andy once told his daughter, "History repeats itself over and again when ignorance allows it. People know what they are taught. Some people are visual learners. Some are hands-on learners who learn from experience. So if people see and receive violence and abuse of all sorts, something in their brain thinks this is what we do, and they will likely repeat them.

"In the days of the Spanish invasions and the building of the missions, our people were kidnapped and enslaved. The babies and elders that were useless were often brutally killed. The people, including children, were brainwashed, abused, and raped by the soldiers and missionaries. Their names were changed to bible names. They were taught by the padres (Father's/priest) to worship a foreign religion and to hate themselves and their true heritage.

"Your ancestors were forced to build the San Gabriel mission, San Fernando mission and the mission San Buenaventura. They were told that speaking our languages or doing anything traditional was evil, and they would be killed if they were caught doing any of it. Of course, they practiced and maintained what they could in secret.

"Tragedies like these happened all over the world. It is not of our Native ways, but the way of power, control, religion, and greed. This is why there are more lost souls today than ever before. People are confused. They don't know how to internalize or think for themselves. Many believe that they must go to church and give money to these rich people on stage, that their god is the right and only one whom to pray. They fail to understand that we all pray to the same force of energy because we are all related, not through blood; we are all connected through the universal energy, the web of life.

"When we die, we leave our bodies as energy, we still exist. It's okay to feel lost sometimes, but when that happens, it's essential to be alone with the earth in silence. There you will find your higher self. The voice within will speak to you, sometimes with words or pictures and sometimes through feeling. All you have to do is sit quietly and listen. That voice or feeling always has your best interest at heart."

Andy equipped Isela with information that he knew she would need on her journey of keeping her culture alive. He also explained how the reinvented story of Aztlan came to be, "At a Chicano Movement meeting in Colorado in the 1970s. These relatives were looking for a way to root themselves in current-day America, so that they would have a defense against the people telling them to go back to Mexico.

"They used the map of 1821; from the short period when Mexico ruled what was previously New Spain, but most importantly, originally villages of our families and many other Native Nations. The men merged the map with the story of Aztlan. In doing so, like the Spanish before them, and the American after them, they created erasure stories of the First Nations that lived on said territories thousands of years before any of these invaders. By fabricating that story, the Chicano movement also attempted to erase Native Nations in Mexico who are not Mexica. If this was their ancestral homelands and villages, they would have sacred burial sites here in our homelands, older than the Missions and modern cemeteries. They don't. We do."

Isela respected her dad and his words. She knew he was always speaking with love. Isela wasn't into gang banging. She picked up the lingo as she grew up with all of the local gang members and was comfortable hanging out with them. The number one thing she had in common with them was smoking weed, joking around, and feeling like an American reject. The game Isela kicked to her peers would make an impact on some of them, including Gabby and Lori, who knew their culture and also understood the qualities of healing.

CAMPING

The night that they had talked about camping, Isela went home and made reservations for a campsite. Surprisingly she found a beautiful spot in Sequoia National Park just two weeks from the day. Using her debit bank card, she reserved the site. She also called Lori to invite her to join them on the trip. Lori excitedly agreed to go.

Come that Friday afternoon, one by one, the girls met up in the Jungles. Denise and Clever were the last ones to show up. They all had blankets, pillows, and backpacks filled with clothes and necessities. Isela said, "Okay, first things first, we're going to drop by the grocery store before we head out. So everyone brought their money to chip in, right?" One by one, she collected twenty dollars from everyone.

They headed to Suzy's van to pack everything up. Isela drove, Suzy sat shotgun, Miranda, Clever, and Denise sat in the first row of the backseat. Gabby and Lori sat in the second row with all of the bags, blankets, pillows, and the stove. In the trunk of the van is where they put the tent, pots, pans, fishing rods, chairs, and the ice chest. They smoked a quick bowl after packing up. Isela headed to the grocery store.

Once she parked, she looked back at Miranda. Isela told Miranda, "Since you and I will be doing most of the cooking, let's do the shopping." Miranda agreed. They bought a big bag of potatoes, veggies, fruits, eggs, barbeque sauce, chorizo, ribs, chicken, and ingredients to make sandwiches (bread, mustard, cheese, sliced turkey, tomatoes and lettuce). They bought stuff for s'mores (marshmallows, graham crackers, chocolate bars), two cases of water and a big bag of ice. They packed the food into the ice chest in the back and covered it with the ice. Then they hit the road.

They pulled over in a small town to stretch and eat dinner. When they reached the entrance of the mountain, Isela pulled over. She asked everyone to get out and speak to the ancestors with her. As they stood in a circle, Isela explained that they were on Mono lands and it was appropriate to ask the mountain and the ancestors of the area for permission to be there. Isela walked around and let everyone grab a pinch of her sacred medicine.

Isela grabbed a pinch as well. Isela announced, "I'm going to ask that you each make your request and offering in your own way." Gabby and Isela sang a song to honor and acknowledge the land and the ancestors of the land. After they each made their offerings, Clever asked, "Now what?" Isela said, "We wait for a sign saying that it is okay, or it's not." Clever asked, "What if it's not okay?"

Gabby answered, "Then we don't enter." Just then, a powerful gust of wind hit them. The wind went in the direction of the entrance. Gabby asked Isela, "Shall we?" Isela nodded. They all got back into the van and drove into the mountain.

They made it to their campsite by 7:40 p.m. Isela told the gang, "Okay, first things first, we're going to set up the tent. Suzy, you can help me with that. The rest of you can look for pieces of wood to throw in the pit and start a fire. Place the wood you find next to the pit." Isela and Suzy got the tent up in ten minutes. Before they hammered down the steaks, they cleared the area of rocks, sticks, and pine cones.

They placed some pine needles down and spread them out evenly. They set the tent over the pine needles. The ladies hammered down the steaks to keep the tent in place. One by one, the gang came back with arms full of wood. They put it in one big pile.

Isela said, "Okay, cool, if you see this pile dying down, feel free to add on to it. Also, something important for all of us to remember, do not leave food lying around anywhere. Do not bring it in the tent or leave it in the car. This storage bin is where we will have to keep our food. There are bears here, and they will break into anything where they smell food, be it cars, tents or backpacks. And I mean it; they have ripped off car doors. Everyone can grab their blankets and pillows and claim your spots in the tent. Clever, can you help me to put the ice chest into that food bin, please?" "Yeah, for sure," Clever replied.

Denise offered to make Clever's bed while he helped Isela. Miranda said she'd set up Isela's spot. Everyone walked over to the van to grab something to help. After putting the ice chest away, Isela said to Clever, "Thanks friend, the last thing we gotta do is grab the chairs and put 'em around the fire pit." Clever responded, "For sure." As they walked back to the van, Clever said, "It feels so dope to be out here G. When I went to get some wood, I was doing a little exploring in the area. It's like nothing I've ever seen." Isela smiled, replying, "Welcome to the outdoors, a.k.a nature loved one." Clever smiled at Isela as he grabbed a couple of chairs.

Once they set out all the chairs, everyone grabbed themselves a seat. Isela went back to the car to make sure there were no drinks or food left behind. She grabbed her backpack, and then locked the doors. Everyone appeared to be sitting comfortably at the fire pit. Isela grabbed some pine needles and threw them in the fire pit. She then placed some small pieces of wood into the pit. She placed three thick pieces of wood at an angle, so they were leaning against each other. She put some more pine needles on top of and in between the wood.

Isela grabbed a lighter out of her backpack. Then pulled up a hand full of pine needles and lit them on fire. She touched the pine needles with the lit bundle then placed the bunch of burning pine needles under the wood. With a piece of cardboard, she blew air into the fire pit. Pretty soon, she had the fire going. Isela finally sat down to relax.

Miranda asked, "Does anyone know any good ghost stories?" It was quiet for about ten seconds as everyone shifted eyes amongst each other. Denise said, "I wrote a chiller for my English class if anyone wants to hear it." No one else could think of a story, so they told Denise to tell her story.

Denise began, "Cold and practically alone, sitting at the edge of the bed looking at pictures of his girl and joking with his acquaintances to the left and right of him, which he could not see. The sheriff called G's number. G stood up, knowing he had court that day. He had been staying in this particular cell for almost a month now. He recently transferred from another county jail. The thought crossed his mind whether or not he would be moved again after his court appearance today.

"G had a beautiful girlfriend showing him support while he was fighting his case. Her name was Izabella. Guys were continually going out of their way to try and talk to her. She would smile politely, but she really wouldn't give them the time of day. All she ever thought about was her and G. She was deeply in love with him. G was sure of it that Izabella was cheating on him now that he was locked up. If only he understood that she was a woman of her word. She told him that she would be faithful to him no matter how extended his stay in jail or prison would be. All she asked was that he did the same.

"All that ever seemed to play in Izabella's mind were images of how it would be when G got released and memories of their past. There was one memory in particular that played continuously in her mind. It was their very last good-bye before G got arrested. It was about three o'clock in the morning; G was sleeping with his head in her lap. As Izabella watched him sleep, she had a bad feeling in the pit of her stomach. G looked so peaceful, that Izabella really didn't want to wake him. Izabella's father would be leaving for work in two hours. She knew if she didn't want to get in trouble, G would have to go now.

"She woke him up by softly stroking his face with her right hand and saying, 'Baby, baby, it's time for you to go home.' Oh how Izabella wished he could have stayed. G got out of the car with Izabella following behind him. He stood in front of the driver door then leaned against it. He then enfolded Izabella in his arms holding her tighter by the second. G leaned in to give Izabella what they never expected to be their very last kiss. In a low tone, G whispered, 'I'll call you tomorrow beautiful.'

"Call her he did. That morning while heading home he got into a high speed pursuit with the L.A.P.D. He blew a tire and eventually gave up. He called Izabella from the station to tell her what happened. He asked her to stick by him through this. She said, 'Don't trip Pa, I'ma hold it down for you.' Izabella needed to go to class for G's first court date due to finals. She did manage to make it to his other court dates. She also would put money on his books every week. Izabella would receive love letters every day. Sometimes she would even receive two or three love letters plus a card in a single day. Every day she would send him a letter or two back.

"There was a girl G used to mess around with a few years before he met Izabella. Her name was Lani. G's sister in law was in the same nursing class with her. She told Lani that G was arrested and reminded Lani how cute she and G were together. Lani decided to ask for his booking information so she could write him a letter. Lani was able to visit G because she was 19. Izabella was only 17. G accepted Lani's visits and began writing her.

"Lani started showing up to G's court trial. The first moment that Izabella laid eyes on Lani she received an awful feeling. Izabella immediately suspected Lani to be there for G. At the next court trial, Izabella was was sitting outside the courtroom on a bench waiting for the doors to open. Lani walked up and asked Izabella, 'Are you here to see G?' Calmly, Izabella replied, 'Yes. How do you know G?'

"Lani smiled, insisting, 'I'm his girlfriend.' Izabella, still calm and showing no emotion, said, 'Oh, that's nice. I'm his homegirl. I just come to show support.' It killed Izabella to say that. Izabella didn't want to fight over a man. Mainly because she wasn't a hundred percent sure who Lani was or how accurate this information was. Izabella maintained her composure and continued to talk to Lani. According to Lani, they had officially become a couple the day before Izabella's birthday.

"The doors opened. Izabella stood up and walked to the front row of seats. She sat down and waited. G came out in his orange jumpsuit. He sat down. He lifted his shoulder so Lani wouldn't see him blow Izabella a kiss, and he motioned his lips to say 'I love you.' Then and there Izabella felt her heart drop. Usually, she would say it back. This time she squint her eyes and motioned her lips to say, 'Why?' as she shook her head side to side. Izabella was disgusted. She felt betrayed, lost, and confused.

"When confronted, G denied Lani to the fullest. He explained that he did know her. He claimed they were friends. He said they lost touch and he hadn't talked to her in years. He told Izabella he could not control Lani's actions and apologized on Lani's behalf. G claimed, 'I long for you. I love only you. Izabella, please don't ever forget that.' Lani didn't show up to the next court date. Izabella thought that was the end of that issue.

"Izabella began to feel better. The very next court date that G had, Lani showed up again. This time with proof that G had been writing her. Lani wanted Izabella to read the letter. The letter mentioned Izabella. It stated that Izabella wasn't shit to G. He said he barely knew Izabella. And that Izabella was from his hood. That's why she goes to show support at court. Izabella couldn't believe it. Her eyes watered up for a split second then she began to laugh. You see, Izabella was not much of a crier. When something bothered her or went wrong, she'd tend to laugh it off. Deep down, the last of Izabella's love crumbled.

"Izabella sent G one last letter. She told him that all he had to do was ask for her support and friendship instead of lying to her. She said that she would have been there for him one hundred percent regardless. Only, she would be able to go about everyday life without such over-concern for him. She told him how he put her in a messed up position with Lani and how embarrassed she felt.

"Izabella wrote that she never loved a man the way she loved him and that she never will. She explained how hurt she was to discover that he and Lani got together the day before Izabella's birthday. She wished him and Lani well. And signed the letter, 'Sincerely, your Ex-Lady.' Izabella didn't hear back from G. She expected that, as she now thought he was the biggest coward.

"G was actually, scared to write her back. Many times he sat with a pen at hand starring at the blank paper before him. He couldn't get himself to write Izabella. He wanted to explain himself to Izabella. He just couldn't stand to hurt her anymore. G really did love Izabella. He didn't care much about Lani. G thought if he got Lani on his team, that it would take the weight off of Izabella's shoulders. He didn't want Izabella to be the one which he asked to be putting money on his books. He didn't realize Lani would go telling Izabella any and everything. G felt awful for hurting Izabella.

"Immediately after their break up, Izabella went out with her friends. Her homies called her left and right to take her out partying. She would go out, drink, and get high in hopes of forgetting it all. Unfortunately, the higher that she got, the more she thought about G. She would think to herself, 'What a fool I was, to think I was just going to sit home and rot my youth away, all for what? For a two-timing fucking loser who didn't have the guts to tell me the truth? Fuck, but I fucking love his stupid ass. Why? Why do I feel like this? Shake it off Izzy come on. You need to think about things that matter.' Izabella had thoughts and emotions that she couldn't understand or know how to control. She was battling with her mind on a constant.

"Four years later, G was released from prison. Two days after his release, he gained the courage to visit Izabella. He wanted to tell her there wasn't a day that he didn't think about her. How every day he hoped she would forgive him.

He wanted to tell her how much he missed her and truly did love her. Every day in prison, he rehearsed this long speech in his head about what he would tell her when he got the chance to see her. Finally, it was time to make things right.

"He pulled up to her house. He took a deep breath, leaned over to the passenger side, and pulled up a beautiful bouquet of blue and white roses. He knew Izabella would love them. His palms became moist as he walked up to the door. This was it; this was the moment that he thought about for years, G rang the doorbell. His heart was racing, but no one came to the door.

"He waited for twenty minutes. G began to walk away with his head down. Halfway down the driveway, he turned around to look at the window. He felt like Izabella was watching him the way she used to when she was mad at him and wouldn't open the door. He shook his head with guilt and continued down the driveway.

"As he got to the end of the driveway, a white car pulled up. The woman got out of her car and said, 'Dios mio, Gabe, is that you?' 'Hello, Mrs. Ongo. I know it's been a while. I was hoping to visit with Izabella and let her know how much I love and miss her.'

"With emotion stricken in her voice, Mrs. Ongo responded, 'Uy mijo, thank you for remembering my Izzy on such a day,' Izabella's mother pulled out a pen and a paper and leaned over the hood of her car as she scribbled down on the piece of paper. She continued to tell G, 'I just came back from visiting with her myself. Here is the address of the cemetery where she is buried.'

"'I'm I I I I'm sorry ce ce cemetery?' G stuttered. Mrs. Ongo turned toward G as she answered, 'Yes mijo,' her eyes got wide, with her hands near the bottom of her mouth and sounding shocked, she asked, 'Oh, mijo you didn't know?' G replied, 'No. I had no idea. I just got out.' G appeared shaken up.

"Mrs. Ongo told G, 'Izabella began to distance herself from us. She began to act different. I thought it was teenage rebellion. I should have seen the signs,' Mrs. Ongo got teary-eyed. Still, she continued to speak, 'I should have known something was wrong with my baby.' Mrs. Ongo began to get choked up as she went on to say, 'We never thought our Izabella would have done such a thing. She never explained or told us why. She just stopped caring about life.'

"Mrs. Ongo now had tears flowing from her eyes, yet she continued, 'She gave up on herself, she gave up on her life. The autopsy confirmed she overdosed mijo. Today is the third year of her death anniversary. Tomorrow is her,' with his hand hiding his mouth, G cut her off, saying, 'Birthday.' Mrs. Ongo nodded her head yes as she handed G the address.

"G still shaken, managed to say, 'Mrs. Ongo I am soo sorry. I would never have thought, I mean.' G began to break down. 'Nooo, not Izabella,' G cried out. Mrs. Ongo said with concern in her voice, 'Hey, hey, everything is going to be alright, mijo. Life pulls it's angels for a reason. Izabella was much more needed elsewhere.' 'But I need her. I need her!' G exclaimed. Mrs. Ongo put her hand on G's shoulder. She told him, 'Don't ever give up on hope. If it is your destiny, then you will someday be reunited.' G wiped his tears as he said, 'I hope so.' He hugged Mrs. Ongo and thanked her for the information. He then got in his car to make his way over to the cemetery to leave Izabella her roses, to pay his respect, and to beg for forgiveness."

Silence took over for a few seconds. Everyone had teary eyes. Clever said, "Damn, Denise, that's some sad shit. I thought we were telling scary stories." Denise laughed and said, "Hey, I heard ghost stories. That was a story with a ghost in it." Isela said, "I loved it mamita. That was a good ass story. What grade did you get for writing that?"

Denise replied, "Thank you. I received an 'A' for that. My teacher said she loves reading my stories and poems. That makes me feel good 'cause I put my heart into my work." Gabby said, "Well, you definitely earned that 'A' mujer. Good story." Everyone agreed. Miranda asked, "Does anyone else know any good ghost stories?" Suzy replied, "We all heard about La Llorona and The Cucuey that's all I grew up hearing." Everyone laughed as they agreed.

Miranda looked up to the sky, saying, "It's amazing to see so many stars. In the city, it seems like I can count the visible stars." Isela replied, "Yeah, that's because of the city lights. I wish we could live this way always; then we could enjoy this beauty every single night. Can you believe our ancestors lived similar to this?" Denise disgustingly replied, "Eww, that's just wrong. They had no running water, plus they had bugs and snakes crawling on them?"

Lori responded, "They had clean running water, it just didn't run through eroding pipes. They often channeled water to their needed locations. And all of that creepy crawler stuff can happen, even in a house. I was sleeping the other night, and a spider crawled on my face. I slapped my face. When I woke up in the morning, I found it dead on the floor. It was huuuge. Seriously though, imagine a life with no house payments. Everyone helps with gathering and hunting food and truly lives as a community.

"That would rule out the poor and the rich as we know them to be. We would eat off of our mother earth with no harmful pesticides or scientific made foods damaging the soil or our cells. Those that know what plants are safe and how to hunt are those that would survive. Where we live now, before it morphed into the city, the water was almost always running and would be healthy and have life." Denise cut in, saying, "Yeah, but we need governance to keep everything in order."

Lori agreed as she responded, "Yes, this is true. The Indigenous people of the Americas were all highly intelligent. They had dependable systems to keep order. America actually took some ideas from the Eastern Turtle Island tribes known together as the Haudenosaunee to make their constitution. Before America, everyone had a purpose and a job to do. They had everything they needed to survive. Everyone had land to tend to and grow food. There were no homeless, with the exception that those who committed crimes had to leave the community.

"I was told in Mexico, the Mexica Empire had plots of land like ranches, for the community to live on and tend to. Everyone could grow what they wanted on their plot. But they were also required to pay taxes in corn. That way, if they came into famine, the Emperor could feed his people with the corn that had been collected and dried. The taxes also paid those that worked for the Emperor. All of our ancestors also figured out how to move the water from point A to point B without pipes. And sometimes point B was uphill.

"Natives before European invasion were doctors, artists, astronomers; I mean the list goes on and on. The only reason their ways and many languages were devastated, was because the invaders had guns and disease outbreaks to rule in their favor. The greed and ignorance of those invaders forced our peoples' intelligence and self-love to be set back.

"These people of the 'old world' claimed the people of the 'new world' to be idiots and savages because they didn't speak or look like them or live in the earth destroying way that they did. They claim that our ancestors were uncivilized savages. Yet, the colonizers carried and introduced diseases because they were not daily bathing people. They dumbed down the people over here with their whacky ways of living and beliefs.

"Now look, where we used to walk to the river to get water to drink and bathe, we can't because they have contaminated everything they touched. Although our ancestors resisted plenty, they came to understand that if they didn't walk in the ways of these invaders, they would die by the gun or be set out to hang. So for the next generations to exist, they adapted.

"It happened and continues to happen all over North, Central, and South America. These invaders conquer mostly to steal resources from the land. But you know what gave the invaders permission to treat our people so evil? Besides them having guns? They had a document that held no legality on our continent, called the 'Doctrine of Discovery,' and its principals are still being used to this day.

"This document claims that if people are not Jesus worshipers, then they can be dominated and converted. And that is how our home lands were taken. It wasn't our people who had it all wrong, so instead of sounding all disgusted, be proud of the things our people did because they had it right. And be thankful they suffered for us to be here today.

"Shit, I think if you lived in those days, you would appreciate the beauty of their lifestyle. I think people of today are too superficial. I mean, if everyone in California today, had to live as our people did, I'm sure a big percentage would die off in 3 months or so. And that's on the real."

Denise looked into Lori's eyes and said, "I never knew any of that. I learned that we were Native by my dad, but I never even thought about my relatives beyond my great grandparents. If I haven't learned any of that in school, where did you learn it?" Lori pushed her chin up towards Isela and smiled. Isela smiled back.

Isela circled her index finger to include Lori and Gabby as she answered, "We spent a lot of our time growing up listening to the stories that our dads and other elders would tell us. Our history is passed on through oral stories and songs. Much of the proof of our civilizations and religious beliefs were destroyed and burned 'at the stake.' It's our relatives and tradition carrying elders that made us care about our real history.

"My dad would say, 'The history we learn in school is his story, but it isn't ours. It isn't fair that all these so-called Americans have to learn about a country that devastated the land in less than three hundred years, and respect the ancestors of the men who Established America, but they don't take the time to learn and respect the ancestors they robbed their so called America from who kept it pristine for thousands of years.' He would also say, 'The good thing about being the winner is that you can rewrite the history, so don't believe everything you read.' When I study history for school," Isela's eyes began to water as she continued, "It turns my stomach, knowing what I'm reading is usually a fairytale lie. My people were forced at gunpoint to sign an agreement not written in their language, but of the English, and gun forced to walk to what is now Tejon Ranch.

"Then, they were getting shoved off of that land, realizing these invaders couldn't even keep their end of the bargain. Claiming there was no such treaty. Fifty years after our families were forced off of the reservation, the document resurfaced. None of this is discussed in school. Instead, we're lied to by teachers who tell stories of our people living the spa life in the Missions. So, I know that I only do these American history classes because I'm determined to get to college for a piece of paper.

"When I first learned of the truth behind Thanksgiving, I cried. I could not believe that our parents would allow us to be a part of those cheesy school plays in elementary school." Surprised, Denise asked, "What about Thanksgiving?" Isela replied, "Okay, well, have you ever heard of a Native man they call Squanto?" Denise nodded her head yes and said, "Yeah, I have the movie at home." Isela, Gabby and Lori smirked.

Isela then replied, "Well, long story short because I don't know it THAT well, I was told this story once years ago. It was explained to me that Squanto wasn't his real name. His name was Tisquantum. He was from the Wampanoag Nation. But in like the early 1600s, the Europeans landed on the eastern coast of North America, right? They collected slaves to take home with them to be traded and sold.

"They also left behind a disease known as smallpox. The Natives in the area had gotten infected with this disease, which they had never known. Naturally, most of these villagers died off. The invaders would later claim this to be god's doing.

"Although I must say, there was a point when these invaders would purposely hand the Native people blankets infected with the disease. Or greet the Natives with a toast to their friendship when really what they gave the Natives to drink was a poison that would kill them. That was all man's doing, not gods. But anyway, back to the story, one of the enslaved happened to be Tisquantum. While in Europe he would spend time with some religious men, he would learn the languages of the Spanish and English.

"One day after hearing a ship would soon head back to his homeland. He spoke with the Captain of the ship heading to Pre-America. He pleaded with the Captain to bring him back with the Captain to Turtle Island. The Captain agreed under the circumstance that Tisquantum worked on the ship while at sea and as an interpreter. When Tisquantum got back to his village, he discovered that the people of his village had died off by the diseases that the Europeans brought. Naturally, he mourned over the loss. He knew these lands well. He would survive.

"Eventually, he ran into a neighboring village. They adopted him into their village. Some Europeans had come to live off of a piece of land off the coast near Tisquantum's adopted home. These people did not know the area at all. They were beginning to die off due to their diseases and starvation. One of the men of the village that Tisquantum was adopted by came and told Tisquantum about them.

"He went to visit and showed them how to live off the land. He showed them how to grow corn and squash. He also taught them where to fish and where to pick berries and nuts. These so-called Pilgrims claimed that Tisquantum was a gift sent to them by their god, for he knew the language of these people. Today, that's kind of the storyline they use to explain why they celebrate their Thanksgiving Holiday.

"But originally when men feasted in celebratory claiming 'Thanksgiving,' they were feasting over a village they invaded, killed, and stole their food amongst other belongings. The more settlers that arrived, the more killings and stealing of communities had occurred. Children and Women included in the wipeouts. The land would then be claimed as available.

"These massive massacres became a tradition for these new settlers, to kill off a village then celebrate the kill with a feast. They began celebrating each massacre anniversary annually. Finally in 1637, it was a governor of Massachusetts Bay Colony who proclaimed an official Thanksgiving Day to commemorate the massacre of 700 men, women and children amidst their ceremonial practice of the Green Corn Dance.

"Eventually, from that evil celebration, the very peaceful Thanksgiving holiday using our harvest gatherings was created using the pilgrims and Indians. You see, the story we learn of Thanksgiving was created to make the country look good and make it okay to celebrate such an evil day. But there is minimal truth behind it. I suppose it is better to tell a child a lie than the haunting evil truth. But I would rather know the truth behind this country's false discovery, history, and holidays. And have the choice not to celebrate with them rather than be fed a bunch of crap to make me proud to be an American and celebrate things that disgraced our Ancestors. I doubt anyone with a kind heart who was told the absolute truth in school would be proud to call themselves an American.

"As Native peoples we have always had a practice of giving thanks every morning as well as many times a day. Our families also have always had harvesting ceremonies and gatherings multiple times a year. These days we struggle being able to do these gatherings the same way due to colonial land grabs and development. Many of us in California are landless Nations today. But we try our best."

Suzy, who was grabbing her heart during Isela's story, said, "Oh my goodness, Isela, please tell me you just made all that up." Isela gave a sympathy smile to Suzy. She replied, "It's a sad truth, my love. But the truth it is. I know the

Wampanoag people can tell the Thanksgiving story better, as it is their story. These immigrants whose children and grandchildren call themselves true American's came to these lands, forcing us out of our homes and either killing us or claiming us as slaves. And when they grew exhausted of the killings, they began claiming peace by forcing their ways and religion on us with boarding schools, and treaties. They used a slogan, 'Kill the Indian save the Man.' Our people didn't live this grimy and ignorant lifestyle before the invader came and dumbed us down.

"We had our own beliefs; we were not Catholic or Christians before they came. Mine and Gabby's people became the slaves that were forced to build the original Missions here in our part of Sunny Southern California. If someone was too weak to build or make these invaders' goods to ship out, they were killed because they were viewed as useless. If they refused to convert, spoke their Native language, or tried to escape, they were beaten or killed. These foreigners killed off as much of our people along with our stories and traditions as they possibly could.

"Their goal was to kill us or our spirit, own us, and own our homeland. They didn't completely succeed, but they took heart to that saying, 'Kill the Indian, save the man.' A big part of that was taking the children away from their families to condition them to forget who they were. They did it all 'In the name of Jesus.' Unfortunately, a lot of our sixth times great grandparents are a product of rape and interbreeding with these evil-minded people who believe they had dominion over us through their god.

"We had bad spirits, but we didn't have a devil or hell here before they force-fed their religion. Any religion that is claiming their god to be better or the only god, and forcing anyone to convert is disgusting and should not exist. If everyone wants to go to this so-called heaven, they have to do good, right? How are killing elders, women, and children or raping them in the name of your religion or god good? It's evil. If people were in tune with their inner spirituality, instead of believing in this 'Sin and be forgiven' mentality, I think this would be a much more peaceful world."

Suzy shook her head side to side. She then responded, "Wow, mija that's deep, thank you both for sharing this information with us. I wish my mom knew this stuff. She grew up knowing she had Native blood. But she was also raised to hate the color of her skin, and I never understood why. I think we have a beautiful skin color." Gabby nodded her head in agreement. She then replied, "Yup. Unfortunately, that was the Europeans doing as well. Out here, the Spaniards would say things to put our people down like: 'Pinche Indios sucios' or 'Negros feos,' things like that. Even when the English had come, it was the same hatred, just a different language.

"We are a beautiful group of people. We are people with connection to spirit. We believe everything has a spirit. We respect every living entity such as stone, the winged, the four, two, six, and eight-legged, plant, and water as relative. We ask permission before hunting and harvesting our food and materials, getting in, or crossing bodies of water. We speak to and give thanks to our food and water. We even give thanks to the sun and moon for rising another day. Many people of colonialism, on the other hand, wanted to take over the whole world and continue to destroy it because they believe it was a gift to them. Every inch of Earth and its inhabitants are supposedly here for their disposal.

"They come in, take what's insight, and take it all for granted. Our people never understood that way. Not only did the invader just force their way and take it, but then they turn around and charge us for any of it, whether it's for land, water, or food. I could never understand that, how could land they stole and its natural life sources be sold for so much money? Why can't any of our families afford to live in what was once our ancestral villages? And why is said land never even genuinely owned by the buyer who now has annual property tax to pay? Even after they are old, and may suffer from Alzheimer's or who knows what, they are to pay or get evicted.

"I know for a fact that the ocean can take any piece of land she likes at any time she likes. And 'Property owners' won't be compensated, right? Yet, here we are, walking zombies following their make-believe ideas, rules, and laws, afraid to disobey and go to their jails. While they never stop to worry, after so much destruction, which they don't go to jail for, that they're going to eventually use up and sell off the last of what they call resources and kill themselves off as well.

"They just pay science to create these dangerous, genetically modified foods to supposedly sustain us. Lucky for us, some descendants of these Europeans disagree and walk amongst us in peace and respect for the land. But we still have more people than not, who are money hungry and can give two shits about geography or climate and how important it really should be for us. And today, with our forced ignorance, these destructive people come in all colors, even ours. They have forgotten that we belong to the Earth and not the other way around."

Lori said, "Oh, then we gotta worry about folks like the white supremacy who enjoy openly being hateful. Even saying they killed the Natives, and they'll do it again. Or that we're better because of them. Every chance they get, they're going around harming our folks. They play a role in our murdered and missing children and people. Sadly, those people are still so dominant minded. They say they're the true American. But ask them what Native Nation they descend from, they get angry and look at you like you're the bad guy." Suzy replied, "Aha, that's funny 'cause it's true. It sucks that the Native American people get treated like second class citizens in their own home, though. Once these people strip this land of everything it has to offer, they can go back to their countries. But where will the Native people go?"

Isela replied, "Well, our people know how to suffer and survive. I'm sure if that happened, we'd be blessed with snow, rain, and probably natural phenomenons that would bring needed water and life. In due time nature would restore itself. I hope suffering wouldn't happen if we (Isela motioned her hands in a circular motion to include her friends in what she was saying) take care of the communities and land we walk on now. We can all do our part."

Denise asked, "How do we do our part, by picking up trash?" Isela responded, "That's always an excellent contribution, everywhere, in the mountains, the beach, off the street and near all water and animal life. Trash easily gets swept in and is dangerous to the inhabitants of the water. We can lead by example and choose to minimize or hopefully eliminate our plastic use, especially things like water bottles and straws.

"Regenerating the land would be ideal as much of our soils are contaminated. Also, we can keep edible plants around our homes. Those of us that live in the apartments can't do too much gardening, but we can have pots with herbs and small edible shrubs. We can get those long rectangular pots and grow something like carrots, little things like that."

Gabby then remarked, "It sure would be nice to grow an entire garden. You know, with the three sisters, tomatoes, chili peppers, mmmm, I'd love to grow stuff like that." Suzy said, "Hey, I saw a spot behind the Park that said something about offering gardening. You might wanna check that out." Gabby replied, "Yeah, that would be cool. I wonder if it's open to the public or if you have to be in a program."

Denise said, "If you guys are serious about a garden, I bet my dad will let you use a piece of my yard. I think my dad will even help you guys get started and show you how to harvest. He's into that kind of stuff. He won't charge you money, but he'll most likely do like the Mexica Empire thing and tax some food!"

Isela giggled, quickly replying, "I'm in on that one. I'd love to get a garden going. We can also help regenerate the soil on your property. And or we can bring some wood and make a raised bed. You think papa Jorge will help us with that too?" Denise replied, "Yeah, he has all the tools in the garage. I'll ask him when I get home."

Clever spoke up, "If you guys start a garden, I'll help to keep it up. It'll probably keep me out of some trouble." Suzy lifted her right eyebrow in suspicion. Suzy then said, "Yeah, that's a good idea. You can learn a little something. Aaaaaand, you'll have another excuse to see Denise every day." Clever blushed and said, "I don't need an excuse to see Denise. I'm over there anyway because she's my roll dawg." Suzy smiled childishly, responding, "Roll dawg? Or looveeer?" Suzy let out a grito, "Chaoow!"

Denise, annoyed, replied, "Okay, okay. Relax, miss twenty one questions." Suzy laughed then said, "I'm sorry,

I'm sorry. But I have to know what's up with you two? You kick it every day. You used to flirt like crazy. But recently, I noticed that when you come around us, you are a little distant from each other."

Clever responded, "I don't know what you're talking about, but I respect Denise; she's a true lady." Denise smiled at Clever and said, "Thank you, Clever, you're always a true gentleman, and I appreciate that quality in you." Suzy laughed again. Suzy called them on it, "So you two are together?!" Denise did not want to answer Suzy's question. Sounding annoyed, Denise said, "Ya, Suzy, leave it alone." Suzy replied, "That says it all right there. Y'all make a cute couple, though. There I'm done!"

Isela cut in, "Clever, I think it's a great idea that you wanna do something to keep out of the streets. Handle it, homeboy." Clever replied, "Thanks Isela, I know this lifestyle ain't how I wanna put food on the table. I rather grow it. And I think it'll be peaceful to be in the garden talking to plants." Miranda responded, "You're right. And the garden won't instigate or get you locked up."

Clever nodded his head in agreement. Gabby said, "I'd like to grow corn and learn how to make tortillas." Suzy retorted, "Man when I smell freshly made tortillas, it takes me back to my grandma. My grandma used to make them every morning. Every single day she would make enough to feed an army. It's a lot of work." Gabby insisted, "I miss your grandma's cooking. She got down on everything she made. For reals, though." Suzy smiled as her mind was stuck on a distant memory.

Isela stood up as she said, "Okay, everyone, the plan is to wake up early tomorrow, eat breakfast and go for a hike. With that said, may I suggest we knock out now?" Everyone stood up and made their way to the tent. Isela threw some dirt on the fire to put it out. She made her way to the tent as well. They joked around a little bit while trying to go to sleep. One by one, they dozed off.

Morning came, Isela was the first one up. She nudged Miranda. Miranda picked her head up. She looked at Isela and threw her head back as to say, "What's up?" Isela whispered, "Good morning, baby doll. Let's go wash up and get breakfast started. Cool?" Miranda really did not want to get up yet. She was a good sport, however.

The two ladies went to the faucet to get some water. They took turns holding the knob to the faucet for each other to brush their teeth and wash their faces and hands. They walked back to the campsite then walked over to the van. Isela pulled the propane stove out of the back of the van. Miranda grabbed some pans and cooking utensils. They both walked over to the table to prepare breakfast.

The smell of chorizo con huevos y papas soon filled the air. One by one, everyone got up to wash their faces and brush their teeth. One by one they came to sit at the table. Gabby was the first one at the table. She asked if they needed help. Isela asked her to grab some plates and napkins. Soon they all sat quietly grubbing on breakfast burritos. Suzy sighed, "Uuuh, those were some bomb burritos. Thank you for hooking it up my loves." Everyone followed suit by thanking the cooks.

Isela announced to the camp that she would be making some sandwiches for lunch. She told the group that when she completed preparing them, they would be off for a long hike. Isela told Clever if he wanted to fish to take the fishing poles and the bait. The girls helped Isela make and bag the sandwiches. They placed some water bottles in a thermal bag, and the sandwiches went on top of the water. They agreed that they would all take turns holding the bag. It was about 7:15 in the morning when they began the hike.

The group must have walked six yards when they walked up on a deer. The deer stood eating from the shrubs. Some of the group had never seen non-domesticated life up close before. They were quietly starring. For Gabby, Lori, and Isela, seeing non-domesticated life, especially deer, was nothing new. But it was always special for them. Isela tended to acknowledge all relatives that she came across.

In this case, it was a doe they had come across. Isela said, "Hello, sister shukaat, we are just passing through. We won't disturb you. Have a blessed day, sister." The deer lifted her head. She looked Isela in her eyes as Isela spoke. Once Isela finished her sentence, the deer nodded and went back to her meal. Everyone was in awe of what they had just witnessed.

They continued walking. Suzy said, "Oh my gosh, Isela, how did you do that?" Isela smirked, asking, "Do what?" Suzy replied, "Dude, you just had a convo with a deer. And she seemed to understand you." Isela said, "When you are a visitor to someone else's home, it is crucial to respect them. By acknowledging them, it lets them know I am here in a good way. Even if you see a mountain lion or bear, whatever you do, do not run, scream or react in fear.

"Remain calm, smile, and say hello in a calm voice. By doing so, you let these relatives know you are not a threat to them. Usually, they will go about their day. If, for some reason, they seem to come closer and you feel threatened, then you would lift your hands in the air and yell aggressively for them to go away. Let them know you don't play that shit. If you have the opportunity to do so, pick up a rock in case you need it. Whenever I hike alone, I carry my knife and rock in each hand. I never once had to use them, though." Just then, Clever reached down on the quickness to pick up a rock.

Suzy said, "Freakin' nature queen over here! But seriously, I think it's pretty cool that you can handle yourself in almost any situation. Not just out in the woods either. You hold your own in the city life too. I would think a man needs you more than you would need a man." Isela laughed, replying, "Haha, thanks love. I try as much as I can to live by the teachings of my elders. As far as the man thing, that's probably why I never had one."

Gabby surprisingly asked, "Isela, you never had a boyfriend?" Isela answered, "Well, I have if you count Tony from middle school." Denise laughed hard. She then said, "Oh my gosh, Isela, didn't you go out with him for like three days?" Isela giggled, responding, "Yes. I broke up with him because he just wanted to mess around. I was like dude I'm 12, relax."

Gabby asked Isela, "So since Tony, you haven't been with anyone at all?" Isela answered Gabby, saying, "Not exactly. I have danced with and kissed a few guys when we go out to a party, but that's it. I never exchanged real numbers with them. None of them have seemed like we would fit right together, you know? And when I have been interested in a guy, it's like they don't even notice I exist."

Clever spoke up, "That's not true, Isela. All of the guys in the apartments think you're a beautiful and amazing woman. But they feel like you're unapproachable. And they say they feel like you're too good for them." Isela surprised, replied, "Really? I wouldn't think of myself as unapproachable or too good for anyone. Is it because I always walk around with my head held high and a serious face?"

Clever answered, "No. They say you're such a good and strong woman that you look like you don't need a man. They don't want to get shot down. Some of the guys are trying to figure out if you're a lesbian or not. And they think you're too good for them because you have your shit together. You go to school, you work, and you have a car. They feel like they don't have shit to offer you, and honestly, Isela it's true. You deserve an equal. You're probably not gonna find him in the hood. So it's a good thing that you're holding out."

Isela replied, "Thank you Clever. That means a lot to me. I'm okay with being alone. I like my space, and I don't feel like I'm missing out on too much." Clever said, "Space is good. But when you find someone you really want to be with," Clever glanced over at Denise as he continued, "You'll ask yourself how you ever got along without them." Denise shyly smiled. Isela said, "Awe, that's beautiful, Clever. I believe you."

Finally, after a six-mile hike, the group arrived at a beautiful lake. Gabby set down a big sheet under a huge tree. Everyone grabbed themselves a seat. Isela looked over to Clever. She said, "Okay, I'm gonna show this guy how to fish. If anyone else wants to try, roll up."

Denise, Clever, and Isela got up to fish. Suzy, Miranda, Lori, and Gabby stayed behind. Suzy looked over at Miranda, saying, "Mind if I smoke a bowl?" Miranda shrugged her shoulders then shook her head no. Suzy packed her pipe with some fluffy potent Kush. She took a hit then passed the pipe to Gabby. Gabby hadn't been smoking as often because of her singing. Since she was camping, she figured, "Why not?" She grabbed the piece out of Suzy's hand and took a hit.

Meanwhile, by the water, Isela put the bait on the hook.

She showed Clever how to cast his line. Isela said, "Okay, so this is the bail arm here. You're going to flip it this way to let the string loose. Keep your finger on the string until you're ready to cast. You're going to put you're pole over your shoulder like this and cast it into the water. As soon as you begin to cast, you let go of the string. Let it get a little distance, then close this bail arm to lock the string. That way, if you get a bite, you'll feel it. When you do get a bite, you'll reel it in really slow with this handle. Okay, go ahead and give it a try."

Clever flipped the bail arm and did everything Isela showed him to do. Isela said, "Good job Clever that was a perfect cast." Clever smiled. He felt a sense of pride, knowing he did well at something he had never before done. Isela explained how the bait will look like its moving and could attract a fish if he reeled it in slowly now and again.

Isela held the second fishing pole out in front of Denise, asking if she wanted to try. Denise said, "Sure." She grabbed the pole from Isela's hand. The hook was baited and ready to go. Isela said, "Let's stand a little further from Clever. We'll cast it in that direction in hopes your lines don't cross." Isela showed Denise where to cast her line. Denise seemed like a natural.

Isela said, "Okay, now both of your lines are out there. The most important part is waiting. Fishing takes patience. Sometimes you get a bite, and sometimes you don't. Sometimes it's within minutes, and sometimes it takes hours." Clever said, "That's cool. We have time. Hey, thanks again, Isela, for bringing us up here." Isela replied, "Thank you, guys, for coming with me. I love doing stuff like this. Maybe we can have an annual camping trip."

Denise jumped in, adding, "That would be awesome,

Isela. I'm down with that." Clever agreed with Denise saying, "Yeah, me too. I want to experience more stuff like this." Isela smiled and nodded her head. Isela said, "I'm gonna go grab a bowl from Suzy. Do you guys wanna take a hit?" Both Clever and Denise said yes.

Isela walked up to Suzy, Lori, Gabby, and Miranda, who were all giggly and seemed to be really into their conversation. Isela said, "Excuse me, ladies." They all stopped and looked up at Isela. Isela then said, "Sorry to interrupt y'all." She looked at Suzy and asked, "Hey Love, can I get you to pack a bowl of that sticky for Clever, Denise and myself?" Suzy replied, "Yeah, for sure."

As Isela waited for Suzy to pack the bowl, she invited the ladies to come by the water where they were fishing. Miranda said, "I'm thinking of getting in the water soon. I'm just taking a little rest from the hike." The other three ladies agreed with Miranda. Suzy handed Isela the pipe and lighter. "Thank you much," said Isela. Suzy replied, "You're welcome much." Isela insisted, "Well, when y'all come down to swim, I'll join you." The ladies were all in agreement. Isela turned and walked back towards Clever and Denise.

While Isela was away getting the pipe, Denise and Clever were discussing their relationship. Denise had been thinking of what Suzy was saying the night before. Denise asked, "Danny, do you think it's time we came public with our relationship?" Clever replied, "Honestly, mi vida, it's whatever you wanna do. I know you're a private person. Keeping a low profile on what we have, that has worked for us. But if anyone tries hating on what we have, that's never gonna pull me away from you, mi amor."

Denise tilted her head to the side, smiling. She loved the way Clever expressed himself when he actually did. Denise confessed, "Thank you, amor, I needed to hear that. I'm so glad that you're my man. Okay then, I don't want to stay low about us any longer. I hate being out and about, and not holding your hand or putting my arm around your waist. I want to do that stuff for now on. Despite what anyone has to say." Clever smiled.

Just then, Isela walked up, rapping, "Guess who's back in the motha fuckin' house, wit' a tasty fat bowl of yerba for 'yo mouth. Hoodies recognize and homies do too, that it's all love when La Laughter pulls through. Whatchu gon' do? Oh, you really don't know? Betta stop frontin' and take a hit off this bowl." Clever and Denise laughed. Isela proclaimed, "It's time to unwind." She took a hit then passed the pipe to Denise. Denise took a hit then handed the piece to Clever. The pipe made rotation two times before it was ash.

A few minutes passed when suddenly, Denise's line got a bite. Denise excitedly told Isela, "I got a bite, Isela! Now, what do I do again?" Isela explained to Denise how to reel the fish in. Isela said, "Slow and steady, ma. I'm gonna go empty the bag. Once you have the fish, just wait for me. Isela ran over to where the ladies were sitting. Clever said, "Good job, love."

Denise smiled at Clever and shrieked with excitement. Isela grabbed the thermal bag and began to take everything out, placing it under the blanket. The ladies gave Isela a look as to say, "What are you doing?" Isela explained that Denise got a fish and ran off with the bag. The ladies shouted, cheering Denise on for catching her first fish. Denise turned toward the ladies and waved excitedly.

Isela put a little bit of lake water in the bag. She placed it down at their feet. Isela then reached for the fish. She unhooked it and placed the fish in the bag. Isela stood up, looking at Denise. Isela commended Denise saying, "Congrats love, you just caught your first fish." Denise exclaimed, "Thank you! That was so dope!" Just then, Clever shouted, "Wait, I think I got something too!" Isela laughed, saying, "Dayum, you guys are on a roll." She told Clever to reel it in.

Clever looked like he was struggling a little. As the fish got closer, Isela got a good look at it. She exclaimed, "Daaang Clever, that fish is huge!" Clever responded, "It feels huge." Clever got the fish out of the water. He asked Isela if he could take it off the hook himself, Isela guided Clever as he attempted to remove the fish from the hook. Clever was so excited. Not only was the first fish he caught about two feet long, but he also got to unhook it. That made Clever blissful. He placed the squirming fish in the thermal bag. Clever hollered, "That was fun. Let's do it again!" Isela giggled, agreeing, "Sure. Let's get you guys hooked up with some more bait."

As Isela was baiting the hooks, the ladies came down to check out the freshly caught fish. Gabby said, "Wow, those are some nice looking fish. Congrats on your catch, you guys." Clever and Denise thanked Gabby. Lori insisted, "Well, I'm ready to take a little swim. You guys aren't down." Lori took off running. Suzy, Gabby, and Miranda chased after Lori to the perfect spot where they all jumped in the water. Before Isela walked away, she told Denise and Clever to call her if they needed any help. They thanked Isela and continued fishing. The ladies jumped in quite a distance away from Clever and Denise.

The water was nice and cool. The water was shoulder-deep for the ladies; they swam around for a bit. After a while of splashing and dunking each other, Miranda shouted, "Who wants to play chicken?" Gabby pointed to Miranda, claiming, "I'm on your team." Miranda jumped on Gabby's shoulders. Suzy jumped on Isela's shoulders. Isela called out, "Ready, set, go!"

The girls started pulling and pushing at each other. The goal was for one of the girls on the shoulders to knock over the other. Isela was good with her balance. Suzy finally knocked Miranda off of Gabby's shoulders. Miranda pulled Suzy down with her. As Suzy fell forward, Miranda let go falling backward. Suzy fell right on top of Gabby, causing them to both go under the water. Isela tilted to the left and fell in. Lori felt left out, so she dunked herself in the water too. Everyone popped up laughing.

After splashing around and racing each other, fifty minutes had passed. Miranda asked the girls, "Am I the only one who's hungry?" Suzy replied, "Na uh. All that laughing was a workout, huh? Let's have lunch." The girls decided to get out of the water and eat their sandwiches. Isela said, "I'll be right there. I'm gonna go check on Denise and Clever."

Isela walked up to Denise and Clever asking, "How is it going over here?" Clever was intrigued as he said, "Look, Isela, we caught another fish." Isela looked into the ice chest. Sure enough, there was another fish in there. It looked about a foot long. Isela acknowledged, "Sweet! For this being both of your first times, I must say you are both naturals. Do you guys wanna break for lunch? Or do you wanna keep fishing?" Denise and Clever looked at each other. Denise replied, "Yeah, sure. I'm pretty hungry." Isela showed them how to put the hooks away as to not catch anyone on accident. Denise carried the poles up to the blanket. Clever carried the thermal bag.

Once they got up to where the young ladies were sitting, Clever excitedly said, "Look, we caught another one!" Clever tilted the bag enough so that the ladies could look inside. Suzy replied, "Right on, you guys. It looks like we're eating fish tonight!" Clever looked over to Isela, asking, "Isela, can you show me how to cook these bad boys?" Isela replied, "For sure, amígs." Denise, Isela, and Clever sat down, joining the ladies for lunch. Suzy handed them each a sandwich and a bottle of water. They each thanked her as she did so.

As they sat there enjoying their sandwiches, a beautiful hawk flew down in front of them. The hawk looked over in their direction and lifted his head as if to say, "What's up?" Everyone's jaws dropped. Isela slowly picked up her hand, facing her fingers upright and tightly together. She said, "Hmm aweeshko'ne xaa nehiinken, thank you, my relative." Isela then whispered, "Wiishmenokre," as she placed her hand over her heart.

The hawk moved his head to the right looking at her with one eye, he blinked his eye, took four steps toward the kids, then the hawk screeched. He opened his wings wide. After a few seconds, he flew over Isela's head and disappeared. Suzy laughed as she said, "Wow. That was freaking amazing." Isela agreed, "Yes. That was beautiful."

Still looking at where the hawk was, Clever pointed and asked, "What is that?" Isela grabbed her medicine pouch. She stood up and walked over to what Clever pointed out. She kneeled and put her hand down. Isela whispered, "Aweeshko'ne xaa, brother." It was a tail feather left from the hawk; Isela said a prayer and dropped some sacred medicine in place of the feather.

She picked the feather up and lifted it to the sky. She then placed it to her heart. As the feather touched her heart, Isela felt pressure in her chest and left leg. Isela believed this was a warning but decided to keep it to herself and keep her eyes open. She went back to where everyone was sitting and showed them the feather.

Denise asked Isela, "How do you do that?" Isela answered Denise with a question, "Do what?" Denise said, "You talked to that deer earlier. Now, this hawk comes down and like, talks to you. Plus, he left you a gift. How do you do that?" Isela smiled big as she replied, "I love animals. I respect them. Maybe they sense it. I don't have an explanation. But I have always felt closeness to the deer. As for the hawk, when I was a little girl, my brother used to spot hawks everywhere.

"We'd be in the car heading to a pow wow or somewhere, and he'd constantly point up saying, 'Look dad a hawk.' Since he passed away, it seems like everywhere I go; I'm the one who spots the hawks now. Sometimes I hear the hawk outside the pad. I'll open the door and look up in the tree by the parking lot. Sure enough, there he is. Once I see him, I acknowledge him. Then he usually flies away. So a part of me feels like the hawk is a representative of my brother."

Denise smiled as she said, "Dang, I do believe that. That's dope, Isela. You're so blessed." Isela nodded in agreement. Isela replied, "Yes I am very blessed, we all are, we all woke up on a good day, we're all healthy, and look around at where we are, we're all blessed baby girl." Denise smiled as she nodded her head in agreement with what Isela was saying.

Gabby said, "I love your outlook on life Isela, ever since the first day I met you, you always had such a positive and loving vibe about you." Isela bowed her head, then said, "Thank you, Gabby." Suzy said, "You know what I notice? No matter where we go, if there are animals around, they stay close by Isela. Whether it's a cat, dog, bunny rabbit, whatever it is, they sit at her feet or lap and chill. Remember when we went to the beach at night, and Gibby's dog wouldn't leave your side?" Isela nodded, yes.

Suzy continued, "Isela went to the restroom, and Gibby's dog wouldn't take his eyes off the direction Isela went. Then she came back, and once again, he would not leave her side. But I never saw anything like what just happened with that hawk. That was simply amazing." Isela smiled then said, "I guess I never paid it any mind Suzy, but you're right."

Isela let out a big sigh. She then said, "Man, today was a beautiful day. But that hawk just made it all the more special." Everyone agreed. Clever said, "I'm glad you guys finally let me go with you somewhere. Now I see why you guys are always so chill." Suzy replied, "Yup. We have a good time no matter where we go. Miranda tried to tell your ass too before you even got put on. Remember? She told you that if you did it, you wouldn't be able to do a lot of the things that we do. You'll be stuck in the hood or locked up or dead. And what did you tell her?" Clever put his head down. He said, "Yeah, I know."

Miranda jumped in, "Yes. But what's done is done. You were too young G. You allowed yourself to get sucked into the hype. You may be from the hood. But you can make a choice now to make positive changes a little bit at a time. I see you distancing yourself from your homies. It might help you to get a little job. That way, when the homies ask why you haven't been around, you can say you've been working."

Clever said, "Yeah, that's true. Thanks, Miranda. I think I'll start looking for work soon as we get back. But those fools really can't call me on much. I put in more work in a day then some of those fools put in six months. Plus, I'm always posted in the hood with my girl. But I do need a job so I can take Denise to the places she deserves to go."

Denise smiled and kissed Clever on the cheek. Denise said to Clever, "You are SO special." Clever grabbed

Denise's hand and squeezed it as he gazed into her eyes. Suzy laughed then exclaimed, "I knew it! I don't know why you guys were trying to be all hush, hush. It was obvious all along that you two were together."

Denise looked at Suzy and said, "I don't like people knowing my business like that. Clever knew we were together. I knew we were together, and there are only two people in a relationship. As long as those two know what's up, no one else needs to know. I love you guys, but I didn't want any of you judging me or giving your input. But now it's out there, you know we're together, it's all good." Suzy said, "Dude, we love both of you mocosos. I wouldn't judge you for hooking up with your best friend. I think if anything, it's a cute love story!" Isela said, "You guys are our family. We accept you, no matter what." Denise smiled, replying, "Thank you. That really does mean a lot to us."

The day felt like it had past reasonably quickly. It was already 3:50 in the afternoon. Isela said, "Okay, I think it's about that time that we head back to camp." Everyone stood up. Gabby folded the sheet. Clever was so proud of the fish that he and Denise caught, that he carried the thermal bag back to camp. On the way back, they had the opportunity to see a mama deer with her baby. It was only for a few seconds. The mama deer looked over to see the group then ran off. Her baby ran after her.

About four miles down the trail, not far from camp, Isela stopped in her tracks. She turned around to look at everyone. Her finger was over her lips, motioning for them to be quiet. She looked up the mountain. Quite a ways up was a ledge. Isela saw something moving on the edge of the ridge. Isela picked up a big rock. She looked up at the ledge again.

The image that they had seen was now walking down

the mountain. Just as she suspected, it was a mountain lion. Isela motioned for everyone to keep walking back to camp. She whispered, "Slowly." Everyone continued sauntering toward camp. Isela said in a low tone, "Relative, you are so beautiful and amazing. We are simply passing through." She then began to walk backward with her eye on the lion.

When they got enough distance from the mountain lion, she said, "Okay, we're good." Clever asked, "So we can walk normal now?" Isela giggled as she replied, "Yes, lil' homie, you can walk normal." Gabby said, "Geeze, talk about intense. To know we were standing under the nose of a predator." Clever added, "I know, I thought I was gonna have to fight him for the fish." Suzy laughed, as she said, "Now you know good and well, you were not going to fight no big ass cat for some fish. You would have tossed the fish at him and booked it!"

Clever snarled at Suzy, "Why do you always have to be the one to put people on blast? Can't you just let me enjoy my little fantasy? Gaaaawd Suzy." Suzy laughed, replying, "Sorrryyy! I was just teasing. I'm sure as chingon as you are, you would have laid that sucka down." Clever shook his head and rolled his eyes. Clever knew that Suzy clowned around a little too much all the time; it was her personality.

Just as the campsite came to view, Isela said, "Clever, we're gonna wash our hands first, then we'll get started on dinner." Clever replied, "Okay, cool." They made it to camp around 6:50 p.m. Clever and Isela went to the spigot to clean the fish and wash up. Everyone else went to the restrooms to clean up. Isela pulled out the foil. She pulled off a few big pieces and set them on the table. Isela showed Clever how to descale the fish and gut it. She did the first one and set it on a piece of foil.

She let him gut the other two fish. As Clever did so, Isela went to the fire pit to get the fire started. She covered the fire with the grill. They squeezed lemon over then seasoned the fish and wrapped them up in foil. They also wrapped some veggies up in foil.

They walked up to the fire and placed everything down on the grill. Clever asked, "Now what?" Isela responded, "Now we wait." Isela flashed a smile. Clever nodded his head. They took a seat and watched the fire. Clever shared, "Damn Isela, this is the most fun I've got to have in a long time, for reals though. It's been a dope experience for me, thank you for bringing me up here and showing me firsthand the kind of activities I can do away from the city."

Isela replied, "It's all good. I'm glad I can open your eyes to new experiences and adventures. I personally love connecting, camping and hiking, so any time you want to get out into the mountains, let me know. We can even go hiking in the mountains by the house. It's about a ten-minute drive, and it's a perfect getaway as well." Clever responded, "I will definitely take you up on that soon."

The ladies walked up to the fire and grabbed themselves a seat. Miranda commented on how good the food smelled. Isela and Clever both smiled in Miranda's direction. Denise said, "Man, it's been a while since I had seafood. But I have never had freshwater fish." Isela replied, "Really? Oh man, you'll soon find out what you have been missing. I prefer freshwater over sea fish. It has an excellent flavor. I think you'll like it." Denise said, "I'm anxious to try it." Isela looked over to Clever then said, "It's about time to flip the fish. Should I do it or do you want to do it?" Clever jumped up, saying, "I'll do it."

Clever grabbed the tongs from the table and walked over to the fire to flip the fish. He asked Isela, "Do I flip the veggies too?" "Actually, you can go ahead and take those off altogether, lil' homie," Isela replied. Clever pulled the veggies off the grill and placed them on the table. He put the tongs next to the vegetables. Clever then made his way back to his seat.

Gabby showed excitement in her face shouting out, "Ooou, can we make s'mores tonight after dinner." Suzy placed her hand on her tummy, saying, "Mmmm s'mores sound good to me." Isela shifted her eyes from Suzy to Gabby, saying, "Well, there you have it, I went and picked up sticks while you all were sleeping this morning. I shaved 'em down so we can roast the marshmallows." Gabby smiled big then said, "You're the best Isela." Isela smiled back, replying, "I got you, baby girl. I know how much you love your sweets."

Clever had a blank look on his face throughout their whole conversation. He finally asked, "What is s'mores?" Everyone burst out into laughter. Clever kept the same look on his face as he looked at everybody one by one. He was waiting for an answer. Denise asked Clever, "For real Pa? You don't know what s'mores are?" Half out of patience, Clever very seriously responded, "No. I don't. So if you are all done having yourselves a good laugh at me, I just want to know."

Denise replied, "I'm sorry, pa, it was just the look on your face and the way you asked the question, it just, I don't know, it was cute and at the same time, funny. But anyways, s'mores are made by roasting a marshmallow over the fire, then placing it in between two graham crackers with a piece of chocolate. The chocolate melts a little bit with the warmth of the marshmallow." Clever got a little excited. Rubbing his hands together with a big smile, he said, "Hells yeah, I'm down for some of those." Isela thought that Clever's reaction was adorable. Back home, he did things with a tough-guy exterior, but amongst the girls, his childlike innocence shined through.

Isela sat quietly as she began to pray for Clever. She prayed that this experience would be everything Clever needed to get his life in good order. She prayed that he would really go home and look for a job. Also that he would turn his life around so that he and Denise both would be able to enjoy life in a whole new light. Once Isela finished her prayer, she stood up to check the fish.

She opened the foil with her right hand and peeked in. She looked over to Clever, saying, "Okay, fish is ready. Can you grab the plate, please?" Clever jumped up to grab the plate; Clever walked back over to the fire. He then took the fish off the grill. Both Clever and Isela walked back to the table together.

Isela lined plates up in front of her. She opened up one of the foil-wrapped fish and placed the fish on a plate. Then Isela split the fish down the center and cut it into four pieces. She left half of the fish on the plate. Isela put the other half on another plate. She did this until all of the dishes had a piece of fish. Isela then filled the plates with the vegetables. Isela announced to come and eat. Isela placed the plates with the largest pieces of fish in front of Clever and Denise. She explained, "Since these two caught our dinner, I'm giving them the biggest piece of fish. Thank you, Clever and Denise for dinner." Everyone shouted out, "Thank you!" Both Clever and Denise replied at the same time, "You're welcome."

Denise insisted after her first bite that she had never had fish that taste as delicious as freshwater fish. She chewed very slowly and savored the flavor as she moaned, "Mmmm." After she swallowed another bite, she said, "Dayum Isela, you weren't lying. This fish is sooo delicious." Isela grinned as she replied, "Told ya so." When everybody finished eating, Suzy and Gabby gathered the plates to wash them. As Gabby walked back to the table, she asked Isela, "Hey ma, where did you put those roasting sticks?" Isela said, "Go grab the graham crackers and stuff from the storage bin. I'll meet you at the fire with the sticks."

The girls came back with everything they needed to make s'mores. Clever had a big smile on his face. He was very anxious to learn how to make one. Not to mention, he was eager to taste one. Isela passed the roasting sticks out to everyone around the fire. Gabby walked around and let everyone grab a marshmallow from the bag. Once everyone had a marshmallow, Gabby announced I'm going to break up the crackers and chocolates. I'll have it pretty much ready for you guys on a plate.

Gabby walked over to the table and placed the ingredients down. She then grabbed a plate and put it in front of her. She broke the graham crackers in halves, placing them in a pile on the plate. Next, she opened up the chocolate bars and cut those into pieces, placing them next to the crackers. She re-stored the leftover graham crackers. She then walked back to the fire with the marshmallows ready to roast along with the plate of graham crackers and chocolates prepared to go.

Everyone roasted their marshmallows and walked over to Gabby to make their s'mores. Clever watched Denise make hers first, then made his with so much excitement. The ladies were enjoying the s'mores with delight. Clever took his first bite. He nodded his head side to side as he chewed, making an unsatisfied face, he said, "Nah, I don't like these things. They are way too sweet." Clever held the rest of his s'more to Denise, saying, "You want this mami?" Denise giggled then replied, "What are you talking about? These things are bomb! Just hold it papas, and I'll eat it." With a stink face, Clever said, "Okay."

Clever admired Denise as she ate her s'more. She wore her brown hair down and straight, reaching her waistline, tight Levi jeans, a grey pullover hoody sweater, and faded black all-star chucks. She sat with her right leg crossed over her left. Clever thought to himself, "I can't believe how lucky I am. The most beautiful girl in the world and she's my lady. I hope I never fuck this up." Denise glanced over and flashed a beautiful smile at Clever. Clever smiled back.

Clever pushed his chair closer to Denise's chair. He grabbed her hand, pulled it to his lips, and kissed it. He then lowered her hand and continued to hold it. Clever quietly sat while Denise talked and laughed amongst her homegirls. He felt so happy at this moment. Clever did not want this feeling of blissfulness to end.

Suzy asked Gabby, "So how is the music coming along?" Gabby's eyes lit up as she replied, "I just talked to a promoter before we left to come camping. She asked me to perform in a couple of weeks at an all-ages hip-hop venue." Isela said, "Fuck yeah, Gabby, are you gonna do it?" Gabby answered, "Honestly, I would like to, but I'm a little nervous because they want me to sell fifteen overpriced tickets and will give me fifteen more tickets to pocket the money."

Suzy asked, "How much are the tickets?" Gabby responded, "Twenty-five bucks. I think if I took the offer, I'd sell em for at least fifteen each. I don't give a fuck about profiting right now. I'm more concerned about getting my voice heard." Isela said, "Don't trip, we'll help you push the tickets. Just tell em' you'll do it." Gabby agreed and then went on to say, "And oh my creator, it has been so fun to be in the studio. I feel at home there. I think the songs are coming out pretty well. You wanna hear a lil' something?" Suzy responded, "Yeah, of course."

Gabby reached into her pocket and pulled out her iPod. She disconnected the one that was plugged into the portable speaker to connect hers. She pulled up her music library and began to play one of her songs. Everyone got very quiet as they sat and listened to Gabby's latest work. Everyone began nodding their head to the beat and smiling. When the song ended, everyone cheered and clapped. Everyone shouted compliments at the same time:

Suzy insisted, "Wow, mujer, you rocked it." Isela said, "That was amazing." Denise added, "You got down, ma." Miranda said, "That's a hit right there." Clever agreed, "Yeah, that was dope, Gabs." And Lori mentioned, "Your voice is beautiful sis." Gabby grew a massive smile on her face. She said, "I'm so relieved to know you like it. I wrote this song for Denis. I titled it 'Change.'" Suzy replied, "Like? I loved it. I kind of figured that's who you meant. You seriously rocked that song. My hat is off to you on that one." Gabby responded, "Thank you, love. That truly means the world to me."

Isela asked Gabby, "So how many songs have you completed thus far?" Gabby said, "About four songs. But I'm not sure about them being one hundred percent complete. I go back sometimes and decide I need to add or change stuff up. My cousin has been a blessing. I wouldn't have recorded anything had he not offered his time to me."

Suzy asked Gabby, "Do you have an album name already?" Gabby answered, "Kind of, I'm leaning towards calling it 51/49 PMB." Isela giggled and asked, "Push me bitch?" Gabby smirked in Isela's direction and slowly nodded her head up and down. Lori asked Gabby, "Are you currently writing any songs?" Gabby replied, "I'm currently writing a song called 'Imagine.'"

Interested in the conversation, Miranda asked Gabby, "Hmm, what's that song about?" Gabby replied, "It's a song describing what life would be like if we stopped being hateful and all learned from our elders instead of going to school. It's also talking about how it might be if we lived as humble, respectful, and peaceful beings." Isela said, "I would love to hear the outcome of that song, baby girl." Gabby replied, "Yeah, I'm stuck on verse one. I feel like the idea behind the song has great potential. It's just so hard to word it to perfection, though."

Denise told Gabby, "Hey, I'm not a songwriter. However, if you need any help, keep in mind that I am an English buff. I got you." Gabby replied, "Thanks, ma, I will keep that in mind for sure. If you do help me write my song, I will be sure to give you the credits." Denise smiled, saying, "That would be tight." Clever asked, "Would that make her a ghostwriter?"

Gabby responded, "Na-uh, a ghostwriter is not mentioned in the credits. In this case, Denise would simply be a songwriter." Clever nodding his head said, "Oh, alright. That would be sick. My girl got some writing skills, for sure." Gabby replied, "Yes, she has impressed me with her work. That's why I would let her help me write a song for sure." Suzy said, "I think with the way Denise tells a story and the way Gabby can bring it to life with vocals, they would get down on a track. Maybe add some bars from Isela and boom." Both Gabby and Denise smiled, Gabby agreed, "I could see that."

Gabby turned to point at Isela as she said, "And being that Isela is a tight rapper, I would let her jump on a verse." Suzy and Miranda shouted, "Get it!" They giggled. Miranda said, "Yeah, she a hella dope rapper. I love when she grabs the mic and busts freestyles at some of the parties." Gabby laughed, replying, "Yup spitting some sick ass rhymes."

Denise challenged Isela, "Are you down to bust out right here, right now, though?" Isela shook her head side to side as she said, "Yeah, I'm down to mess around, give me a beat." Gabby nodding her head, scanned her iPod for an instrumental. Gabby found one and said, "Okay. Here goes a good one. You bust a verse and cue me in. I got your hook. Then you can take over again. We'll do it 'til you spit three verses. Sound good?" Isela agreed.

Gabby played the instrumental. Isela nodded her head, trying to get the feel of the beat. Isela busted out, "Uh, I'm feeling this beat, bringing this heat, killing this verse, for what it's worth, I'm a straight-up beast. Ain't no one stepping to me, cuz they fear won't allow, I'm on my level, spotting ants when I glance down, I spread my wings and fly like ol' perv Kellz. I'm glancing down on the world now. How you like my style? You say you love it. I drop the kinda sounds you wanna thump in public. At any party, I can flow all night. Hearing 'em scream dayum, that femcee is so tight. So is my choncha, but my music's all you can feel, bring me that hook, and let 'em know the deal."

Gabby brought the hook in, "We on a whole other level these haters can't touch, music, we droppin' the best of, we puts it down we getting mad love, said we on a whole other level these haters can't touch, music, we droppin' the best of, we puts it down we getting mad love."

Isela jumped back on the beat, rapping, "Yup, that's us, all day we droppin' the best of, music, said someone's gotta do it, leave it to my team to make yo' ass bounce, ladies clap your hands, men pick up your tongue and close your mouth, throw your hood up eight one eight's in the house, best area code, in case you didn't know, givin' it up for them Vallero's, unstoppable, so don't waste your time, hold your change tight cause out here we don't drop the dime, I mean you can if you wanna be the next victim laying cold, but I suggest you keep your eyes straight and live by the code, there's a lot you gotta learn to survive, these streets ain't no joke, I walk them with pride."

Gabby took over again with the hook, "We on a whole other level these haters can't touch, music, we droppin' the best of, we puts it down we getting mad love, said we on a whole other level these haters can't touch, music, we droppin' the best of, we puts it down we getting mad love."

Isela came back with the third verse, "Verse number 3 on this one listen close. I'm gonna tell y'all a story of the day my homie became a ghost, It was a Friday afternoon, I was coming home from school, seen my homeboy at a distance, four guys ran up, They all dissed him as they began to rush. But my boy put in work, he laid the biggest one out, left him face down in the dirt, he phased out two more, he never hit the floor, he knew it was time to run when they grabbed for the guns.

"I was on the phone letting an O.G know, he came out with two straps, as my homeboy was getting shot up from the back, it all felt like time slowed, he dropped to one knee, then his hands hit the floor, he began to crawl, one guy ran up and finished him off once and for all. The O.G held two guns up at point-blank, took two of those guys out the game, the other two ran as fast as they could, the O.G chased them out the hood, I kneeled beside my boy, I put my hand over the wounds, no point on calling 911 there was nothing anyone could do.

"I gave my boy a hug, followed by a kiss, removed my jacket, and placed it over him, didn't want the nosey ass neighbors to see my boy like this, I saw his spirit standing there, he was in disbelief, this is what to expect when you live life on these streets, I said a lil' prayer to send his spirit home, I miss him very much, but I know he's not alone, he's with all the other homies who passed away as well, I know they made it to heaven now that they left this hell."

Gabby sang, "This is just a taste of life from our view, it's not always fun, but some days can be cool. Said this is vida in the eight one eight, some give some take, some real some fake, some drink some blaze, gotta accept our fate at the end of the day." Everyone clapped and cheered for the two ladies. Gabby and Isela grasped hands and gave each other a hood style handshake.

Suzy said, "Daaaang, that was hella tight, you two. Man, my girl still got them rhymes. And of course, Gabby, you got beautiful vocals and words." Gabby and Isela both smiled. Clever said, "I like how you fit in that story about the homie. That verse came out clean." Isela responded, "Yeah, I replay that moment a lot in my head. I wish it could have gone differently. You know, sometimes I wish I would have had a strap that day. That way, I could have given him a chance to get away.

"I hated myself for a while for not doing anything." Denise said, "Trust me, mija, you don't want that kind of stuff on your conscience. You were right to call the big homie. Anything more that you could have done would've

got you caught up in some way. You could have got it too."
Isela replied, "I almost didn't even make that call, I started
to go into a panic. I had to pull it together. It sucks that
anyone should have to die like that."

Denise responded, "Well, unfortunately, that's all a lot
of us kids in the neighborhood know. You seemed to have
held yourself together pretty good after that. I'm proud of
you." Isela replied, "Did I? I had nightmares every night for
months straight. Now and again, I still have nightmares
about it. I didn't want to talk to anyone about what I saw that
day. The cops were vicious on the subject. They harassed
the crap out of me. They kept telling me, 'We know you
were an eyewitness. If you don't comply and tell us what
happened, we're gonna have to throw you in jail for with-
holding information on a crime.'

"It made me really not want to comply. I was like, 'What
the fuck? I didn't see shit, I heard shots, I ran outside, and
my friend was laying on the floor bleeding to death. How
many times do I have to replay this awful picture 'til you
assholes get it through your head?' I swear, man, some of
these cops are bullies who think it's better to harass people
to get the job done than to show genuine concern. Maybe
if they were friendly and showed compassion toward the
people they're supposed to be protecting and serving like
offer up counseling for the horror one may have experi-
enced, they might get some help from us too. But all they
seem to serve us is harassment and jail time."

Clever nodded his head as he said, "And that's on the
real. These fools cuffed me just for standing around doing
nothing. I'm like, 'Seriously?' That's why Denise never lets
me carry shit on me. They will look for any excuse to throw
my ass in jail." Denise agreed with Clever. She said, "Oh my

gosh, one day he was waiting for me outside my house and by the time I come out, he's got his hands on his head, and these assholes are searching him.

"They found a dub sack of Kush on him, okay? What do they do? They arrest him and claim it to be 'Over an ounce of marijuana.' I wanted to be like bitch please I got a scale in the house we can weigh this shit right now. But of course, I said nothing because I didn't wanna get Clever into deeper shit. I watched them take him away. I thought how fucking stupid. A kid just died on the boulevard, and they're taking my man in for a dub? Shouldn't they be investigating a crime?"

Clever added, "Oh, they were investigating!" Clever chuckled. He continued to say, "They had a chingo of us, youngsters, in there for dumb shit. And they made sure to question us all on that matter. I tripped, I was like for real? You brought me in for a weed sack, and here you are interviewing me for murder? Yeah, it was sad that someone had died. But I found it hilarious the way the cops decided to handle it. But that's the juras for your ass.

"They're like doctors; sure there are tests they have to take and pass before they get the job. But not one of those tests is fully preparing them for real situations. So when faced with real-life situations, they're playing the guessing game on how they should handle it. A lot of them handle it poorly if you ask me. But they have to live and learn just like us."

Suzy sounding shocked, responded, "Wow, that's a pretty good analogy. It's true, these cops today don't have a clue what to do when faced with real-life situations. It's as if they are taught to shoot first and ask questions later. It seems more and more broadcasted these days, that they're just killing people like it's a casual thing. I think if they're gonna be doing that, they should change that quote on the cop cars from 'To protect and serve' to 'Kill or be killed' or something like that. I can't understand why they have to kill someone who looks like they're holding a gun.

"I say tase him in the arm or hand holding the supposed gun, and if he was committing a crime, let the guy do his time. I mean, I guess they think they're doing the taxpayers a favor, it's just kind of harsh." Isela said, "Dah, doing the taxpayers a favor, that's funny. But you're right. It feels like those guys come in to cause more pain in our neighborhood than good most of the time. I mean, I like to believe they don't all start out that way. I think that a lot come in with good intentions. And I know for a fact that there are a few nice guys in the game. I feel like there are more corrupt ones, though. I imagine, after seeing the things they see in these streets, they all begin to change. I imagine it feels like the corrupt cops are the majority because when one cop is trying to be good, they have a handful of cops against them, and it's hard."

Gabby said, "The cops of America's beginning were meant to lock up and torture Blacks and Natives and return them to slave owners. They always been like gangs themselves. And they're still torturing Blacks and Natives. My cousin quit her job as a cop because of all the corrupt things that she witnessed. She couldn't turn anyone in because no one above her would take her side. She didn't agree with anything that was going on inside of their little cop circle, so she just decided to walk away and went to school to become a nurse. She just wanted to do something where she could help people. She loves her job now."

Miranda said, "In my line of work, I can't afford to hate the cops. I smile and say hi when I see them. It's like don't fuck with me, and I won't fuck with you. I haven't had a problem with them. In fact, Ramirez is always giving me this look like he wants me. So I'm not even trippin' off of it."

Gabby reminded Miranda, "I know. Remember that one time he had his homie pull over in the squad car? He was practically drooling as he asked you how your day was, and telling you he sees you walking alone sometimes and how that worries him because anything can happen to you. I was thinking, 'Staaalker, if anything happens to her it's because you couldn't hold back any longer!'" Everyone laughed. Miranda nodded, saying, "Yeah, he's always telling me stuff like that. I remind him I'm just a kid. So he does keep a slight distance. But I'm pretty sure he's waiting for me to be eighteen."

Clever asked Miranda, "Would you date a cop?" Miranda replied, "Hmm, I don't know. I think all the homies would frown upon it and call me a traitor. Some of them might even think I'm giving up info and accuse me of being a 'Rata,' plus it would be a dangerous thing to do being that I slang, and not to mention my bro's big in the game. If I dated a cop, it wouldn't go far, it would be a few dinner dates, and that's it. I guess I'm going to have to answer your question with a no. Why lead him on? You know? If I hurt him by denying him a relationship or whatever he may be looking for, then that might burn my spot as well. I wouldn't mind, however, dating a lawyer. But to be honest, I don't even want to date until I finish college."

Denise questioned Miranda, "Why are you waiting so long?" Miranda responded. "To be perfectly honest, because I know from now until then, my mindset is going to change. Also, I want to put all of my focus on me and my school-ing. I know a guy would take away from that. But once I complete school, I'll consider dating. Plus, if I become a doctor, I might just date one." Suzy said, "Wow, you really have thought this through, haven't you?"

Miranda nodded as she replied, "Yeah. Well, Miguel and I have been talking about stuff like this recently. He wants me to do great things with my life. I don't want to disappoint him. If I bring random Joes around all the time, I know that he'll be a little disappointed in me. I'm sure that I will have to date a few guys before I find my match, but at least I'll have my life together. By that time, I will be much surer of what I want."

Isela said, "Good for you, baby girl. Stay true to yourself. As long as you're happy, I'm happy for you." Miranda smiled. Isela stood up and said, "Well, I'm going to change and knock out. Do you guys want to stay up or should I put the fire out." Suzy said, "I'm right there with you, ma. I know all about your 'No one sleeps in rule.' So I believe I'll knock out now too." Everyone agreed with Suzy. They stood up and made their way to the tent. Isela double-checked that everything was put away. She then walked over to the fire to put it out. Isela turned on her flashlight and walked over to the tent to go to sleep.

Since the truth was finally out about Denise and Clever being together, they decided it'd be fine to cuddle up and sleep together. Denise whispered in Clever's ear, "This feel's so right." Clever whispered back, "I can't wait to do this every night with you." They kissed each other on the lips and went to sleep.

The next morning Isela was the first one up. She walked over to the spigot with her toothbrush and toothpaste at hand. As Isela was brushing her teeth, she heard movement behind her. She turned to see what it was. It was a bear. The bear was about twenty feet away from her. Isela finished brushing her teeth and rinsed. She looked up to watch the bear; the bear strolled by. As if he hadn't a care in the world. Isela smiled and whispered, "Thank you, creator, for blessing me with this moment. Thank you for allowing me to share space with such a sacred relative, hmmm."

The bear stopped in its tracks; he looked over to Isela. He stared directly into her eyes for about twenty seconds. Isela smiled as she looked back into his eyes. She nodded, saying, "Thank you for blessing me with your presence, relative." The bear then looked directly in front of him and disappeared through the trees. Isela touched her heart with a closed fist.

Suddenly it dawned on her; he should have still been hibernating for a few more weeks. Isela knew hibernation varied with California bears. She figured it was a 50/50 chance that was a spirit bear. Isela asked her guides to help her understand the reason for seeing the bear.

Isela walked over to the food bins to pull eggs, bacon, onion, and potatoes out of the ice chest. She closed the bins. Isela then walked over to the table to place the food down. She grabbed two pans, two cooking spoons, a cutting board, and a knife. Isela diced up the potatoes and onions; then, she started the propane stove. She placed the pans on the stove. Isela put some olive oil in one pan. Once the oil was hot, Isela put the onion and potatoes in the pan. Ten minutes later, Isela began cooking the bacon. Isela covered both pans. She then went to sit down by the fire pit.

Isela took a deep breath and calmly released it. She loved this feeling of being in the woods. Something about the smell of the woods in the morning always felt so comforting to Isela. Nothing could quite calm her as this smell could.

She could feel the presence of the ancestors that occupied these lands so long ago. Isela sat quietly, feeling very relaxed.

Miranda stepped out of the tent with her toothbrush and toothpaste at hand. She walked up to Isela and asked, "Good morning, mamita. Why didn't you wake me up to help you with breakfast?" Isela smiled. She replied, "Good morning, baby doll. I just thought I'd let you sleep. It's cool though I got it." Miranda replied, "Thank you. But it doesn't bother me when you wake me up FYI. I'm gonna brush my teeth and wash my face. I'll come back and help you." Isela nodded her head in agreement.

When Miranda walked back to camp, Isela was at the table, cracking eggs into a bowl. Miranda asked, "What shall I do?" Isela said, "You can check the bacon and papas." Isela seasoned the eggs and began beating them. Miranda announced that the bacon was ready. She grabbed two paper plates, layering the bacon on top of one plate. She took the other plate and placed it over the bacon.

Isela walked over to the stove and poured the eggs into the bacon fat. Miranda checked the potatoes. She covered them back up with the lid. The potatoes were ready, so she removed it from the fire. She took it to the fire pit and placed it on the grill. Miranda then went to grab some tortillas. She also grabbed the tortilla holder to place the cooked tortillas in.

Gabby stepped out of the tent and took a deep breath. She let out a loud "Ahhhh." She walked over to the stove where the ladies were standing. Gabby said, "Mmmm, it smells like some good cooking. Do you need any help?" The ladies both said, "No, thank you." Isela said, "It's just about ready. You can go get Suzy, Lori, and the love birds, though." Gabby obliged, she walked back over to the tent to wake everyone up.

Gabby came back to the table and sat down. Lori, Clever, and Denise came out to join the ladies. Everyone said their good mornings. Suzy came out last. She sat at the table and said, "Ugh, good morning. Man, I had a crazy-ass dream right now. I dreamt that Jose was following me. I remember feeling scared. But he was charming. I asked him to leave me alone, and that's when the look in his eye turned evil.

"I was on a mission to getaway. Every time I ended up somewhere away from him, there he was. He finally got a hold of me. He took me to a barn. He put me on my knees and put a gun inside of my mouth. Then Gabby woke me up." Gabby said, "Oh my gosh. Thank goodness you woke up before he pulled the trigger. I've heard when people die in their dreams, they never wake up." Isela said, "Luckily, it was just a dream, and you woke up to this beautiful scenery. I'm sure you'll figure out what it means. In the meantime, let's enjoy some breakfast." Suzy nodded her head.

Isela and Miranda served everyone a plate. Isela placed Suzy's plate in front of her. As she did so, she put her hand on Suzy's shoulder and kissed Suzy on the top of her head. She whispered, "It doesn't mean anything horrible; you're going to be just fine." Suzy reached to her shoulder and squeezed Isela's hand.

After breakfast, Isela announced, "This is our last day here. I suggest we get on the road no later than 1 p.m. Let's clean up now and pack everything up except the ice chests. We'll save those for last. I'm going to take the tent down right now. So, if you can all get your stuff and put it in the car, that would be greatly appreciated. Again big thanks to Clever and Denise for catching our dinner last night. Since we had fish for dinner, we still have chicken and ribs. Might I suggest that we barbeque when we get home?" Everyone agreed.

They went to pull their belongings out of the tent. They piled their bags and sleeping gear into the back of the van.

Clever helped Isela take the tent down. Together they put it back in the casing. Clever took it to the van. Isela asked, "Well, before we put the chairs away, I gotta ask, do y'all wanna post up here at camp? Or do you want to go on another hike?" Clever said, "Can we post up here and play cards or boneyard?" Isela asked, "Is everyone else cool with that?" No one seemed to have a problem with that request. Isela said, "Okay, games it is. Let's put these chairs away still, and we can post up at the table." Everyone grabbed a chair and put it away.

They sat down at the table, ready to play. Isela brought the games out. She asked which one they wanted to play. Suzy and Gabby said poker. Miranda, Clever, and Denise said boneyard. Isela shrugged her shoulders, saying, "Majority rules, we'll play cards next." Isela dumped the dominoes onto the table. Everyone flipped all the dominoes face down, and then Isela washed them. Before she let anyone pull their dominoes, she said, "Wait! Let's smoke a bowl before we play, you know, make it interesting."

Miranda laughed, shaking her head side to side. Suzy pulled out the pipe and packed a bowl. The piece made its way around for one rotation. After they smoked, Clever slapped and rubbed his hands together, saying, "Okay, let's play." They all reached for their dominoes. Once everyone had all seven dominoes, they set 'em up in their own way and waited.

Miranda had the double six, so she slammed it on the table. Clever matched a six to the center of the double six. On the other end of his six was a three. He called fifteen. Denise played next. Next, it was Lori's move. After Lori, it was Isela's move. Gabby played after Isela. Then it was Suzy's turn to put a domino down. That was the order of rotation for the game.

Clever was winning at the beginning of the game. Halfway through, Gabby picked up her points. She wound up winning the game. Everyone congratulated Gabby. Gabby said, "Thank you, this was fun. I used to watch the guys play boneyard all the time. But this was the first time I ever played, though." Suzy responded, "Well, for this being your first time, you sure did kick ass." Gabby smiled at Suzy, replying like a southern belle, "Why thank you."

Isela asked, "Do you guys wanna play another round of boneyard? Or shall we play poker?" Everyone decided on poker. They all helped Isela put the dominoes away. Isela grabbed the cards and handed them to Suzy. Isela said, "Here, you can be the dealer." Suzy grabbed the cards from Isela's hand. She then began to shuffle the cards. Suzy distributed the cards one by one, starting to her left. She said, "You can draw or get rid of up to three cards. Place them flat on the table. Two's are wild." Once Suzy passed out all of the cards, she placed the deck at the center of the table.

Everybody picked up their hands. They all started moving their cards around as they tried to evaluate how strong their hands were. Gabby placed two cards on the table saying, "Hit me." Suzy picked up two cards from the deck and handed them to Gabby. Isela kept her hand. Denise placed three cards down as she said, "Hit me." Suzy gave Denise three cards from the deck.

Clever placed one card on the table as he said, "Hit me." Suzy asked Clever, "Are you positive that you just want one card?" Clever answered, "Yeah, shoot it." Suzy handed Clever one card from the deck. Miranda Placed down three cards. She, too, said, "Hit me." Suzy grabbed three more cards from the deck. She handed them over to Miranda. Suzy glanced at Lori. Lori tilted her head to the left, scrunched her lips to the right, she then said, "Okay, yeah. Hit me." Lori put two cards down on the table. Suzy gave Lori two new cards. Suzy placed two of her cards down. She then grabbed herself two more cards from the deck.

One by one, they revealed their hands. Gabby put her cards down first. Gabby had a lousy hand. Isela had a full house; a pair of kings, and three of a kind of tens. Denise had a pair of fours. Clever had four of a kind; three aces and a two. Miranda had a straight; five, six, seven, eight, and a nine. Lori had two pairs. Suzy announced that Clever won as she placed her cards down; she had three of a kind, a pair of two's and a king. They played two more games until Suzy collected the cards. She neatly put them away and handed the cards back to Isela.

Isela said, "Welp, are we all ready to go back to reality?" Everyone shouted, "Nooo!" Isela laughed. She said, "None the less we gotta bounce soon, my darlings. First, let me make some lunch for the road." Isela made some sandwiches and placed them in a container. She chopped up some celery and carrots and put them in a separate container. "Alright, we're good to go," shouted Isela. Isela and Clever packed up the ice chests, while everyone made their way to the van. Everyone found themselves seated in the same seats as when they came up.

The conversing on the drive home mainly consisted of how much fun camping was. Clever said, "This was a weekend, unlike any other. My lady and I caught our first fish together. I witnessed Isela talk to animals. That hawk is something I will never forget. I cooked the fish that we caught with Isela. I tasted my first s'more, and it tasted like shit. But I enjoyed watching my lady laughing and enjoying herself." Clever turned to look at Denise, "You looked so beautiful in the light of the campfire." Denise smiled big.

Clever announced, "The only bitch is that it went by too fast. But I can't wait to do this again, you guys." Isela said, "Clever, this trip was for you, so I'm glad you did enjoy yourself. We did talk about making this an annual trip. I think that would be a great idea. Espeeecially knowing school will be coming to an end soon. Whether we like it or not, we're going to begin to get too busy to kick it daily eventually. Some or all of us will go to college; some of us will hold down jobs as well. So I think to put a weekend aside to spend quality time with each other once a year, would be much needed." Suzy said, "You can count me in." Everyone else followed with a, "Me too." Isela smiled as she said, "Alright, cool."

The girls and Clever made it home around 5:30 p.m. When they reached the apartments, Clever grabbed an ice chest and walked it over to the jungles. Suzy and Denise grabbed the other ice chest and walked it over to the jungles as well. Gabby brought down the plates, utensils, and spices. Isela went to her apartment to get a barbeque. Isela came back with a small table and a grill on wheels. Isela went back to the house one more time to grab charcoal for the barbeque.

Isela put charcoal in the barbeque pit. Miranda set up the table to prep the meat while Isela started up the fire. Isela also chopped veggies and placed them in the corner of the grill. Isela told Suzy, "While we get the meat started, can you roll one up with my clear wraps? They're in the side pocket of my bag right there, and my container is next to it." Suzy nodded, yes. She walked over to Isela's bag to grab the clear wraps and weed. She then sat down next to Gabby and began to break up the bud.

Isela helped Miranda season the meat. The ribs went on the grill to cook as well. Isela and Miranda went to wash their hands at Miranda's house. As Isela washed her hands, she asked Miranda, "Do you think we should cook up some beans for the side dish?" Miranda said, "Yeah. You know what? I have a couple of cans of sweet pork and beans. I'll heat them in here. You go watch the meat and smoke your weed." Isela smiled as she replied, "You're too sweet. Thanks, love." Miranda smiled back and said, "De nada, mujer."

Isela walked back over to the jungles, Suzy asked if she was ready to smoke, Isela said, "Did that question for real just come out of your mouth? Let's do this." Suzy shrugged her shoulders and lit it up. As Suzy hit the blunt, Denise called out, "On this blunt, you can't release the smoke from your lungs until the blunt makes its way back to you. Anyone who releases it early gets a titty twister." Isela laughed. Suzy nodded yes and gave thumbs up. The blunt made its way around two times with no problem.

Before it could make its way back to Clever, he choked on the smoke and let it out. Denise looked over at Suzy and raised her eyebrows twice. Suzy and Denise leaped over to Clever, they each twisted a nipple. Clever yelled out in pain. The ladies wanted to laugh hysterically, but they held in their smoke. It was Isela's hit when Clever choked. She took a hit then walked over to check the ribs. She flipped them over, and then added some chicken to the grill.

Isela still had the smoke in her chest. She walked back over to the circle and waited for her next hit to release the smoke in her lungs. When the blunt finished, the ladies turned their attention to Clever. They clowned on him because he couldn't hang, whereas the three ladies held in the circle without choking. Clever knew if he made an excuse, the clowning would escalate, so he just sat there and took it.

Isela went to check on the meat again. She removed the veggies. Just then, two O.G's from the neighborhood walked up. Isela greeted the men saying, "Q-vole big homies." They both said, "Hi, mija." As they walked up, they gave her a hug and a kiss on the cheek. One of the O.G's, Big Slick, said, "Mmm smells good mijita. What are you cooking?" Isela said, "Barbeque ribs and chicken. Ol' girl Miranda is making some pork and beans. You guys are more than welcome to eat with us."

The other O.G, BooBoo, said, "Simon gracias baby girl. What's the occasion?" Isela said, "Well, I just came back from taking the homegirls and Clever camping. The intention was to eat this up there, but Clever and Maldita caught us some fish yesterday, so we ate that for dinner last night instead. We just figured let's use up the meat now since we all chipped in on it."

BooBoo nodded his head, saying, "Firme. Where did you guys go camping?" Isela said, "I found a spot near Sequoia. Ah, it was so beautiful. There was a stream that ran behind the campsite. Instead of chilling there, I took these guys on a long-ass hike, though. Eventually, we came to a big lake and had a little picnic. That's where they caught the fish."

Big Slick said, "That's what's up. I wish you would have invited." Isela replied, "Awe, I'm sorry big homie, but we decided while we were there that we would make it an annual thing. If you guys want to put the date in your calendar, you're both more than welcome to join us. It will be around the same time next year."

Big Slick said, "On the serio, I would want to go. It's been a cool minute since I went camping." BooBoo agreed. He said, "Shit I know dawg, member back in the days we would gather up homies and do the same thing. Those were some good times we had que no homie?" Big Slick nodded in agreement. He looked at Isela and said, "Yup. We used to have some good times in the mountains. We would roll up like four carloads deep."

Isela said, "Wow, that's a lot. It was just a few of us this time. Clever had never been camping before. So the point of this camping trip was to show him that there are other things to life than just the hood life." BooBoo said, "That's good, mija. That's why we would go tambien. Being stuck in this concrete jungle can drive a motherfucker to insanity. With all the struggles, it sometimes feels worse than being in the pinta. But when you get away into the forest and take them deep ass breaths of fresh air, it's like medicina." Isela agreed, saying, "Well, I have never been to the Penn, but I know life can get hectic. Everyone can use a quick getaway now and again."

Big Slick said, "And you ain't never going to the Penn mija. You're smarter than we were at your age. You're on the fast track to success. I see you holding down your job and your school shit, that's the business right there baby girl, keep that up." Isela smiled and thanked Big Slick for his words of encouragement.

Isela said, "But every day that you wake up is like a second chance at life. That means every day is a chance that you can make a choice to change it up, do something positive and exciting in your life too. You know, like going back to school." Big Slick said, "You're right, little mama. It's just hard to break bad habits, you know?" Isela said, "I know. But it can be done."

Just then, Miranda rolled up with a pot of beans. She placed it down on the table. She greeted the O.G.'s with a hug. She then asked, "Are you guys staying for dinner?" BooBoo Said, "Is that okay, mija?" Miranda said, "Yeah, of course. It wouldn't be a hood barbeque without the hood." The O.G.'s smiled. They both made their way to the bench to give their respects to Clever, Denise, Lori, Suzy, and Gabby.

When BooBoo reached Gabby, he said, "Orale Chiquitita, I've wanted to hear a live performance. How's about you kick out some "Angel baby," by Rosie and the Originals? Gabby laughed. She asked BooBoo, "Are you for reals?" BooBoo reached in his pocket, pulling out a five-dollar bill. He said, "I got five on it right now. What's up?" Gabby said, "Say no more homeboy." Gabby stood up and grabbed the five out of BooBoo's hand. She neatly folded it and put it in her pocket. Gabby stood back and began to sing.

The O.G.'s enjoyed hearing Gabby sing. When Gabby finished singing, everyone clapped. BooBoo said, "Thank you, Chiquitita. Man, I just love hearing you sing. You're going to make it someday." Gabby touched the pocket that she placed the money in and said, "Thank you, BooBoo." Gabby took a seat. Big Slick told Clever, "What up little homie? How did you enjoy your camping trip?" Clever said, "It was a good time. These ladies know how to have fun. Oh, and I caught two fish. Bullshit you not; one was over two feet long."

Big Slick asked, "Oh, serio?" Clever excitedly said, "Yeah. My girl caught a fish too. Isela showed me how to cook them up. So last night, we grubbed good." BooBoo said, "That's cool lil' homie. From what I smell, we're about to grub good right now too." Clever said, "Man, these females been hooking up meals all weekend. Some bomb food too."

Miranda grabbed a plate from the table. She walked over to Isela and held the plate out. Isela piled the ribs on the plate. Miranda placed that plate down on the table. She grabbed another plate. Isela piled the chicken up on that plate. Miranda walked back to the table and set that plate down. Miranda began to brush sauce on the ribs. As she did that, Isela grabbed some more raw chicken from the table. She put the last of the chicken on the grill.

Miranda finished up brushing the cooked chicken with barbeque sauce. She looked over to Isela and said, "Okay, babe, we're good to go." Isela said, "Let's go ahead and make everyone a plate. Together they filled plates with ribs, chicken, veggies, and beans for everyone.

Isela turned around, shouting, "Come and get it!" Everybody stood up and walked over to the table. Isela said, "Go ahead and grab a plate. Forks and napkins are at the end of the table." Everyone grabbed a plate, fork, and napkin. They made their way back to the benches. After everyone else had a plate, Isela and Miranda grabbed a plate and sat down to eat. The entire circle was silent. There was an occasional "Mmmmm."

Once he finished what was on his plate, Big Slick told Isela and Miranda, "Damn, you ladies got down everything was bomb as fuck, gracias." Everyone agreed with Big Slick. The girls thanked everybody for the compliments on the food. One by one, as people finished with their plates, they would walk over to throw trash in a paper trash bag that Miranda had under the table.

The plates were placed on the table with the utensils. Clever waited until the last bit of trash was in the bag. He jumped up and grabbed the bag explaining that he would throw it away. Denise asked, "You want me to go with you?"

Clever replied, "Na, I'll be right back, mamash." Denise smiled. When Clever walked away, BooBoo smiled at Denise, asking, "Oh, what?! You guys finally hooked up, huh?" Denise smirked as she replied, "What are you talking about? Clever's been, my man." BooBoo hit his knee, exclaiming, "I fucking knew it! That's cool, mija. He's a good guy, and you're a good girl. I know you two will be good for each other."

CAN'T KEEP A GOOD MAN DOWN

Clever walked out to the parking lot where the trash bins were. He lifted the lid and tossed the trash. As he began to turn around, he heard someone shout a diss to his neighborhood. Just then, gunshots rang out. As soon as she heard the shots, Denise jumped up and ran to Clever. As she got closer to the gate, she could see him lying there in pain. With a hand on her gun in her pocket, and eyes squinted, Denise quickly scanned the perimeter. After realizing the suspect bounced, she ran back and told Isela to get the van and meet her in the second lot where Clever was lying.

Without question or hesitation, Isela ran to the van. Denise ran back to Clever. BooBoo and Big Slick followed Denise out to the lot. Denise kneeled beside Clever. She was afraid to touch him. At the same time, Denise knew it was necessary to apply pressure on the wounds. She frantically told Clever, "Hang in there, my love. Isela's coming; we're going to take you to the hospital. You're going to be okay, mijo."

Isela pulled up. The guys placed Clever in the van. They offered to go to help, but Denise didn't think it was a good idea because they looked like Cholos. Denise hopped in the back with Clever. BooBoo closed the van door. On the way, Clever was moaning in pain. He told Denise, "I think

I'm gonna die, Neecie." Denise said in a shaky and quiet whisper, "Shhhh, you're going to be just fine. I know you are."

As painful as it was to do, Clever reached over, grabbed Denise's hand, and squeezed it. He said, "I fucking love you, mija." Denise told Clever that she loved him too. Isela pulled up to the county hospital. When they got there, Denise ran into the lobby and grabbed a wheelchair. Isela and Denise lifted Clever and put him in the chair.

Isela went to park the van while Denise raced to the emergency room, she got to the front desk frantically asking for help. The lady behind the counter looked over to see Clever bleeding out from the chest and leg. She called for the staff to get him. The lady told Denise they would come right out to get him. Denise, still frantic, thanked the lady.

Denise kneeled on one knee. She then kissed Clever on the cheek. She whispered in his ear, "They're going to come to get you, papash. They're going to help you. You just gotta hang in there a little longer." Clever had blacked out by that point. He had lost a lot of blood. Denise silently cried and prayed for Clever. By the time Isela came into the E.R, the staff was barely coming in to get Clever.

Denise tried following them, but the nurse said, "I'm sorry, miss you have to wait out here. We'll keep you updated on his status." Denise said okay and sat down with Isela. Just then, Denise began to sob. Isela held Denise in her arms. Isela said, "I'm confident he'll make it through this. I'm praying we'll take him home tomorrow."

Denise quietly whimpered, "Me too." Isela handed Denise a sweatshirt and said, "Go to the bathroom and clean up." Denise thanked Isela and went to scrub the blood off of her.

An hour had gone by. The girls hadn't heard anything from the hospital staff. Denise very nervously picked up her cell phone and stared at it for a minute. Isela asked, "Do you want me to call her?" Denise's eyes began to water again. She shook her head no as she held the phone to her heart. Denise replied, "I'll call her. I'm gonna go to the front lobby. Can you stay here just in case they come out to let us know anything?" Isela replied, "Of course I will, mamas."

Denise walked to the front lobby and sat down. She stared at her phone again, then let out a long breath of air as she built up the courage to call Clever's mom. As the phone rang, she nervously rubbed her thigh. Rosita picked up the phone, immediately asking what was wrong. Denise told her that Clever had been shot and gave Rosita their current location. Rosita said she would be there as soon as she could. After they hung up, Denise let out a small whimper. She put her head down and let a few more tears release. She shook her head then stood up to join Isela in the E.R's waiting room.

Rosita had the worst feeling in her heart; the very second her son got shot. She heard the gunshots, but she stayed inside and prayed that her son was still in the mountains safe. When Denise finally called, Rosita expected the conversation that took place. Rosita told her boys to get their shoes on.

They got in the car and drove to the hospital. On the ride up, the boys were asking where they were going to. Rosita explained to her sons that their older brother was in the hospital. She told them that she didn't know yet how serious it was. She then asked her boys to pray for their brother. The rest of the ride up was silent.

Rosita and the boys showed up in the E.R. When Denise and Rosita caught eyes, they gave each other a look of concern. Denise stood up to hug Rosita. She hugged the two boys and pointed out some seats. She told the boys to go sit down. Rosita asked, "Have you heard anything yet?"

Denise shook her head no as she shakenly replied, "Mama Sita, he lost a lot of blood. By the time I brought him in here, he had blacked out. They shot him in the chest and the leg. It's been two and a half hours, and we haven't heard anything." Rosita nodded her head as she took in this information. As Rosita opened her mouth to speak, the nurse came out, asking to talk to Denise.

Denise grabbed Rosita's hand and walked over to the nurse. The nurse asked Denise, "Is this his mother?" Denise responded, "Yes." The nurse looked over to Rosita as she explained Clever's status. The nurse said, "Okay, the young man is in recovery. He is stable. He had a bullet wound in the left quadriceps. The doctor also pulled a bullet from his chest cavity. The bullet was a few inches away from the lung; however, no organs got punctured."

Denise asked the nurse, "Can we see him now?" The nurse replied, "Yes, but he's non-responsive right now. We had him under anesthesia. Also, there are some forms I need you to fill out for the patient. Please follow me. I'll take you to him."

Denise turned to Isela, asking, "Can you stay with the boys, please babe?" Isela nodded her head yes and made a gesture with her hand as to say scoot along. Denise and Rosita followed the nurse to Clever's room. They were so relieved to see him lying there breathing. The nurse said, "I'll be back with the forms."

Both Rosita and Denise rushed to Clever's side. Rosita looked him over thoroughly just to reassure herself. Under her breath, Rosita said, "Oh, thank you, God." Denise wrapped her left arm behind Rosita's back placing her right hand on Rosita's arm. They stood there with such gratitude as they watched Clever breathing.

The nurse came back with the forms for Rosita to fill out. Denise told Rosita. "I'm going to go get the boys and tell Isela to go home. Rosita nodded as she said with a shaky voice, "Mija, be sure, and thank her for me for bringing my baby here." Denise said, "I will, mama Sita."

Denise walked out to the waiting room. She walked up to Isela and said, "He's good, just sleeping. Mama Sita said to thank you for bringing her baby here. I wanna thank you too, baby girl, for being here for us." Isela replied, "Of course, mami, that's what family is for." Denise smiled, then told Isela, "That's right. I'm gonna stay with Clever babe. You should go home and get settled in from the trip. I'll clean the blood out of the van tomorrow."

Isela stood up, replying, "Okay, love. Don't worry about all that. I'll have the youngsters clean it. If you need me for anything at all, just call me. K?" Denise nodded as she replied, "Okay. Thanks again, ma." Isela gave Denise a big long hug followed by a kiss on the cheek. They said their goodbyes. Isela turned and wished the boys good night. She then walked out to go home.

Robert, one of Clever's brothers, asked Denise, "Neecie, is Danny going to be alright?" Denise smiled at him, replying, "Yes, mijo, he's alright. He's just taking a nap right now. Do you guys wanna go and see him?" The boys nodded their heads, yes. Denise said, "Okay, I'm going to take you. But you have to behave and don't touch anything, okay?" The boys agreed. Denise took the boys to Clever's hospital room.

The boys walked up to the bed to see their big brother. Clever's little brother Andy poked at Clever's hand, asking, "What's up with Danny? Is he really just sleeping?" Denise patted Andy on the head. She answered his question, saying, "Yes, mijo, he is sleeping. So let's let him rest okay, papa?" Andy shrugged his shoulders. He walked over to sit next to his mom.

About thirty minutes later, the nurse walked in to check on Clever. As Rosita handed the nurse the paperwork, she asked, "Is it possible to take him home tonight?" The nurse answered, "No. He may be able to go home tomorrow. I really couldn't say. It's up to the doctor."

"Oh. Okay, thank you, nurse," said Rosita. The nurse smiled. She told Rosita, "I'm going to take the paperwork to get processed. If you would like to go home, someone will give you a call to let you know when he's ready to go home." Rosita thanked the nurse. The nurse nodded her head and turned to exit the room.

Rosita looked over at Denise, saying, "Mija, I gotta get these boys into bed. We should go home. There isn't very much we can do here." Denise replied, "You go home, mama Sita. I wanna stay with him." Rosita said, "Okay, mija, just please call your parents to let them know. Tell them if they want to, that they can call me." Denise agreed.

Denise walked with Rosita and the boys to the lobby; she gave Rosita and the boys a hug and a kiss. They wished each other a good night. Denise called her mom to let her know what happened and that she would stay with Clever. Her mom was thankful that both Clever and Denise were okay.

Denise came back into Clever's hospital room. She kissed Clever on the forehead. She softly said, "Thank God that you are okay, mi vida. I love you so much. I don't know what I would do without you in my life." Denise pressed her cheek against Clever's cheek. She turned her head to kiss him on the cheek. She then kissed his lips. Denise walked over to sit in the chair. She closed her eyes and began to pray silently. Finally, she rested her head against the wall and eventually fell asleep.

When Denise awoke, Clever was sitting up eating breakfast. She sat up, rubbing her eyes. "Good morning, beautiful," Clever greeted his lady. Denise smiled. She replied, "Good morning, papi. How are you feeling?" Clever smirked as he replied, "Like I got shot." Denise laughed. She said, "I fucking love you, mijo." Clever smiled, saying, "I love you too, mamash. Thank you for staying with me last night."

Denise nodded as she said, "I don't think I could have got much sleep if I went home. Your mom was here last night with the boys." Clever asked Denise, "Oh serio? Was she mad?" Denise replied, "What the fuck? No. She was relieved like me, that you were okay." Clever smiled, asking, "Awe, you guys were worried about me?"

"You have no idea what went through our minds. I didn't know if the bullet hit an organ. Or if maybe you had lost too much blood. I didn't know if the doctor would come out announcing you deceased or alive and well. It all played through my head at different times. I just kept praying; please let you be okay. I'm so happy that you're still here with us, my love." Denise said with watery eyes and a concerned voice. Clever called Denise over to him for a hug and a kiss. He then offered some of his breakfast to Denise. She picked at his plate a little.

Two police officers walked in. Clever invited them to have a seat and get comfortable. They rejected his offer. One cop said, "We just have a couple of questions for you. Then we'll be on our way." Clever said, "Sure, ask away." The cop asked how he came about getting shot. Clever said, "Well, we had a barbeque at my house. After we all finished eating, I offered to take the trash out. I went out and placed the bag of trash in the trash bin. As I began to turn around, someone shot me, and I went down. I didn't see anyone around me before I tossed the trash. I didn't even think to get a glimpse of them or see anyone after I hit the floor."

The officer asked, "Are you sure that's how it happened?" Clever lowered his eyebrows, looking a little angry that the cop would second guess him. He replied, "Yes, I'm sure." The other officer asked, "Are you planning on retaliating?" Clever retorted, "Against who?" The cop said, "Well, against the person who shot you." Clever replied, "I'm gonna have to say no, being that I have no idea who shot me or why." One of the cops asked Clever what gang Clever banged.

Clever answered, "I'm an innocent bystander who happened to get shot while taking out the trash." The same cop responded, "Well, I wish we could help you, but we need your cooperation. I guess we're done here. If you hear anything on the person who shot you, give us a call." The cop handed Clever a business card. Clever smirked, saying, "Thank you, officer, I will be sure to do that. Also, if you hear anything on the person who shot me, give me a call. "

After the cops walked out, Clever and Denise smirked at each other. Denise said, "Oh my gosh, I can't believe those cops were serious. That was like an awful comedy skit." Clever shook his head. He said, "I know. It was hard to keep a straight face talking to them fools. I wonder if they talked to any witnesses at the apartments." Denise replied, "For reals, though. Damn babe, now I'm over here legit thinking; I don't think you should ever take out the trash again." Clever exhaled loudly, shaking his head. He said, "Seriously, huh."

The doctor walked in, grabbed Clever's chart, and looked it over. The doctor asked Clever to wiggle his toes.

Clever did so. He asked if Clever felt up for leaving already. Clever replied, "Yeah, I think so." The doctor then said, "Okay. The nurse will come in with crutches. She'll show you how to use them. Once your mother comes to pick you up, you're free to go." Clever smiled. He said, "Alright, Thank you, doc. I appreciate everything you guys have done for me." The doctor reached out to shake Clever's hand and wished Clever luck on his recovery.

Shortly after, the nurse walked in with crutches. She opened the package. She helped Clever to get out of bed and stand up. The nurse showed Clever how to use the crutches. He was in pain, but he picked it up rather quickly. "Okay. It looks like you're good to go, son. Go ahead and relax. I'm going to call your mom. I'll ask her to bring a change of clothes. What you were wearing last night had to be cut off of you."

Clever exclaimed, "Awwwwe those were my favorite jeans!" The nurse shrugged her shoulders. She said, "Hey, you're alive. You can buy a new favorite pair." Clever nodded his head. He replied, "You got me there. Thank you." The nurse said, "No problem. You two have a great day." They both thanked her as she exited the room.

Clever's mom showed up about thirty-five minutes later. As soon as he saw her, he said, "I'm sorry, mom. I'm sorry you had to stress or worry for me." Rosita said nothing. She gave her son a gentle hug and a loving kiss on the cheek.

Rosita then said, "Here go your clothes. I'm going to grab your release forms and go down to the OSHA office since I'm already here. You two meet me down there when you're ready." Clever asked, "What's OSHA?" Rosita explained that they might help to lower the hospital bills. Rosita said, "So when you get out of the waiting room, make a left. Then follow the signs." Denise said, "Okay. We're right behind you." Rosita left the room.

Denise helped Clever to put on his clothes. As she did so, he continuously looked at her with admiration in his eyes. When he was all dressed and ready to go, he said to Denise, "I got the best woman a man could ever ask for." He looked up to the sky, saying, "Thank you." He then gazed into Denise's eyes; he touched her cheek and said, "Thank you." Denise pressed her lips together. Then she smiled as she nodded her head.

Very slowly, Clever and Denise walked down to the OSHA office. When they stepped inside, Rosita was already speaking to someone about the bill. Denise told Clever to sit down while they waited. Clever was a little nervous to sit down because the chair looked too low for him. He offered Denise the seat explaining he would rather stand. Denise went ahead and sat down.

Rosita thanked the man for his help, gathered all of her papers, and walked towards the exit. Rosita paused in front of her son. She asked him if he was okay. Clever nodded his head yes as he answered, "I'm good." Rosita said, "I gotta make a stop to put in your prescription for pain killers. Then we can go home."

They all started for the exit together. Rosita decided to run ahead to grab the car and meet Clever and Denise at the pick-up/ drop-off location. When Rosita sat in the car, she put her arms up in the air, saying, "Thank you for keeping my son as safe as possible. I love you so much. I appreciate all that you do for my family and me."

Rosita drove up to where she said she would meet Clever and Denise. She could see them walking toward the exit. Poor Clever was walking so slow with a look of discomfort on his face. When he finally got to the car, he slowly inched his way onto the front passenger seat. He felt intense pain in his leg as he attempted to sit down. Once he was seated and somewhat comfortable, Denise closed the door. She went to the backseat. The crutches went in first; then she sat down next to them.

As they pulled onto the street, Clever asked, "Mom, can we stop to get some burritos? I'm hungry." Rosita snapped her tongue against the top of her palate. She replied, "Fool, you just got out of the hospital. Do you know what that means? That means I have hospital bills to pay. So you can eat what we have at the house. I made chicken enchiladas yesterday. There's also beans de la olla."

Clever smirked. He looked over at his mom and said, "Fuck it, I like your enchiladas. Hey mom, don't worry about the bills. I'll pay whatever it costs. How much did it come to?" Rosita responded, "It was over six thousand dollars. I got them to lower it to one thousand." Clever replied, "Damn, what a difference, huh? I'll give you half of the money when we get home." Rosita nodded.

She laughed as she said, "Well, in that case, do you want a burrito, honey?" Clever laughed too. He tried to rub his hands together, but it hurt too much. Clever responded, "Naw mom, I'm good. Now you got me thinking about those enchiladas." Rosita asked Denise, "What about you, mija? Do you want me to stop and get you something to eat?" Denise replied, "No, thanks, mama Sita. I'm Okay."

Rosita pulled into the shopping center parking lot off of Glenoaks. She parked and ran into the pharmacy to drop off Clever's prescription. When she got back into the car, Rosita tossed the bag at Denise. "I'll let you give them to him when he needs them," Said Rosita. Clever chuckled then jokingly said, "Oh, so you trust her with my medication more than you trust me?" Rosita didn't answer. Instead, she started the car and drove towards home.

They pulled into the apartment parking lot. Rosita shifted the gear into park. She turned to her right side placing her hand atop Clever's arm. She calmly said, "You have no idea how relieved I am that you are okay, mijo. I have to head into work for a little while. I'll be home with the boys in a few hours. Take it easy and rest."

Denise grabbed the crutches and met Clever outside his door. She opened up his door. She said, "Okay, tell me what you need me to do papash. I don't wanna hurt you." Clever insisted, "It's alright, mamash, I got this." Denise stepped back and let Clever get out of the car. Clever was in so much pain. Denise wished she could do something to make him feel better. She thought it might be more helpful simply to stay out of his way.

Denise bent over to thank Rosita for the ride home. Rosita answered, "Thank you for taking care of my baby. Call your parents. I love you, mijita." Denise touched her heart with her right hand. "There's nowhere I'd rather be than by his side and in this family. I love you too, mama Sita. Have a good day at work. We'll see you when you get home," replied Denise. Rosita smiled and winked at Denise. Denise closed the passenger door.

A couple of the guys were having a smoke session near the parking lot. One of them pointed, saying, "Mira no mas, Clever's already back from the hospital." They walked over to meet Clever. They wanted to see how he was doing. Clever shook Johnny and Manuel's hands. They asked how he was feeling. Clever said, "I'm in a little bit of pain. But I'm not even tripping dawg. It could have been worse, you know?" Manuel responded, "Símon, you got real lucky G. It's good to see you and know you're alright. That would have been a tough pill to swallow since we're still not over the loss of the homie Grumps."

Clever nodded, "I know my boy. I wondered if I was going to see him and the other homies or live to see another day." Johnny said, "Well, thankfully, it was another day you got to see. Que no? Listen, G, we'll let you get inside and chill. Si quieres, we'll hit you up with a smoke session mas alrato G." Clever said, "Actually, smoking isn't a good idea. They shot me in the chest. But if you can get me some edibles, that might help." Manual shook his head and said, "I got you, G." The guys shook both Clever and Denise's hands.

Clever and Denise made their way into the apartment. Clever slowly sat on the couch. Denise walked over to the kitchen, calling out, "Do you want frijoles too or just the enchiladas?" "Los dos por favor," answered Clever. Denise warmed his food in the microwave. As it heated up, she moved a dinner tray table in front of him. Denise placed the pills down with a cup of water. She walked back into the kitchen to get a fork and napkin. When the microwave beeped, Denise grabbed the plate out and walked it over to Clever. Clever smiled, saying, "Thank you, baby girl." She leaned toward Clever slowly, kissing him on the forehead. Denise walked back into the kitchen to make herself a plate as well.

Denise was getting nervous about being alone with Clever. Everything happened so fast that she didn't have time to process any of it. Now that the craziness had calmed, Denise didn't know if the topic was safe to talk about or not. So she decided she wouldn't bring anything up at all about the shooting. If Clever ever wanted to talk about it, that was fine too.

Around 3:30 p.m., there was a knock at Clever's front door. Denise opened the door to find it was Miranda and Isela. They tightly hugged Denise at the same time. Denise hugged them both equally as tight. She then welcomed them in. Miranda sounding very concerned, asked Clever, "Awe, Clever, are you alright, mijo?" Clever, looking relaxed, sighed, and said, "Yeah, I'm good."

Miranda then slapped him on the back of his head, shouting, "Well, good menso. You scared the shit out of us! I fucking told you. Didn't I fucking tell your stupid ass?" Miranda looked like she wanted to keep scolding Clever. She caught and collected herself. Tears ran down her cheeks. Very quietly, Miranda said, "It's not cool what you guys put your loved ones through for mere ignorance and selfishness. Please let this be your second chance to get your life together."

Clever sat very still as he heard Miranda out. He put his head down as he replied, "It's not that easy to just walk away. I chose to bang. But I will slow my roll eventually. I know I have to grow up and take care of my family. I want to give them the best. Denise deserves that and more. But I can't just give them my two weeks' notice and say it's been fun. I committed. I tell myself that once I earn enough stripes, I'll slow down or stop. That's why I been so active. That way, my days of putting in work might be over much sooner. But even then, I'm marked for life to all enemigas. They don't give a shit if 'I don't bang anymore.'"

Miranda rubbed Clever in the back of the head where she had previously slapped him. She leaned his head on her stomach, saying, "I know how it is Danny. I know. That's why I asked you not to get involved in the first place. Just know that you don't have to stay trapped in this world forever. There are ways to distance from this life, as we talked about this weekend. I'm glad you're okay, menso."

Denise sat quietly. Although she agreed with Miranda, Denise was on the same boat as Clever. They got put on the hood together, and they claimed that they would gang bang for life. Isela held up the hawk feather that Clever spotted on the camping trip. She peyote stitched it with a design using red, white, black, and yellow beads. She said, "I made this for you, G. I wanted to tell you to keep it the day you spotted it, but I wanted to hook it up for you first."

Isela walked in front of Clever, saying, "I have been taught that the hawk brings clarity, insight, and guidance. Hawk is one of the messengers between us and spirit. Hawk was warning us. I take partial responsibility for not listening. This feather is for you. I'm going to gift it and hand it to you in the way I was taught to gift a sacred medicine item. I will hold it out to you three times, and when I hold it out the fourth time, it is yours to take."

Isela extended her arms and brought them back three times, the fourth time she stretched out her arms and held them out, Clever slowly reached towards Isela's hands to grab the feather. As he admired the feather and beadwork, he said, "Wow, Isela, this is dope. Thank you so much, homegirl." Isela smiled and said, "You're welcome, G."

Isela suddenly felt flushed; she excused herself and stepped outside for some air. Isela saw a couple that she knew; they were arguing on the sidewalk near the busy street. It seemed pretty one-sided from the looks of it. Adolfo was shouting some very vulgar words to his girlfriend, Annette.

Annette quietly stood there and took everything he said and did to her. She didn't fight back or try to walk away. Isela wanted to tell him something. She also felt like it wasn't any of her business. Maybe Annette accepted this treatment because she grew accustomed to it. Or perhaps she just didn't know her power.

Growing up in the apartments, Isela had seen how some girls would get abused as children. Those same girls grow up, psychologically damaged, finding these kinds of relationships. She believed this wasn't the case with Annette. Isela decided to walk over to the couple. With her back to him, she stood in front of Adolfo.

Isela looked Annette in the eyes as she said, "You hold more power than you know. You are a woman. Women are powerful beings. Mija, you have every reason to love yourself. Respect yourself. As soon as you realize that you are greatness, everyone around you will see it too.

"Please don't allow yourself to get treated like this. Many generations before us, our men respected their women because they knew how powerful we are. We are givers of life. Somewhere in this new world of un-civilization, we lost ourselves. We forgot our ways. But it's time for you to find yourself, Mija. I believe you were placed here for a reason. Look inside and find your reason. You will achieve great things when you realize your own potential. Remember what you told me on the steps? It's time."

The whole time Isela spoke to Annette, Adolfo was yelling at Isela to mind her business while saying vulgar things. It was background noise to Isela, as she didn't hear one word of it. Isela never once acknowledged Adolfo. Still, Adolfo knew better than to put a hand on Isela, so he continued yelling. Isela grabbed the young woman's hands and gazed deep into her eyes. As Isela did this, she thought, "Stand in your power. Move forward with your greatness." Isela let go of Annette's hands and walked away. Annette heard every word Isela said.

On the day Isela was referring to: Annette sat out on the steps smoking a blunt. Isela walked out of Suzy's apartment. She smiled and waved to Annette. She took a second glance at her, Isela's eyes grew wide.

Isela walked up to Annette and looked her face over as she whispered, "Tell me this puto didn't put hands on you again, Annette?" Annette took a hit off of her blunt. She rolled her eyes and head to the right, as she nodded her head yes. Isela said in a low tone of voice, "What the fuck dude? Why do you stay?"

Annette looked up to the sky as she let out a cloud of smoke, she replied, "It wasn't always like this, you know? In the beginning, he treated me like a queen. Fuck, homie even used to open doors for me. For the first year and some change, he was such a gentleman. I know it's the drugs that have him acting like this fucked up asshole. As of right now, I don't have anywhere to go. My pride won't let me go to my parents.

"I'm saving up little by little. Eventually, when I save enough for a down payment and a few months of rent, I will pack my shit and leave." Isela shook her head side to side as she began to say, "I hope you do get away from this situation. Some people just become accustomed to it and stick around. That's a horrible way to live or die. If I can help you in any way, please ask." Annette nodded with gratitude and replied, "I know, this isn't the life I want at all, trust. I feel a little stuck between a hard place and a rock right now, but this shit won't last."

ANNETTE AND ADOLFO

nnette lived in Panorama City with her two brothers, mom, and dad. Her father was Acjachemen from San Juan Capistrano, and her mother was Kumeyaay from San Diego through her mother and Cahuilla from Coachella Valley through her father. When Annette was 19, she hung out a lot with a guy named Eric. Eric's sister Lesly lived in the apartments. One day Annette went to hang out with Eric and his sister at her residence.

Lesly was dating a guy named Albert. Albert, Lesly, Eric, and Anette hung out in the living room with the door open. Albert's sister and brother lived next door; they were Yaqui and Mayo from the Cáhita tribe in Sinaloa. As Albert's brother passed by, he noticed Annette. Albert hadn't talked to his brother in over two months due to a previous argument. So Albert was tripped out when his brother suddenly stood at the front door, talking nicely and offering to buy them some beer.

Albert's brother Adolfo introduced himself to Annette. He asked her if she would like to come with him to the store to choose her drink. Annette didn't think anything of it; she agreed to go. When they got to his truck, he opened the door for her.

They got to the store, and Adolfo said, "Hold on, let me get your door." Annette said, "That's okay; I can get it." Adolfo responded, "I know you can. When you're with me, I would like it if I could open your door. Is that okay?" Annette smiled and nodded. They walked into the grocery store headed straight to the liquor and beer aisle. Annette grabbed a 32 pack of beer and handed it to Adolfo. Together they talked while walking to pay at the cash register. It was mostly Adolfo who asked personal questions trying to get to know Annette better.

When they got to the apartment, Adolfo parked his truck in the street. They walked toward the entrance. Once in front of the gate, Adolfo asked Annette to hold the beer while he unlocked and opened the gate door. As she held the case of beer, he pulled his keys out, then turned toward her and attempted to kiss her. Annette turned around, dodging his kiss as she shouted for Lesly.

Adolfo turned to open the gate door. He held the gate open then grabbed the beer. Lesly came running out, asking what was wrong. Annette told her, "Your cuñado just tried to kiss me." Lesly laughed as she asked sarcastically, "Really, Adolfo?" Adolfo apologized to Annette, explaining, "You're just so beautiful I had to try." Annette responded, "Whatever man, don't do that shit again."

When they got to Lesley's apartment, Annette went straight to Eric and sat right next to him. Adolfo stayed for a bit to drink and chop it up. He asked his brother Albert, "When are you going to let me cook some of my famous fish tacos for you?" Albert said, "Shit, whenever." Adolfo said, "But Annette's gotta be here when I make them."

Albert turned to Annette, insisting, "He makes the best fish tacos, man, you gotta try em." Annette replied, "I don't care to eat things that smell like an unclean choncha." Adolfo laughed then replied, "These don't smell bad, and they taste like clean choncha." Annette smirked as she shook her head, and rolled her eyes, then responded, "I don't know. We'll see what's up."

Adolfo felt he had overstayed his welcome with Annette. He stood up and excused himself, claiming, "It's about that time; I gotta go feed my girl." Eric asked, "Your girl?" "Yeah, my horse," explained Adolfo. Eric nodded his head, gesturing that he understood. Everyone, including Annette, said goodbye to Adolfo.

A minute after Adolfo walked out of the apartment, Albert turned to Annette, claiming, "Yo, my brother has a huge crush on you." Annette replied, "Yeah, I got that after he tried to rush me." Surprised, Albert asked, "He tried to rush you?" Lesley laughed, saying, "Yup, he tried." Albert laughed, explaining, "He hasn't even talked to me in weeks, so I knew it had to be about you."

A week or so later, Annette went back to Lesley's place. They were playing cards at the table when Adolfo knocked on the door. He came in and sat with them. After some time, Annette excused herself to smoke a bowl in the bathroom. Adolfo asked if he could join her. Annette stared into his eyes. She raised an eyebrow then shrugged her shoulders as she said, "Sure."

Adolfo sat on the bathroom counter as Annette prepared to pack the bowl. She asked, "Do you smoke often?" Adolfo replied, "No, I don't like yesca." Annette made a baffling noise and asked, "So why did you want to smoke with me?" Adolfo answered, "Because I like you." Annette nodded her head and looked to the right of her. She quickly looked back at Adolfo and asked, "Do you have a drug of preference?" Adolfo said, "Yes. I do coke." Annette said, "Well, do you want to put some on the weed?" Adolfo's eyes got big as he asked, "You like coke too?"

Annette answered, "Nope. But I'll do a coco puff with you this once." Adolfo grabbed his vile and sprinkled some cocaine on top of the weed. They sat in the bathroom, smoking and talking. Adolfo asked Annette, "Do you like guys who do coke?" Annette answered, "No. I think that guys who do coke are woman beaters. Now, I don't care if I was with a guy that did coke. But if he hit me, I'm not going out like that." Adolfo said, "Well, I'd never hit that beautiful face."

When they came out of the bathroom, Adolfo asked Albert if it would be okay to ask Annette out on a date. Albert said with an attitude, "I'm not her keeper, ask her." Adolfo said, "I just didn't want to upset you or Lesly by asking your friend out." Albert said, "I don't care, bro. Go for it."

Adolfo asked Annette out on a date. Annette said, "I'm not really into dating." Adolfo added, "It doesn't have to be considered a date. I can take you to meet my horse and take you for a ride." Annette smiled. She said, "That sounds like something I would like." Adolfo smiled too then said, "Can I pick you up tomorrow around 4:00 p.m.?" Annette replied, "I'll meet you here." Adolfo couldn't hide his excitement. He excused himself by explaining he had to get ready for work for the following day.

The next day, Annette met Adolfo just as she said she would. He took her to a ranch in Sylmar; it was a huge yard. Adolfo showed Annette around first. Afterward, he took Annette to meet his horse Cherry. Cherry and Annette had an instant connection. Adolfo brought Cherry out of her stall and saddled her up. He explained how she needed to put her foot on the stirrup and pull herself up. He also helped her up.

Once Annette was comfortable, Adolfo jumped on behind her. They went on a ride around the neighborhood. They rode down in a small canyon behind El Cariso Park.

They talked the entire time and found they had a lot in common. Adolfo's birthday was the day after Annette's. Both of their birth sun signs in astrology were that of the Leo. Annette felt bliss as she put her guard down, sitting on the back of the horse with Adolfo's arms around her waist. Adolfo felt the same way. He was glad she was opening up to him.

They trotted back to the ranch. Adolfo helped Annette to get off of Cherry. He unsaddled Cherry and washed her off. He then walked her into her stall. He set Cherry up with some food then stepped outside of the corral to stand near Annette. Annette was still admiring Cherry. She told Adolfo, "You are so lucky to have her." Adolfo smiled and said, "Yeah, I agree; she's wonderful. Any time you wanna see her or go for a ride, just let me know." Annette smiled and said, "Thank you."

Adolfo looked over towards the west and told Annette, "It's getting late. Can I get you home?" Annette agreed. On the drive home, Adolfo asked if he could keep in touch and text her. Annette wanted to know Adolfo better at this point, so she said, "Yeah, that's okay. What's your number? I'll text you." After Adolfo stated his phone number, they continued talking non-stop the whole drive home. Once they got to Annette's house, they sat and talked for another hour and a half before Annette excused herself to go inside.

Adolfo and Annette started talking every day and night. They began growing feelings for each other. Within days they became nearly inseparable. Two weeks after their first date, Annette started spending the night at Adolfo's place. Lesly and Albert placed bets on whether or not Adolfo and Annette were having sex.

One day Annette stopped into Lesly's pad to say what's up. Lesly decided to ask Annette, "Keep it real foolia, does he know how to work it?" Annette made a face, asking, "What? How would I know?" Lesly said, "Come on, you stayed there night after night already. You expect me to believe you guys haven't done the damn thing?" Annette lightly shoved Lesly at the shoulder and responded, "Just because you have sucia tendencies, doesn't mean that I do. He's been charming."

Lesly studied Annette's eyes and laughed as she said in surprise, "Oh my gosh, you truly didn't do anything with him yet. I owe Albert twenty bucks." Annette put her hand to her chest as she gasped. Then with a giggle, she raised her voice, saying, "Oh hell naw, you guys are so freakin' petty. Bye." Annette got up to leave. Lesly shouted, "Oh, come on, you know you love me!" Annette lifted her middle finger in the air as she walked toward the door. She opened the door and shouted, "I felt it, and it was huge!" She then slammed the door behind her. Lesly screamed out in laughter.

That night as Annette and Adolfo lay in his bed cuddling, he asked her, "I was wondering if you would like to move in here with me?" Annette backed away from Adolfo. She looked him in the face and asked, "Are you serious, pa?" Adolfo smirked and said, "I mean you been here every night, and now I can't imagine a night without you here. And I don't want to." Annette said, "You gotta meet my parents before I can move in. Can we plan a date to have dinner with them?"

Adolfo replied, "Yeah, mija, that'll be cool. And I will be the one to ask for permission if that's okay." Annette nodded her head in excitement. She quickly leaned in to kiss him. She playfully pushed her way on top of him as she continued kissing him."

Two nights after they discussed living together, they went to dinner with Annette's parents. Both parents told her that they just wanted her to be happy. They all shared a pleasant dinner. Annette and Adolfo thought it went well. When they got to the car, Annette's parents cringed and agreed they didn't care for or trust Adolfo.

The next day Annette went home to grab her clothes and necessities. The next few months were magical for Annette. She felt blessed to be a part of not only Adolfo's life but all of his nieces and nephews who she grew close with while she lived with them. Adolfo and Annette shared a room with his 12-year-old nephew.

Getting out of the shower one day before work, Annette broke her toenail from the tip of the nail to the cuticle. It was bleeding out pretty bad. Annette called into work, but no one answered, so she left a message. She called back later and again, no answer. Annette left a second message. She cleaned her toe up and stayed off her foot all day. When she went in to work the next day, her boss fired her for 'no-showing' without warning. They claimed not to have gotten the messages. She got home bummed out.

Adolfo told Annette, "You don't need a job any way mi vida. I'll take care of you." Adolfo convinced her to stay home. It wouldn't end up being a good idea for Annette because she found herself smoking more weed and being less productive. It wouldn't take long for Annette to realize that work was necessary for her. She got a new job doing clerical work.

A year into living with him, Adolfo met a woman who started renting a trailer at the ranch where he housed Cherry. Adolfo started hanging out with her, which led to them doing speed together. Sooner than later, he began an affair with the woman. The more addicted he became to speed, the more the trust issues that he had festering within, began to show.

He started causing arguments with Annette over nothing. Every other day Adolfo was accusing Annette of cheating and talking to other guys. He put his hands on her a couple of times. Annette fought and hit back. There were times they physically rumbled. He always apologized with lovely gifts and a weed sack.

For her twentieth birthday, she got angry with him and left. She started on foot to go hang out with some friends. On her walk, a man grabbed her vagina and took off running. Filled with rage, Annette began to chase him. The man ran down a dark street, Annette came to a halt. She ran down the busy street to a church nearby. She called Adolfo and told him what happened.

Adolfo was there within three minutes. She got in the truck and said, "I just need you to drive me down that street and watch me mop his ass up." As they drove toward the dark street, Annette spotted the man. She shouted, "There he is!" He was walking back, possibly to look for Annette or maybe another victim.

Before she could open the door, Adolfo put the truck in park. He ran up and socked the man in the face. Just then, the man pleaded, "It wasn't me." Adolfo beat the man brutally, then walked back to the truck and drove off. By that point, whatever anger Annette felt toward her man entirely melted away.

Adolfo drove home, parked the truck, and said, "Wait here." He went inside and grabbed blankets and pillows. He walked up to the truck door and opened it. Adolfo gestured his head, signaling for Annette to follow him.

Annette got out of the truck and walked towards the back of it. Adolfo climbed into the bed of the truck. He laid the blankets and pillows down. He reached his arm out and helped her get into the bed of the truck. They spent the night under the stars cuddling and talking until they fell asleep.

In the morning, they woke up to a flock of green parrots flying overhead squawking and circling the block for a few minutes. Annette said, "This is a birthday I will never forget." She leaned in and kissed Adolfo. Adolfo said, "Let's get ready, and I'll take you for your birthday breakfast."

The next couple of weeks were back to normal until Adolfo came home one day with a candle that had something that looked like the grim reaper on it. Annette asked about it. He said, "It's a prayer candle. La Santa Muerte. She'll watch over me and keep me safe." Annette asked, "Safe from what? What's going on?" Adolfo hugged her and responded, "Just safe." Annette let it go.

One night Annette was awakened by a voice in her head that warned her, "Get up, look to the left!" Annette arose, sitting in the bed. She glanced over to see Adolfo crawling on the floor on his hands and knees. He had his head down, but his eyes fixated on her with a butcher knife in his left hand.

Annette heard the voice say, "Run." Annette leaped out of bed and ran out of the bedroom. She ran toward the living room and ran outside; Adolfo followed her out and chased her for five blocks. Frightened and barefoot, she stood at the corner of a busy street, realizing she was in her pajamas and didn't know where to go.

When Adolfo reached her, he no longer had the knife in his hand. He looked perplexed as he asked her what she was doing out there. Frantic, Annette said, "Stay away from me." Adolfo responded, "Baby, what's wrong?" Almost in tears, Annette replied, "You Adolfo. You're what's wrong. Why would you stare at me like that?" Adolfo asked, "Like what?" Annette continued, "And chase me for blocks?"

Adolfo looked extremely confused as he looked around. He pleaded, "Look, it's late; you can't be out here by yourself; you might get hurt." Annette angrily said, "I might get hurt being home with you, so I'll take my chances."

Annette no longer felt threatened. She sat on the curb, placed her elbows on her legs, and plopped her head on her hands. Adolfo didn't know what else to do or say, so he sat next to her quietly. After a few minutes, Annette walked home. Adolfo said nothing and followed behind her. She kept looking over her shoulder to keep an eye on him.

When they got to the front door, she said you're sleeping on the couch. She walked into the living room, ran to the room, and locked the door behind her. She checked to make sure the window was locked in the room and laid in the bed staring blankly at the ceiling. As she laid there, she thought about everything that had just taken place.

Annette thought about leaving. She didn't have as much money saved up as she would have liked to afford a decent place alone. This event would be the push needed to start looking for a place. She found a small apartment complex that offered a studio apartment that she felt she could soon afford. Annette would continue tolerating Adolfo as she continued to save money secretly.

THE SHOW MUST GO ON

Two days after she got back from camping, Gabby called the promoter back and agreed to do the music event. The lady asked her to come down to do a photoshoot for promotional purposes.

Gabby and Miranda showed up to the photoshoot, ready to get Gabby's pictures snapped. They met two of the promoters in charge of the event, Sid and Lisa. Lisa complimented Gabby's beauty.

Lisa heavily touched up Gabby's make up. As she did so, she explained that the makeup makes all the difference once Gabby gets under the lighting. When Lisa finished, Miranda said, "Dang, what a huge difference; you were gorgeous before, but, wow, you look gorgeous, Gabs."

Gabby smiled, asking, "Can I see?" Lisa handed Gabby a mirror. Gabby moved her head side to side as she checked out her makeup. Gabby said, "Oh my gosh. I am gorgeous." The ladies laughed at Gabby's response. Lisa looked to Sid, saying, "Okay, she's ready for her close up." First, Sid took Gabby outside to pose in the natural sunlight. After about forty minutes of being outside, Sid brought Gabby back inside to take pictures and make a promotional video in front of a green screen.

Before the video, Sid presented Gabby with the contract to sign. He told her what to expect at the venue, "There's gonna be fun festivities for the kids, we'll have a mechanical bull, food, drinks, over thirty performers, we're going to have some hilarious comedians." Lisa asked, "Do you have C.D.s and shirts or other merch made?" Gabby answered, "No, but I can have a mixtape, and I can have shirts ready." Lisa responded, "Okay perfect, bring your mixtape and shirts. We'll have a table ready for you to set up your booth."

Gabby asked, "What time will I perform?" Lisa replied, "We'll have you up sometime between five to six O'clock in the evening. Gabby thought it all sounded great, so she filled out her information and signed the contract. Without asking for a copy of the contract, Gabby and Miranda shook the promoters' hands and now had thirty tickets to sell.

Sid let the girls look through the pictures. They were very impressed with the photos. Sid said, "Okay, let's do the promotional video, and then we'll let you go." Gabby took two blooper takes before getting it right on the third take. Gabby and Miranda were at the shoot for about five hours.

Gabby sold tickets as soon as they got to the apartments. After buying tickets of their own, Miranda, Isela, and Lori each took some tickets to sell. The thirty tickets sold within nine days.

Isela made shirts with a picture of Gabby holding a fist extended out in a punch before her with a microphone at hand. In the corner of the image at an angle, it read Gabby V.

The day of the event came. The girls all piled up in Suzy's van. They brought an E.Z. up tarp and some lawn chairs, along with Gabby and Isela's merchandise. They got to the venue at 11:50 a.m. The event time started at noon. The venue looked empty. Gabby text one of the promoters asking if the gate was open so they can begin setting up. The promoter text back, "Come back at 3:00 p.m."

Gabby told the ladies, "They're tripping, they just said to come back at three." Suzy said, "Well, what should we do 'til then?" Gabby asked, "Well, do you guys wanna park the Van and walk around Hollywood Blvd?" The girls agreed. They killed time walking around, snapping pics, acting like goofballs, and having a great time.

Isela realized and pointed out that it was already 2:50 p.m. The girls headed back to go set up. The gate was still closed. The girls could see the stage was barely being set up. Gabby said, "That's weird; the first act was supposed to be on by 1:00 p.m. Gabby called Lisa, who didn't answer. She texted Gabby, saying to come back around 5:00 p.m. Gabby didn't like that. Gabby text back saying, "No. I'm here, and I expect someone to open the gate so I can set up." Minutes later, the other promoter Sid, drove up and opened the gate. The girls set up and hung out while they waited.

Some background drama occurred with the promoters, which would end up affecting the sound and the artists. Gabby's set got pushed back further and further. By the time 11:00 p.m. came around, Lisa brought Gabby backstage and began arguing with another promoter over who would go next. Lisa demanded Gabby go up next. Finally, they agreed. Gabby was uncomfortable as she felt the intensity of the tension between both promoters.

When Gabby got up on stage, the sound man was over-powering her vocals with the music. Gabby was straining to try and make it work. Frustrated, Gabby told the d.j to stop the music. She apologized to the crowd. The whole audience began cheering her on. She was surprised there was not one boo from the crowd.

She knew if her brother Denis were there, he would have booed. Gabby tried the song again but had the same results.

Still, she finished the song. She told the d.j not to play the next track. Gabby decided to go acapella with the following two songs. To her bewilderment, Gabby received a standing ovation. She felt so emotional from the whole experience.

As Gabby walked back to her booth, people were stopping her to give her props for her set. On the drive home, all the girls excitingly talked about Gabby's performance. Gabby said, "Man, that was unreal fam! They should have booed me off the stage. Instead, I watched the hope in each of their eyes as they cheered me on. They all seemed to believe in me. And it made me feel like; I don't know, like they saw something in me.

"Something I don't think I saw in myself. Like I'm really gonna make it somewhere in this career." Isela said, "Baby, you are going to make it far in this game. You have everything going for you. You got the sound, the words, the look, you are the whole package." Gabby was beaming as she said, "Thank you. In our own ways, I think we're all going to be successful. You just wait and see."

The next day Suzy and Isela took a trip to target. On their way back, they were posted at a red light on Osborne St. and San Fernando Rd. heading east. Isela was sitting passenger. The light turned green, Suzy pushed the gas, but the car shut off and refused to start. Turning the key and pushing the gas and brake pedals, Suzy looked at Isela with a look of fear on her face. Isela asked, "Oh no, what the fuck just happened?" Suzy replied, "Dude, this van's tripping." Suzy placed her leg outside the door and began giving the car a push while pressing on the gas. It started to go. Suzy said, "That was fucking weird."

As they pulled up to Osborne St. and Glenoaks Blvd, they hit another red light. They were in the furthest left lane to make a left turn. When the light turned green, once again, the car wouldn't go. Suzy looked over to Isela. She said, "Okay, you're gonna have to steer. I'm gonna go behind the car and push. No matter what happens, do not hit the brakes just drive." Isela nodded. Suzy put the hazard lights on. She stepped out of the van and walked to the back. Isela moved over to the driver seat.

As Suzy reached the back of the van, her aunt Lola noticed her. Lola was in the car behind the van. Lola looked towards her oldest daughter asking, "What do you think's wrong?" Evelyn replied, "I don't know, mom. Should we stick around just in case?" Lola agreed. Lola had her two daughters Evelyn and Andrea in the car with her.

With her back to the van, her hands under the bumper, and wearing skinny jeans and heeled boots, Suzy began pushing. Isela stepped on the gas. The car started to pick up momentum. Now the van was on Glenoaks heading up hill.

Suzy ran alongside the van, placing her hand on the passenger door, she flung the door open. She kept up with the van as she tried to gain the courage to jump in. She threw her left foot up first allowing her right foot to follow. Unfortunately for Suzy, her right heel slipped. Suzy stumbled out of the car and rolled onto the street. As she fell out, she yelled, "Keep going!"

Suzy bounced up almost as quickly as she fell. She dusted herself off, quickly checking that she was intact. Her pants tore on the left knee. Her left knee was cut and throbbing. More than anything, she was embarrassed. Suzy's aunt and cousins watched the whole scenario happen before their eyes.

Suzy's aunt Lola was freaking out. Her cousin Evelyn was giggling. Lola shouted, "Oh my God, oh my god. Do you think she's okay?" Lola pulled over immediately. Evelyn laughed out, "Mom, it's Suzy, of course, she's okay!" Suzy ran over to her Aunt Lola's back passenger door and jumped in. Lola asked Suzy, "Mija, are you alright?" Suzy quickly responded, "Yeah, Tía, I'm fine." Evelyn giggled again and shouted, "See, I told you, mom!"

Isela couldn't believe she had just watched Suzy slip and fall out of the passenger side. She wanted so desperately to stop and help Suzy. Isela also didn't want to Anger Suzy. Just as directed, she kept driving to the apartments.

On the remainder of the drive, Isela replayed the image of Suzy falling out of the car. Isela couldn't stop laughing. Luckily for Isela, the gate to the parking lot was open. She sloppily pulled the van into Suzy's parking spot. Isela waited nervously by the van. Unsure of what Suzy's reaction would be.

Lola pulled in right next to the van. Suzy hopped out, thanking her aunt for the ride. Suzy walked over to Isela. Isela said, "I'm glad you're okay. I felt so fucked up not being able to stop." Suzy replied, "Naw, my main concern was getting the van home without a tow truck! Thanks for your help, ma."

A group of the guys stood around the staircase. As Suzy and Isela walked up, one of the guys asked Suzy, "What the fuck happened to you?" Suzy, still filled with adrenaline, hadn't quite processed what just happened. As soon as the question came about, she burst out in tears. Isela looked at the guy and shook her head. She quietly followed Suzy up the stairs.

The two ladies walked into Suzy's room. Suzy's left knee was bleeding through her jeans. She went to the bathroom to clean it up. When she returned, she jumped on her bed and stared at the ceiling. "Ugh, I still can't believe that just happened." Isela agreed. She said, "I know. I swear that kind of shit would only happen to you." The girls giggled.

Later that same night, Gabby was in the parking lot chilling with her homie Tripps and a kid named Ricky. They were sitting in Gabby's car, smoking a blunt. Ricky sat shotgun, Gabby sat in the driver seat, and Tripps was in the back seat. Tripps told Gabby that Ricky wanted to get put on the hood. Gabby shrugged. She didn't feel like Ricky had what it took to do what these guys do.

Tripps stoned off his ass, decided to pull out his Desert Eagle handgun to show it off. As he did so, he fired a shot. It was so close to Gabby's ear that she heard a constant loud ringing after the gunshot. Ricky got shot in the shoulder. Gabby turned back and gave Tripps a look of anger. "What the fuck, Tripps?" Gabby shouted. Tripps responded, "My bad. It was an accident."

Gabby said, "Alright, look, you need to get the fuck out my car, stash that shit and go home. I'm gonna take him to the hospital. Tripps nodded and began to exit the car. Gabby called out, "Tripps." He turned back, looking into Gabby's eyes. "Go home or go to Lil' Listo's house, but don't go anywhere else," Gabby said sternly. Tripps nodded again and took off.

Gabby told the kid to get in the back seat. He was holding his shoulder. His face expressed pain, but he didn't make a sound. On the drive to the hospital, Gabby instructed Ricky on what he would say. "Listen, when we get to the hospital, the staff and cops are going to question the shit out of you. They will ask the same questions over and over. Stick with the first story that you tell them.

They're gonna want you to make a statement in detail on what happened. You're gonna tell them that you were walking on Glenoaks and Pakooynga when some guys hit you up and shot you. You didn't hear where they were from. You didn't catch faces. All you remember was the gunshot.

I was coming home and saw you. I don't know you, but I couldn't leave you out there, so I told you to hop in, and I drove you to the hospital. Do that for me, and when your arm heals, I'll let you go rounds with Tripps. You guys can shake hands and call it a day. Is that clear?" Ricky answered, "Yes." Gabby said, "I hope so, cause if you fuck around and put Tripps on blast, you're gonna get it worse than a gunshot to the arm." Ricky nodded.

Gabby pulled in to the E.R. She parked and ran over to help Ricky out. Two of the hospital staff walked up, asking what happened. Gabby told her part of the story. The staff guided Ricky into the hospital. Gabby went to park in the lot; she sat there for a few minutes with both hands on the steering wheel. She replayed the scenario in her mind's eye, which had gone on 25 minutes prior.

She covered her face with both hands and shouted, "Holy fucking shit!" Gabby began to think, "That could have been me. He could have shot me point blank in the fucking head." Gabby was so mad at Tripps. She wanted to let him have it when she saw him next. She sat there for a while in such gratitude for being alive.

Gabby got off the car and walked into the hospital, she asked for Ricky. They directed her to the room where Ricky was. When she got to the room, Ricky's parents were already there. Ricky said, "This is the lady who brought me here." They thanked her for taking care of their baby boy. Gabby smiled. She looked over to Ricky and said, "Now that you're folks are here, I'll go ahead and leave you be. I hope you feel better soon, and I'm really sorry for what happened to you." Ricky said, "That's okay. Thank you." Gabby nodded her head. She turned to walk away.

As she drove home, she thought about Tripps and how he had become trigger happy lately. He had got his hands on four different guns that she knew about, and he was always itching to shoot at somebody. Before bed, she texted Tripps, telling him she'll visit in the morning. Then she said a prayer of gratitude.

The next morning Gabby got up and got ready. She walked over to Tripps' window. Gabby knocked on the window. Tripps looked out to see that it was Gabby. He put his index finger in the air, signaling to hold on, and disappeared. Gabby walked over to the nearest staircase. She stood on the stairs waiting for Tripps. Tripps approached Gabby and hugged her; they sat down on one of the steps together.

Gabby said, "You know I want an explanation." Tripps replied, "I know. First of all, fuck that fool. It wasn't really an accident. He's been chilling with enemigas, and I don't trust him." Gabby asked, "So why did you tell me he was gonna get put on?" Tripps replied, "I was just talking shit. He keeps pushing the issue that he wants to get put on. I let him talk about it, but fuck him. He could never be from my hood. I don't let him kick it hard because I think he's a fucking mole. I gave him something to go back and report que no?"

Gabby laughed as she told Tripps, "Well, I wish you would have put me up on game before I told him he could go heads up with you when he heals." Tripps said in an angry tone of voice, "I don't give a fuck I'll go heads up with his punk ass." Gabby shook her head side to side. She said, "You're stupid as fuck." Tripps laughed then proceeded to say, "Honestly, honestly, I thought about giving him a dome shot, but I couldn't do that in your car, though."

Gabby paused, looked down to her feet, and then glanced over at Tripps, Gabby looked him straight in the eyes as she said, "Last night after I took that kid to the hospital, I sat in my car for a while. After my ears stopped ringing so loud, I started thinking about how that could have been my head. One shot, just like that. I could have been taken out the game. That shit broke me down for a minute."

Tripps shaking his head side to side, said, "Na, that could never be you, man. Let me tell you why, 'cause you're real. You're one of the realest females alive. People like you, get respect. I would never hurt you. None of the homies here would ever hurt you. Matter of a fact, if anyone ever fucks with you, you have every right to come tell one of us, and we'll handle it."

Gabby had a quick flash of George on top of her. She nodded her head up and down, responding, "Yeah, I know Tripps. Thank you for that." Tripps nodded his head and placed his left hand over his right fist. Tripps asked Gabby, "Are you okay, homie?" Gabby shook her head as she quickly replied, "Yeah. I'm cool, G." Yearning to change the subject, Gabby asked Tripps to go with her to check her mailbox.

She scanned through the mail, looking for anything with her name on it. She had received a letter. Fabiola Jimenez was the name on the return address. Gabby looked over to Tripps, asking, "Isn't Fabiola Jimenez Locs' Rest in peace big sister?" Tripps replied, "Símon, she sent you a wíla?" Gabby said, "Yeah, I wonder what she has to say." Gabby closed the mailbox and locked it. She put her keys in her pocket and walked out to sit on the steps that lead into the mailroom. Tripps sat quietly next to Gabby as she opened the letter. Gabby read it out loud:

Dear Gabby,

First and foremost, I pray this letter finds you healthy and doing well in esta vida. I know you don't know me well. I'm sure you're wondering why the hell I'm writing to you. My name is Fabiola. I am Ivan Jimenez, aka Locs older sister. I am writing to you because I understand that you are a singer and a songwriter. I heard you have mad skills in the songs that you write. I would like you to write a song about what happened to Locs and me. Some hyna here who wrote short stories approached me. She asked me if I would let her tell my story. At the time, I didn't want it out there like that, so I said no. But as time passed, I thought more about it. I would rather have you get it out there, Gabby. You knew my brother, you know our story, and you know that this will be a meaningful story and song that many families can relate to when performed with the right passion and words. I'm going to tell you my version of the story in hopes that you decide to take this project on. I'm going to leave names out for obvious reasons. It's like this: Locs came and told me that he had gotten into a fight with a chump up the street. Locs put manos on him pretty good. The guys' homies didn't like that, so they decided since he fucked up their homie, they would take matters into their own hands and jump Locs. This was the start of it. After they jumped my carnal, they told him that he fucked up and he was going to get it. Locs told me that he felt like their threat was real, and he was going to die. I told him, "Bitches always say shit like that. You'll be fine." My brother had a look on his face that I never saw before.

He knew that his time was coming. One week later, he went to meet up with one of his homies in the apartment (I imagine to smoke some yerba.) Before he reached his homies pad, three guys approached him. He boxed with one of them and beat the guy up. The guys pulled out guns, Locs turned to run, but they shot him from the side and back. It was the three guys who he told me were going to do it. I heard gunshots. Shortly after, I heard tires screeching. One of Locs' homies came running to my door knocking non-stop until I opened it. He had a look of fear on his face; he saw everything from his window. All he had to say was, "Locs," and I took off running in the direction I had heard the shots fired. My baby brother, my right-hand man, was lying in the grass. I dropped to my knees, shaking him. I picked him up and held him as I screamed hysterically. Both of us now drenched in blood, I looked at my right palm and seen his blood covering it entirely, suddenly I snapped. I looked at his homie, the one who came to my door, in rage, I asked, "Who did this?" His eyes opened wide. He said he didn't know them. The cops questioned everyone, including Loc's homie, who witnessed it and me. Of course, no one said anything. Instantly Loc's homie knew when I snapped and what I had in mind. He kept saying the guys were too far to see their faces. I talked to another man who seen it happen. He was also scared to speak up. I told him, "Look, don't tell me nothing, I'm going to describe the guys who did it. If I'm right, I just need you to nod your head, yes." He ended up nodding yes. Now me, myself, personally, I am not into that gang bang, cholo shit. I wouldn't even date a cholo. But something clicked in me when I lost my brother. I decided to take these guys out myself. I killed two of the guys who killed my brother. I followed them as they walked up the street. I parked my car up ahead. I got out and waited for them to reach me. One of them asked, "How's your brother doing?" I replied, "Ask him when you see him." I shot the one who said that first. I went for the head. Then I shot the other guy twice in the back as he ran away from me. He clearly didn't get far. I hopped in the car and went home. There was one more guy I needed to get. I don't know if anyone saw me or what, but the third guy suspected that I was the one after them, and he ratted me out before I could get to him. The cops came to my pad and gaffled me up. They served me with a search warrant, as well as a warrant for my arrest. They found the strap I used for the murders in my room. Moms couldn't believe I could have been capable of such a thing. Fuck, maybe I wouldn't have had to do it if we lived in a safer community and if Locs didn't live that fucking lifestyle. I hated that he was a little gang banger. But anyway, I told moms that I was a big girl, I made this decision, and I was willing to face my consequence for my actions. The Judge sentenced me to life in prison with the possibility of parole. I lost my baby brother and, shortly after, my own life. With the possibility of parole, though, who knows, maybe I can make my life right again one day. I know I'll never be the same sweet innocent girl I once was. To be honest, it's a hard life in here. Most of these ladies are walking around with unhealed traumas of all kinds. Those issues lead to

them lashing out in reckless ways. I have to pretend
to be this hardcore, badass chick that I never was
before. I guess you can say I adapted pretty well.
The other ladies respect me, or maybe they fear me.
It doesn't matter, as long as they don't fuck with me.
When I first got to chowchilla, I fucked up the first
bitch that came at me crooked. She tried to punk me
on the yard. I smashed in her face. I went to solitary
confinement, and it sucked. But that wouldn't be my
last visit. I hold my own weight in here, that's for
sure. I'll be damned if I let anyone punk me, you
know? Now and then I drink some of that 'home-
made' to try to escape this hell, it doesn't work that
way though. But that's my story in a nutshell Gabby.
If you want to take it on, cool, if not, that's cool too.
Either way, I pray you do good and become suc-
cessful in your life, mujer. One day, I wanna hear
your success story on the radio or read it in one of
those big-time magazines or something. Get out
of that place where nothing good seems to happen.
It's with love and respect that I send these words.
Take care of yourself, Gabby.

Sincerely,
Fabiola"

Gabby and Tripps looked at each other. At the same
time, they said, "Fuuuuuuuuck." Tripps asked, "So are you
gonna do it, Gabs?" As Gabby folded the letter up and put
it back in the envelope, she replied, "I don't know, I mean,
how could I not? She asked me to do it. It's an honor to have
her permission. Yeah, fuck it, I'll write it. I'll write it and
send her the words or, better yet, visit her and sing it to her."

Tripps said, "That's what's up." Gabby opened her notebook and began writing on the spot. She wrote the first verse and thought of a hook she heard from a well-known rapper's song who she knew. He took and revised some words from an older song called love TKO. She changed his version as she wrote it down; she sang what she had written down for Tripps to hear and give feedback. Tripps nodded his head as she sang. When she finished, he said, "That's badass. Keep going."

Gabby started on the second verse and got stuck. She closed her book and said, "I'll pick it up later." Tripps said, "Let's smoke a blunt, and maybe that will motivate you. I gotta get my stash from the pad." Gabby agreed. They stood up and walked back to Tripps' pad.

Gabby sat at the stairs and waited. As she waited, she continued writing the second verse. She added the hook. When Tripps came back, Gabby said, "Verse two is complete. Now I need a third verse y ya." Tripps said, "You'll have it done before the day is over." Gabby nodded in agreement. As Tripps broke up the weed and rolled a blunt, Gabby sat working on the third verse. The song wouldn't have all of the descriptions that Fabiola mentioned, but it flowed well. Gabby decided this would sound better as a rap.

Gabby wrote a letter back to Fabiola to thank her for giving Gabby the honor of writing Fabiola's story. She wrote that she began writing the song immediately, and it was already complete. Gabby offered to visit Fabiola to read her the song.

HARD TO LET GO

Miguel received a phone call. It was a man Miguel dealt with a couple of times named Javi requesting some work. Miguel never had the best feeling about Javi, but they met through a mutual friend. This time, Javi mentioned twenty grand. Miguel agreed to make the trade.

Miguel immediately prepped the work and loaded his car up with his merchandise. Miguel came back into the house looking for Miranda. She was sitting at her desk doing homework. He stood at her doorway, admiring her for a minute. She looked up and shyly smiled.

Miguel said, "Mija, you make this family proud." Miranda's smile got bigger. Miguel continued, "I know you're gonna go far in life, mamash. You may not have the same financial opportunity as any rich kid. But you have both streets and book smarts; it's what you do with it that matters."

Miranda replied, "I know, Carnal." Miguel said, "Mira, I'm gonna go drop some work off to this man named Javi. I have his info written down on the table. If anything happens to me, I need you to share that info with Listo." Miranda asked, "What the fuck you mean, if anything happens to you? Like what?" Miguel replied, "You know this job is dangerous, mamash. I'm just saying."

Miranda insisted, "Well, let me go with you. I'll hold the strap." Miguel disagreed, "No, mamash, it's a school night. I need you to stay at home. I'll be back in a couple of hours.

Don't worry about me." Miguel walked up and gave Miranda a big hug. When he did so, Miranda felt what Miguel had been feeling. It was an uneasy feeling. After Miranda finished her homework, she sat in the living room, waiting for Miguel.

Miguel placed his wallet in the glove box, locked it, and drove off to the spot where he agreed to meet Javi. Javi was sitting in another car alone. He got out of his car with a suitcase at hand and walked up to Miguel's passenger door. He sat in Miguel's car. They briefly talked about business.

Javi opened up the suitcase to show Miguel the money. They both got off of the car to get the work from the trunk. Once the work was exposed, a man quietly hopped out of a dumpster. He was holding a handgun with a silencer attached to the barrel. He crept around the driver's side of the car and shot Miguel in the head. Miguel's body dropped to the floor. Javi and the man grabbed the work, the money, and everything in Miguel's pockets, including his cell phone.

A couple of hours came and went. Miranda called Miguel's phone. When there was no answer, Miranda felt the worst feeling she had ever felt in her gut. She sat on the couch the entire night, staring at the front door.

The time came for her to get up and get ready for school. Miranda headed over to the apartments to pick up Suzy. Suzy got in and hugged Miranda. Suzy said, "You look exhausted, mujer, que paso? Looking and sounding worried, Miranda quickly responded, "I don't know." Suzy asked, "You don't know?" Miranda repeated, "I don't know." Miranda began to drive off. Suzy said, "You don't know about what?"

With a shaky voice, Miranda responded, "Miguel. Last night Miguel said he'd be home in a couple of hours. He didn't come home at all. Miguel felt something before leaving; he didn't say it. It was in the way he looked and talked to me. When he hugged me, I felt it too. I don't know. I don't know where he is. I don't know who he's with. I don't know if he's alone. I don't know if he's okay. I don't know." Miranda's eyes watered up. Suzy asked, "Have you tried calling him?" Miranda replied, "Yes. I called him once. I don't wanna keep calling because I just don't know." Suzy said, "I'll say a little prayer for him, babes." Miranda thanked Suzy.

They got to school and sat in the cafeteria. Miranda seemed so anxious and zoned out. The bell rang; the ladies separated to go to class. They met back up at lunchtime. Suzy asked Miranda, "Have you heard anything from Miguel?" With concern in her face, Miranda shook her head no. They walked to the car and headed home. When Miranda got to the gate to drop off Suzy, she noticed a police car in the apartments. Miranda drove in and parked the car. The girls walked up to Miguel's mom's door; it was wide open.

Lita and Ana were crying as the police were talking to them. Miranda walked in and asked Ana, "Que paso ma?" Ana gave Miranda a look with the gravest concern in her face. Miranda scrunched her eyebrows as she shook her head no. Ana nodded her head yes as she continued to cry. Fighting back her tears, Miranda whispered, "No, no man, no." She walked up to Ana and hugged her tight. Miranda said, "I'm sorry, ma. I'm so sorry." "Me too, mija," replied Ana.

The cops asked Miranda who she was to Miguel. Miranda explained that she was the next-door neighbor. The police asked the ladies some questions such as, "Did Miguel have any known enemies." The ladies weren't any help toward the investigation. The police explained that someone would call them to have them view the body and verify that it was, in fact, Miguel. They gave their condolences one more time before leaving. When they left, Ana asked Miranda, "When was the last time you seen him?" Miranda said, "He left last night and said he would be back in a few hours, but he didn't come home."

Ana nodded her head. Then she asked, "Well, he didn't tell you where he was going?" Miranda put her head down and said, "No." Ana grabbed Miranda's chin and pulled her head up. Ana said to Miranda, "Miranda if you know anything, you have to talk to the police. Let them do their job."

Miranda looked into Ana's eyes and said, "I don't know." Ana put her hand down and said, "Okay, pues." Ana knew Miranda was hiding something. Ana was aware that there were codes around the neighborhood that you just don't break without possibly facing the consequences. Ana kept in mind that Miranda was a good girl suffering from the loss of her adopted brother.

Ana wrapped her arms around Miranda, and together they cried at the loss of their loved one. Lita rubbed their backs as she cried too. Miranda threw her arm around Lita and pulled her in. Seeing the ladies crying over the news, of Miguel's death, brought Suzy to tears, she stood quietly crying in the kitchen. After a few minutes of crying in a huddle, the ladies broke it up and took a seat. Miranda invited Suzy to come to sit with them. Suzy gave each of the ladies her condolences along with a tight hug. They sat reminiscing and sharing stories of Miguel.

A couple of hours passed, the phone rang. It was the coroner. She asked them to come down to the morgue to verify Miguel's body. Ana hung up the phone and blankly stared at the wall across from her. "I can't," she said. Miranda asked Ana, "Do you want me to go with you?" Ana looked over to Miranda, saying, "Mija, I can't get myself to go. I'm not ready to see him. Can you go, please?" Miranda gulped her saliva. She nodded, saying, "Yeah, I'll go, ma. I'll be back." Miranda and Suzy stood up and walked outside.

Suzy asked Miranda, "Can I go with you, ma?" Miranda said, "Please." As the ladies were walking to the car, they bumped into Gabby. Miranda told Gabby what was going on. Gabby threw her arms around Miranda without saying a word. Gabby pulled her head away from Miranda and looked into Miranda's eyes; Gabby said, "I'm here for you, Miranda. If you need anything, help planning the services, help to cook or clean or whatever, please let me be there."

Miranda nodded her head and said, "Thanks Gabby. I appreciate you, mujer." Gabby gave Miranda another tight hug before letting go. Miranda told Gabby, "We're going to go verify his body. Do you wanna roll with?" Gabby said, "Yes, of course."

The ladies hopped in the car and headed to Los Angeles. There was silence in the car for about 10 minutes. Gabby finally broke the silence, saying, "Remember that time we went to six flags fright fest and Miguel dared you to fake a seizure the next time someone tried to scare you?" Miranda laughed, "Yes! I told him, 'No, I can't just drop to the floor. I'd have to place myself down gently, and then begin convulsing. It wouldn't be believable.' Then I dared him to do it."

Gabby laughed out, "Oh my god, and he did it so clean! I'll never forget the look in the man's face when he thought he caused a seizure. He was so panicked." Suzy added, "And the way he laughed as he teased the monster when he stood up." The ladies laughed at that memory.

Suzy rubbed the door panel as she said, "Man, I'll always remember when he first got this car. He must have wiped it down with his special rag like 50 times a day. He'd sit in it, put his arm out the window, and pretend he was cruising.

Then get out and start wiping it down again. That must have gone on for like a month."

Miranda said, "Yup, I remember that. He used to watch this car drive by and say, 'I'm gonna buy that car.' He couldn't believe the man actually sold it to him. He was proud of this car. Shoot, I'll never forget when he gave it to me. I thought it was a joke at first. Only 'cause I knew how much he loved it." Gabby said, "Yeah, he did love this car. But he loved you more. He told me he didn't want you to take the bus to school because it was too dangerous. He's always wanted the best for you. I love how he's always looked out for you."

The girls pulled up to the morgue. Miranda parked the car and took a deep breath before getting out of the lowrider. Suzy squeezed Miranda's hand then said, "We're here with you, ma. You can do this." Miranda nodded her head. They got out of the car and headed into the building.

The girls explained their reason for being there. A man led them to the body; the man folded the sheet down to reveal Miguel's face. He asked, "Is this Miguel Villanueva?" Miranda's eyes grew wide when she saw the gunshot. The man asked again, "Ma'am is this Miguel Villanueva?" Miranda nodded and said, "Yes. That's Miguel." The man thanked Miranda as he placed the sheet over Miguel's face. Miranda grew furious as she thought about the conversation she had with Miguel before he left.

Miranda asked about Miguel's belongings; the coroner suggested they go through the police department. The ladies thanked the coroner and walked back to the car. Gabby said, "Man, was it just me, or did that place feel creepy as fuck." The ladies agreed. Suzy said, "I would hate to work there, especially for a night shift." Creeped out at the thought, Suzy shook her body.

Gabby put her hand on Miranda's shoulder, saying, "We're right here. We're gonna get through this together, ma." Miranda nodded her head, gesturing yes. Miranda said, "I'm just tripping out. He knew it was going to happen, gave me the whole pep talk about how successful I'd be in life. I asked if I could come with him so I can hold the strap in case shit took a left, and he told me chales because it was a school night. I knew I should have gone." Gabby said, "I hear what you're saying, baby girl, but he felt something was going down, and he didn't wanna put you in harm's way, that's love. If you would have been there, you'd be lying right next to him."

With tears flowing down her face, Miranda responded, "I know this is selfish, but the way I'm feeling now, I wish I were lying next to him. He's the biggest part of my life. He's like my fuckin' dad and my big brother rolled into one. What the fuck am I supposed to do now? How the fuck am I supposed to go on in life when my number one supporter in every aspect isn't here to back me up anymore? My fuckin' rock dude, I don't know life without him. I'm sorry I know I sound like a selfish brat saying some shit like this, but I just feel lost without him." All the girls were shedding tears as Miranda spoke about Miguel.

Gabby sobbing, replied, "You have every right to feel the way you feel mamash. But I am grateful that he told you to stay home. Cause I don't know what I would do without you in my life. I've known you since we were chamakita's. You're one of my trues. And I want to grow old with you in my life and become comadres, you know? You have a whole familia with us girls, and we will be your supporters whenever you need us. I love you, Miranda, and I'm relieved that you stayed home last night."

Miranda said, "Thank you, Gabby. I know I still got good people on my team. I just need some time to process all this shit. My mind is running wild." Suzy said, "I love you, Miranda, and I second everything Gabby said. You mean so much to us and to so many people." Suzy reached over and rubbed Miranda's back.

The ladies drove to the police station. The woman behind the counter told her where they towed his car. They released his keys and wallet to her. She thought to herself, "He had his phone." She asked the woman behind the counter, "Are they holding his phone for evidence?" The woman replied, "I have no knowledge of him having a cell phone. It's not on the list of belongings." Miranda thanked her for his belongings. The ladies walked back to the car and headed to the apartments. Miranda thanked the ladies for going with her. Gabby said, "Don't trip, ma. We got you."

The ladies got out of the car and proceeded to walk to Ana's front door. When they got to the front, Miranda turned to the ladies, saying, "I really do appreciate you being here for me, loves. I'm gonna go in and drop these off. Then I'm gonna call it a night. I'll see you tomorrow Suzy, same time."

Suzy asked, "Are you sure? Maybe you should take some time and chill." Miranda replied, "Na, I rather keep busy and get school handled. We only got a couple of weeks anyway." Suzy said, "Okay, ma, see you tomorrow, good night." Suzy gave Miranda a tight hug followed by a kiss on the cheek. Gabby did the same as she wished Miranda a good night. Gabby and Suzy walked away together.

Miranda walked into Ana's apartment. Ana was sitting at the Kitchen table, looking at pictures. Miranda picked one up. It was of Miguel and Miranda making funny faces as they showed off the pumpkins they had just carved for Halloween. Miranda smiled as she studied the photo. Miranda was five years old in the picture. She placed the photo down as she grabbed a seat at the table.

Ana was still staring at the same photo since Miranda walked in. When Miranda sat down, Ana said, "This kid was so adamant about being the man of the house. He always wanted to make sure his three women were happy and had everything. I never approved of what he was doing. But what could I do to stop him? I know my mijo meant well."

Miranda nodded, "I spent almost every day up until this point being extremely happy. Thank you for raising the most amazing man I will ever have known, and allowing me to be a part of this family. You can live the remainder of your life, knowing you raised a great man and had a wonderful relationship with him. A lot of these moms around here can't do or say that, but you can."

Ana put the picture on the table; she placed one hand on top of the other over the image. Ana let out a loud sigh as she looked straight ahead. She then looked into Miranda's eyes as she said, "Mija, things are going to be very different from now on. We have a lot of things to discuss and plan, not just for his services but for our lives and lifestyles."

Miranda nodded, saying, "I know, ma. I'll be with you every step of the way." Ana said, "Thank you, mija. You knew him better than anyone, so I do want your input on everything." Miranda said, "I'm here, ma." Miranda pulled out Miguel's belongings and said, "They gave me his wallet and his keys. They said his car was in the black and white tow lot. I can get it out tomorrow with Suzy if you want. Because I think the price goes up by the day. I just need you to be there to sign anything."

Ana agreed, "That would be a great help. Just take it home and leave it there." Ana opened up Miguel's wallet; there were hundred dollar bills equaling up to one thousand dollars. Ana handed it to Miranda, saying, "Here, use this." Miranda looked at the money and told Ana, "No. I just want his license. You keep that for whatever you need. I'll take care of the car."

Ana's eyes squinted at Miranda. She raised her hand in the air as she said, "Otra, mija, I hope you put that shit to rest. Look where it got Miguel. Don't get caught in that lifestyle too." Miranda put her head down. She defensively said, "I know. I'm not a big-timer like that. I just sell petty sacks to normal Joes. I've only been doing it to pay for college. Miggy saved all my money so I wouldn't have to struggle with student loans. I'm going to be a doctor, ma, not a dope dealer." Ana asked, "Mija, you want to be a doctor?" Miranda nodded her head, yes. Ana looked up to the ceiling, smiling. She held her head proudly, as she raised her arms as if seeing it written out in front of her, and repeated, "A doctor."

Ana looked over to Miranda, saying, "Mija, I hope you do it. I hope you do it and get far away from all this danger." Miranda nodded and said, "That's always been the plan. I already got accepted into college. But truth be told, danger can be any and everywhere, even at college. Ma, it's late, and you need to rest. I'm going to school tomorrow. When I get out, I'll come to pick you up so we can take care of the car, and we can figure out what else we need to do, okay?" Ana agreed, they hugged, then kissed each other's cheeks and said good night.

Instead of getting rest as they agreed, both ladies laid wide awake in bed, crying and thinking of Miguel. As Miranda lay in bed crying, she had so many thoughts rushing through her head. One thought, in particular, made Miranda sit straight up. Miranda heard Miguel on his phone the night he passed away. When she collected his belongings from the morgue, there was no cell phone.

Miranda walked over to her desk. Miguel had an app on his phone that Miranda set up for him in case he ever lost it. She logged on to the app's website. Miranda tracked the phone down to the last known location. She compared the address to the info Miguel left for Listo. It was the same address.

Miranda decided to drive to the house to check it out. As she parked a couple of houses away, she noticed two guys walking out of the house. Wondering if one of them was Javi, Miranda thought of all the ways she could kill him. As she stared out of her windshield, she envisioned herself pinning her hair close to her scalp. She placed a nylon cap on her head, covering her hairline.

Miranda then put on makeup, including fake lashes. She placed a wig on her scalp made with short red hair, which barely reached the back of Miranda's neckline. After pinning the wig in place, Miranda was entirely unrecognizable. She wore skin toned nylons. She then slipped into a tiny black dress. She wore a long coat to cover her dress and put on fishnet stockings.

Miranda glanced in the mirror, making seductive faces, then walked over to her desk, opened the top drawer, and pulled out a sharp knife and some medical rubber gloves. The blade was 11 inches long; she placed the knife and gloves in her boot. Reaching back into the drawer, Miranda grabbed four bus tokens. She stashed the tokens on the side of her boot in a zipper intended for looks. She grabbed some winter gloves and put them on.

Miranda walked to her backyard with her boots and keys at hand. She locked the door behind her. Miranda stashed her keys in a bush, hopped the gate into her neighbor's yard, and tiptoed around their house. She was relieved when she reached the sidewalk with no one seeing her. She walked down the darkest streets.

About two blocks into her walk, she sat on the curb in the dark to put her boots on. She kept the knife and gloves inside her right boot alongside her calf. Miranda walked to a bus stop three miles away from her house. She got off two miles away from Javi's home. Before stepping onto his street, she took her coat off, rolled it up into a ball, and dropped it in the corner of someone's lawn and wall.

She walked on to his street and began stumbling as if she was drunk, zig-zagging on the sidewalk. Javi was exiting his car. He glanced over to his left and seen Miranda. He decided to wait for her. As Miranda got closer to Javi, he asked, "Hello, miss, how are you doing this evening?" Miranda looked up, slurring, she replied, "I'm doing wonderful thank you." Javi asked, "Where are you headed if you don't mind me asking?" Miranda said, "I'm heading home from a friend's house."

Javi asked, "Where do you live?" Miranda replied, "I live in North Hollywood." Javi responded, "Wow. North Hollywood is pretty far. You're going to walk out there?" Miranda said, "Sure, why not? It'll give me time to sober up." Javi replied, "Well, you can always chill here with me until you sober up and let me take you home later."

Miranda smiled saying, "Awe, that's very sweet thank you. But I'm sure you have better things to do. I don't want to burden you." Javi replied, "I was going to call it a day and kick it at home for the rest of the night. But I'd rather hang out with you if you're cool with it." Miranda held her right hand out and said, "I'm Destiny." Javi grabbed her hand and said, "Nice to meet you, Destiny. My name is Javi. Come on, let's go inside." She smiled in agreement. He walked her to the bedroom, locking the door behind him.

They sat on the bed. Miranda giggled as she said, "Hmm, you seem tense. Here let me massage you, Javi." Miranda directed him to lie on the bed. Javi lay on his belly with his arms folded under his head. She crawled onto and straddled his back. She began to massage his neck with her palms. Miranda asked, "Do you like that, papi?" Smiling, Javi said, "Yeah, that feels good, better if you take your gloves off." Miranda said, "Okay." She took her hands off of his back.

She reached into her right boot, grabbing the knife. Miranda reached her left arm over Javi's forehead and quickly slit his throat. She stood up near the bed and watched him bleed out. Miranda removed her gloves, leaned over, reached into her boot, and traded out gloves, grabbing the rubber gloves. Miranda put the rubber gloves on.

She cleaned the blood off of the knife using his bed comforter. She placed the blade back into her boot. Miranda began looking around for Miguel's phone. She found it hidden in Javi's sock drawer. She looked over to Javi's limp body holding the phone up, asking, "Really top drawer?" as she closed the drawer.

Miranda walked over to the window. She opened the window and jumped out, quietly closing the window behind her. Miranda took the rubber gloves off and placed them back in her boot. She walked back towards the bus stop. She grabbed her coat from where she left it and put it on. Miranda took two buses to get to Santa Monica Beach. When she got off the bus, she took the rubber gloves out of her boots and threw them in the trash can at the bus stop. She walked toward the ocean. Miranda took her coat off and dropped it on the sand with Miguel's phone.

She continued walking along the beach. After walking along the ocean quite a ways, she walked into the water. She walked until she was chest-deep into the water. Miranda lifted her right leg as she reached for the knife and then cleaned it in the water. She dug into the sand with her boot and dropped the knife. Miranda tried to bury the blade in the ocean floor.

She took off her false lashes and scrubbed her face with the ocean water to remove her make up. Her eyes burned from the salt water. Next, she removed the pins from her wig. Miranda took a deep breath; she went under the water and began to swim. She took off her wig, nylon cap, and the remainder of pins under the water. Miranda came up for a quick breath and went back under the water. She swam a little further. Miranda popped up and faced the extending ocean, placed her face in her hands, and sobbed. She asked for forgiveness as she cried.

Miranda removed her boots. She then turned toward the sand and walked along the shore, up to her coat. Miranda picked it up, dropped the boots down, spread the sweater neatly against the sand, and sat down. She stared at the ocean as she talked to Miguel. Miranda cried, "I know it doesn't make things right, I know it's not going to bring you back to me. I'm sorry, Miggy."

As Miranda sat there in the car imagining this, she heard Miguel's voice say, "Go home." Miranda gasped, looking over to the passenger seat. Miguel was vividly sitting there looking at Miranda. Miranda questioned his image, "Miguel?" Miguel nodded as he said, "Mija, you're going to be somebody important in this world. You have your whole life ahead of you. Don't worry about me. I'm okay. You'll be okay too, mija, go home now, don't ever come back here."

With tears streaming down her face, Miranda started the car and began to drive home. Miguel began to fade. Miranda said, "I don't want to live without you, Miguel." Miguel said, "And you won't, I'll be with you when you need me. I will never stop loving you, baby girl. I will always support you." Miranda nodded her head. Holding her tears back, she said, "I know Miguel, thank you, and I'll never stop loving you." Miguel faded a little more. Miranda didn't want him to leave yet. She held her arm up to him as he faded away.

She understood why he came to her, and she was grateful. She pulled into her driveway, put the gear in park and turned off the car. She cried uncontrollably for a few minutes. Miranda stepped out of the car and into the house; she walked over to his bedroom. She lay in Miguel's bed, staring out of the window.

The next morning Miranda sent Suzy a text message which read, "Good morning. Bring your license. I'm going to need help in getting Miguel's car home after school." Suzy texted back, "Okay, see you soon." After getting ready, Miranda drove over to pick up Suzy. Suzy hopped in and gave Miranda an extra big hug. This time they both looked exhausted. Neither of them questioned it. They went to school and went about their day as usual. This day would be a little tougher for Miranda than the previous. She excused herself from each class to go to the restroom and cry a bit. She would gain composure and get back to class.

When lunchtime came, Suzy knew Miranda would want to get out of there as soon as possible. The girls met up and rushed straight to the car. They drove off to pick up

Ana, then headed to the black and white tow lot to retrieve Miguel's car. When they got there, the ladies walked up to the window and explained the situation. Miranda handed them her license along with his birth certificate, social security card, and license.

Miranda said, "The only thing I don't have is his death certificate cause, well, it just happened yesterday." The man behind the counter shared his condolences and sympathy. The man slid everything back to Miranda. He told her to meet him at the gate.

Suzy, Ana, and Miranda walked to the gate. It opened just enough for the ladies to walk into the yard. He walked them over to the car; the man opened the door inviting Miranda to drive it off the lot. Miranda opened the back door and told Suzy to hop in. Ana sat passenger, Miranda sat in the driver seat. She thanked the man then drove the car off the lot.

Miranda pulled over near her impala. She held her keys over her right shoulder, saying, "Be careful." With sarcasm in her voice, Suzy responded, "Oh see, now you're making me nervous." Suzy got out of the backseat and walked over to the impala. She unlocked the driver's door. Once inside the car, she locked the door, started the car, and put on her seat belt.

Miranda waited for Suzy to pull up behind her at the edge of the driveway. They drove the cars back to Miranda's house. The whole drive home Miranda could smell this cologne like fragrance. She kept sniffing, as she did so, she thought to herself, "Miggy never wore cologne that smelled like that."

Miranda pulled the car into the garage. Suzy parked in the driveway. After Miranda shut the car off, she waited for Ana to exit. Then she turned around to smell Miguel's seat. The seat vaguely held his scent. She then leaned over to the passenger side, she sniffed the seat, and there was the strong scent. She sniffed the chair a few times to get familiar with the smell; she knew that was Javi's scent. Miranda went into the house to grab some Lysol. She came back out and sprayed the seat down.

Suzy asked Miranda, "Are we going to Ana's pad right now?" Miranda said, "Yeah, we need to plan the services and figure out what to do with his stuff. I just need to grab the will that Miggy wrote." Suzy asked, "Do you want me to go with you two ladies?" Miranda replied, "You don't have to babe." Suzy asked, "But I can?" Miranda said, "Yeah, of course you can. I mean, I'd appreciate it." Suzy smiled and nodded. Miranda went into the house, straight to Miguel's room. She opened his safe and pulled out the will that he wrote a few months back.

The ladies got in the impala and headed to the apartments. As the ladies approached Ana's door, Miranda caught eyes with Gabby, who was sitting outside waiting for her. Gabby jumped up and walked up to Miranda, giving her a big hug. Gabby gave Ana and Suzy a big hug too. Gabby said to Miranda, "I know you're going to go over arrangements and such so I figured I might take notes to help you guys stay on track of what needs to be done. Miranda responded, "Thank you, Gabs, that's sweet of you." Gabby briefly bowed her head as to say, "You're welcome."

The girls walked into the house. They all sat at the kitchen table to discuss arrangements and what they'll do with his things. They agreed on everything from where the services and reception would be held to where he'd be buried.

Miggy's will stated that, although the house was under his grandmother's name, he left his house and belongings to both Ana and Miranda with the confidence that they will care for Lita. They were both the only two documented as beneficiaries. He knew that they loved each other enough not to fight, but rather, they would come to an agreement and care for Lita.

Ana told Miranda that she wanted Miranda to keep the house along with anything in it and Miguel's car. Miranda said, "Ma, you have full rights to that house, I just live there; if you or Lita want to move in or sell it, I'm okay with that." Ana said, "I know mija, but you live there now, that's your home, so I think you should keep it." Miranda nodded. She placed her head down and started to cry.

Ana jumped up and hugged Miranda. Ana couldn't hold back her tears any more either. Ana spoke through her tears, "No parent wants to lose a child no matter how old. That's not how it's supposed to be. Whether we like it or not, these instances are a part of life. Together, we'll get through this mija." Miranda nodded her head as she said, "I know. I know. I love you, ma. I'm sorry that this happened."

Ana kissed Miranda on the forehead, she said, "It's not your fault, mija. It was his time to go. He was a good man with a big heart, which makes it easier to accept." Miranda looked up into Ana's eyes; she gulped and slowly said, "I admire your strength and wisdom. I hope to be as strong as you one day." Ana acknowledged Miranda's compliment with a nod. Miranda said, "Uy, I'm gonna go outside and get some air. I'll probably just head home in a bit unless there's anything you need." Ana said, "No, mija, we're okay. You need to rest."

Miranda and the girls said their goodbyes to Ana and Lita. The girls walked over to the jungles and had a seat on the bench. They sat quietly for a moment. Miranda broke the silence saying, "I have a confession, you guys." The girls both responded, "What is it?" Miranda took a deep breath, and then she said, "Ok, here it goes, I know who killed Miguel."

The girls gasped. Gabby asked, "What? How do you know?" Miranda quietly spoke, "Miguel knew he was gonna die that night. He gave me the guys' info. He said to pass it along to one of the homies. I didn't tell anyone because I didn't have proof that it was this guy for sure. When we went to the police station to get Miguel's things, there was no cell phone. I knew Miguel took it with him because I called him once that night and I didn't hear it at the house. He has a phone locator, right? So I logged on to see where his phone was, it was at the same address that Miguel gave me." Suzy asked, "So what are you going to do?"

Miranda told the girls, "Fuck, I parked by the guy's house last night. I sat there imagining in detail how I can murder his bitch ass and get away with it. I mean a clean murder. But something happened." The girls both had their mouths open, anxious to hear what happened. Miranda continued, "Miguel showed up. He was sitting in my passenger seat."

Gabby quickly covered her mouth with both hands; she raised her eyebrows. Suzy grabbed the bench with one hand and Gabby's leg with the other. With tears in her eyes, Miranda continued saying, "He told me that I was gonna be someone great. He told me to go home and never go back to that house. He assured me that he was okay. I really was planning on handling this lop by myself. But I trust and respect Miguel, so I am going to listen to him. But man, you guys, it was so unreal. He was sitting right there. I could see and hear him so clear. It was so emotional."

Gabby said, "Damn ma, that's fucking crazy. He never ceases to amaze me with his amount of love for you. So are you going to pass along that info or let it go?" Miranda shrugged as she said, "I just, I don't know if I should, you know? What's done is done. No matter what I do, it won't take my life back to where it was. I do believe that this bitch ass motherfucker needs to face a consequence for what he did. But I don't want to involve anyone else and risk feeling responsible for someone getting locked up or dying. I mean figure karma will handle that fool eventually, right?"

Suzy nodded, saying, "He will definitely get his. Just keep in mind that taking bitch ass lops out the game is what the homies do. They understand the consequences of their actions. No one will hold you responsible for nada. Listo is probably already on the hunt for this fool anyway. By you passing along the info, will simply be seeing to it that no one other than the responsible party pays the price of your carnal's death."

Miranda looked up to the sky and took a deep breath. Miranda looked at Suzy and said, "I hear you, it makes sense, really it does. But it's still hard to think of someone going down for a crime that I instigated. Who's to say I won't then receive karma for being the middle man to someone else's death? Especially after Miguel assured me that he's okay, ugh, I don't know, it's just a lot to take in. It was easier to think of me doing it and accepting responsibility for my actions rather than having someone else handle him."

Gabby said, "Miranda speaking of karma, do you remember what you told me the day that shit went down and I slept on your porch? You said, 'Don't be a victim, cause when you are, he wins,' right? Now it's on us to choose how we perceive our experiences. Miguel already told you he's fine. It was his time to go. This guy so happened to be the tool creator used to bring Miguel home."

Miranda replied, "You are absolutely right, Gabs. It's all part of something greater than my comprehension. Miggy is on his path, and I am on mine. I do know in my soul that one sweet day our paths will cross again. Gosh, I wish the spirit world had a cell phone, so I could text him and call him when I miss him." Gabby responded, "If only."

Gabby asked Miranda, "You haven't eaten anything since all this have you?" Miranda just looked down. Gabby looked over to Suzy and made a helpless face. Suzy said, "Baby girl, you have to eat to be strong for Miggy's mom. She needs you more than anyone. If you're weak and frail, you can't help her." Miranda said, "I know you're right. I just have zero appetite."

Suzy said, "I get it. Even if it's one piece of multi-grain toast a day for the next two weeks, just something to keep you going, I can't tell you that everything is gonna get better or that you'll get over it soon, cause that's a lie, but babe, I know you'll do the work to heal. You will be okay eventually, and life will be amazing when you're ready to allow it to be. Miggy's body may be at rest, but you know his love for you lives strong. This is a huge hurdle to jump over, but you're gonna do it gracefully, and we're gonna be here every step of the way."

Miranda said, "Thank you, Suzy, I need you guys right now, and I'm glad you're here." Gabby sat next to Miranda and put her arm around her, saying, "We love you, mamash." Miranda stayed silent as she put her arm around Gabby. The ladies tried changing the subject to clear Miranda's mind. It didn't last long. With her mind still racing, Miranda felt the urge to speak to Isela, whose brother passed away the year before. Miranda excused herself, wishing the ladies a good night and thanking them again for their words.

Miranda picked up her phone to dial Isela's number as she walked away. Isela answered with concern in her voice. Miranda asked if she could see her. Isela said, "I'm home come through."

Isela was waiting at her front door when Miranda walked up. Isela hugged Miranda tight. They cried together for a few minutes while they hugged. Isela invited Miranda to her room. As they took a seat in her room, Isela asked, "What's going on, love?" Miranda explained, "I'm trying to go through the motions of processing it all. I keep going back to some horrible thoughts in my mind. I just, I guess, maybe hearing you're story with your brother might help."

Isela nodded her head. She began, "Well, as you know, I was mad at him before he passed. I called him a bitch and told him that I dis-own him. The morning of the day he passed, I woke up from an intense dream. In my dream: I killed my cousin and turned her into ash. I swept her up in a glass jar and placed it on a wooden table.

"When my mom walked in, I opened my arms wide, as I did that, I knocked the jar to the ground. It shattered. I stood there fearfully repeating, 'It was an accident,' until I woke up. I sat straight up in bed and said, 'someone's gonna die today.' That night he went out with his friends, and on the way home, he fell asleep behind the wheel, just before the exit to get here. The car flipped over the side of the freeway bridge and landed upside down on the street below.

"At first, I acted as if I didn't care because I was still so hurt by him. It wouldn't be until I saw his lifeless body lying there, that it hit me like a ton of bricks, this was real, and my brother was gone. That was the first time I cried over it. Then the guilt started to kick in, you know? 'I shouldn't have said what I did,' 'I should have forgiven him when he asked me to.' Those kinds of thoughts started to race through my mind. But what was done was done.

"The blessing was; when he came to me in a dream, he took me to the beach. We walked along the shore, blazed, and talked. We both apologized to and forgave each other. We were able to let it go, which I think was more necessary for my healing then it was for him. The crazy thing too was, my mom and dad decided to cremate my brother just like my first dream had stated.

"The whole experience helped me realize that we are spiritual beings temporarily borrowing these outer shells so that we can accomplish and endure the experiences necessary to take back with us. I don't know if any of this helps, but I believe one of Miggy's accomplishments was to guide you on to your road, which includes your successes.

"This is a big bump in your road but not the end of it. My loss differs from yours Miranda. My brother was in an accident that I can't blame anyone for. Miggy was murdered, and I think that might be harder to handle because the thought of revenge might come up now and again. But let Locs' sister be a lesson for us. You'll move forward with Miggy always by your side when you need him most."

Miranda threw her arms around Isela, without saying a word, they cried and hugged each other for a couple more minutes. When Miranda did pull away, she told Isela, "I love you and respect you for your strength, ma." Isela said, "I love you too. You're just as strong, baby girl." Miranda said, "I'm so exhausted, Isela, I'm gonna go home and rest." Isela nodded and walked Miranda to the front door. They gave each other one more long-lasting tight hug and said goodnight.

The day came; Miggy's funeral services and burial were held at a mortuary and cemetery in San Fernando, California. They bought a beautiful casket for Miguel; the funeral was a closed casket ceremony. Ana had a catholic priest do the speaking. They asked for very little bible scriptures because Miguel didn't like it. The day was a massive blur for Miranda, Ana, and Lita. There were about a hundred and fifty people who came to pay their respects.

Listo was nervous that cops would be surrounding the funeral service, so he didn't go. He showed up at the reception. He paid his respect to Miguel's family. Listo handed Ana a sealed envelope with three thousand dollars inside, and he said, "I'm so sorry for your loss. Miggy was like a little brother to me. You raised a good man. If there's anything at all that you need, furniture moved around or anything at all, please know that you can call me. I put my number on the envelope." Ana smiled slightly; she raised the envelope shoulder height as she thanked Listo.

Toward the end of the reception, Denise whispered to Clever, "I didn't think anything of it before, but I missed my period this month. And lately, I been feeling weird and like I have the urge to quit smoking yerba." Clever asked, "Serio? You think you're pregnant mamas?" Denise said nothing. Instead, she smiled a nervous smile. Clever said, "On the way home, do you want me to buy a pregnancy test to ease your mind?" Denise nodded her head, yes.

The girls and Clever helped to clean up in the reception hall. They packed flowers, pans, and anything left over at the reception hall into both Ana's and Miranda's cars. Suzy said, "We'll meet you at home to help you unload."

Ana drove home with Lita. Gabby went with Miranda. Clever, Denise, and Suzy took the van. On the drive back home, Clever asked Suzy, "Do you think we can stop by the grocery store so I can buy a bag of chips real quick?" Suzy agreed, she pulled into the shopping center on Glenoaks and dropped Clever off in front of the store. Clever asked if anyone else wanted anything. Both ladies said, "No, thank you."

Clever asked the lady at the service desk for a pregnancy test. Together they walked to the isle where the pregnancy tests and condoms were locked up. She asked which one he wanted. Clever pointed to the cheapest one he saw. She grabbed the test and locked the glass door. "Is that all for you today?" asked the woman. Clever nodded and said, "Yes, ma'am." They walked to a register together.

The lady left the test with a young lady at the register. While Clever waited in line, he grabbed a bag of hot fries. Clever bought the pregnancy test and chips. He stuck the test in his pocket and walked out of the store. Clever got back in the car and said, "Long line, but I got what I wanted, good looking out Suzy Q."

They drove back to the apartments to unload all the stuff in Miranda's and Ana's cars. Every one grabbed things from the cars and brought it into Ana's house until everything was unloaded. Ana thanked everyone for their help. She offered them more food. The crew hung out to keep Ana and Lita some company for a while.

A few hours passed until they all decided to call it a night. They hugged and wished Ana and Lita a good night. Miranda said, "Don't bother with this stuff, ma. Go to bed. I'll come by tomorrow to help sort and put things away." Ana nodded her head in agreement, she wrapped her arms around Miranda and gave her a tight hug followed by a kiss on the cheek and said, "Thank you for the help baby girl." Miranda nodded and kissed Ana on her cheek. Ana thanked everyone for their help and hugged them good night.

Clever and Denise anxiously walked to Clever's apartment. When they got there, Clever asked, "Can I be there with you?" Denise asked, "Eew, you wanna see me pee on a stick?" Clever laughed and replied, "Well, I just wanna be there with you." Denise said, "Let me do my thug dizzle, then we can look at the results together." Clever sunk his head in disappointment and said, "Fine then."

Denise grabbed his face in her hands and lifted his head, trying to get him to look at her. Denise said, "You are the most beautiful man, I swear." Denise admired Clever for a brief moment. Then with her hand out, she said, "Damé lo esté chingadera." Clever pulled the test out of his pocket and handed it to her. Denise leaned in for a quick kiss, then turned and walked to the bathroom.

Denise came back out and laid her head on Clever's lap as they waited. Clever asked, "If the test says you are, are you going to be okay with that?" Denise said, "It sucks that we barely had sex this one time. I think we're young to be parents, but I accept whatever comes my way. How do you feel about it?" Clever replied, "I wouldn't want to have kids with anyone else. I think we'll have beautiful children. And if you are pregnant, I'll be there every step of the way."

It was time to get the results of the pregnancy stick. They went into the bathroom together to see the results. The test results were positive. Denise cried as Clever hugged her tight. They were both just as happy as they were scared. They agreed that they would both stay in school and try to work until the baby came, then Clever would do both, and Denise would just attend school. They also agreed that they would tell Denise's parents and Mama Sita together.

THE GRADUATION

Suzy took a shower and put rollers in her hair the night before graduation. She covered her head with a blue bandana, and then went to bed. When she woke up in the morning, she went to the bathroom to take a birdbath and brush her teeth. She went back to the room to put on her makeup. Suzy pulled a beautiful dark brown and beige dress out of her closet and slipped it on. She slowly pulled the curlers out of her hair then slightly combed her locks. She put her beige pumps on and called out, "Okay, mom, I'm ready!" Lisa and Suzy met in the living room.

Lisa gasped. She grabbed Suzy by the arms and said, "Uy mija, you look gorgeous!" As Suzy and her mother faced each other, grasping each other's forearms, Suzy said, "Dang mommy, I can see where I get it from, va va voom!! I never saw you look so stunning." Lisa smiled then said, "Today is a very special day. My baby is graduating from high school."

Lisa put her palms to the ceiling and pumped her arms up and down as she said, "Wooo wooo!" Suzy giggled, she scrunched her nose as she said, "Uy ma, you're crazy, but I love it." Lisa's eyes opened wide as she exclaimed, "Well, now you know where you get that from too! Let's go get you that diploma loca." Suzy and Lisa walked down the stairs to the car and headed to "The High."

Miranda was standing with her mom, Ana, Lita, Gabby, and Gabby's mom Tiffany on the football field. Suzy and

Lisa walked up to greet the ladies. They were all filled with nervous excitement. Lisa told Suzy to group up with her friends so she could take pictures. All the moms, including Ana, started snapping pictures. Lori walked up and was told by Gabby to get in and pose. The group of ladies posed for several pictures. There was an announcement for all the young adults to begin taking their seats in preparation for the acceptance of their diplomas. The girls walked over in a single file line and sat together.

Miranda was asked to speak as valedictorian. She walked up to and stood at the podium. She began, "First off, shout out to my girls who recently seen me through the toughest tragedy of my life. I love you ladies and will forever hold gratitude for your friendship."

Miranda gave a subtle nod as she continued, "Fellow graduates, today I commend you as we have accomplished a great hurdle in the beginning stages of our young adult lives. We all know the system that we live and go to school in has often been meant to keep us down. We watched some of our classmates go to jail, some pass away too soon, and some dropped out to help their parents by working.

"Yet still, here we stand. We now speak and write the language of those who tried so hard to keep our voices from being heard by the world. As we move forward in our lives, we must remember that we have to work harder and be more determined than the privileged to enter their level of success. But it can and will be done. Because we have to show our ancestors that they did not suffer or die in vain. And show our future generations, we will be their heroes. We will show them the way. Each one, reach one, teach one.

"Today is the beginning of the rest of our lives. What we do with it, who we become, is entirely up to us. We have a choice to stand in our own way, lose faith in ourselves, and maybe settle for a paycheck that's mediocre. Or, we can rise high, strong, and know that we are here to change our world for the better. Let us choose the latter. I am extremely proud of you all for making it this far. I look forward to seeing or reading about the amazing gifts you offer the world. So go forward and continue to be amazing." Miranda shouted, "We did it!" The crowd instantly cheered in excitement. Miranda followed her speech by chucking the deuces. Miranda turned around and walked to her seat.

Isela, who already graduated from her home-study program, came to support her friends. She sat with the girls' families. When her friends took their turns on the stage, she would scream as loud as she possibly could. Isela wished she could walk that stage with the ladies, but she was still content with the way things worked out for her.

After the graduation ceremony, the ladies went out to eat with their families at Carrillo's Mexican restaurant. They packed the tables in the back. They had a great time filled with a lot of laughter.

Isela made a toast; "I would just like to once again congratulate each of you ladies for busting your butts and finishing high school. My middle school and high school memories were made so memorable due to each of you. Thank you for being the best friends and sisters a girl can ask for. I know as we move on to the next chapter, we'll make so many more amazing memories to share with each other. I love you, ladies." The ladies all shouted, "We love you too," and cheered to Isela's speech.

Fast Forward...

ANNETTE

Four months later, at her lunch break, Annette went to check out a studio apartment. It was a decent little space about seven miles away from work. It was three cities away from Adolfo. Annette prayed that would be far enough. She signed a 12-month lease, gave the manager the down payment and rent for the next two months.

The manager gave Annette two keys to the apartment along with a gate key to enter the parking lot and a master entrance key to all of the doors leading into the building. Anette locked everything in the glove compartment of her car.

Annette played it cool, afraid to tell Adolfo that she was leaving. That night, she acted as if it were any other night with Adolfo. Annette waited until Adolfo fell asleep. Her eyes were fixated on him for quite a while before she got out of bed. She only packed up all of her necessities, with enough clothes for a week.

She didn't want to spend too much time packing for the risk of getting caught. In her mind, she figured that she had enough clothes and necessities to make a fresh start and that she could shop for clothes later. She left a farewell note for Adolfo and his family on the kitchen table. Annette left with whatever she could carry in one trip to the car.

She placed her bags in the backseat and drove over to her new apartment. In the first few weeks, Annette slept on the floor. Little by little, she eventually furnished the place, starting with a bed. She swore to herself that she would never go back to Adolfo.

Annette decided to take the bus to work in hopes that she could dodge Adolfo. She thought it would throw him off, not seeing her car at work. She took the bus to work for a few weeks. After work, a co-worker would drop her off at her new place. Every day, life seemed to improve for Annette.

She did have occasional nightmares about Adolfo. One, in particular, was of a flashback to a real-life event. It was evening; Annette was in the bedroom watching T.V. when Adolfo walked in, high on something, and drunk from beer. He began calling her foul names. Annette told him that he was acting dumb and told him to get out of the room and leave her alone.

He told Annette that she was the one acting stupid, and she needed to cool off. Adolfo lifted Annette off of the bed and carried her to the bathroom. With her clothes on, he threw her in the shower under the cold running water. Annette scram, "What the fuck is wrong with you?" To which Adolfo replied, "You need to cool off."

Annette kept trying to get out of the shower, but Adolfo continued to shove her, holding her in there. Annette shouted, "You're not okay, Adolfo, you're sick in the head!" Adolfo reversed it by saying, "Naw, it's you. You're always tripping on stupid shit." Freezing in the shower, Annette realized it was pointless to say anything more. She thought about the bathroom door; it was open. She needed to reach the exit.

Annette dove under his arm and ran out of the bathroom door. As she ran down the hall toward the front door, which was open, she noticed Adolfo's niece and realized by the fear in her eyes that his niece had witnessed some of the abuse. She was scared and crying from what she could hear between her uncle and Annette.

At the same instant that Annette saw her, Adolfo's hand grabbed Annette by the hair, pulling her back toward the bathroom. Annette's legs swung forward as Annette flew backward and was getting dragged. Adolfo's niece screamed loud. She ran into the hall where Adolfo could see her. She yelled, "What are you doing to my tía? You're hurting her; you're mean. You're mean, and I hate you. You're not my tío. She's my tía." Adolfo released Annette's hair.

Annette knew Adolfo loved that little girl more than life itself, and no matter how crazy he was, he would never harm her. She also knew that if his niece was there, that meant his sister came home too. The front door was open, so Annette took that opportunity to run.

She ran through the front door as fast as she could. She ran around the corner of the apartment building and hid under a car. She could hear Adolfo's footsteps running as he searched for her. Annette just lay there silent for as long as she felt she had to. Adolfo ran back to the house to get his truck keys. Annette heard him drive off. Still, she stayed.

Adolfo's sister came outside, whispering Annette's name. Annette rolled out from under the car. Adolfo's sister said, "Come on, you'll be safe now." That's when Annette always wakes up. When Annette awoke from the dream, she spoke out loud, "I can't believe I stayed that long." She kept telling herself it was the drugs making Adolfo this way. Although it was the drugs that had Adolfo acting like a psycho, it was the weed he was supplying her with, that had her putting up with so much. She was addicted too. She should have left sooner.

After having that dream, she laid in bed thinking of their past together. She recalled another instant where Adolfo was driving and kept calling her a hoe as he accused her of being with someone else. Annette socked him in the arm each time he called her a hoe. Adolfo said, "Hit me one more time, Annette, and I'm gonna backhand you."

Annette replied, "Stop calling me a hoe, and I won't touch you." Adolfo said, "Don't act like a hoe; I won't call you a hoe." Annette socked him in the arm again. Adolfo reached up and swung the back of his hand into Annette's face. Annette opened her door and jumped out of the moving truck. She got to her feet and ran. Adolfo drove around, looking for her.

He spotted her walking, drove beside her, and asked her to get in the truck. Annette refused to get in. They argued back and forth a few times before Adolfo drove further ahead. He put the truck in park, got out and walked away. He turned around after he was a safe distance from the truck, and said you take the truck and I'll walk home. Annette agreed to that. She jumped in, locked the doors, and sped off. When she got home, his niece asked, "Where's my tío?" Annette responded, "He's coming."

Adolfo walked through the front door forty-five minutes later. He went straight to Annette, and with a raised tone of voice, he said, "Why'd you leave me?" Annette laughed as she replied, "Because you told me too." Adolfo tried to be mad, but as he watched Annette smiling, knowing good and well that she should be heated, he smiled too and hugged her tight.

Despite how hard she tried staying off the radar now, Adolfo soon found Annette. She was at the bus stop. The bus pulled up to the curb. The doors opened; Annette placed one foot on the step, just as she began to pull her other foot into the bus, Adolfo grabbed her from behind and threw her over his shoulder. "I just want to talk to you," He explained.

Annette frantically kicked and screamed, "Let go of me, put me down." Witnesses on the bus freaked out. A few people called the police, but the bus driver kept going. Annette squirmed out of Adolfo's arms and took off running.

Adolfo caught up to her and once again scooped her up and tossed her over his shoulders. He was trying to shove her in his truck when the cops arrived. Annette had both feet at the top of his truck, with one hand on the front passenger door and the other hand on the roof above the back passenger door, trying to keep from going into the truck.

One policeman exclaimed, "Put her down right now!" Adolfo saw that it was the police and put her down. He tried to explain that she was his girlfriend. The policeman asked Annette, "Do you know this, man?" Annette responded, "He's my ex-boyfriend. I want nothing to do with him." The policeman said, "Ma'am, this is considered kidnapping. We're going to need you to file charges so that we can take him in and file a case."

Annette grew up by the hood code, "Never pull rat." She sighed, sounding worried. She said, "I'm sorry I don't have time for that. I have to get to work. If you can just hold him, I can run and make that bus." Annette pointed to a bus passing by.

The cops agreed, and Annette took off running. She made it to the bus and put a token in the machine. She found a seat up front and sat quietly until she reached her designated stop. Annette went into work as if nothing happened. After work, her co-worker drove her home. They talked about sports and shallow subjects.

The following morning, Annette woke up to tons of missed calls and messages from her friends and mother. She called her mom back to find that her brother had over dosed and transitioned to the spirit world. Annette made a call to her boss explaining the situation and that she would go to work the following day. Her boss insisted that she take two weeks off.

Friends and family showed up all day long to give their love and condolences to Annette's family. One of her brother's best friends walked up to Annette as she stood in the driveway. He tried to give her his condolences, but he fell apart as he hugged her. Annette hugged him tight and consoled him. At that exact moment, Adolfo drove by.

Adolfo knocked on Annette's apartment door the following morning. She looked out of the peephole to see that it was him. Annette quietly tiptoed away from the door. Adolfo said, "I know you're in there. I just want to talk. Can you open the door, please?"

Annette sat quietly and still. She wondered how he found her exact apartment. Adolfo waited a couple of minutes before saying, "Well, I don't wanna bother you anymore. I just wanted to talk and bring you some of your stuff that I know you love. I painted your bike. I'll leave it right here for you. I love you, Annette, and I'm sorry for everything." Adolfo walked away.

Annette still did not move. She sat quietly for about 20 minutes before she peeped out of the window. Scanning around outside to see if Adolfo was anywhere in view, he wasn't. She looked at her bike, posted at the front of the door. Slowly Annette walked to the door.

She opened it and began to bring in her stuff. Within seconds, Adolfo was inside of her apartment. Knocking her onto the couch, he punched her face. Then he wrapped his hands around her throat, squeezing it tight. She swung at his face. He accused her of sleeping with her brother's friend. He sat on top of Annette's stomach as he continued to squeeze her neck. He no longer said a word he just held on tight.

Annette attempted to move his hands by grabbing from the outside of his wrist. Adolfo had a firm grip. Her grip and swings became weaker as she began losing consciousness. She thought to herself, "This is it, this is how I die. Fuck it then." Annette stopped moving. Adolfo finally let go.

Adolfo immediately slashed open her couches along with the pillows. Annette's body began gasping for air. In-between gasps, she attempted to cry out, "What the fuck is wrong with you?" Adolfo said, "Shut the fuck up. Stop being so dramatic bitch. I didn't fucking kill you." He pushed her DVD rack onto the floor then walked out. Annette jumped up and locked the door behind him. Still gasping, she slid down the wall next to the door.

Annette pulled her phone out of her pocket. She called Isela. She asked Isela to stay on the phone with her until she could calm down. Annette's hands shook in fear. It took a few minutes of heavy breathing before she could calm down.

Finally, Annette calmed down enough to explain to Isela what had just happened. Isela held her hand over her mouth as she listened. Isela was concerned for her friend. At the same time, she felt helpless. Isela asked, "Do you want me to go over there and stay with you for a couple of days?"

Annette answered, "No, mija, I'll be okay. I just needed to talk to you so I could chill the fuck out." Isela replied, "I'm here if you change your mind, ma. But if you don't take me up on that offer, I think you should stay with your parents for a few weeks because they need you right now. And this fool is highly unstable."

Annette thanked Isela a few times for staying on the phone with her before ending the phone call. When Annette hung up the phone, she said, "God, please remove Adolfo from my life before I end up in prison for self-defense. I have been through so much with him. I just want to move forward and have a good life that I deserve. I deserve to have peace. Please remove Adolfo from my life."

After leaving Annette's apartment, Adolfo went to his connects house to pick up a teener of scanté because that was all his connect had at the moment. Adolfo wound up at his side girl's trailer. He asked the woman if she wanted to get high with him. She invited him in; they hung out and got wired. They were up together for two days.

When the tweek and high were gone, the woman told Adolfo that he had to go too. That made Adolfo feel rejected. He punched her in the jaw. She yelled at him, "Get the fuck out before I call the cops!" Adolfo became even more furious. He pulled out a gun and pistol-whipped her a few times.

Adolfo said, "You know what happens to rats, don't you? I swear to God if you ever call the cops on me, I'll fuckin' murder your bitch ass, don't fuckin' test me." He slapped the woman one more time. He continuously called her names like "Stupid fuckin' dirty bitch," before finally leaving.

Even after being threatened, the woman went to the cops. They had her fill out an affidavit. Then they took pictures of her injuries. There was a warrant issued for Adolfo's arrest. The police caught up with him the following afternoon, on his way to the liquor store. Isela happened to see the arrest. Isela knew Annette had a lot to deal with, so Isela held back from telling her about the arrest.

Annette had no choice but to show up to her brother's funeral arrangements and service with a busted lip. Of course, people had questions. Annette was embarrassed, but she had no answers to give to anyone asking what happened.

A week passed, and Isela hadn't seen Adolfo in the apartments. Word went around that he got arrested for assault with a deadly weapon. When the cops arrested Adolfo, they also found some speed on him. Isela found out that he would be looking at twelve to fifteen years in the state penitentiary.

Isela called Annette to see how life was going for her. Annette told Isela that although she continuously had bad flashbacks and dreams of the abuse that she endured throughout her and Adolfo's relationship and after, that, everyday life was getting a little better for her. Annette was grateful to Isela for the push and support.

Annette said, "One thing that I do truly hate, though, is always looking over my shoulder and staying on my toes. I have anxiety and fear that he's going to pop up out of nowhere and attack me. My heart races when I hear footsteps behind me. And before I can put my key in the lock to open the door to my apartment, I walk around the entire building and even look under the staircases to make sure he isn't going to shove me into my apartment and pull that shit again."

Isela decided to ease Annette's mind by telling her what she had seen and heard. Annette was shocked to hear about Adolfo. Yet, at the same time, she thought it sounded like something he was fully capable of doing. Annette did feel a sense of relief to know Adolfo wouldn't be around for a while. She started thinking that it would give her time to save more and get further away before Adolfo's release. Three months later, Annette found out that Adolfo did get sentenced to fifteen years in prison. Although she felt safe knowing he couldn't hurt her now, she had ongoing nightmares about him for two years. Annette was also left to deal with PTSD.

Annette and Isela never lost touch. Isela started a movement to guide the local communities to heal themselves, where she called on Annette often to share her story and council people who needed it. Annette felt fulfillment in helping others overcome their traumas.

Annette's job announced it was moving from Northridge to Burbank. They offered her a promotion if she was willing to move with them. Annette took the promotion as lead manager, receiving excellent health benefits and a 401k retirement fund. She worked for the company until retirement. Although Adolfo attempted to reach out to Annette on social media outlets, he never paid her any surprise visits. Annette never felt comfortable entering another relationship. She lived with her two pit bulls in a small quiet neighborhood in Burbank until she quietly passed away at 78 years old.

GABBY

After high school graduation, Gabby went straight to UEI in Van Nuys to become a certified massage therapist. A month and a half into attending school, her best homeboy Tripps was murdered at the apartments. Gabby went through it pretty hard. Although she thought about dropping the class, she knew how proud Tripps was of her for going in the first place.

Gabby knew he'd be proud if she graduated. So, she continued going to school, and while she was there, she put on a show like nothing drastic recently occurred in her personal life. Gabby began smoking a little more yesca and drinking energy drinks that contained a small percentage of alcohol in it.

One day after school, some guys from the hood jumped into her car to go to the store. One of them said, "There go the guys that killed Tripps. Gabby knew one of the guys in the car had a strap, and she had been fantasizing the murderer's deaths. She pulled into a parking lot to turn around and catch them slipping.

Just then, her bumper tapped the wall loud enough to catch the attention of a cop passing by. The police told her to put her car in park and put her hands out of the window. They instructed everyone to get out and get on their knees with their hands on the back of their heads and fingers intertwined. The cops called for back-up.

When the other squad car got there, they began searching Gabby's car and asking questions.

Stroller was one of the guys in the line-up. He kneeled beside Gabby. He had previously done time in the pinta and was hated by the LAPD. He whispered his booking number to Gabby and said, "If anything happens, I want you to write to me." Gabby responded, "Nothings gonna happen to you. They got nothing."

One of the cops who went through Gabby's car, pulled her aside after seeing her schoolwork. He said, "You're a good kid. You got your whole life ahead of you. What are you doing with these low-lives?" Gabby angrily said, "They're not low-lives; they're my neighbors." The cop shook his head, replying, "Well, they're gonna get you caught up if you keep hanging around them. We have to take you in for questioning. I'm gonna leave your car here, and you can pick it up later." Gabby knew they found the gun.

Everyone was arrested and taken in for questioning. Gabby was detained separately from the guys. When the investigators pulled her into the interrogation room, they asked her questions about how she knew the guys in the car. They questioned whose gun it was that they found in the vehicle. Then, threatened that Gabby would go to prison for the firearm unless she could agree to say that it belonged to Stroller. Gabby refused to co-operate. All she could say was, "I don't know."

She was put back into the holding tank by herself. Eventually, two ladies got thrown in the holding tank with her. Gabby said nothing to them. One of them attempted to put her crack in Gabby's dinner trash that the cops would be picking up any minute. Gabby quietly said, "I'll go down for that without saying a word to them. But just know I'll take your ass out the fuckin' game when I do."

The lady went back to the trash, grabbed her crack, and swallowed it. The other lady who was pregnant, and clearly, a crack head started trying to make small talk with Gabby. Gabby asked if this was her first pregnancy. The lady responded, "No, I have three other kids. My mom's been raising them." Gabby asked, "If you couldn't take care of those kids and you left them with the woman who raised you, who's now a crack head, how the fuck are you gonna bring another child into this world knowing you have no intention to be the mom they deserve?" Before the lady could say another word, Gabby said, "I'm done yo. Don't say another word to me, or I'm taking face shots."

Gabby was called and moved to the Van Nuys station, where she would spend the night until morning. She entered a room filled with thin metal bunk beds. She sat on her bunk that had a slim mattress. She took off her shoes and wrapped them in the sheet that the officer gave her. She put the sheet wrapped shoes on the bed and used it as a pillow.

As she lay there with her eyes open, she thought about how her car hit the wall earlier that day. She put the car into drive, and still, it went backward. She couldn't understand. Then she thought of Loc's sister, who was in prison for retaliation. She also thought about what the cop told her earlier that day when they were getting arrested.

All she could think was it was probably a blessing they got pulled over before they went after those guys. When morning came, she was transferred by bus with other inmates who had been bussed down from county jail to the San Fernando courthouse. She waited there to speak to an attorney. She was called and told to sit at a window where she would meet a D.A. Twenty minutes passed until she asked a C.O. about what was going on. The C.O. came back to her and said, "D.A. reject, let's go." He walked her back to the holding tank with all the other women.

Gabby got called out again come late afternoon. Luckily it was Friday so she would be released. She sat against the wall with thirteen other women. The C.O.'s teased her the whole time. One of them asked if she was Jennifer Lopez, Gabby made a face. They asked her name. She told them her name. Then one of them said, "No, we don't have a Gabriela, but we have a J.Lo. You sure that's not you." Gabby would be the last to be released as they continued messing with her. Finally, when they let her go, they said, "See you soon." Gabby replied, "No, you won't." To which one C.O. responded, "That's what they all say." Gabby rolled her eyes and said, "Man, you guys have a weird way of flirting."

The gates opened up, Gabby walked outside and sat on the grass. She called her dad from her cell phone to tell him where she was. She asked if he could pick her up and help her get her car back. Her father denied her request. The gate opened up about twenty minutes later. Gabby turned around to see all of the guys she got arrested with minus Stroller. Stroller wouldn't be out until Monday. One of the guys used Gabby's phone to call someone to pick them all up.

Gabby picked up her car. She made it to class Monday and made it a point to make up the work she missed on Friday. After that experience, Gabby made sure to make it to every class. After she graduated from the nine-month massage program, she tried to get a job. She realized that she didn't like that she needed to be certified in teachings from foreign regions when she had her own teachings from right here on her ancestral land. She definitely didn't like that these courses and teachings were being taught by Europeans for way too much money when they were teachings of the people of Japan and India. She started her own mobile massage company called La Chi-Spas Mobile where she could freely practice her way.

Gabby would take her table, sheets, bolsters, and music to the clients' house and set it all up. She offered a variety of different modalities such as therapeutic, deep tissue, relaxing, pressure point, reflexology, pregnancy, hot stone, energy, and mental work. Gabby offered something she called massage parties. At these parties, the host would invite up to seven friends. Gabby would massage them each for an hour at a lower rate. The host would receive their massage for free. If the host wanted to have more people, Gabby would bring a chair and charge by the minute, with twenty-five minutes being the max. Sometimes Gabby worked free of charge or worked out deals with people who couldn't afford luxury spa massages. Thanks to word of mouth, Gabby stayed busy.

When she was 22, Gabby finally decided to live a sober lifestyle. She went to Los Angeles Mission College in Sylmar to get her general classes done. While she was at school, she also took nutrition and kinesiology courses. While attending Mission College, Gabby settled for a job at a small massage place, making twenty dollars an hour plus tips. She continued seeing her personal clients as well. The tip money from both jobs was what paid for the entire creation of her first album.

At the age of 23, Gabby met the love of her life, Raymond, in Community College while she was taking a nutrition course. He was interested in the health field and later became a food inspector. They dated for four years until

Raymond proposed to Gabby. Gabby asked Denise to be her maid of honor. Miranda, Isela, Lori, and Suzy agreed to be the bride's maids.

The day of her wedding, as the girls were surrounding Gabby to help get her ready, they made a pact that they would all be bride's maids at each other's weddings. She and Raymond had their wedding on a ranch. Gabby had a glamourous gown. Her father walked her down the aisle and gave her away to Raymond. They had a small reception in the ranch barn. Gabby's family sang some traditional California songs. Each family introduced different cultural dances. Everyone who attended had so much fun at their wedding.

Gabby continued performing for fun and extra money. She did both rapping and singing. She did many car shows and hip-hop venues. Now and again, Isela would feature on some songs and jump in at a concert. Denise was Gabby's manager and made sure to keep Gabby busy.

By the time Gabby was twenty-nine, she had a supportive husband, a beautiful three-year-old son, a home, a secure connection to her Nation, and fans all over the world requesting her performances. Gabby decided to give her fans what they wanted and began touring. She mostly did weekend tours so that her husband and son could join her.

When her son's summer and winter breaks came about from school, Gabby usually had gigs lined up and mostly took her boy on the road with her. These gigs were both in and out of the country and always paid. No matter where she performed, she made sure that the Indigenous people of the area did a land acknowledgement and were compensated before her show could begin.

Gabby continued massaging her personal clients on her downtime. By the time Gabby was thirty-three, she had received a call from Denise telling her to turn the radio station to 93.5. One of Gabby's songs finally made it on the radio. Gabby started performing at even bigger venues. She was performing at radio station concerts as well as shows of her own. When Fabiola heard Gabby on the radio for the first time, she smiled big and said, "Yes. That's right, Gabby. You did that."

Denise worked very hard for her friend and boss. Gabby was very thankful. Denise wouldn't retire as Gabby's manager, nor did Gabby ever consider firing her, the two of them made a strong team. It was surreal to Gabby to hear fans screaming and chanting her name. Some venues had lines around the corner of people waiting to get in to watch Gabby perform. By the age of thirty-seven, Gabby had released three albums over the lifespan of her career. She had three children, two boys, and a girl, as well as a massage business.

Gabby's massage business did well. She owned a building in Reseda, California. Gabby rented office spaces to different companies. She used one office space for her spa; it had six rooms, two bathrooms, an office, and an employee lounge. She had seven employees working at the spa at all times during business hours.

Gabby's children were hard workers. They grew to be successful. Her son Hunaar was an engineer, her other son, Honor, was a major league baseball player. Gabby's daughter Ochuur was just as talented a writer as Gabby. Instead of music, she wrote stories and articles. Ochuur worked as a magazine editor for a high-end Magazine.

Eventually, Gabby would be a grandmother and great grandmother and was proud of each of her babies and grandbabies. Between music and her family, she stayed swamped with activities. She sold her massage business when she was seventy-six. She also gave the building to her children.

Gabby did her last tour at the age of seventy-nine just before learning her husband had colon cancer. Gabby wanted to spend as much time with him as possible. He chose to eat healthily and avoid any medical care. He kept his cancer at bay. They did some traveling on cruise lines while he still felt up for it.

A year and a half later, he called Gabby to his bedside; Gabby came in to see what he needed. Patting the bed, he asked her to sit beside him. Gabby sat on the bed. Raymond grabbed Gabby's left hand, he looked her in the eye and quietly said, "I feel so honored to have had the pleasure of being your husband and best friend throughout all of these years Gabs. You have been an amazing mother to our children. You have been the best wife I could ever have hoped to have. I have always been so proud to watch you live out your dream and be damned good at everything you ever wanted to do. You could have had any man in the world, and you chose me."

Raymond flashed a tremendous smile as he continued, "Wow. Thank you mi vida, for being by my side through it all, I love you. I love you un chingo." Gabby smiled a warm, loving smile at her husband. In a low, warm tone, she said, "Oh Viejo, I wouldn't have had it any other way, you're the most wonderful husband and father, te amo un chingo tambien mi corazon." Gabby could feel a whirlpool of energy surrounding her; she closed her eyes as she acknowledged it. Gabby leaned in and kissed her husband on his lips. She opened her eyes to see Raymond smiling at her as he took his final breath. She continued to hold his left hand in her left hand. She raised her right hand over her mouth and nose. Gabby quietly released tears of pain.

Gabby lived for four more years after her husband's passing. She grew exhausted. One day in her living room, she saw Raymond in broad daylight. She spoke to him, "My love, have you come for me?" Raymond responded, "Yes, mi vida, I am waiting for you." Gabby asked, "How is it, Raymond? Is it beautiful?" Raymond replied, "You'll know soon enough, my love." Two days later, Gabby also died in the house where she and Raymond made a home and raised their children. Raymond was the first to greet her as she made her journey to the other side. She was joined and welcomed by many of her loved ones in the spirit world.

MIRANDA

Miranda did what she and Miguel discussed. Her high school grades were at a 4.0, allowing her to go straight to UCLA to start on the path to becoming a Doctor. Miranda had decided to be a surgeon. While attending her second year at UCLA, Lita passed away, making it hard for Miranda to focus for a few months. Still, Miranda stuck it out and helped Ana as much as she could.

Miguel left behind enough money to make payments on the house for five years. Although Miranda had her cash set aside for school, she applied for and received scholarships that paid for a big chunk of her schooling. When Miranda graduated as an M.D., her mom and Ana threw a big party for her. It was the biggest deal for the two women. They couldn't be more proud to have a doctor in the family. Miranda had a great time celebrating with her girls and family.

After four years of college and a year of internship, she took a position at UCLA medical hospital where she practiced general surgery. Miranda continued higher education to get into cardiothoracic surgery.

One day while in the school library, Miranda was walking to a table to study. With her head in a medical book, she accidentally bumped a man causing him to drop his books. Miranda felt flushed when she looked up to see his handsome face. She apologized and leaned down to help him pick up his books. They stood up straight around the same time. He put his hand out and introduced himself as Henry.

Henry was studying law and was an intern for some big guys in Los Angeles. Miranda's beauty struck Henry. He didn't know what to say or how to talk to her, just that he wanted to. He sat at the same table as her to study. When Miranda finished up at the library, she stood up holding a few books and looked at Henry. Miranda asked, "You coming?"

Henry, surprised, quickly closed up his books and followed Miranda out of the library. They walked to a coffee shop on the campus. Henry bought two coffees. The two of them sat and talked for a few hours. They spoke of the struggles of growing up and what brought them to school. They talked about future goals and family. That was the start of a hectic and wonderful life for Miranda and Henry.

Both Miranda and Henry lived intense lives with schooling and internships. They tried to hang out most Sundays. But sometimes studying and life got in the way of that.

Eventually, they would both graduate and end up with their dream jobs. For them, life had many overwhelming and stressful moments. As Miranda grew older, she would remind herself and Henry that a little stress was normal for their line of work, but not to give it too much attention or let it affect their work and personal lives. Her favorite saying became, "Let go and let God."

Two years into their dream jobs, Henry moved in with Miranda. He contributed to all of the bills. Henry and Miranda both agreed to dedicate themselves to the next six years of their careers and save money as much as possible. Miranda made it a priority to have Gabby come over once a month to massage her for an hour and a half. Every other month or so, Henry would try to be home to get a massage as well.

After attending Gabby's wedding, Henry started thinking of marriage. Henry called Lori and asked for her help getting Miranda's family and friends together. The plan was to go on a date at Universal City walk. As they walked up to the restaurant, Miranda noticed people standing in front, holding big signs that altogether read, "Miranda Will You Marry Me?" Miranda read it out loud.

She looked over to Henry. He was already on his knee with a ring box open. Miranda made a face of emotion as she nodded yes. She finally found her words, exclaiming, "Yes, Henry! Oh my gosh, yes!" Henry jumped up to hug and kiss her. He leaned her backward into a dip as they kissed. Miranda and Henry's loved ones cheered and came up to congratulate the two. They all went into the restaurant to celebrate.

Miranda and Lori began planning the wedding to be held a year from the engagement. Miranda wanted it to be beautiful yet simple. She decided they would have the entire wedding at her house. Maggie, a friend of Miranda's, was an Ordained Minister. She would be the one to marry Miranda and Henry. Miranda hired a crew to set up and take down the tables and the decorations that she and Lori, picked out, bought and made. She hired a catering service as well as a D.J. Although she would give anything to have Miggy walk her down the aisle, the wedding was just perfect in Miranda's eyes.

Miranda's mother walked her down the aisle. Lori was Miranda's maid of honor. Gabby, Suzy, Isela, and Denise were the brides' maids. They all had their hair and makeup done by two professionals who went to high school with them.

For their honeymoon, the two went to Yucatán. Per Isela's request, they dropped tobacco and asked the Ancestors of the area for permission to be there. They spent two weeks exploring the area. From the Pyramids, the freshwater pools called cenotes, beautiful ocean, and an underwater museum, they had a fantastic vacation that neither of them could ever forget.

The two had a happy marriage. Kids never seemed to fit into the equation. They were able to vacation once a year and enjoy the life they had created. After being married for thirteen happy years, there would be a shift in Henry's demeanor.

Henry had a couple of secretaries come and go. After his last secretary gave her two weeks' notice, Henry put out an ad for the job. He interviewed three different women and two men. Two of them were overqualified, and two were underqualified. That left him with a woman named Vanessa Sweeny. Vanessa seemed to do her job and followed directions well. After two years of working for Henry, they would begin getting closer. He spent more long nights at his office, where Vanessa would join him for dinner and conversation.

Eventually, the two would end up having casual sex. Henry kept this up for another two years before finally being caught in the act by Miranda. As hurt as Miranda was, she just wanted Henry out of her life. The next day after catching him, while he was at work, Miranda changed the locks on all of the outside doors. She gathered his belongings and put them outside the front door. She kicked him out of the house and told him she didn't want anything from him. Henry didn't mean to hurt Miranda.

Unfortunately, he wasn't thinking of her when he began his affair. He was only thinking of himself. After the first time it happened, and he didn't get caught, it became intriguing. With love in his heart for Miranda, he insisted on giving Miranda a big lump sum. He didn't take anything from her and gave her a peaceful divorce.

With part of the lump sum Henry gave her, she created a C.D. at her credit union. She decided to swear off men for a couple of years. Miranda chose to keep herself busy and be home as little as possible. When she wasn't working, she decided to spend some of her free time at the homeless shelter where she would cook and serve hot meals.

On top of being a surgeon who saved many lives, Miranda founded a non-profit organization that worked with other programs to help bring therapy, health, education, clothing, and housing to people in need who were willing to do the work to better their lives.

In some points in her career in the medical field, Miranda faced discrimination for being a brown woman in her field. She demanded her respect. Aside from that, Miranda felt a lot of happiness and satisfaction in her life.

Miranda never had children. She dated off and on vaguely. At the hospital she worked at, there was a Doctor named Jesse Dominguez. He had been single for quite some time as well. He was four years older than her. She dated him for a year or so before finally entering a committed relationship with him. Jesse's children were all adults. They liked Miranda.

Jesse's children felt that Miranda would be suitable for their father, so they treated her well. His grandchildren would call Miranda gramma. Miranda and Jesse moved into his home together. They agreed that they didn't need to wed to be in a loving, committed relationship. They had a reasonably happy life together. Miranda felt surrounded by love as part of Jesse's life with his family, including his children and grandchildren.

Miranda rented out her home and always saved the money left over after paying insurance and property tax. She kept the money in another CD where it would build up in case of an emergency as well as for house fixes. Jesse had his home paid off as well.

Jesse made smart investments. He would end up retiring at the age of fifty-eight. He took up exercise classes and woodwork to keep himself busy. Miranda would follow suit four years later. They spent the next fourteen years traveling and taking the kids and grandkids camping.

At the age of seventy-six, Jesse would pass in his sleep of heart failure. He left the house to Miranda. He made sure Miranda, his children, and grandchildren all had his assets distributed evenly. His children and Miranda were peaceful and loving as they made plans together in agreement for Jesse's funeral services. They set his ashes out at sea as he wished.

Miranda and the children sat down to dinner together that night. While there, she asked if the children would handle her services when she passed on. She stated that she wished to be at sea with Jesse. The children agreed that when the time came, they'd make arrangements for her.

Jesse's children always invited Miranda to events involving the family and grandchildren, including birthday parties and graduations. Miranda maintained a good relationship with Jesse's family. She decided at her age that it was best not to get involved with another man. Miranda continued working with the non-profit until she was seventy-nine years old. She passed the organization down to a young woman named Debbie.

Miranda spent the rest of her days quietly at home doing exercises, gardening, walking to the grocery store with her roller cart, cooking her meals, and seeing her grandkids whenever possible.

Miranda called Jesse's daughter Nelly one day and asked her to come over the following day. Nelly agreed. When Nelly showed up, Miranda didn't come to the door. Nelly waited a few minutes before using her key to enter.

Nelly found Miranda sitting in a beautiful gown, lifeless on the couch. Next to her were legal documents for her assets, which she was giving to Jesse's children and grandchildren. Nelly called 911 to make a report. She then called her siblings from outside the house. They agreed to make their way over. The kids spent the evening saying beautiful things about Miranda. They held a quiet service and laid her ashes to rest where they put their father's ashes. Not only was Miranda ninety years old when she passed, but she was also healthy and happy.

ISELA

sela continued silk screening while attending multiple courses on botany, and self-growth. She delved within on healing herself. She also picked up and added an embroidery machine to the business when she was nineteen. Tim grew tired of the company. He left the silk screening business and sold all of his equipment to Isela. She took over the shop full time.

She would also continue to set up shop at the big car and biker shows with her custom made clothing. People loved the designs that Isela sold. It was rare if she went home from an event with a box of clothes. Gabby also hired Isela to create her merchandise to sell at the venues where she performed.

Isela hooked her homegirl up on prices, and Gabby brought lots of customers to Isela. Isela stayed so busy that she didn't want to make time for a boyfriend. She saved as much money as she possibly could. At the age of twenty-six, Isela put a ninety thousand dollar down payment on her first home in the hills of Lake View Terrace.

After a year living in her new home, Isela finally allowed a little more time to fit a boyfriend in her life. Although her free time was limited, Nick, the man she began to date, was on the same boat. He was California Indigenous too. Nick grew up on a reservation in Northern California until he left for college. He stayed involved with his tribe but lived in Los Angeles, California. Nick often gave lectures at different high schools and colleges. He was also a councilman for his tribe. Work had Nick traveling a lot.

Isela and Nick had known each other for many years from the Native gatherings that their families would attend. They always had an interest in each other and remained good friends throughout the years. When they finally agreed on dating, Isela and Nick made it a point to see each other twice a month. Eventually, their time together blossomed into a relationship. Their relationship worked perfectly for them.

With the nudge from Nick, Isela committed to walking the red road. Meaning she became completely sober and went deeper into the ceremony ways. Now and again, she and Gabby attended ceremony together.

After five years of being together, Nick proposed to Isela after their anniversary dinner. The waiter brought a chocolate cake. The rim of the plate read, "Isela Will You Marry Me," written in chocolate. Nick pulled a turquoise ring out and kneeled by her side. Isela happily said yes. They had a beautiful wedding outdoors where they incorporated a blend of Native and Westernized American culture.

Isela wore a rabbit fur top sewn to buckskin that wrapped around her back and tied together with yucca rope. She had a buckskin skirt that had seashells on the front. She wore a half skirt made of a California plant named Tule over the backside of her buckskin skirt. She wore her long wavy hair down and wore a traditional headband made of keyhole limpet seashells around her forehead. Suzy was Isela's maid of honor. Gabby, Miranda, Lori, and Denise were the bride's maids at the wedding.

The bridesmaids and maid of honor all wore turquoise and grey ribbon skirts, which Isela made. They hosted two hundred people at Isela's house in Lake View Terrace. They hired a taqueria to cook tacos and quesadillas as well as serve beans. Isela's family also made a big pot of deer stew and acorn bread. Isela changed into a dress to party in; she looked stunning. Everyone partied the night away until about 3:00 a.m.

Isela moved in with Nick, who was now living in Tujunga. As rent went up, Isela decided she would close down the shop that she had been renting and work from home. Her team still had their jobs. She shipped out most of her silkscreen orders. She also continued to work venues.

Isela rented her home in Lake View Terrace to a sheriff and his family for about ten years before deciding to sell the house. Isela put some money from the sale into trust funds and other savings accounts for her and her kids.

Isela and Nick had two children, a son named Spotted Feather and a daughter named Dancing Fawn, who they raised in the Native ways and circle. Isela began paddling with Chumash relatives in the Tomol, which is the Chumash description for their plank canoes.

Most of Isela's life involved community work. She was an ocean protector who stood against oil drilling and toxic dumping in the ocean. She was a water protector, which meant she stood up against anything threatening fresh water. She educated folks about the Salmon and other life that lived in and along the Los Angeles River. She was a land protector who stood up against contamination and disrespect of our mother Earth. She went to many protests, board meetings, and sit-ins. Some demonstrations, she dragged her family or Gabby along to stand and or sing with her.

Isela worked with a couple of ladies, including Annette and Gabby on hypnotherapy and self-healing. After proving successful with these ladies, she created a community program that dealt with healing traumas of people's personal experiences as well as the traumas carried from their genetic DNA.

Isela's guided healing techniques included healing of mind, body, and soul. She demonstrated the use of food, meditation, eliminating self-sabotage stories as well as self-limiting beliefs, and physical exercises to help people heal themselves and grow.

Isela understood how the Natives of Turtle Island carried trauma through the knowing and feeling of what has happened to their relatives from the multiple cases of harsh invasions of the Europeans. Most Natives contain a lot of pain in their personal life from domestic abuse and or for being treated as second class citizens or worse than animals mostly by European Americans.

Many European Americans dealt with hurt, guilt and or hate passed down from their genetic DNA and social shaping. Other BIPOC folks also had traumas instilled in them by Westernized colonization. Isela understood that emotional, spiritual, and systemic wounds weren't only in her Native community.

Isela had a great passion for helping all people to find healing of self. She knew this would create a better future for the Earth and all life forms, including water. When Annette took on a position as a part-time counselor for the program, she and Isela became much closer. Annette was a great asset to the team and found her true calling in the work of guided healing.

Isela and her family lived a blessed life. Spotted Feather grew to be a community guidance counselor. He also worked with the Native brothers in the prison system. In there, he ran sweat lodge and helped the men to stay on a spiritual path. Eventually, he went on to be the Mayor of Los Angeles. Dancing Fawn grew up dancing fancy shawl like her mother.

When she was 20 years old, Dancing Fawn went on the road with a Native rapping crew and other dancers. On occasion while on the road, she competed at the local pow wows. Also, on her downtime from dancing with her group and at pow-wows, Dancing Fawn mentored in Native workshops throughout the states and Canada. Dancing Fawn would spend life on the road for many years before finding a place in Oxnard to call home. She spent time with her family on holidays, as well as some ceremonies.

Nick died at seventy-six from a violent heart attack. Isela spent the rest of her years with her Native community doing ceremony and social gatherings. Isela also began doing opening prayers, blessings, and land acknowledgments at events. She died happily in her sleep at the age of ninety-eight.

DENISE AND CLEVER

After the news of Denise's pregnancy, Clever stepped up. Both of them juggled a job with their schooling. Clever spent most of his downtime in the garden that the girls created in Denise's parent's yard. Denise gave birth to their beautiful baby girl named Adelena Rose.

She and the baby lived with Clever, mama Sita, and Clever's two brothers in Arleta, in the home that Rosita finally purchased. Rosita and Denise's parents were a great help as they encouraged Denise and Clever to stay strong at finishing out school. After high school, Denise went to a trade school to learn dental assisting. She graduated in seven months and found a job.

On top of being a mom and a dental assistant, Denise was Gabby's music manager. She was sure to book Gabby a paying gig at a minimum of every other weekend. More often than not, it was every weekend. Denise traveled with Gabby often.

When Gabby would get paid, Denise would get her ten percent. Denise made seventeen dollars an hour as a dental assistant. Her job also offered medical benefits. Clever got a job working as a carpenter, where he earned about eight hundred dollars a week. Clever made sure to keep that job.

Although they did pay rent and contribute to bills and food, Clever and Denise managed to save money monthly. Denise made a monthly visit to her credit union to put money away.

When they were twenty-three, Clever took Denise and their daughter Adelena Rose to Denise's parents for dinner. The house was quiet. They walked to the backyard. Denise was surprised to see Rosita and the boys standing there with her parents. She looked over to Clever in confusion. He was already kneeling on the floor with a ring out.

Clever said, "Denise, I have been beyond blessed to have you as my girlfriend and mother to my child. I'd be grateful to be able to legit call you my wife. Will you marry me?" Denise was crying through his entire speech, when he finished, Denise dropped to her knee's she embraced Clever's face in her hands, she stared into his eyes as she excitedly said, "Yes, baby, yes I'll marry you!"

Clever placed the ring on her finger. Denise was still in tears of happiness. Their parents stood clapping, smiling, and feeling proud. After a long, loving kiss, Denise and Clever stood up and walked over to join their parents. Denise went straight to her mom with her left hand out, running in place, she excitedly said, "I'm getting married!" Denise looked over to Rosita, shouting, "We're getting married!" Denise and Clever received love, tight hugs, and congratulations from the family. Then they sat down to a beautiful meal.

Denise decided, like her girls, to have a simple wedding. They were married in a beautiful garden in Camarillo. Miranda was Denise's maid of honor, Isela, Gabby, Suzy, and Lori were bridesmaids. Adelena Rose was the flower girl.

Denise, Clever, and their daughter lived with Rosita until they discovered they were having another baby. Clever decided they should have their own home where they can raise their children. Clever and Denise bought a house in West Hills, California. There, they raised three kids, two girls, and one boy. All three attended college and became good people who contributed to their community.

Their daughters Adelena and Arlene were seven years apart. They got along very well and created their own bakery business. The bakery did good enough to keep the girls' families fed, clothed, and allowed them to have reasonably lovely homes in the west end of the valley. Their son Danny Jr. was the baby of the family. He became a politician as a Los Angeles city council member. Later, Danny Jr. would join the Assembly in Sacramento. He was sure to take notes from Gabby and Isela on how to be a good relative and ally to Native People.

Clever and Denise lived out the rest of their lives happy and comfortable. Clever made a garden when they first moved into their home. He tended to it a couple of days a week until his last days. A month short of turning eighty, Clever passed away suddenly in his man chair. The doctors say he had a heart attack. Denise died two days later in her sleep. Their kids say she died of a broken heart.

With Isela's help, their children gave them a beautiful transitioning ceremony. Clever and Denise were buried together in a rose garden where the children would gather a couple of times a year to honor them.

SUZY

Suzy had worked as a model after high school graduation. She started doing small-time modeling gigs as she pursued her college education. The small-time stuff did get her recognized. She went on to do photoshoots with some famous clothing lines. Suzy also featured in some big magazines. She joined many catwalks internationally. Modeling paid for Suzy's schooling, Suzy graduated with her MBA.

When Suzy was thirty-three, she retired as a model. She opened a modeling agency, hiring mostly young women with a similar background as hers. Her clients were successful, making Suzy very successful. When she was thirty-six, Suzy bought a beautiful home in Topanga. She had a home office there and loved every second of her life.

At the age of thirty-seven, Suzy met a businessman named Vic on her vacation in the Bahamas. She discovered that he also lived in Los Angeles County. He owned a home in the hills of La Cañada. They had their first date in the Bahamas. Suzy stayed in touch with Vic after they got home.

Vic asked her on a few more dates when they had returned home. He was a very classy and tasteful man. Each date was amazingly romantic. They dated for half a year before Vic asked her to be his woman. Two more years passed, Vic took Suzy to Italy on vacation.

He proposed to her while standing before a beautiful sunset on their second to last day in Naples, Italy. With tears of joy, Suzy said, "Honey, to be your wife would be a dream come true. Of course I'll marry you." The wedding took place six months later. The tradition continued, in the sense that all the homegirls were bridesmaids at each other's weddings. Gabby was Suzy's maid of honor.

My mom's brother, Uncle Saul, walked Suzy down the aisle. I walked on the other side of Suzy down the aisle. I stood by Suzy's side for the entire wedding. The wedding took place on the sands of Malibu, and the Reception was at a house they rented in Malibu. Vic and Suzy both kept their homes and stayed in each one as they pleased. Suzy lived a great life. Traveling both for work and vacation with Vic. She has seen hidden treasures in the world that most will unfortunately never see in this lifetime.

When she was sixty-two, Suzy and Vic attended a modeling show in Hollywood where some of her clients walked the runway. Before she left the show, a magazine editor asked Suzy, "Do you have any words of encouragement for young girls who dream of being a model?"

Suzy replied, "To all the children of the world, not just the future models, no matter what you want in life, go after it. Love yourselves enough to know that you are worthy of having your dreams come true. It doesn't matter your current circumstances. What matters is that you want and need it as much as you need air in your lungs, and you go for it. Believe that it's already yours.

"The only person in the world who can stop you from reaching the height of your success is you. My homegirls and I grew up in a poor and gang-infested community. We were surrounded by negative people with little to no hope. We all had dreams of our own, we pursued our dreams, and we succeeded because we believed that we could. If we can make our dreams a reality, I know that wherever you are, you can too."

Suzy thanked the editor for her time and shook her hand. Suzy wished everyone she encountered on her way out a blessed night as she and Vic made their way to the valet. Vic opened the passenger door for Suzy to enter. He closed the door behind her then walked to the driver's side and headed for home.

Vic took his exit off of the 210 freeway west. He proceeded to make a left-hand turn, a car speeding out of nowhere t-boned them on the passenger side. The driver of the other vehicle was drunk, he failed to have his seat belt on, and his body flew twenty feet away from his car. Suzy's neck snapped from the pressure of the impact.

Vic held firm to the steering wheel, but his forehead still hit the driver door window hard enough to knock him out cold, he was pretty banged up. Vic was passed out until about five minutes after the ambulance got there.

Vic was frantic to find that Suzy didn't survive the accident. She died a quick death. I was there by her side for the accident too. I was the first one to greet her. My mom outlived us both.

Vic never entirely stopped mourning Suzy's death. However, he did allow himself to live a long, healthy, and happy life to the best of his ability. Vic ran Suzy's business for six months after Suzy passed away until finding someone to take over. Instead of selling her business, he became a silent partner. He also cared for my mother until she passed away five years later. Eleven years after Suzy passed, Vic died a single man, but he was never alone because my sister continued to stay by his side as much as she could until he came home.

LORI

ori was a full-time student at Stanford law school. She graduated within three years with a BA. Lori continued education throughout her career, advancing her position frequently. She went into environmental law. Lori knew as a kid that the court dismissed Native people's knowledge because they didn't have college degrees to back them up. She wanted to change that. She did what she could for her Native community as well as her other relatives who have a voice but aren't being listened to, being the water, animals, plants, and the land.

While Lori focused on the original people, animals, waters and plant life of the lands that she was fighting to protect, it was evident that the non-Native people in the courts cared only and at times very little for the plant life and animals and not the people at all. The Natives have always been very well aware of this.

Lori would ask to join meetings with the Natives whose lands she was fighting to protect. She would bring Traditional gifts to offer the members on the board. In this way, they knew she was connected to the Earth the way that they were. They would open up to her and explain the stories and sacredness of the area.

She would ask them to stand before the court and explain this, but the answer was always similar to: "We cannot share our truth with the European minded American. Their history wrote us out for a reason. When we try to explain why an area is sacred, the American seems to want to destroy it further, or study it with no respect and take our artifacts to their homes and museums. These people, their greed, it keeps them from understanding the ways, being connected to the land. If it doesn't benefit their wallet, they hold no interest in protecting it."

These explanations were understood immensely by Lori. It also frustrated her; she wished the Natives could speak up in the courtroom to help her protect the areas. She wished that the Non-Natives would listen to the insight of the original people of the land and understand and respect the Earth and its Native inhabitants. Lori often felt stuck between a hard place and a rock. She worked hard and did the best she could with every case that she took.

The passion Lori carried for Environmental law shined through. Lori represented the Native American Heritage Commission. She fought hard and enforced civil rights and anti-discriminatory laws, and she served as Chief Counsel and Deputy Director of Legal Counsel and Investigations. Lori was a straight-up Warrior Woman with so many accomplishments under her belt.

Lori found her time frequently occupied with work. She also helped to mentor youth who were interested in law. Annually she tried to make time in her calendar to visit with the Native community for ceremony as well as make time for family and friends as much as she could. Every year for forty years, the girls and their families kept up their camping trip.

Lori had a small garden and some of her traditional medicines that she tended to in her backyard. She also bought 80 acres of land under a non-profit and shared it with Gabby and Isela's Nations. They kept it well maintained and were able to conduct ceremony any time there.

Lori tried dating on multiple occasions. Unfortunately, Lori didn't find herself attracted or compatible with most of the men she dated. A few times, she met someone date-worthy. Although she had two long-term relationships, time would always prove these men not to be as confident in them-selves to uphold a relationship with such a strong-willed, financially stable, and outspoken woman. It never took away from Lori's confidence or happiness. She had self-love and was very much in love with the life she worked hard to create.

Lori retired at the age of 65. She took up sewing and beadwork for hobbies. She'd often sell her work at pow-wows. Sometimes she followed the pow-wow trail into other states and met some very humble elders in every community. Often times she still counseled Native folks on Law and protecting their lands and rights.

Being a part of the Native community kept Lori feeling young. However, when she reached the age of 82, it became time to allow the young ones to pick her up and help her in different ways, which they were more than happy to do. There were a handful of young Natives who made it a point to Call Lori and check on her weekly. They would call Lori, "Gramma Lori." Being that she had no husband or children, she was happy to receive the love and care of the young ones.

When Lori was 86, she was in her backyard meditating; she heard the powerful singing voices of Native women. The song was in her Yoeme language, and her spirit knew it was her ancestors. They had come to guide her home. With her eyes closed, Lori smiled and began to lay flat. She breathed deeply until her last breath; her spirit flew out of her body in the form of an eagle. She was welcomed to the spirit world with so much love.

Lori had a will written up that would disburse her assets to some of these caring young people. There was a young couple named Rita and Freddy that Lori knew since they were children and shared significant memories of their lives. They had two young children who Lori loved dearly. Lori wanted to leave them her home and twenty thousand dollars. She left some of her money to five other youngsters who were always quick and generous to tend to Lori. Lori signed the 80 acres of land over to the local Tribes with some money and an explanation of how to maintain the non-profit. Lori left a positive impact on the community.

Each of us in this lifetime has a path that we will walk, mostly alone. Throughout the journey, our paths will cross with others. At specific points, our paths will allow us to walk side by side for moments in time. Within these young women's lifetime, they grew knowledge and understanding with every relationship and experience. They each lived the life they chose to live. I wish that I can say they all lived happily ever after, I think the best way to describe it really, is that they all lived. May you too, go out and put your best foot forward, walk in love, and prosper. You got this.

'Aweeshkone Xaa 'Wee Nehiinkem

I want to send so much love to my son Honor, who has helped me change my lifestyle and pulled me back to the Native ways. When I wasn't at work helping people through massage therapy, I was going down a miserable path, but the day I found out I was pregnant, I knew my life had more meaning and that I had a lot of changes to make to prepare myself to be the kind of parent I knew you needed. I sobered up and made my way back to the Native community. I have been healing and growing a little more each day with the strength to push forward and do the work. I had to learn to love myself unconditionally, so that I can understand what it means to love you and my people unconditionally. I am grateful beyond words son to have you be such a big part, teacher, blessing, and friend of my life. I love you.

My parents, we haven't always had the best relationship, mostly because of my experiences and traumas that wouldn't allow me to trust or get too close to anyone. Through my healing journey, we have shed tears and truths, which have brought us closer. I thank you for the life you have given me, the teachings you have taught me, the roof over my head, and the love you offer my son and me.

I'm grateful to my entire community (many whom are my sisters). There are way too many to name, but if you've cried with me, encouraged me to follow my dreams, gave me a hand when I needed it, opened up to me, shared a meal with me, danced with me, laughed with me, shared ceremony space with me, and or taught me something, please know that I love and appreciate you.

I want to shout out a couple of Native women who inspire me and inspired the careers and educational choices of some of my Characters. First off, UCLA graduate, Anmarie Mendoza of the Tongva Nation, and Solange Aguilar of the Mountain Apache, Yoeme, Kalinga and Kapampangan Nations thank you both for your contributions to help me complete this book. University of California, San Francisco graduate, Dr. Andrea Garcia of the Hidatsa Nation, thank you for being a trailblazer for Native women Doctors. Stanford University Law School graduate, Antonette Cordero from my Chumash Paddle family, you are a powerhouse. Thank you for your hard work and dedication to justice for the Native Nations and our Natural world.

The Honorable Deborah Sanchez (Wewla) who is a practicing Judge of the Los Angeles Superior Court. Wewla graduated from California State University, Long Beach with a BA in Sociology. Wewla also has a JD (Juris Doctor/ Law Degree) from Loyola Law School. Auntie Wewla, thank you for having so much passion for the language, and showing us the beauty in learning and speaking the Chumash language. Stanford Graduate, Tanaya Winder of the Duckwater Shoshone Nation. Thank you for providing a safe space for our heart work and guiding me on my journey of music and teaching workshops. Lyla June, your strength, courage, and love for your people that you carry as you heal through your traumas has been an inspiration to me. Bethany Yellowtail, not only have you shown us how to make a dream come true with passion, hard work and dedication, but you share the dream as you uplift the voices of other Indigenous People and artists. You also have been loving and respectful as a visitor on Tongva lands and I hope you know that doesn't go unnoticed. All of these women work hard for their community and are the perfect example of a woman who stands in her power.

For the record there are hundreds of other beautiful, strong, dedicated, hardworking, talented Native women out there. Many of whom I know personally. Some are directors, some are business owners, some are writers, some are chefs, some are artists (rappers, singers, poets, actors, producers, painters, beaders, basket weavers, story tellers), and some are cultural bearers. All are amazing women. This book is dedicated to these women.

Let us not forget our men. Our men are our balance, our equals. We appreciate our men who lift us up, work with us in community, stand with us, heal with us, pray with us, and respect us. We need you great men. We see and appreciate you men. Thank you for being you.

Made in the USA
Monee, IL
28 September 2023